THE EMPIRE OF THE DEAD

Johns Hopkins: Poetry and Fiction
John T. Irwin, General Editor

The Empire

of the Dead

Stories by
Tracy Daugherty

Johns Hopkins University Press
Baltimore

This book has been brought to publication with the generous assistance of the Albert Dowling Trust and the Writing Seminars Publication Fund.

Printed in the United States of America on acid-free paper
9 8 7 6 5 4 3 2 1

Johns Hopkins University Press
2715 North Charles Street
Baltimore, Maryland 21218-4363
www.press.jhu.edu

Library of Congress Cataloging-in-Publication Data

Daugherty, Tracy.
[Short stories. Selections]
The empire of the dead : stories / by Tracy Daugherty.
pages cm.— (Johns Hopkins: Poetry and Fiction)
ISBN 978-1-4214-1580-2 (pbk. : acid-free paper)—ISBN 978-1-4214-1581-9 (electronic)—ISBN 1-4214-1580-1 (pbk. : acid-free paper)—ISBN 1-4214-1581-X (electronic)
I. Title.
PS3554.A85A6 2014
813'.54—dc23 2014012498

A catalog record for this book is available from the British Library.

Special discounts are available for bulk purchases of this book. For more information, please contact Special Sales at 410-516-6936 or specialsales@press.jhu.edu.

Johns Hopkins University Press uses environmentally friendly book materials, including recycled text paper that is composed of at least 30 percent post-consumer waste, whenever possible.

◇ ◇ ◇

For Margie and Hannah

◇ ◇ ◇

CONTENTS

I

II

III

I

◊◊◊

I Have the Room Above Her

Every evening at 5:30, Bern walked from the storefront office of the small architectural firm he worked for on West Eighth Street to Glasco's, a bar one block north of the Cedar Tavern on University Place. There he had a sandwich and a beer. After dining alone in the melancholy comfort of noisy anonymity, he strolled along West Eleventh in the direction of the river, taking in the mild midwinter night. The steel gratings in the walls of the old brownstones emitted blasts of hot air smelling oddly of hair oil. Through the street-level basement windows of the First Presbyterian Church (sooty Gothic Revival), he glimpsed women sweating over an industrial stove.

A few paces later, Bern prickled at the bland modern façade facing the street where anarchists had blown up their 1840s-era townhouse in the 1970s. These days, the front window of the first floor showcased a teddy bear dressed in a yellow slicker, holding a black umbrella—the occupant's wink (Bern assumed) to the Weathermen, the group that had built the bomb.

A young man marched past Bern, hoisting a boy onto his shoulders. "Mommy's *stressed*," the man warned the boy. Mommy was nowhere in sight.

The sidewalk, a mix of new and old concrete squares, sloped and dipped. In the bare little garden of PS 41, a black and broken umbrella lay on the ground. A bearded man in a heavy coat and a Mets cap climbed over a rail fence onto the school property, gripping a plastic trash bag, and began searching for scraps among the garden's twigs.

Usually, Bern stopped at the end of the block to contemplate the Wall of Hope and Remembrance on the south side of St. Vincent's Hospital. Hundreds of notes and photos commemorated people never found after the attack on the World Trade Center. On the sidewalk, someone had left a child's light blue sweater and a pair of baby shoes. Pigeons cooed in the building's concrete eaves.

Bern was startled to find the brick wall blank, emptied of its elegiac icons. A siren shrieked. An ambulance pulled up to the curb. From its rear, two paramedics unloaded a man on a stretcher.

Still dazed by the hard, cold wall, Bern turned from the hospital's emergency entrance. Across the street, in the front window of a shop called Fantasy World, faceless mannequins lounged, wearing sheer pink lingerie. Down the block, wind ruffled the red canvas awning of the Village Vanguard. Bern shuffled up the street to the White Horse, where he stopped for another beer.

At a table next to him, two women conversed:

"How's her father?"

"*Which* father?"

"I know, I know..."

Someone had left part of the *Times*, wet and rumpled, on a chair. Distractedly, Bern raced through the paper. Why did the hospital's cleared wall disturb him? He had not known anyone who died in the attack. From the beginning, he had resisted the media call to public mourning and the government's shameless fear-mongering.

Here, now, was a headline declaring that Governor Spitzer had signed off on the Freedom Tower. A mistake, Bern thought. Who would occupy the thing? It was terribly designed.

He finished his beer and paid. His agitation—over what?—was too great for sleep, so he walked some more, retracing his steps. He ducked into the Strand.

"Was Ishmael the whale," he heard someone say, "or the guy that tried to kill the whale, or—?"

On the table of New York titles, Bern found a reprint of E. B. White's *Here Is New York*, a volume he had loved twenty years ago as a fresh arrival on the island, not long out of college... though even then the book had had a musty air about it. White's New York was that of the Beaux Arts urban canyons of the 1920s and '30s, full of brick buildings with cozy window ledges and niches sheltering restless doves: a city long vanished. Since 9/11, White's book was spoiled for Bern because its prophetic conclusion—"A single flight of planes no bigger than a wedge of geese can quickly end this island fantasy"—had been quoted so often in the press and on the blogosphere.

On the shelves Bern found a pristine paperback entitled *A Hut of One's Own* by a woman named Ann Cline. On impulse he decided to buy it. He liked the cover illustration: a black and white photo of a simple square table, a kerosene lantern, a pitcher and a pan, all in a small wooden room. Like most old-school (i.e., middle-aged) architects he knew, Bern was fond of huts—of the *idea* of the hut.

He hiked to Seventh and caught the subway, then darted over to West Twenty-third Street. His apartment was on the fourth floor of a building with wide glass doors, next to a new thrift shop called McGee's, whose sign was painted to appear beat-up, old, and faded. In the lobby of his building, a worn blue carpet once plush—ten, fifteen years ago—kinked like popcorn beneath his shoes as he moved toward the elevator. A dull, gassy odor filled the lobby, rising from the sofa squeezed against the far wall between two potted ficus plants with cobwebs stretched among their leaves. The smell came from old leather that had been too much in contact with soiled clothing over the years—the sweaty dresses and slightly damp bottoms of long-forgotten visitors to the building.

A hand-drawn map of Paterson, New Jersey, now mostly faded, was framed on the wall above the sofa, next to a chipped mirror whose smoky, yellowed glass flattered even a weary Bern after a trying day. Its smudged spots smoothed the lines under his eyes and seemed to straighten his mildly crooked nose. On the sofa slept Mrs. Mehl, about whom Bern knew little. Widow. Third floor. Light snorer, often asleep here in the evening. Tonight there were two bags of groceries—cat food and chocolate cookies sticking out—on the floor at her feet, as if she had made it just this far, surviving the bustle on the streets, and could walk no more.

Gently, Bern nudged her shoulder, nearly lost in the padding of a purple coat. "Mrs. Mehl. Dear," he said. "You'll want to go up now. It's getting late."

"Oh yes, yes. Certainly," she said, primping her sparse white hair as if she hadn't been napping but was prepping backstage, somewhere, for her moment in the klieg lights.

"Can I help you with your bags?"

"No, no. Well, just the one, perhaps. Thank you," said Mrs. Mehl, and they rode the lift together in mute dignity. When the doors, heavy wood with copper trim, sighed apart, Mrs. Mehl wrestled the bag from Bern's arms, thanked him again, and swiftly turned the corner in the dim, greenly lighted hallway. Bern smelled leaden fried foods—perhaps pork chops and onions? And he also detected... some rare Asian leaf? Was it kaffir lime?

In his apartment, he added water to a blue vase on his kitchen counter holding a single moss rose—a reminder of his East Texas childhood, just outside of Houston, where moss roses grew in abundance. He switched on his bedside radio. Another car bomb in Baghdad. Another condemnation by the vice president of war critics, whom he implied were traitors to our brave and steadfast republic.

Before turning off his light, Bern flipped through Ann Cline. "St. Anthony in a hut, immobile in the face of worldly temptations," he read. The hut, he read, was the "taproot of inhabiting."

Bern closed the book and lay in the humid dark. Cline's remarks reminded him of Carlo Lodoli, an eighteenth-century Venetian architect he had learned about in grad school. Apparently, Lodoli had much to say about wood, stone, and bone, and their uses in construction. Bern remembered that, in addition to promoting radical building designs, Lodoli was suspected by the inquisitors of the republic of spreading seditious ideas. Upon his death, officials confiscated his papers, including his architectural jottings, and locked them away under a leaky roof in the Piombi, where they rotted. Only through the subsequent, and much embellished, writings of his students, Algarotti and Memmo, did Lodoli's thoughts survive, as rumor, hint, and innuendo.

Back in school, Bern had deduced that the master's teachings, if they could ever be known, said the point of architecture was to understand the nature of the materials it employed. Perhaps this is what disturbed me earlier, Bern thought now. Isn't the aim of all human activity—violence, remembrance—to plumb human activity? Taproots. First principles. So damnably hard to trace.

2.

He had not visited the WTC site in five years. Early this morning, before heading to work, he felt a desire to see the area again. On the subway he stared at the cover of the Ann Cline book. The table, the pitcher, the pan.

Of course, there was not much to see at the site. A vast construction zone, with little construction in progress. Pataki's Pit, everyone called it, deriding the former governor's politics, which had kept the hole a hole longer than it needed to be.

Bern was not as pleased as he thought he would be by the new structure—knife-edged and opaque—on the pit's north lip: 7 World Trade Center, the newspaper reviews of which had been mostly positive. To Bern, the building's blocky base screamed *fear*. The first ten floors housed an electrical substation powering most of Lower Manhattan. But did it have to *look* like an electrical substation? Bern thought. The Jenny Holzer installation—a series of ghostly words marching across the front glass wall, including lines from *Here Is New York* and celebrations of the city from the poems of Walt Whitman—charmed him but left him feeling irritated that he couldn't stay all morning to read it.

Bern made his way past Vietnamese street vendors hawking New York sweatshirts and woolen caps, as well as pamphlets with TRAGEDY printed in red across the top.

Bern's office on West Eighth was small and drab, outfitted only with a desk, a rarely used computer, a few chairs, and a smattering of file cabinets overflowing with paperwork. The dirty windows overlooked a secondhand clothing store. Usually at lunchtime, Bern left the building, passed through the dreary lobby—almost always empty—caught a subway, and strolled up to Madison Square Park. There, under the pleasant shadows of curling oak trees, he'd eat a sandwich he'd packed at home.

Today, he worked into the early afternoon on a project for a small foundation whose office space on West Broadway lacked sufficient light in the interior, despite floor-to-ceiling windows facing the street. Where Bern would normally place tubing for a light scoop, an old fire escape interfered—a pretty little problem that kept him from fully realizing his hunger until well past midday. When he *did* knock off for a while, he walked and stretched, ending up at a nice little Italian place on West Eleventh called Gene's. While he waited for his salad, he sketched hut designs on his napkin: flat-roofed, pyramid-shaped, open to the air.

He took a meandering path back to work. Children's drawings of the neighborhood filled the front window of Ray's Pizza: happy families clustered beneath the Jefferson Market Library clock or around the flower garden where the women's prison used to stand (long before the children could have known about it).

For three more hours he worked on the foundation design. At 5:30 he wandered over to Glasco's, to find it locked and dark. A handwritten sign taped to the front window cited plumbing problems and apologized for the inconvenience. A tall young woman in jeans and a green wool sweater stepped up beside him, squinted to read the sign, stepped back, and gripped the straps of her tan leather purse tightly against her body. Bern recollected having seen her in Glasco's now and then.

"Well," she said. "I guess it's the Cedar tonight." She set off down the street, her auburn hair bouncing on her shoulders. After a moment's delay, Bern followed her.

The only seats inside the tavern were jammed into a corner. Bern squeezed next to the woman in green. "May I?" he asked. She answered, "Sure." Separately, they ordered drinks and food. The place was too bright. Acoustically bad.

Bern scribbled on his napkin.

After a few sips of her beer—Guinness, Bern noted; this woman was serious about her beer—she said to Bern, "Nice," and indicated the napkin with a lift of her chin. "Are you an artist?"

"No."

"Make houses?"

"I'm an architect, yes."

"Cool," she said. She drank some more. "Say something... I don't know... architecturally *cool*."

Bern laughed. She had a way of speaking loudly, over the crowd, which sounded soft: the low timbre of her voice, perhaps. "Well, I'm not sure I..."

"Come on. Amuse me. It's been a long day."

"Okay. Let's see. The seventeenth-century Jesuit Athanasius Kircher attributed to demons all of Roman architecture, because of the nudity in its statuary," Bern said.

"No kidding?"

"The philosopher Vico believed the bastard children of Noah's sons became giants by feeding on the nitrates in their own feces, which they rolled around in—primitives that they were—and that their large stature and fat fingers led to crude and awkward building practices."

"You're... something else," the woman said. "I'm Kate."

"Wally. Wally Bern."

"So, Wally, what are these little houses all about?" She tapped the napkin, leaving two or three wet spots on it. "Is this how architects doodle?"

Their sandwiches arrived and Bern swept the napkin into his lap. "I suppose... periodically, most professionals seek a renewal," he said, aware of his shyness, his formal manner. "A return to first principles, right? When the business starts to feel stale or the ideas dry up? We try to remember what drew us to our work in the first place—that initial euphoria, the falling-in-love—and we reach back to basics."

"Sure," Kate said. "When you get in a rut."

"Yes. Well, in my profession, the hut is often seen as the most basic building design. The source: column and roof. The idea that it must have been raining the day Adam and Eve left Paradise. They had a sudden need for shelter, you see, so they grabbed the first things they could find. Tree limbs for structural support, leaves and grasses for their ceiling."

"Cool," Kate said.

"There's something very appealing, very elegant, about the *spare*."

"So." She brushed foam from her lips. "Your ideas are stale, huh?"

"Excuse me?"

"These doodles. Back to basics. You're feeling a need for renewal?"

Bern wiped his mouth with the napkin. Kissing the hut, he thought. Falling in love once more. "I'm not sure. The truth is..." Did he really want to explain? To someone just killing time after work? "...I've been thinking, in the last day or so, about the wrangling over the World Trade Center site...the rebuilding process, you know, the *meaning* of it...how we've lost sight of the basic needs for that area, our community values..."

"Like?"

He didn't know *what* he wanted to say. Why had he prattled on so? "We have a fundamental desire to understand what happened there and why, so whatever we do with it should involve, I think, first principles."

"Wally? You want to put a *hut* at Ground Zero?"

Bern stared at her.

"Well, well. You are *crazy*, baby." She ate her sandwich.

* * *

Did he believe what he had told the woman at dinner? He hadn't said so many words—to anyone—in weeks. Nerves. The unexpected break in his evening routine. The loss of the Wall of Hope and Remembrance.

A need for renewal?

He walked and walked, all the way up to Bryant Park, past the statues of Goethe and Gertrude Stein, then back down to the Strand. The E. B. White book still sat, prominently displayed, on a table near the front entrance. Next to it, Henry James's *The American Scene*. Bern picked it up. Published in 1907. After a twenty-year sojourn in Europe, James had returned to New York to find its "Gothic" pride "caged and dishonoured" by "buildings grossly tall and grossly ugly." Some of these, Bern knew, were the Beaux Arts beauties E. B. White would find charming, but for James they were filled with too many windows, ruining their "grace."

New York's style had changed, wholesale, at least twice—if such a thing could even be measured—since James had first observed it. Bern made his way over to Twenty-third Street, taking another circuitous route past the Flatiron Building, past Edith Wharton's birthplace—an old Anglo-Italian brownstone—and the Hotel Chelsea. At home, he tried to read himself to sleep. "Sweet, sacred, and profane"—this is the "hut dream," said Ann Cline.

In the street in front of McGee's someone yelled obscenities. "She don't *want* my skinny brown ass no more!" another man barked into a cell phone. A car horn brayed.

Bern closed his eyes and tried to picture a garden, a soothing space in which he could slumber, but various thoughts intruded: E. B. White; auburn hair; leaky roofs. Lodoli seems to have believed it was humanity's aim to perfect Nature. Imperfect in itself, Nature offered materials to men and women of genius who, in choosing certain substances for particular designs, improved the makeup of matter. In this way, the world strove to return to Paradise.

Bern imagined moss roses, hoping to will himself into a dream. Acres and acres of orange and yellow blossoms around the family house and near his grandfather's grave, north of Houston: the small granite stone under swelling Gulf Coast clouds, the swoon-inducing sweetness of pollen, and the dense, rich loam underneath.

3.

Glasco's remained closed the following evening. The plumbing sign had been removed. A new sign said, "Vacation. Back in Three Weeks." Bern suspected something more sinister at work. Elsewhere, he had witnessed the gradual letting-down of clientele, as in the saga of the Gotham Book Mart, which had apparently been dying of high rent for two years now without admitting as much to its customers. No one knew the store was in trouble until the steel fencing came down in front of its windows, shutting out of reach the first edition Joyces and the copies of *The Sun Also Rises* signed by Papa himself. Had Glasco's lost its liquor license? Had the building been sold?

The Cedar was even louder than last night. Bern didn't see an empty chair until one sailed across his sight line, dragged by a booted foot. The foot—a lovely and perfectly functional ornament—belonged to Kate. "Okay, hut-man. I've been waiting for my turkey and mayo for thirty minutes now. I'm hungry and bored. Tell me something crazy," Kate said.

Bern sat beside her. "Well, then," he said. "All right. Have you heard of Carlo Lodoli? History's greatest architect. He was cursed with ambitious students who distorted his teachings. He felt—or we *think* he felt—that all architecture, even the 'primitive,' had value, but his apprentice Algarotti dismissed whole continents of builders."

"You don't say."

"There are peoples on the Earth, Algarotti said, who, lacking materials or a 'certain kind of intelligence,' make their huts 'out of the bones and skins of quadrupeds and marine monsters.' It's clear he disapproves."

Kate cased the busy room. "I'm *thirsty*, too," she said. "Tell me more."

"Trouble arises naturally. Pleasure has to be planned for."

With cool gray eyes Kate appraised him. "How did you spend your day, Wally?"

"Sketching, on paper—"

"Not a computer guy?"

"Not a computer guy. Sketching, on paper, methods of squeezing a light scoop past a fire escape."

"How old are you?" Kate asked. "What's the matter with computers? ... Oh, bless you," she said to the waitress who arrived with a pint of Guinness and took Bern's order for a pilsner.

"Forty-nine. And computers..."

"No, it's okay, I get the picture. A Luddite in love with huts... I mean, you know, a little out of touch, aren't we, Grandpa?"

"What's wrong with computers is, they minimize the hand," Bern said, trying to resist Kate's humor. This girl, he feared, could make him giddy. Unseemly, at his age. *Focus.* "Building comes from nerve endings. Fingertips. It's all about the body. But also"—as he spoke, he twisted the cardboard coaster in perfect little circles on the tabletop, and Kate watched him, amused—"with a sketch, you can't tell just by looking at it if it predates the structure or if it's a rendering of something already there. Drawings have this magical quality, past and future all at once... they're preposterous."

"You lost me there," said Kate.

"*Pre* and *Post*, *before* and *after*, all in the same word. *Pre-posterous*. The ideal architecture."

Kate laughed.

Was she put off by him? Charmed? Bern thought the latter, but he wasn't sure. She *had* asked him, the other night, to entertain her. Now, maybe she was just being polite. At least she didn't get up to leave right away.

"Forty-nine, eh? So this 'renewal' business," Kate said. "Midlife crisis? Maybe a little late in your case..."

"I don't know. What *is* a midlife crisis?" Bern said. "Something dreamed up by magazine editors to sell copy."

"But you all have one, right? Sooner or later? All you guys. Wife?"

"No."

"Girlfriend? Boyfriend?"

"No."

"When was your last affair?"

"A couple of years ago," he said before he could check himself, prompted by the easy sway of their conversation. She waited for more. "I was married for two years in my late twenties. A Texas girl who hated the east and went back home. I'm okay, you know, being alone. I like solitude."

"Sex?"

His face burned. "Well, yes."

"So what do you..."

"Are you always this forward with strangers?" Bern asked.

She smiled. "You're not a stranger. Life is short, Wally."

Her sandwich appeared, and Bern ordered a garden burger. "Okay, old friend," he said. "How did you spend *your* day?"

"I'm a staff writer for a magazine called *Theatre News.*"

"Oh. I'm sorry. What I said before... I don't really have a gripe against editors."

"It's okay." She touched his arm. "Naturally, the old hands get the plum assignments and reviews—*Vertical Hour*, *The Coast of Utopia.* I get the off-off-off stuff. But last week I got to meet Wallace Shawn—the lispy guy in all those Woody Allen movies? Another Wally! That was exciting. And the editors let me do a capsule review of *Translations* over at the Biltmore—the Irish play? It's the leprechaun in me."

"Hence the Guinness?"

"Cheers." She raised her glass. "My family's roots are in Ireland. As whose aren't? Anyway, we have a small but avid readership and I write small, avid articles."

"How long have you been in Manhattan?"

"Four years."

Still a tourist on the island—as was he after two decades. "From?" he asked.

"New Orleans." Before he could speak, she added, "I haven't been back since Katrina. I'd find it too devastating. I want to remember it the way it was."

Bern mentioned the muddy bayous of his upbringing.

"Houston! So! You and me, Wally," Kate said. "Big storms in common."

"Moss roses?"

"Oh, my god! You should see, in my apartment—I couldn't get over it when I saw them for sale at a street market here. In January! How do they do that?"

"Boyfriend? Girlfriend?"

"Boyfriend. Sort of. A lighting technician over at the Beckett."

"Sort of?"

"We're...volatile with each other, which is sometimes good, sometimes bad. You know? So we're on-again, off-again."

Bern played with the coaster. Kate watched him. "Tell me, Wally. How's your hut?"

"You laugh," he said, "and of course it's just a fantasy. But there's a certain *rightness* to the notion."

She *did* laugh at him.

"I'm serious," he said. "A return to origins. What better place for it? And it needn't be crude—the savage *box* most people picture when they hear the word *hut*."

"What do you mean?"

"I mean..." Should he? "Where *is* your apartment, Kate? Can I walk you home? I'll show you on the way."

"Wally. Are you a weirdo-psycho-creep?"

"Not weirdo-psycho."

"No rolling in feces? That sort of thing?"

"Not lately."

"Okay. Let me finish this."

Her apartment was on West Twelfth—part of an old condo, she said, that had been partitioned into hotel rooms and rental units with community baths. On the way, she mused, "I know what your trouble is, Wally. If you're thinking about Adam and Eve and *preposterous* and giants on the earth, but you're spending your days with fire escapes, well then, you're bound to feel a bit..."

"Displaced?"

"Yes."

"Perhaps. And the closing of Glasco's...but..."

She laughed. "You *do* like to talk, don't you? For a quiet sort."

A silent beat. Then: "Lodoli—the guy I told you about?—he liked to walk with his apprentices, looking at buildings. He saw his 'lessons' as a series of strolls and talks—*conversation*. His favorite mode was the allegory."

"And yours?"

"The apology, I think." He stumbled over a curb. "Among Lodoli's students were young women. Unusual for that day and time."

"Is that what *I* am tonight? Your student?"

Was she flirting? Was *he*?

"Not at all. But here," Bern said. "Here we are."

They had come to the Presbyterian church. Bern took Kate's shoulders and positioned her in front of the grand entrance. At first, she winced at his touch, but then she seemed to settle. "All right. Imagine this building made of wood instead of stone," he said. "Slender tree trunks framing the entry, and the arch at the top formed by flexible willow limbs, curved and tied together. Can you see it?"

"Yes!" Kate said.

"Good. And the ornamentation, the busy carvings above the doorway—like foliage. In the spring, when the rooted willows sprout new life—"

"Is *that* where the design comes from? Those Gothic monsters in Europe?"

"It's a theory. So: simple wooden construction—the hut—as prototype for our greatest creations. The echo of origins. It needs to be there, like an old message in a bottle, for anything we make to have meaning."

"At Ground Zero?"

"Anywhere," Bern said. Lodoli would object. Apparently, the lost master was anything *but* a traditionalist. Still, if you love him, you must fight him, Bern thought. How else to keep the mental conversation going?

Kate nodded at Bern but looked uncertain.

"You're cold. I'll get you home," Bern said.

They strolled quietly up West Eleventh. Near Gene's, the Italian restaurant where Bern had eaten lunch the other day, they came upon a clump of small, mossy stones just off the sidewalk. "What's this?" Kate said.

Twenty or so jagged markers in the shadows, behind a tiny iron gate. "A cemetery," Bern said. "Of the old Spanish and Portuguese synagogue. Some of the city's first Jewish immigrants are buried here. In fact, this is one of the oldest graveyards in Manhattan."

"It's lovely."

"Yes, it's a favorite spot of mine. I walk by here every day."

They squinted to read the dates on the stones. 1683. 1734. 1825.

"This plot used to be much larger," Bern explained, "but city commissioners ran a road through West Eleventh and cut it in half about 1830 or so, disturbing a few unlucky souls."

He started to point out the unusual number of relief carvings on the headstones—remarkable, given the Jewish aversion to graven images. A snipped-off flower (life cut short), the Angel of Destruction waving a flaming sword at Gotham. He stopped himself. No more Teacher tonight, he decided. Why *did* he go on so, hiding behind his moldy old facts? To protect his thin and shabby inner life? From what? Kate seemed to enjoy him in a smirky sort of way—an Irish tolerance for blather?—but he didn't want to press his luck. He didn't flatter himself he was sexy; on the other hand, he didn't want her to think him an old pedant.

A green Mystic Oil truck rumbled past them. Garbage spilled from ripped bags on the corner. A rat scurried behind a low stone wall. Bern glanced down Seventh to the Vanguard. When he had first come to the city in the early 1980s, he spent an evening in the club listening to Woody Shaw. Shaw was dead now. So was Max Gordon, the club's old owner. Ghosts of jazz. Bern remembered Shaw's drummer as ham-handed and loud.

A man in a motorized wheelchair, hunched and smoking madly, whizzed past them, nearly knocking Kate over. Bern steadied her, touching her arm. Two men in blue cotton overcoats strolled by them. "What I'm saying is, all of our daily encounters with people, even with our friends, are essentially *financial* in nature," one man said to the other.

Kate led him up West Twelfth. She pointed to a lighted window in her building. "There. Can you see?" she said. Bern followed her gesture to the fifth or sixth story: creamy yellow light through rippled panes of glass. A wrought-iron railing just inside the window frame. Wrapped around the railing, orange blossoms. "Moss roses!" he cried.

"Welcome home," Kate said. "Thank you, Wally. For the lesson, the tour."

"I'm sorry, Kate. I get carried away. Pompous."

"It was fun."

"Sleep well."

"You too. Forget about fire escapes, just for tonight. Dream of…"

Bern pecked her cheek and backed away.

4.

A few days later he read in the *Times* that St. Vincent's Hospital, which had "lost money for several years," planned to demolish its current building and erect a sleeker, more efficient facility across the street. The paper cited "New York's shrinking hospital industry" and said that St. Vincent's old "mazelike layout," with some rooms dating to the 1930s, had become too expensive to heat, light, and cool.

In the early afternoon, walking up Fifth to scope out a new project he had been assigned, he saw that a shop for skin creams and facial care now occupied the high-windowed space (with old leaded frames) where Scribner's Bookstore had formerly displayed its treasures. The culture had declared its priorities: vanity over history, art, and literature.

Well, Bern thought, recalling Kate's gray eyes. On one level, hard to argue.

I like solitude. Had he really told her this? However true it was, she had tapped into a deeper reality. "Rut," she said. "You get in a rut." Loneliness had become a habit with him—a common enough malady, he supposed. Especially here. Especially now.

Kate had evened his keel. Nowadays, his melancholy over the rapid changes all around him was mitigated by the pleasure she took from the regular walks they made together, from "his knowledge," she said, "of the city's many layers."

"This talk of many layers," he said uneasily one afternoon. "There are scads of books..."

She squeezed his arm. "But you're my *personal* Baedeker."

"Me?" he thought. What about Lewis Mumford? E. B. White? But he held his tongue. That day with Kate, Bern worked assiduously to stem his commentary—he faced no such problem alone, but now, in her presence, he became aware that his *thinking* could be antisocial, a hostile, distancing act if it wasn't parceled out.

"Like *this* neighborhood," Kate said abruptly, tugging his sleeve.

They had turned onto Greenwich Street, between Rector and Carlisle, just south of Ground Zero. The Pussycat Lounge. A peep show, a topless bar. "Your timing is uncanny," Bern told Kate. "This is actually a very interesting area."

"I knew it!"

What was he to do? It was difficult not to recede behind lectures when she prompted him like this, encouraging his natural propensity. Like dear old Lodoli, Bern considered strolling—the cold experience of *touching buildings*—a means of learning "in blood." "You really want to know?" he said.

"Absolutely."

"From, say, the 1790s to about 1820, this was the poshest real estate in Manhattan."

"Mansions?"

"Sure."

"To-die-for clubs?"

"The jet set of the eighteenth century wouldn't party anywhere else. New York City got its start here at the southern tip of the island." He waved his arm. "This was the home of the mercantile elite until waterfront shipping changed the dynamic."

"Hey, Professor," a greasy-haired man with an eight-ball tattooed on his chin called to Bern from a smoky doorway, "we got lap dances from ten bucks. Your lady friend's welcome too."

Kate pressed close to Bern without actually touching him. He ignored the man's black chin. "A developer wants to tear all this out now."

"Good riddance, yes?" Kate said. "Like when they cleaned up Forty-second Street."

"Except—and there's always an exception—the building housing the Pussycat, here, is over two hundred years old, a Federal-era townhouse and, as such, unique and valuable. It's the old story. The developer claims to envision a better New York—wiping out blight, hmm? The Pussycat's owner claims to want to preserve the city's rich heritage. Up to a point, both men have a legitimate position. And of course, no one's listening to the ghosts of the old well-to-do, who gave the city its start and were swept away long ago."

"What kind of ice cream do you like?" Kate asked. On most afternoons, despite her apparent interest in his stories, she had about a twenty-minute limit for his oratory.

"Plain vanilla, I'm afraid."

"I could have guessed it. Let's go. I know a place just around the corner here, and it won't be crowded this time of year."

Her bounciness, an almost desperate craving for distraction, convinced him his "lessons" really did delight her—"*All* Southerners are history buffs," she said. "You've read Faulkner, right?"—and this helped Bern swallow *her* first principle: "No sex between us, okay, Wally? It's not an age deal, or anything." Bern judged her to be around twenty-five—she wouldn't come right out and say. "It's just that, what with Gary"—her man—"I need a *friend*."

"Sure," Bern had said, wondering where the opening lay in this genteel arrangement. There was always an opening. Her solicitude had tempered his fears of unseemliness. He could be patient. In a shockingly short time, he had learned to depend on her company, as he had formerly staked his comfort on solitude.

Now, today, on Fifth Avenue, anticipating supper with Kate at the Cedar (Gary—whom Bern had not yet met—had a late evening at the theater, with rehearsals for a new play), Bern reflected on how his renewal had arrived: not with the Ann Cline book or his sketches of huts, but from the conversations Kate tripped him into, the challenge of articulating his cherished principles to a person who had never heard them before. New people! Who knew?

He wished he could share his revival with the city. Apparently, post-9/11, the thirteenth century was "in" again. Barricades. Blocky walls. The old/new urban style. He thought once more of the Freedom Tower. The prismatic glass panels planned for its base couldn't hide the *flinch* in its frame. The other day in the office, one of Bern's young colleagues had joked that, in the age of expanding terrorism, architects required military training: "Mark my words. We're going to see Rem Koolhaas marching around Rockefeller Center in a helmet and a flak jacket."

If only the city had kept its *lightness*. Bern missed the "Phantom Towers," the twin beams of light cast into the sky from Ground Zero, six months after the shock: a powdery afterimage of what had once existed on the spot and a public echo of the private vigils that had taken place with candles in every neighborhood. An architecture of the imagination.

He also missed the spirit of sober whimsy visible in the attacks' immediate aftermath: for instance, the suggestion (who had made it...some artist?) that the barricades around the smoking pit be replaced by plastic piping—shifting, soft, ringed with buckets for flowers. Instead, burdened by habitual politics and the egos of celebrity architects, the site's fate had locked into a predictable pattern, with little hope of renewal.

Either way, Bern thought—vulnerability or an impregnability so forbidding even citizens felt imprisoned—suicide was the end result.

Perhaps a giant marble head of Robert Moses was the most appropriate marker for the site. Vandal planners could sneak into the area at night, swords at the ready, zoning codes hand-printed on vellum clutched to their armored bosoms. Ritual dances could be aimed at cursing the mayor. Chanting, drumming, spray-painting Jane Jacobs's face on the Power Broker's pockmarked nose, a nose the size of a motorboat.

The city's many layers. If Bern had helped Kate manage them, she had enabled him to tunnel back into and forgive himself his first reckless enthusiasms here: the art parties he'd been invited to on upper Broadway and in SoHo and Chelsea when he'd just arrived, a fresh young professional. For a few years he'd stayed active in the art scene, shyly attending openings, until the high energy of mingling with strangers finally wore him down.

He recalled Dan Flavin's wedding in the Guggenheim—'92? '91? A friend of a friend, a staffer with the Landmarks Preservation Commission, had gotten Bern an invitation to the gala because the artist's young bride, a painter, was a Texan. Bern's acquaintance thought he might know her, as if Texas were no bigger than a kitchen. The bride was stunning, tall and dark-haired in a shimmering white Isaac Mizrahi dress. All night, Bern skirted the edges of the ceremony.

He didn't long now for the awkwardness of grand public occasions, preferring his sandwiches in the corners of quiet bars, but jogged by Kate's fondness for the city's tchotchkes he remembered the mystery and magic of certain moments. For Flavin's wedding, the museum's inner walls were bathed with ultraviolet light, with yellows, pinks, and greens turning the corridors into rivers, the walls into warm energy. That night, Bern felt the building and everyone in it would lift into the air; he imagined the bride's dark hair grazing his face as they rose hand in hand into paradise, scented with blossoming moss roses . . .

The one blemish on Bern's private wall of remembrance was his ex-wife's unhappiness. Marla came from an old Houston family with conservative politics and narrow social values, yet she had always seemed easygoing and nonjudgmental—until New York. The prodigious drinking and sexual energy at art parties rattled her. She claimed she wasn't homophobic, yet Bern felt her stiffen in the presence of gays. Manhattan acted as a palette knife, scraping off the unfixed surface of her personality and revealing the coarser base underneath. A common enough story. But this isn't fair to her, Bern thought. Even in 1983, when she complained about the city's squalor, its noise and dirt and heat, its exorbitant prices—"Back home, for this rent, I could get the fucking Astrodome!"—he understood that deeper currents shocked her into smashing against her surroundings, and he may have been part of the problem. Just as the city's rhythms unlocked movements in her behavior that Bern hadn't sensed before, it unleashed his latent capacities for self-absorption, obsessive work, quiet anxiety. This much he had learned about himself in twenty years: whole swamps of his quirks remained hidden from him. He had known from the first that Marla didn't have patience for his pronouncements, not the way Kate did now.

What continuing part, if any, did Bern play in Marla's mental life? A few years ago, a friend informed him her father had died, a gentle man whom Bern had always liked, and he had given her a brief condolence call. He hadn't spoken to her since then—over a decade now.

Remembrance. Hopeless.

Over the years since Marla's departure, he'd developed a reputation in the office as a loner, slightly off-kilter, seldom dating, seldom leaving early for the day. He worked hard, earning the firm a small, steady profit, so his job was secure. But the young guns (he was about their age when he started), these kids with their software lingo, their gossip about Robert Venturi and postmodernism, viewed his passion for history, his "seeking the truth in building" as quaint. Behind his back (but not so softly he didn't hear it) they called him the "Utopian." In the coffee room, one of them would quip, "You know, Wally, eventually every utopian experiment ends in tyranny and disaster," and they'd all crack up. Bern thought it a serious point, worth pursuing.

What he really wanted to tell them, if they had granted him the courtesy of entertaining his ideas, was that he didn't care about Utopia. From his office window he could point to billboards, tenements, distant shipping cranes, sewer pipes exposed beneath jackhammered sidewalks, the used clothing store... he could turn and ask his colleagues, if they had ever gathered in his office to listen (as he often imagined them doing—on a pleasant late afternoon, say, the sun in bright squares on his carpet, a lazy warmth in the room), "What do the things we see around us have to do with our inner lives? Is this blandness a reflection of who we are? Or do we come to reflect the objects we live among?"

But the original young guns had all moved up or out, leaving Bern in the same old spot surrounded by fresh faces, men and women whose years he *did* now exceed. Considerably. The youngsters got the corner offices, the sexy commissions (trendy night spots, restaurants in Trump's benevolent shadow) while the nonprofits trickled down to Bern, the social service agencies in need of a bit more room, old churches looking to remodel, foundations with cash restrictions—projects for which a slow pace and a simple approach could still turn a profit for the firm and earn Bern's bosses citizenship points throughout the community.

Lately, *function* was the firm's motivational catchword, according to Jerry Landau, Bern's immediate supervisor: workplace as System, with each component fulfilling its designated capacities. Bern understood function in more natural terms, as the *suffering of a process*, the way wood weathers over time or the body experiences mild discomfort as it goes about its sweet digestive task.

He stood now facing St. Patrick's Cathedral. Shadows of birds moved lazily on the white marble arches. A man with a camera bumped his shoulder, mumbled "Sorry," and moved to take a picture of the church's shaded steps. The man said something in French to a female companion. Bern caught the words *sacre* and *cité*. *Sacre*, he recalled from school, meant "cursed" as well as "holy."

He remembered reading, years ago on an airplane, a not-bad thriller about an IRA man who rigged the cathedral with bombs.

The church's treelike spires and gently bending portals reminded him of his moment with Kate the other night in front of the Presbyterian's arch. Mysterious groves, these houses of worship, forests encased in stone, hiding secret rituals. Wind wheezed in the gaps among the rose-colored windows. The breath of orphans, Bern thought, children now forgotten, whom monks once tended on this site, long before the cathedral was built. The structure's thin arcs resembled oak limbs laden with ornaments: animal skulls, pelts, and hides—the leavings of a sacrifice, the attempt to dress up murder as a thoughtful gift to the gods.

Bern shivered, the sunlight cold on his skin. A group of Japanese tourists joined the French couple in a digital snap-fest. Bern turned. He didn't want to hurry back to the office, to the chatter of his young colleagues. Moving slowly down Fifth, he was startled to see a pair of homeless men kneeling under a makeshift shelter in the space between a clothier and a bank. Since Giuliani's Days of

Stomp-and-Thunder, the homeless had become largely invisible in New York, especially in an area such as this. The men recalled recent photographs of post-Katrina New Orleans.

A shopping cart, cardboard, blue plastic tarp...but the squatters had also outfitted their space with metal buckets of differing sizes and paper kites arranged to create an airy, split-level effect, almost Oriental in its aesthetic. Ingenious. While in grad school, as part of his dissertation project—an investigation into architectural origins—Bern had traveled to some of the world's political hotspots. Nicaragua, Yemen. He had witnessed brilliant adaptations of the "primitive" to the modern, to organic necessity, to cultural arrogance: in Managua, he had marveled at the marriage of native stone to Spanish colonialism, and in Sana'a, at the use of dun-colored mud in sheltering animals, children, and the elderly—but never, he decided now, as he admired what these men had done with their scraps, had he seen such elegant adaptability.

Dread. Bern thought, Isn't that what drives construction—fear of harsh sunlight, wind storms, lightning? Honoring terror, a precondition for beauty, instead of trying to stave it off? One of the men shared with the other a slice of uncooked frozen pizza.

This spot, with an asking price of nearly $1,500 per square foot, was, Bern knew, one of the most expensive strips of real estate on the planet.

He passed an IRS branch office. With each ticking second, an LED sign above its door tabulated the national debt. The numbers, in the trillions, flashed as quickly as the burps of a Geiger counter he remembered using in his middle-school science class. One day, he had sat with twelve other sweaty kids in the center of a football field to measure the assault of the earth by solar rays.

On the north side of Union Square, Bern saw a billboard touting "Lifestyle Buildings." He didn't know what a "Lifestyle Building" was, and he experienced a moment of panic. Was it possible that eventually you lost your edge in the city? Dulled by overwork, so you couldn't even spot a wedge of geese . . .

When he reached the office he spoke to no one. Two of his colleagues argued in the hallway outside his door—something about a realtor "flipping a building, repping a new client." "We *all* know product doesn't move that far south of the fucking park," said one of the men. "Everyone in America knows that!"

5.

The wide glass doors of Bern's building infused him with relief from half a block away. A quick change of shirts, a fresh tie before running to meet Kate... when he entered the lobby, he saw Mrs. Mehl sitting hunched and red-eyed on the sofa. Ryszard, the super, knelt beside her, dabbing her face with a wet cloth. Two tall blondes and a dark woman with taut, boxy hair (a look Bern associated with fashion magazines and stoned stupidity) stood in the center of the room. They held whippets on diamond-studded leashes. The dogs were gorgeous, vividly sculpted, gray with wispy orange streaks down their legs.

"I told him, 'Why shouldn't I style my personality after my pet?'" one of the blondes said to her companions. "Style is style, darling. You take it where you can get it."

Bern thought, No animals were harmed in the making of this psyche.

He nodded hello to Ryszard and asked Mrs. Mehl what had happened. She said she was taking her cat to the vet, making her way through the lobby when "these three harridans stomped in with their smelly old beasts and scared my little poopsie. She ran out the door."

"We should have known we had the wrong building," the dark woman said to her friends. "*Look* at this dump. Stephane would never stay here. He'd be ill."

"All right, all right," Ryszard grunted, waving his arms. No matter the concern—a burst pipe, a minor break-in, a scuffle in the elevator—from Ryszard it was "All right, all right" and a choppy wave of the arms. He was Polish, pretended he had never learned much English (though he managed just fine with the language when he wanted to), couldn't repair a paper clip, yet somehow had earned the landlord's trust. He'd been a fixture in the building for years.

True, he was strangely effective in emergencies involving livid people. Bern figured this was because Ryszard's presence was such an anomaly, people backed off rather than engage a fellow with whom it was clear there could never be any resolution. He reminded Bern of a puffer fish he'd seen once in a wildlife documentary.

The whippets left the building, tugging the harridans behind them.

Ryszard pressed the wet cloth into Bern's hands and shuffled to the stairway. Bern helped Mrs. Mehl into the lift. She was the very image of reduced yet indomitable dignity, like the homeless men on the street. "I'll draw up some fliers. We'll post them around the block and over at McGee's," he told her. "We'll find your cat." For once this week—the fire escape still nettled him—his drawing skills might be useful. Mrs. Mehl described the animal to Bern. "Her name is Madame Anna Mona Pasternak," she said. "After my aunt, in Minsk."

"That's unusual."

"It's her *name*."

"Yes, yes. Of course."

"Put it on the flier."

"I will."

The old woman moved slowly down the third floor hallway, and it occurred to Bern she could pass away before they found her pet. He wouldn't be surprised to hear in the morning that she had died in her sleep. Well, he thought: life among others.

The phone in his living room blinked its round red eye. A message from Kate. The moment he heard her voice, he convinced himself she had called to cancel. "Wally, I walked by the Cedar today at lunch. It's closed!" she said. "There's a sign in the window, saying the disruption is only temporary."

He stared at his moss rose. What was more distressing—the news about the Cedar or the insecurity Kate's voice had just caused him? Was he becoming too dependent on this girl?

"Why don't you come to my place?" Kate said.

Her place.

"I'll fix us some gumbo. A salty little taste of the Gulf, how's that? And Wally? I know what you're thinking."

Flame in his cheeks.

"You're thinking it's another loss—the Cedar."

His shoulders fell. Once again, his insecurities had forced him face to face with his vanity. Naturally, it didn't occur to Kate that her invitation would arouse him, even mildly. She didn't think about him the way he thought about her. Wasn't that clear by now?

"The sign *does* say 'Temporary,'" Kate observed. "Let's wait and see, okay? It doesn't mean the sky is falling again."

Sweet girl.

"I'll see you around six?" she said. The loud click of her hang up echoed the ticking of the numbers on the national debt sign.

Bern pulled from his closet a fresh white long-sleeved shirt. Should he iron it? The collar was askew. Wouldn't ironing suggest—*reveal*—to Kate a hope on his part?

It's said that Carlo Lodoli was perpetually disheveled and dank, distracted as he moved through the world. Yet young people flocked around his tattered, tottering frame, eager to hear his talk.

In the bedroom, Bern considered his face in the mirror of his dresser. Querulous. Pale. An expression of frozen surprise. He recalled the lost eyes and mouths on the wall at St. Vincent's. Tucked inside the wooden edge of the frame around his mirror was a newspaper clipping, yellowed now, about the discovery of an old burial ground in Lower Manhattan. Workers had unearthed ten to twenty thousand slave remains when they dug a pit for a new federal building. Bern had kept the clipping to keep alive in his mind knowledge of what Kate called the city's layers—the island's onion skins. Paper and bone. A passing breath.

The clipping nudged another scrap on the mirror, also beginning to yellow: "Ten Rules for Cardiovascular Health."

Bern's dresser was thick with relics from his past: a framed quote from an Isaac Babel story: "You Must Know Everything." Marla had given it to him for his twenty-eighth birthday. A cherrywood box for paper clips and pennies, also a gift from Marla. A comb, rarely used. An empty container for "Cactus Candy," a souvenir of Houston, vividly blue and green with a hot yellow streak on the side of the box. Probably these things will outlast me, Bern thought. Through the years, their hard edges will soften but remain, and here they'll stay: testimony to the life I lived, good or ill.

Kate's place resembled a parochial school, with framed, out-of-register prints of St. Patrick and the Virgin on the wall above a bookshelf. On the shelf were candles in thick glass containers imprinted with the faces of saints and prayers for salvation, fortitude, and luck.

The solemn atmosphere, broken only by a couple of sports magazines left open on the floor, was bolstered by Faure's *Requiem*, playing softly on the CD player. Bern recognized the stately Kyrie.

In the lobby, on his way to the elevator, Bern had noticed the grime on the walls, the tiles like weak, malarial eyes staring at him. The stench of old cabbage and rotting meats in black plastic bags piled in a side room next to the elevator shaft caused his stomach to clench, the odors clashing with the scent of the single rose he'd brought for Kate. The feathery erotic charge tickling his skin since her phone message dissipated in the lobby's pungent assault.

The building's hallways appeared to be part of a wasp's nest, cells within cells. Rough, sandy walls. Holiday decorations—all out of season (red Christmas bells, cardboard skeletons, brittle and dry four-leaf clovers)—sagged on a few apartment doors.

When Kate let him in, her roses and the cayenne prickle of the soup carried him back into East Texas bayous: the hunt for crayfish in muddy bottomlands packed with steamy brown leaves, warm seepage from rice paddies . . .

"How nice," Kate said, taking the rose from his hand. She placed it in a glass of water and set the glass on a wood plank atop her antique radiator, next to pots of roses. Starlike blossoms strained toward the window and the lights of the street. "Portulaca, the man at the market told me these were called," Kate said, touching the flowers. "I'd never heard that name. I guess that's what they say up here. Wine?"

"Yes, thanks," Bern said. Through her window he glimpsed satellite dishes, ash cans, rainspouts.

She pulled the cork from a bottle of cabernet.

"No Guinness?" Bern asked.

"I only drink Guinness in bars, to impress older men," Kate said. She saw him eyeing the saints. "I know. It's like a K-Mart convent in here. I'm lapsed, don't worry. What can I say—I like the kitsch. It comforts me. Childhood, you know. You?"

He thought she meant the wine, to which he had already assented, and he stood puzzled. Then he realized she was asking about his religious upbringing.

"Oh. Nominally Jewish. What the newspapers call 'cultural Judaism.' Little to do with faith, so I never had a chance to lapse—though my grandfather tried to interest me in the rituals. I must say, I've noticed in others that 'lapsed' is a pretty murky category."

Kate laughed and raised a thick brown brow. "A Texas Jew..."

"It's true, we were rare in our part of Houston. But not ostentatious...which is why my wife's family, good Southern Baptists, finally accepted me in spite of their doubts."

"You married hellfire?"

"She told me she had lapsed."

"I see."

Now the *Requiem* soared. The minor strains of the "Offertory" gave way to the "Sanctus." The violas wept.

Kate didn't join him in the wine. For herself she poured a glass of mineral water. He felt the odd treat of seeing her beyond public arenas, among her private things, at a rhythm of her choosing. He would watch. He would learn.

"Gumbo's almost ready," she told him. "Relax. Mi casa es tu casa... does that apply to rentals? Anyway, kick those magazines out of your way... Gary's old baseball stuff..."

At the mention of the name, Bern stiffened involuntarily. He stepped around the magazines as though they were predators whose sleep he shouldn't disturb. The wine tasted like pepper.

She ladled the gumbo into fat yellow bowls, topped off his glass of wine, and placed a stiff baguette, wrapped in a tea towel on a platter, on her tiny dining-room table. She switched off the lights in the kitchen. Candlelight perked across her forehead, nose, and cheeks. They toasted. The *Requiem* reached its climax—in "Paradisum." The piece's martial pacing opened up into lighthearted trills: for one jaunty measure, Bern caught something like a Rodgers and Hart beat. Perverse of him to hear, in sacred strains, the Great White Way. What kind of philistine was he? What was he doing here?

"—stereotypes," Kate was saying. "Two summers ago, in Northern Ireland—my first and only time there—and it was strange because I felt a pull from the place, given my family history and all, but I wondered how much I had talked myself into... you know, tourism and prefab nostalgia... and how much of my attraction was genuine? What did 'genuine' even mean?"

Bern watched her face and nodded as she spoke. He brought a spoonful of steaming soup to his mouth. "This is delicious," he said.

"Could have used more salt. Anyway," she said, rising, "what was I responding to? Some smell from the stones? The moss? The air? Were the genes stirring inside my body? Or was this feeling just bullshit, the magic of my Visa card?" She laughed, placing a new CD in her player. "Now for something *completely* different. Do you mind?" A computerized thudding imploded in her speakers.

"Not at all," Bern said.

"Death Cab for Cutie," Kate said, tapping the CD case. "I just discovered them. But Ireland. It was weird, Wally, because *my* family's experience wasn't the happy-go-lucky... you know... drunken revelry, storytelling, that sort of thing. The O'Dochertaighs—my ancient relatives—were the last of Donegal's seventeenth-century clan lords. The summer I visited, I'd drive my rental car into some village on the coast, stop and ask directions, talk to folks. When they found out I was an O'Dochertaigh, their faces crumpled. 'Ah God,' they'd say, 'not another one.' They'd squint at me: 'Yes, yes, you'd fit in any ditch around here.' I mean, four hundred years had gone by, and *still* the O'Dochertaigh name was associated with brutality and war."

"Pleasant group, your folks. Available for weddings, wakes, and plunder."

"In a pub one night, a nice old gent even suggested to me... gently, politely, but *still*... that the O'Dochertaighs were just like the Israeli army, occupying Gaza. *Centuries* in the past!"

"Well, but look what's happening now in Belfast," Bern said. "Gerry Adams and Ian Paisley breaking bread together. Unthinkable, right, even a few years ago."

"Yes, it's confusing," Kate said. "Incredibly hopeful, on the one hand, and on the other... you should have seen Derry, Wally. So moving. The 'Free Derry' murals at the Bogside, commemorating the Bloody Sunday martyrs. But there again... someone had come along and spray-painted pro-Palestinian graffiti across several of the pictures. Like there was no difference between... ah, hell..." She laughed. Her cheeks had flushed with excitement, the color of warm copper, a color Bern wanted to touch, the way he often felt compelled to run his hand along smooth staircase banisters in vintage buildings—the slow, comforting ascent, a retreat from the world outside.

"I'm one to talk," Kate said. "One of my ancestors, a warlord named Cahir, sacked Derry in 1608—a deliberate provocation of the British. He burned the place to the ground. So that's *my* family's legacy. Great, right? I've got the death of a city on my conscience, and the people there won't let me forget it!" She laughed again.

"What if I designed a hut for you?" Bern said. " 'The Atonement Hut.' You could offer it to the Derry city council."

Kate smiled but her mood had slipped. "Wally?"

"Yes?"

"Do you think we'll ever get over it?"

He searched her eyes.

"You know."

He had splattered soup on his shirt. He dabbed the spot with his napkin. "Naturally, certain individuals will never get over it," he said. "But it seems to me that—except for the site itself—the city has moved on, for the most part. Doesn't it seem so to you?"

"Yes. I guess. But—*should* we move on? Maybe *that's* what I'm asking."

"Ah."

"I mean, I know we have to. Sort of. But your hut—isn't it…"

Bern slid his hand toward hers—aware of the stain on his shirt, of the sweet smell of roses in the room. "Kate. By any chance, is this about New Orleans?"

"I don't know," she said. "I—"

"Maybe you should go back and see it. You still have friends there, right? Places that meant a lot to you."

"Yes. My friends the Lindahls have…well, they lost…" She shook her head.

"I'm not a believer in 'closure,' " Bern said. "But I do trust reconnecting. Grounding oneself. When you told me you hadn't been back since the storm, I confess I was shocked."

"First principles."

"Yes."

She removed her hand from his. "Well, this is awfully gloomy talk for such a lovely evening. I'm sorry. How did we get into all that? I was telling you about my family, my trip to Ireland." She refilled his wine glass.

"Will you join me?" Bern said. "I can't drink the whole bottle."

"I shouldn't." She wrinkled her nose. A little girl's face: an attempt to pass off as trivial something quite serious. Bern sensed this immediately. "It's annoying, and I can't believe myself," Kate said rapidly, her eyes full of reflected candle flames. The room's low light and its shadows made her face fluid, her nose and lips resembling tips of underwater reeds, now foreshortened, now elongated as the candles flickered. "This morning I realized... I think I'm pregnant," she said. "Pure carelessness. I haven't told Gary, not until I'm absolutely certain, and he's going to... Wally? Wally, what is it?"

She stared at him as though she feared his heart had exploded. And his heartbeat *did* quicken, surprising him.

"It's nothing, really. Just a little morning sickness," Kate said. "That's why I'm avoiding the alcohol."

Bern wiped his mouth and stood. He walked over to the bookshelves. Dizzy. The wine. The roses. He studied the face of a saint on one of the tall glass candleholders: an androgynous, childlike figure in a blue-plumed hat, with brown curly hair, dark eyes, and a rose-petal mouth. The saint, seated on a wooden throne, held a basket and a golden staff. "The Holy Child of Atocha," said a paper label on the glass. "Purify our hearts by the example of your meekness."

He turned to Kate. Though she sat in shadow, he saw she had registered what surely marked his face. Sexual jealousy. A man of his age! Yes, yes: he was a pathetic gag gift at someone else's party. A trick can of peanuts... pop the lid... the fake, ungainly snake.

"Oh shit," Kate said.

Bern stared at his shoes: smeared with the dirt of the streets.

Kate carried the yellow soup bowls to her tiny kitchen sink. Death Cab shook the room. The flowers trembled. "I thought we... I thought you understood," Kate said.

"Yes," Bern said.

"But?"

"But."

She whirled to face him, her wet, soapy hands on her hips. "Can we get around this, Wally? I really enjoy our friendship."

Her words sent heat through his arms and caused an amorous swelling. Kate glanced at his pants. "Do you..." he said. "Excuse me, where is you-your..."

His stutter appeared to enrage her. "Down the hall. To your left," she said tersely.

She didn't have a hallway. He stood rooted, a disoriented, carnal clown. Then he remembered that, on each floor of this old building, three or four units shared a single bath. She meant the hallway outside her apartment.

Architecture!

He walked to the door.

Institutional green tiles lined the bathroom walls. A toilet and a shower missing its curtain filled the miniscule space. Someone had left a plastic bag stuffed with pink soap and a hairnet hanging by a cord from the shower nozzle. The nozzle dripped black water. The toilet bowl was plugged with shit and enough paper to fill a Brooklyn phone book. The odor dampened his lust. Oh my god, he thought, recalling Kate's outraged look, the firm set of her mouth, did she think I'd run in here to—?

His vision blurred. His shirt stain seemed to spread, like the smell in the room. He tore off a piece of toilet paper and wiped his forehead. His stomach pitched. He took slow breaths until his pulse returned to normal.

By the time he got back to Kate's living room, rage coiled in the muscles of his arms, though he couldn't locate its source. She stood in the kitchen where he'd left her, drying her hands on a towel. A sting of pepper in the air. The gumbo. His eyes watered. A smell of smoke. One of the candles had guttered.

Kate wouldn't look at him. "I'm sorry, Wally. Maybe it's not possible to... I mean, for a man, a man who's been lonely for a while, and a young woman—"

"It's possible, Kate. We'll do it, okay?" His words sounded harsh.

He had no control. "It's just that, I didn't picture myself babysitting some young couple as they worked out their little soap opera..."

Mistake, he thought. Erase. Erase.

"Babysit?" Kate said.

"You're right. I'm feeling sorry for myself. I shouldn't..." Act your age, old fool. Tighten the screws. "I apologize."

Kate crossed her arms over her breasts. The dish towel hung from one of her hands and covered her torso, demurely. "I think you should go, Wally."

He made a formal bow. A bobbing punch-clown. "I'm sorry, Kate."

"I'm sorry, too."

"Thank you for dinner."

She nodded.

Only steps away from Kate's he felt his shoe crack—a slapstick flapping of the worn right heel—as he crossed Seventh where, apparently, the new St. Vincent's would be built. Bern went through shoes at an alarming rate: three pairs in the last six months. Shoddy craftsmanship, he thought. Then: Of course she doesn't want me. I'm just an old curmudgeon.

In the middle of the avenue, a crumpled Starbuck's cup blew against his instep.

His heart beat fast again. His hands smelled of salt and cayenne, and faintly of the flower he'd cut for Kate.

The western sky was glassy violet with a smear of orange. From the shadows of the hospital a dirty, khaki-clad figure reeking of gin and onions lurched at a pair of girls. "Cigarette," he said. "Fuckface. Fuckface." The girls fell back against a wall. Bern thought of stepping in—but why? To do what? Assert himself? At his age? These girls were old enough to stroll around the city on their own, to cope with whatever the streets tossed up at them. One of the young ladies fished a cigarette from her purse.

Bern started to head up Seventh toward a subway station. On

Kate's corner, a raucous party erupted out of a brownstone's doorway, down the building's concrete steps. Young people laughing and drinking beer from silver cans. Many of them appeared to be interns at St. Vincent's—they wore wrinkled green medical smocks. A basket of blue paper slippers, the kind doctors pull over their shoes for sanitary purposes, stood on the stoop. The revelers seemed to be using the slippers as party favors, wearing them on their heads or hands, or stuffing them into their pockets so they resembled boutonnières. Inside, the crowd danced to laborious hip hop while dressed to treat gunshot wounds, burns, and lacerations.

Bern glanced back one last time at Kate's place. Would she let him in now if he showed up, hangdog? Probably she'd gone to bed. He veered away and, thinking of her, missed the subway station. Well, it felt good to walk. It always felt good to walk. His shoe heel clattered on the street like the ceramic tiles hung on a chain-link fence, three or four blocks back, commemorating 9/11. The tiles came from New York well-wishers: "Oklahoma City is Thinking of You!" and "Arizona Says God Bless NYC!" When wind blew and shook the fence, the tiles rattled like seed-filled gourds.

Tomorrow he would telephone Kate. Yes. He was the mature one here: it was up to him to make things right. They *would* forge a friendship, by God—against all odds. Men and women: it could be done. Belfast, right?

Don't get carried away, Bern told himself. After all, "making things right" meant taking small steps. Building a hut one mud brick, one pole, at a time. An apology. A design for a fire escape. A poster for a missing cat. He had learned his lessons from Lodoli, had *become* Lodoli, watching the great cities of his time wax and wane, and wax again. Live lightly on the earth, he thought, and leave all pages blank.

On a sidewalk grating Bern paused impulsively, then steadied his feet as a subway train thundered beneath him.

◊◊◊

Suitor

The cabbie pushed a button and rolled down the windows rather than ease out of his coat as he drove. Shivering in the back seat, Bern concentrated on an ad posted in front of him in a small silver frame: a Lincoln Center staging of the Romeo and Juliet ballet. A few years ago, he had seen a production of *Romeo and Juliet*. The show's second half featured few dances because, by intermission, most of the characters had been killed.

Not the best story line, perhaps.

Like his little pirouette with Kate. He was eager and afraid to see her now.

The cab dropped him near the Dakota. A boy with skin as dully textured as Miracle Whip led a knot of tourists to the corner of Seventy-second Street. "The ghost tour begins in five minutes!" he called. "Spirits of the famous dead..."

Bern slipped into the park across the street, between idle horse-drawn carriages. In a tiled circle inside a small plaza, a mosaic spelled the word *Imagine*. People sat on benches gripping Met bags, eating pretzels the size of babies' fists, or reading papers—"Celtic Tiger!," a piece about Irish entrepreneurs snatching up Manhattan real estate. A bald man with a blue dragon tattooed on his neck sat by a tree reading a biography of Einstein. Bern found a spot on a bench next to a Jamaican woman, apparently a caretaker hired to watch an elderly lady. The lady shook violently in a wheelchair, precisely in everybody's way. Her companion waved a bagel in her face. "But I dropped it on the ground!" the old girl said. "Well then, I guess you can't *eat* the damn thing now, can you?" said the nurse.

Where was Kate? Making him wait. Punishing him for that terrible night last week.

Of course, he deserved it. He had known she was living off and on with a guy. He had learned she was carrying Off-and-On's kid. How could he have violated their friendship?

We're buddies, Kate had always said to him. *Yes?*

He was too damn old for this. And she was far too young to tolerate his sorry needs (midtwenties? she'd never said). The perils of the city. This is what happened when you packed people tightly on an island. It was impossible not to feel the *warmth* of the body beside you.

What the hell, he thought. In a few more years, maybe at sixty-five, sixty-six, I'll get prostate cancer. Maybe *that'll* put an end to this miserable daily ache.

Dried flowers formed a circle around a splintered guitar lying on the sidewalk. People dropped coins into the instrument. "Peace and love. Yeah, right," said one boy to another, walking past. They wore Harvard Business sweatshirts. Japanese teenagers pushed through the crowd, snapping digital pictures of each other, whispering, "Beatle John! Beatle John!" Nearby, a fiftyish-something husk slumped in a wheelchair, a more ragged contraption than the bagel lady's. He held a German Shepard on a leash. A Cat-in-the-Hat top hat wilted on his head like a Neapolitan ice cream cone. "Welcome! I'm the Mayor of Strawberry Fields!" he called to the strollers. "Oh yes, oh yes, we loved Johnny Rhythm, didn't we?"

He pointed to the dark apartment building towering above the trees. As an architect, Bern knew he was supposed to love the structure's ornate grandeur. But it was *fussy*. Thick. "See that black railing in front of the white shutters... up there on the seventh floor... that's where he lived. Yoko still sleeps there. Wasn't it just the greatest love story of the century, folks? *Wasn't it?* "

A few minutes later, with a lull in the sightseeing, he wheeled his chair to the scuffed guitar, picked it up, and shook the money out of it. He stuffed the coins into his coat. "Hey! Fuck! I need me some juice!" he yelled at a small Hispanic man sitting on a bench. "You! Pancho! What say you push me on down to the corner store?"

"Man, I got no time for this!" the fellow said.

The Mayor said, "Fuck you. You got the fuckin' time. What are you? Late for a fuckin' Security Council meeting at the fuckin' UN?"

Bern rubbed his eyes. Maybe this was a mistake. Maybe he should just slip into a coffee shop, warm up for a few minutes, and take a subway home.

Then Kate appeared, hunched and flushed, from around a curve in the path leading to the street. She wore a long wool coat, charcoal gray, and a green scarf. "Sorry I'm late," she said, squeezing next to Bern on the bench. It occurred to him she had chosen a popular spot to fend off intimacy.

"Are you all right?" he said.

"Nausea. You know."

"Should we—"

"I don't have the strength for a long discussion, Wally, but I needed to see you."

"Me, too."

"I didn't want us to end on that badness from the other night."

"We don't have to end, Kate."

"We do."

He stared at his hands. "I'm a grown-up. I can control myself."

"Of course I know you have the best intentions, Wally. And I miss spending time with you. I enjoyed our friendship. But what's there is there... actually, I'm glad you confessed your feelings... it's good to get them out... but I'm not strong enough... *you're* not strong enough..."

Wait, he thought. Had she just admitted *she* was attracted to *him*? Or did parsing her words prove her case: despite his good will, he'd always press her for more?

"No, Kate."

Her cheeks, already crimson from the cold, reddened further.

"You're never not sure, are you?" she said. "But that's not the point. I'm sorry. I'm sorry. The point is—"

"Katie, please—"

"...the point is, your certainty is another reason we're *wrong* together, Wally. You're the teacher. The expert on everything."

"No, no, no."

"Absolutely. That's how you see us. That's how *I* saw us, too, at first. I liked it. Your little lectures to me. From that very first night we met at the bar."

"I thought they were conversations."

A sad, brittle laugh. "The gap between Venturi and...who was it?...Gehry? Pediments and dormers...I'm sorry, Wally, what were they?..."

"I'm no expert, Kate. Especially about...you know. I'm a fool. I'm ashamed. I apologize," Bern said. He felt for her fingers. "Really. I won't say anything more about my...my..."

"You don't understand, Wally. I *crave* your certainty." She smiled. "It's comforting, so different from people *my* age, and I don't want you to change. But given what's happened..."

"No, no, no."

"Stop 'no-noing' me!" She puffed her cheeks. Then she doubled over, holding her stomach. She's right, Bern thought. The body will have its way.

Without speaking, he seized her hand and pulled her out of the park. Down the block he spotted a Greek deli, not too crowded. He pointed to the facilities in back. "I'll wait for you here," he said. A roast pig turned slowly on a wooden platter in the window. Several minutes later she joined him again on the sidewalk.

"Can we get a cup of coffee?" he said.

"No. I have to meet Gary," she said.

"Ask him to take you straight home. You need to lie down. Kate. Can I call you? Please? We need more time. I *am* your friend. I won't try to be anything more than that. I promise."

"Wally. No. I—"

A carriage driver passed them, whipping his horse. The animal did not respond to the blows: its exhaustion seemed saintly, beyond the possibility of pain. "Hey! Stop it! Stop it!" Kate yelled at the man. He glanced at her contemptuously and raised his whip again. Kate turned to Bern, outraged, as though *he* had staged this incident for some unfathomable reason. She looked dangerously weak and pale. "I'm going to be sick!" she muttered. She scurried away.

Bern felt certain he would not see her again.

The perils of the city.

He stared after the carriage at the spot where he'd got his last glimpse of her. The horse whinnied. Any minute now, Bern thought, this beaten brute will crumble to the street. At least its agony will have ended.

He laughed bitterly at his self-pity. A self-pitying man is not capable of being *anyone's* friend.

Oh, now—*that's* self-pity, too, he thought.

He turned for his apartment.

2.

Too much. He was talking too much.

Conscious of the need *not to teach*, he tried to keep his mouth shut. But Kate! A week after their last meeting, she had called and asked to see him again, yet now she sat glumly in the restaurant, twirling her fork, poking at the head of a langoustine in its bed of yellow rice.

Nervous, Bern gulped his first glass of wine, asked for another. He stared at the crab meat on his plate. It glistened warmly. Waiters bustled around him in the narrow aisles between tables where diners came and went, bulked up in wool coats and floppy cashmere wraps. Every now and then, cold gusts from the opened door swirled the caramel-cocoa odors in the air.

Bern's nose ran. He dabbed at it with his napkin. Kate's usually clear gray eyes seemed drained of color. "Are you feeling better?" he asked her. "The nausea?"

"Fine," she said forcefully, as if this was the last word she ever meant to utter.

So Bern—halfway through his second glass of wine—described for her a recent walk he'd made past the ice rink at Rockefeller Center. A work crew in green caps and maroon coats maneuvered quiet machines across the blade-scritched ice, glazing it with water, he said, while impatient skaters huddled around the ring, chatting, laughing, munching bagels or hoagies. Bern stood and watched the scene from the sidewalk, dwarfed by the shiny metal statue of Prometheus.

"Sounds nice," Kate said, clearly underwhelmed.

Bern nodded. What had been the point of telling her this? Honestly. Was he suggesting they go skating sometime, like a pair of young lovers? No. No point, really.

The things that struck him that day at the rink were so private, so completely beyond sharing, and so fleetingly insignificant, *awareness* might as well take a hike, he thought.

It was ridiculous. *He* was ridiculous.

How could he tell Kate—and why should he—he had stood there, that afternoon, recalling the frozen lake in Dante's *Inferno*, one of his favorite books in college? Satan brooding in the center of the earth. Then he'd noted the joke (were the center's architects and designers in on it?): Prometheus, the bringer of fire, guarded the ice. Then his mind swelled with jigsaw scenes from silly old television shows—visual bric-a-brac as tangled as the ice tubes, electric wires, and water mains invisible beneath the street. Only later did he realize he'd thought of these shows because RCA, Rockefeller Center's old tenant, had churned them out from its studios here when he was nine or ten years old. Somehow, deep in his brain, he had made a connection... just as, moments later, he underwent an auditory hallucination—chopper blades. Vietnam. Cambodia. And why? Because General Electric, maker of napalm—the bringer of fire—also lived in the Rock.

TV. College. A well-edited war. O, what a mix of miracles was a man!

A young girl, leaving the restaurant, said to her friends, "I hear they're tearing down Coney Island. Let's go out there and get high."

Glancing at Kate across the table, Bern considered communication—even *failed* communication—a minor amazement. "More wine, sir?" asked a passing waiter.

"Yes, please," Bern said. Accidentally, Kate dropped a clam shell on the floor.

"So," said Bern. He cleared his throat. "Have you written many new pieces?"

He'd looked for her byline whenever he came across a copy of *Theatre News.*

"A few. The usual. You know."

"Seen some good shows?"

"Nothing to shout about."

She was watching him like an animal eyeing a snake, Bern thought.

"Is this what you did, growing up?" she asked.

"What do you mean?"

"Questioning everything. Like, Talmudic study."

"You feel I'm interrogating you?"

"A little bit. Yes."

Bern was about to ask why she'd wanted to meet tonight, but she pressed him. "What *was* it like for you, growing up Jewish?"

"Oh, I don't know."

"Really. I'm curious. We nun-beaten micks don't get outside our circle much." She laughed, and seemed to relax for the first time. "Your education...did you read the Bible a lot? Or the Torah—what's it called?"

He fingered the stem of his glass. He would have to slow down if she continued to stall. Don't push, he thought. Give her some slack. "Well. The most intense reading I ever did—religious reading—was in a study group when I was a teenager," he said slowly, drawing out the words. Filling the social space. "We read the Five Books of Moses with our rabbi." He took a sip of wine. "He was very good, insisted we pay attention to the literary qualities. Characterization. Narrative arc. Metaphors, repeated images. He steered a course between the way most lay people read sacred texts—looking for heroes, inspiration, that sort of thing—and the Midrash, the laws and meanings rabbinical students are supposed to take from it. We saw Abraham and Isaac, Esau and Jacob, David, all the rest, just as people. Flawed, ordinary people who—granted—did extraordinary things sometimes."

Kate nodded thoughtfully.

"We refused to draw morals from the stories. We tried to live them, walk with these folks, find parallels with our own lives. It was a very fine education in... empathy, I would say, as well as reading."

Oh Lord. He was dangerously close to *teaching* again. And he caught himself totting up risks: the suggestion of a movie later this week, a concert, a walk through Central Park? These activities masked his true concerns: his body weight and hers, his middle-aged stamina, the pesky aches in his joints in the mornings, the care he should take with his heart.

She sat silently.

It is what it is, he thought, trying to picture *him* with *her*, a view from above, the two of them sitting at the table. Two characters in a story. A love story. But you don't have to act on it.

Still, he decided, is anything sweeter than two people who genuinely enjoy each other anticipating, moving toward, then consummating new sexual bliss?

How do I let this go?

The waiter passed again. What the hell. Bern asked for another glass of wine.

This seemed to prompt Kate to come to the point at last, before he was beyond absorbing it. "Wally, I need your help. This weekend," she said. "Two old friends of mine from my New Orleans days are coming to town. A couple—Glenn and Karen Lindahl. They lost nearly everything in Katrina."

"I'm sorry," Bern said.

"They've been living in a Best Western in Houston. Anyway, a couple of weeks ago I got the idea of throwing a small party for them, inviting some of the theater folks I know, really generous people, collecting money and supplies. Just enough to get the Lindahls through this little stretch of time. I've talked to my friends here. Most of them are willing to give, and so... I'm going to do it. A small gathering at my place on Sunday."

"That's wonderful," Bern said.

"Well. I'm calling on everyone I know. I need help getting ready for the party. Shopping. Straightening the apartment. Moving furniture."

"Sure," Bern said. "Absolutely. Count me in."

What was she withholding? Nothing she said explained why she had wanted to meet for dinner. A simple phone call would have done for the party. Her reserve restrained him, as well. He waited patiently, watching her pick at her rice. Her gestures were delicate and contained. Observing her, he understood with some regret (because he wanted to be a better man, more present and giving in the moment) he was intrigued with Kate *philosophically*; that is, he was compelled by her necessity to him as a woman, the need he had for a certain kind of feminine beauty offering grace, grief, acceptance, and lament: qualities he also asked of the architecture he loved and, yes, romanticized.

Construction *always* fell short of its promise. Okay. So what?

Kate pulled a chicken bone from her mouth and set it on the table next to her plate.

In his contemplations of beauty, he was only seducing himself. Oh, for the lightness of a Ladder to Heaven, he thought. My life weighs too damn much.

"Gary left me," Kate said quietly, setting aside her fork.

He removed his fingers from his wine glass. "What did you say?"

"He's gone."

And just like that, gravity seemed to drain through a hole in the bottom of the earth.

"First things first," Bern said. He steered Kate past a circle of people milling in the halo of their collective breath on the sidewalk outside the International Film Center. He took her down bright lanes, warmed by quickly moving bodies, skirting Washington Square Park. "The party on Sunday. Let's get through that. If you'll give me a list, I'll do the shopping. Food, drinks, whatever. On Saturday I can come over and help you arrange the apartment. Your friends, the Lindahls, will stay with you for a while, right, so that'll be a comfort. After that, Kate, whatever you need, however I can help..."

"He said he couldn't handle the baby," Kate said. "Can you believe that? I expected him to be nervous about it—hell, *I'm* nervous about it—but..."

"I know."

"Wally, I didn't think he'd leave."

He patted her back. Near the park's south entrance, a man sold jewelry, clothing, and books. He prowled behind loose boxes wearing a gray sweatshirt and furry Sherpa boots. At his feet, spread across quilts, turquoise, a lifelike baby doll, a broken-spined volume, *Journey of a Soul*, written by one of the popes, and a Jimmy Durante album.

The park shone under spotlights mounted on spindly metal stands; a portable generator growled among twiggy bushes. Perhaps someone was filming a movie scene or a television commercial. Under the arch, a klezmer band performed a Tom Waits song. The spotlights burnished dancers. Swirling shadows moved against the limbs of the trees, a large half-moon above.

Kate pressed her body against Bern's left arm. "I'm scared," she said. "Raising a baby alone..."

"A lot can happen in the next few months."

"And I'm scared about us."

"I understand."

"I need you, Wally. I need you to be my friend."

"I *am* your friend, Kate."

Laughter and applause for the players. Wooly dogs on leashes. Leaden air. A man sold individual flowers from purple buckets: irises, lilacs in green water. A car backfired as the band began again. Lemon light through the trees. The rasp of an airplane engine broke the moon-tinted darkness beyond the boundaries of the park, at first as soft as a grasshopper whirring, then louder as the plane came into view. Everyone stared, as though its appearance signaled something uniquely important to each of them. What does it mean? Is my life going to change?

Bern watched the bobbing heads. Against all odds, we're bred to endure, he thought. He reached for Kate's hand. At first unsure, she relented, and offered a tentative squeeze of the fingers.

3.

The Lindahls were delightful. Easygoing, down to earth. Glenn was a tall man in his early thirties, pale and blond. Karen's shoulders swayed as she talked. Her eyes glistened like chicken broth in a pot, verging on boil.

Kate's smart-talking actor-friends could lead a parade. Loud and gaudy. One young diva wearing…what *were* those godawful things—toreador pants?…glared at the CD player as if soldering its parts with the heat of her gaze. A middle-aged woman, clearly used to attention, wore a tall, wiry wig: like the whirling brushes in an automated car wash. In the kitchen doorway, an old woman squeezed past Bern, her face a welter of marks. Time had chewed her up and spit her out.

Kate stood across the room from Bern, plainly exhausted. He circled the dining room table, served himself salad. The spoon in the bowl was hot to the touch, the handle slightly sweaty. On a blue dish, slices of lime, their delicate curves reminding Bern of the planet Venus, the green crescent he had seen once through a planetarium telescope. Next to the dish, melon rinds, tossed like dentures in a stainless-steel bowl.

Three young men, exuding a powerful musk, huddled near Bern, discussing the Tonys. "Brian F. O' Byrne," said one. "*Coast* is going to sweep this year." "No no," said another. "If Frank Langella doesn't win it, I'll eat my Equity Card. As for Vanessa Redgrave, I mean, really honey, doesn't she get *enough* adulation?"

"The awards will never recognize them, but the best shows this year were all south of Fourteenth Street. Those little storefront theaters?" the third fellow insisted. He tried to snatch an apple from the table, couldn't manage it around the bulk of one of his pals. Bern reached over and handed it to him. He glowered.

A producer. Who else would suspect kindness?

He had a thrusting tongue—warping his teeth—and a splashy heart, no doubt, pumping his body full of blood. A man whose business probably involved legal robbery. Just what the GNP demanded. He turned away from Bern; a whiff of cologne, dusty, like walnuts.

How do I appear to these people, Bern thought. Do I hide my feelings well enough? *Too* well? Can they tell I'm adrift in abstractions? Behind on my taxes?

He leaned against a radiator next to a window. The glass was strangely discolored as if streaked with English tea. Light filtered through it, turning, near the ceiling, the green of felt on a well-worn billiard table. Bern saw a truck in the street, moving laboriously, burdened, it seemed, by a weak heart. He believed he could smell the block's wretched garbage, lolling in plastic bags up and down the curb, but perhaps it was his own panic he smelled, the sense of not belonging. He had felt it the last time he'd come to Kate's apartment.

We're friends. Yes?

Grand gestures, frantic talk. Makeup, piercings: tribal markings. Men and women poised to ambush one another. In every corner, sexual etiquettes clashed: the courtly and the cool. Pressure. Languorous flirtation. Romeo and Juliet. John and Yoko.

Right in front of him, neuroses simmered to erotic excitement, like the reduction of rich sauces over a burner's high heat.

He inched toward the Lindahls. The producer had herded them into a corner. "*Godot*," he was saying. "In the Ninth Ward. Staged on the rotting porch of a flooded old house. Now wouldn't *that* present a powerful message?"

"All due respect," Glenn told the man, "it's hard for me to see the city as a theatrical backdrop."

"Well, but art can be a powerful healing force."

"Well, but money is better."

Bern overheard Kate speaking to a woman whose diction was a mix of College Drama Department and *Sex in the City*. He was relieved to see annoyance cross Kate's face. Was she, like Bern, always out of place, no matter where she was? Lines etched the drama woman's chin. A pale space, like an inoculation mark, separated her eyebrows. These genetic dispositions would look unflattering soon, but for now (she was *just young enough*) they gave her an off-kilter beauty.

The producer, failing to elicit from the Lindahls the awed response he sought, stepped away. Bern approached them and told them he was sorry for their losses. They thanked him for his kindness. "How *is* the city?" he asked.

"Mildewed. Putrid. Gone," Glenn said.

And then Kate stood beside him. "I'm bushed," she whispered. They stood in a corner in candlelight.

"Your party is a great success," Bern said. "You've done a marvelous thing for your friends."

"Yes. I'm happy. I just wish I could sneak away and rest for half an hour."

"Come home with *me*."

Kate patted his arm—impatiently, he thought. Why couldn't he keep his damn mouth shut? He had no business at a party. If he had ever possessed social skills, they had long since eroded.

One by one, the actors made their exits.

Kate assured Bern the Lindahls would help her clean the mess. They'd stay for another couple of days. She'd call him after that.

"You're sure?" he said.

"Yes, thank you, Wally."

He said goodbye to Glenn and Karen. No idea what to wish these sweet people.

Evening had chilled the sidewalks. St. Vincent's upper-story windows blazed yellow down the block. The actors vanished up the street, in search of Zoloft, in search of fame.

"Good night!

"Good night!"

"Good night!"

Bern lingered on Kate's front stoop, its top step spilling him gently toward a raucous noodle factory next door. He felt deflated; his pre-party expectations had leaked away, into the ether. Was he disappointed now? No. He had fulfilled the function of friendship, the best thing he could do for Kate. It's what she wanted of him: right behavior. *Reasonable*. A tepid substitute for *passionate*—a bland leftover, like something cold and soggy smothered in Cling Wrap. Still, it was a takeaway from the party. Possibly, now, he'd be invited to the next celebration.

Through an open window, he heard clattering forks and plates, the rattle of trash bags. Three old friends from the Easy. One of them, he couldn't tell who, cried.

Three days later, he met Kate at Grand Central to see the Lindahls off. Glenn and Karen had witnessed enough of New York. "Your city's still here," Glenn said. "But, I mean, it can't be said to *work*, in any sense *I* understand."

Beneath the figures of the Zodiac, painted on the blue-domed ceiling, Kate hugged and kissed her friends. Then they ran to catch their bus to La Guardia.

Bern took Kate to the oyster bar downstairs. In the vast, open room, under coils of light bulbs wrapping stone arches, they wolfed clam chowder. At the table next to them, two delicate Japanese women struggled for dignity while wearing oversized lobster bibs, then gave up and tore ravenously into their lunches. Shells sprayed the hard, cold floor.

"I feel accused," Kate said.

"Of what?" Bern asked.

"Betrayal, I guess. Glenn's indictment of Manhattan. Like, why am I living here when New Orleans needs me?"

"Number one: your friend's still in shock. Two, you *do* have a life here, Kate. A job, a network of pals."

"But with Gary off the rez—"

"And *three*, you've got to take care of yourself. Volunteer workers are swarming the streets of N.O. What could you add?"

"A while back—when we first met, remember?—you urged me to go. As a friend. Reconnect, you said. It'll do you good."

"Well—"

"It broke my heart, hearing them talk. Did you *listen* to Karen? Muddy beds in the alleys. Cars stacked against walls. Sea straw, broken trees..."

"You knew this, Kate."

"But I hadn't faced it. You were right about that. And the cleanup..."

"I know."

"A trailer or two, a little fiberglass, a little plasterboard, and FEMA's finished for the day. How are Glenn and Karen *ever* going to get home? What do they have to return to?"

"I agree. But Kate, please, concentrate on what's in front of you."

"The baby, you mean."

"The baby."

4.

In the next few days, they developed a sweet ritual. After work, Bern met her on Ninth Avenue, at the Alvin Ailey American Dance

Theatre. She had enrolled in a beginning ballet class taught by one of the company dancers. "Pregnancy-friendly," Kate said. "I can push myself as hard or as easily as I like. It'll keep me limber before I'm too huge to move." Bern sat on the building's front steps or on an egg-shaped concrete stool just inside the revolving door during the hour and a half Kate sweated in class. Through a slender window he watched her bend, stretch, roll her arms. Live piano music rose from a small room at the bottom of a stairwell. On most nights, dusky blue rain-light poured through the building's front glass walls. Bern became enamored of the storklike young ladies passing through the lobby. Chatting on cell phones, they dropped to the gray carpet in front of the elevators to stretch their legs. Gay black boys in old Tupac or Jimi Hendrix T-shirts pressing the lift buttons with long fingers were the essence of grace. The sensual mix of ethnicities—Hispanic, Asian, black, white, in-between—made the place shimmer. It seemed everyone here was on a path to purification, in body and spirit, with discipline and great good humor: preparing for some higher level of evolutionary development. It got so Bern felt an erotic charge whenever he saw from a distance the orange banners—"Ailey!"—on the side of the building.

Each day after class, he walked Kate to an unpretentious Italian place, Puccini's, for dinner. Only a dozen or so tables; an old brick wall along the back. It was early March: evening mist shrouded the streets. The fresh scent of invisible blooming things softened the chill in the air. The restaurant was BYOB. Bern would settle Kate at a candlelit table and walk up the block to a liquor store for a bottle of Chianti. By the time he returned, their salads had arrived.

He and Kate recovered their mutual ease, their *friendship*—though Bern was afraid to touch her. And though he basked in her company, longed for her when she wasn't with him, he wasn't sure what he wanted from this arrangement.

One night after dinner they strolled past a Middle Eastern restaurant. Loud Israeli men lingered by the door. Each spoke into a cell phone, authoritative in some obscure capacity. Around the corner, Bern and Kate spotted half a dozen black limos displaying government plates, and three or four taxis parked on the street, the drivers smoking cigarettes next to their cars. "What is *this?*" Kate whispered. "A call-girl neighborhood for the fucking high and mighty?"

"Or maybe a bunch of foreign dignitaries, holding a hush-hush meeting," Bern said.

The intrigue (even if Bern and Kate only imagined it), the hint of secrecy and money, titillated them. Kate grabbed his arm and giggled, pressing her breasts to his side. Bern's face flushed. Then, as they stood there, a fire truck stopped silently at the corner. For the first time, Bern noticed a crumpled figure on the sidewalk. An ambulance arrived, then two police cars. "Some billionaire who had a heart attack in a hooker's bed?" Kate wondered, squeezing Bern's arm. "A Russian mob hit?" he countered and they walked, laughing, up the street, prickled by deepening mist and the warmth of each other's bodies.

Kate asked him to stay the night.

"You're sure?" he said.

"It'll be the most innocent night of your life, believe me. I'm sure."

She made a pot of chamomile. "That's nice," she said. He'd been stroking the back of her hand. "You know, so far, the worst thing about pregnancy..." She squeezed her thighs. "It's what it does to your conception of yourself. As a woman, I mean. I watch others in the dance class. I look in the mirror and think, any day now, what a bloated, ugly..."

"No," Bern said.

"I didn't think he'd really leave."

"I know."

She turned to him. "Do you think I'm—"

He placed a palm on her belly. "I think you're exquisite, Kate."

Tears came. She tried to laugh. "I'm being vain."

"Shhh."

They watched part of a Tracy-Hepburn movie on TV. Affectionate repartee, romantic wit. Kate wanted him in her bed. Chastely. He stripped to underwear and a T-shirt. They spooned beneath the sheet. Bern asked himself what he was doing. Kate needed care. And him? Maybe he was needier than he'd dreamed. A baby? A little girl or boy? Kate slept. Delicately, he rose and stood by her bedroom window.

In the street, a young couple jogged past a pizza place. Bern watched them in the neon bath of a Pepsi sign. I'd like a small deep-dish, extra cheese, with pepperoni and X-Y chromosomes, please.

He lay back down, wondering what good, if any, remained in him. Here he was, clinging to a woman for ease and assurance, when *she* was the one needing attention. A fine thing! Tomorrow morning, he would get up, shower, towel himself off...pretend he was just another decent man!

That night he dreamed pregnant dreams: rising dough, hot-air balloons, great windy dirigibles.

The Village Cinema just down the street was showing Jean Cocteau's *Beauty and the Beast*. Bern talked Kate into going with him. She wore a yellow smock. She'd tied her hair in a lazy bun; it wasn't going to stay, and he found himself gleefully eager, waiting for the soft and sexy tumble.

The film—an old, scratchy print—broke twice, blurred. Beauty looked as bristly as the beast. The crowd booed. Bern didn't care. He was happy, holding Kate's hand. He cried at the end when the handsome lovers kissed.

Afterward they walked to a hamburger shop to split a basket of fries ("I'm craving grease," Kate said, "platters and platters of grease"). Kitschy paintings of Marilyn and Elvis lined the light-green walls, old 45s ("Telstar," "My Boyfriend's Back, "Love Potion Number Nine") stocked the restored, ancient jukebox, and a pair of fifties car fins crowned big silver doors marked "Guys" and "Gals."

The Cokes came in thick glass cups with paper straws.

Bern loved the good-old-days décor, the laughter, the talk. Men and women at play. "They do nostalgia very well here," he said. "Kind of romantic."

Kate nodded.

"Anything wrong?"

"No. Well. Gary and I used to come here."

"Oh," Bern said. "Of course. Of course. We can go somewhere else."

"It's not the place, Wally. Really. I like it. It's... when you mentioned nostalgia..."

"What?" He touched her arm.

"That was Gary's whole deal. I mean, look around."

He considered the tables, the curved booth seats, plump leather angles spilling people into each other, accommodating the body's desires. "I'm not a kid. But here I am, in this neighborhood, right in the middle of the Nikes and the back-assward baseball caps. Why?" She shook her head. "Gary wanted to 'stay young.' He liked living like these New School students. Reminded him of his best days, as a fraternity jock."

"Football?"

"Soccer and track." She slurped her Coke. "And fucking."

Bern squeezed her fingers.

"I knew of at least a couple of affairs he had after we were together. He's probably having one now." She rubbed her eyes. "He doesn't want a baby because he's an immature little piss-ant."

"A deadbeat."

"A son of a bitch."

They laughed together.

Anyone who'd strand ample Kate...

"Well," she said. "It's a weary old story."

"Not to you. It's your life."

She looked at him over the cooling basket of fries. "You're a nice man, Wally."

"I like you."

"I know."

They walked back to her place in misty, prickling rain, bright from reflections of buzzing curbside signs. On the sidewalk in front of her apartment building, her bun finally unraveled, a shock, a gift. "Kate," Bern whispered, and kissed her lips.

In bed she rubbed his thighs. He spread almond oil on her belly. "That's wonderful," she said. She closed her eyes. "My doctor says some women, when they're pregnant, lose all interest in sex."

Bern tickled her navel: a pink, oval bloom. "Yes?"

She took his face in her hands. Fertile Kate! "Wally. We're still going to be chaste, okay?" she said. "But bring that oil over here." She lay back and unbuttoned her blouse. "My breasts are a little sore. Go easy."

"How's this?"

"Mmmm."

"Yes?"

She nestled in his arms.

5.

On Saturday morning, Bern took Kate to the Irish Hunger Memorial. She had always wanted to see it, to "get in touch with my heritage... you know, especially now the baby's on its way."

From Vesey Street it appeared to be a castle's ruins. Up close, it resolved into a craggy, manmade hilltop overlooking the Hudson on one side and the financial district on the other. Plants native to Ireland hugged low granite walls surrounding a two-room cottage shipped from County Mayo. It had been reconstructed, stone by stone, as a tribute to New York's Irish immigrants. A small turf fire burned between four flat rocks, lighting the slim, grassy slope.

Kate wept silently, walking the winding path around the cottage. She looked peaceful. Wistful. She folded her hands on her belly. She was just beginning to show. Bern followed her at a respectful distance, leaving her alone with her thoughts. Words carved into the memorial's walls commemorated the Declaration of Human Rights.

Irish ballads were chiseled into the stones, and Gaelic proverbs: *Ar scáth a chéile a mhaireann na daoine* ("People live in each other's shelters and shadows"). Sparrows nested in moist niches.

Afterward, Kate stayed quiet as she strolled with Bern along the river, past a children's park with a wading pool and a fountain, a merry-go-round and a pair of slides. Jersey City and Ellis Island rose in the distance. A helicopter passed overhead, reflected in the glass wall of a tall mortgage firm. Bike paths and new construction—the city was hustling to lure people back down here.

They meandered past Stuyvesant High School, up Chambers to the Soda Shop, a pleasant breakfast place with dark wooden walls, showing just a touch of brick, and an old-fashioned bar topped with white marble and glass cases full of candy. From his seat, Bern could see across the street—the Mudville 9 Saloon ("Wings/Ribs") and a rickety fire escape festooned with potted purple flowers just beginning to bloom. Above it all, painted on the side of a building, an ad for beer: a sweating green bottle.

The room smelled of lightly seared chocolate.

"Wally, thank you," Kate said. "The memorial... it reminded me of my summer visit to Derry, a few years back. My *first* crack at my roots." She laughed and brushed her hair. "There was a genealogy center a few kilometers from the city—a larger version of the cottage we just saw. I went there one day hoping to find information about my family, but the only person I met, the caretaker, was shit-faced. At nine in the morning! He begged me to help him lock the place up and drive him down to Lough Derg, in County Donegal. He wanted to visit Purgatory, he said, and atone for his sins." The waitress brought them coffee. "Apparently, it's an old legend—the mouth of Purgatory is said to be on Station Island. Anyway, I kept trying to get away from this guy without hurting his feelings. Finally, I said, 'What sins?' And he said, 'Well now, what did you have in mind, missy?'" She laughed again but her eyes remained cloudy.

"Are you feeling all right?" Bern asked.

"Fine."

"No discomfort?"

"Don't nag, Wally. I'll let you know, okay?"

The conviction remained: she was teetering on a precipice. He'd try to keep her moving. Laughing. Relaxed.

He spent the afternoon showing her two of his favorite objects in the city: El Greco's painting of Toledo at the Met—"A city made of chalk," he said—and, at MoMA, Giacometti's little wooden sculpture, *The Palace at Four a.m.* The dream of a castle, a romance, a life, as fragile as a child's drawing. In both museums, people chattered about the recent deaths of Bergman and Antonioni. "The age of great filmmaking is over," said a bearded professor-type in line next to Bern. He smelled of tweed and ink.

Outside, on Fifty-third, the afternoon sky arced over silver buildings, spectacularly purple and blue; against it, the city looked sharp and flat, like construction paper.

Times Square, for the hell of it. A digital avalanche. In the cavernous Toys "R" Us, people lined up to buy the last Harry Potter book ("The age of great publishing is over"). Ads for coming films, *Hostel, Saw, Live Free or Die Hard.* It would be a summer of torture.

On the subway, three blonde high school girls handed out pamphlets: "Jesus Made Me Kosher."

For dinner, Bern tried to take Kate to a refurbished Italian place in the Village, one of his favorites. It was closed, "For Sale or Lease," its windows shuttered. Shaken, Bern let Kate lead him up Hudson to a place called Fatty Crab. "Fusion," Kate said. Bern didn't know what this word had to do with food. But his dinner was excellent: scallops and jasmine rice garnished with shaved bonito.

"So," he said when he'd ordered the wine. "In the museums today... did I become pedantic at any point? Too much the teacher?"

"You were fine, Wally." She smiled distantly. Butterfish glistened on her plate. She sighed and rubbed her belly. "I guess I'm getting too big for the dance classes."

"Is that what's hampered your mood?"

She shrugged.

They ate quietly, Kate staring at her stomach, Bern grieving for the old restaurant. How quickly worlds vanished! Villages. Cottages. City blocks. He could fill a book with place names and streets, and within a year it would be a guide to nowhere.

By the time their desserts arrived—coffee for Bern, frozen *fusion* for Kate—he wondered what could salvage their evening. For separate reasons, they were bound by lassitude, and it was tugging them to the bottom.

They walked to the Fourteenth Street station and caught a train to her neighborhood.

He reached for the almond oil.

"That was an astonishing meal, didn't you think?" Kate said, falsely cheery, setting her keys on her dresser. "Thank you, Wally."

"Rub your belly?"

She stared at him. She sat on the edge of her bed. "Wally?"

"Yes?"

"You should know. Gary called me last night," she said quietly. "I wasn't going to tell you."

His scrotum tightened. "Oh?"

"I think it finally struck him. He's going to be a father whether he's with me or not—and his baby's going to grow up without him."

Bern swallowed hard, surprised at the breadth of his panic, stunned by his commitment to this woman. He was just a friend. He understood that. He sat beside her. "Does he want to come back?" he asked.

"I don't know. I don't think he knows. I *do* think he's having a fling."

"This is what's made you so glum."

"You've said that twice tonight. Have I been glum?"

"What do *you* want, Kate?"

In the glare of a streetlamp, the leaves on the sidewalk trees made slow, gentling shapes on her walls. Just below her windowsill, a store sign pulsed, purple and green. She reached for his hand and held it. The curve of her belly reminded him of a cedar trunk in the back of his grandfather's closet. As a child, he'd always wondered what was in it.

Well. Tonight, all he could do was continue to astonish. "Shall we?" he said, sure of nothing else, waving the bottle of oil.

"Okay."

Purple. Green. Purple. The leaf-forms on her walls squirmed like little fists. She unbuttoned her blouse. "Wally?"

"Yes?"

"Tell me. Please. What are you thinking right now?" she said. "Are you mad?"

He unscrewed the bottle cap. "I'm thinking I don't understand how you can resist me."

"I don't know." She smiled, smoothed his hair, his brows, his lips. "I really don't know."

But *he* did.

Of course he did. Who was he fooling?

Just now, he had flirted with her like a kid. She liked the oil and their little ritual, but he realized his hands were rough, his skin loose and beginning to spot. She did not recoil from him, physically, but that was because, and only because, she'd put limits on their intimacy. This wonderful, funny, lovely girl. He was supposed to know better.

Yes.

But where did *that* assumption come from? The Almighty Authorities had no place in this apartment tonight. Who needed—what *was*—conventional behavior?

How far was he willing to go? How much latitude did he have here?

And really, shouldn't he be embarrassed that Katie seemed so much smarter than he was? She knew before he did that his best bet as a suitor was not as a sexual specimen but as a knight errant, serving his sweet lady. Chivalry was his strength. Empathy. Obviously, Gary lacked courtly impulses. But no. No.

The point was, Bern was no suitor at all. When Kate said "friend," she *meant* friend, notwithstanding her vanity (just enough to be charming) and the pleasure she took in the power of her body.

Still, the context was clear: for Kate, flirting with Bern was just an aspect of friendship, like the touching she allowed him during rubdowns. Her nonchalance stupefied him—a generational matter, he supposed; endeared her to him, and certainly aroused him. He kept looking for an opening, but the oil was only oil, pleasant on her skin, not an elixir (*Spirits of the Dead*!) intoxicating her into ignoring his flaw: his incontrovertible, irreversible age.

He squeezed out twice as much oil as usual tonight. One last chance to use it up.

"Mmmm," Kate said.

"Yes?" Bern said.

"Yes," Kate said.

◊◊◊

The Empire of the Dead

Bern was scheduled for a routine colonoscopy on Wednesday morning, forty-eight hours from now. Today, carefree indulgence. Tomorrow, penance and prep.

He showered, dressed, and fixed himself three scrambled eggs, bacon, and two flour tortillas warmed in the oven. Glancing at the flowers he'd bought on a lark yesterday to cheer the place up—they were arranged in a vase on his kitchen counter—he pictured his ex-wife as she had looked in her New York days. It was Marla who first discovered moss roses for sale here, at a street market on Third Avenue. She decorated their small apartment with them (then, they lived on Christopher Street, above a shop that sold sex toys).

One morning, she told Bern she wanted to get pregnant. He laughed and said a baby wouldn't make her happy. Lord, how callous had he been? The fact was, he wasn't prepared for a child; he wanted to make a mark at work, and he didn't bother to try to understand what Marla needed.

The day, nearly twenty years ago, she returned to Houston, where they'd met, she laid a riding crop she'd bought at the sex store on the kitchen table. "Work seems to be the only thing that whips you into a frenzy," she told him. "*I* can't do it. Take that to the office with you. Maybe you can use it on your colleagues. Or yourself. Think of me when you do." She picked up her suitcase and walked out the door, gripping a single orange rose against her cream-colored sweater, right between her breasts.

Several times, Bern had tried to imagine the moment she braved the erotica boutique. He had not been able to do it. What had that moment cost her? What had she hoped to gain from it? Did she ever regret her impulse—or did she see it now as the finest moment of her life? A mark of independence?

The week she left New York, he *did* tuck the whip (creepy-slick, heavier than he would have thought) into his briefcase and took it to the office. He stuck it in a desk drawer. For about two weeks, he'd open the drawer with his left foot in the late afternoons, stare at the thing, and weep. Eventually, file folders covered it over. Bern hadn't seen it in years.

He finished his eggs and left the sticky plate in the sink.

Down in the lobby, Ryszard, the building's super, swept the black-and-white-tiled floor. He bent above his broom like a crone in photographs of early-twentieth-century Russian bread lines.

"Good morning," Bern called to him.

Ryszard nodded.

Behind him, Mrs. Mehl, perhaps the building's oldest tenant, basked in a pear-shaped slant of sunlight on the couch, below the slow but increasingly apparent fade of a painting of New Jersey on the wall.

"Oh. Hello," Bern said.

She was trying to remove a wool scarf but it was caught in her furry coat collar. Bern gave her a hand.

"Thank you," she said. "People don't help people anymore. Especially in this part of town." She wiped her dry lips with the back of a papery hand. "Pained me something fierce to relinquish my uptown place, years ago." She eyed Bern to make sure she had his attention. In the past, she'd rarely acknowledged him—though he had tried and failed to help her find her lost cat, once. He'd left fliers all around the neighborhood.

For some reason, this morning she needed to talk. Bern stood patiently, smiling. "Rent-controlled, fifty years' worth of our stuff in the closets, coats, board games, scrapbooks...now, *there* was a neighborhood. Harlem, between Second and Third. People took the time to introduce themselves and say hello on the streets. They considered your burdens their own. True neighbors. Herbert and I settled there in '32. The El used to run right past our window."

Ryszard carried his broom across the room, as far away from the couch as he could get. Clearly, he'd lived many times through Mrs. Mehl's travails.

"When they tore down the El and the war started in Europe, we heard what this nation did. Sold the iron from the El to the Japs, and they turned it into bombshells to use against our brave, good boys," Mrs. Mehl said.

"I don't think that's true," Bern said.

"What do *you* know about it?"

"Nothing, I guess. Nothing much."

"Now here I am, all on my own." She dabbed her eyes. Her fingers trembled. Bern produced a handkerchief from his coat pocket. "Thank you," said Mrs. Mehl. "Nobody helps anybody anymore." She clutched Bern's handkerchief to her bosom. He didn't try to retrieve it.

2.

He caught a local to work. In his office, he tossed his briefcase onto a wooden chair and hung his coat on a wall peg next to a glossy poster. DISASTER TIMELINE, it said. Beneath this heading, a list of dates: July 18, 64 AD, The Great Fire of Rome; October 21, 1868, The San Francisco Earthquake; October 8, 1871, The Great Chicago Fire; September 8, 1900, The Galveston Hurricane…

Bern took five minutes every morning to stare at this dismal roster and contemplate what he should learn. Increase the space between buildings; decrease population density; use fire debris to fill in low-lying places, where malaria and other diseases might fester in standing water; restrict the heights of houses in relation to street width.

Next to the poster, he'd hung a copy of Hammurabi's Code, the world's oldest known building law, the original of which was carved into ancient Babylonian stones: "If a builder build a house for someone, and does not construct it properly, and the house which he built fall in and kill its owner, then the builder shall be put to death," it said.

Bern straightened the papers on his desk and laid out his most recent sketches for the light scoop of a building he'd been asked to renovate. He'd been pondering the project for two months now. Below his window, a man in the street yelled at a speeding cabbie.

"Wally? Got a minute?" A rap at the door. Jerry Landau, Bern's supervisor—florid, pencil-necked—stuck his head in. "There's someone I'd like you to meet," Landau said. Behind him, a pale young man with slick, black hair, biscuit cheeks, and a slender nose stood with his hands in his pockets. "This is Murphy. Sam Murphy. He'll be joining our team," Landau said.

Bern rose. He and Murphy shook hands. The boy's knuckles were unusually white. Eyes like a gull's. "Where you coming from?" Bern asked.

"MIT," Murphy said.

Not just another young gun. A whole armory, rolled into one.

"Next few weeks, Wally, share your thinking with Sam on the projects you're working on. Help him learn the ropes, see how we do things around here," Landau said.

"Sure. We could start with this." Bern turned to the sketches on his desk. "Right now, I'm designing a light scoop for a local foundation. Their building is rather unusual, and the problem is, this fire escape on the east wall—"

"Oh, Sam's already taken care of that," Landau said. "I gave him the specs yesterday, as an example of what he might expect at first."

"Yeah, it was a little perplexing," Murphy said eagerly. "But after studying it a while, I figured we could combine the light scoop with a ventilating chimney, roof-mounted…" He pointed to Bern's sketches. "Enhance the stack effect there, see? And we install these motorized trickle vents. You get your natural airflow, and the occupant can control the operable windows."

Landau beamed. Bern thought: Oh my. *This* shmuck—who *is* he? He's my goddamned pallbearer! Quick! Get me my pension.

"There's a basement in a brownstone over on East Fifty-fourth, by the river... some water damage, too small for the owner's needs. He wants to expand the laundry facilities for his tenants, provide better access. I'd like you to take a look at it, Wally," Landau said.

"What about that building over by Fifth?" Bern asked. "The one you asked me to survey yesterday?"

"Oh, I think we'll give Sam the lead on that one. It's pretty straightforward, no? Why don't the two of you chat for a bit, get to know each other, then you can stop by my office, Wally, and pick up the basement specs, okay?" Landau withdrew.

Bern set his briefcase on the floor and motioned toward the empty chair. Murphy sat and studied the DISASTER TIMELINE. "Whoa," he said.

"Reminds me of the seriousness of our calling," Bern said.

"I think it would freeze me up to look at that every day."

"So. What gets you moving?" Bern asked.

"Oh! Possibility!" Murphy said. "All the ways to *do* this terrific city. Parks, for instance. You work much on parks? They're such marvelous liminal spaces."

"Meaning—?"

"Well, the way I see it, city parks are ironic, right? I mean, we all live here because we like the urban fabric. But we demand, along with our elevators and automated bric-a-brac, groomed trees, spiffy gardens..."

"Contrast. Relief," Bern said. "Seems natural."

"Yeah. Clearly, we crave both. So parks... maybe we play around with them a little, right?... *extend* the city into the park, say, with metallic sculptures... concede to nature, but *remind* the stroller—"

"I don't follow you," Bern said. "What—you'd soften the ugly by *adding to it?*"

"No, no, no!" Murphy said, laughing. "Don't be so literal, Wally."

"Designs *are* literal."

"I'm just saying, introducing a little whimsy, a bit of the unexpected, into something like a city park can educate public taste, so—"

Bern rolled up his drawings of the light scoop. "It's easy to laugh at public taste," he said, standing stiffly. "But it can't be dismissed. People's preferences are based on pretty sound principles. Comfort, shelter. They're not as unsophisticated as they seem." He hated his scolding demeanor. This young man... the perceived threat of him... had put him on the defensive, forced him into a more conservative stance than usual.

"But," Murphy began, "a sudden ironic awareness..."

"What about the poor slob who just wants to sit somewhere nice and eat a sandwich?" Bern said.

Murphy rose. "Well. I'm sorry, Wally. We seem to have gotten off on the wrong foot. I was just thinking aloud with you."

Bern shrugged. "It's nothing. I'm sorry, too."

Murphy pointed at the rolled-up sketches under Bern's right arm. "I didn't mean to steal your thunder. Landau gave it to me as a kind of test, I guess. I didn't know."

So. Smart *and* nice. Bern couldn't stand him.

Murphy turned to leave. He waved at the tragedies on the wall. "Seriously, though. I'd think about something else here, Wally. This can't be good for you. How about a pinup of Lindsey Lohan?" He grinned, an attempt at lusty camaraderie, but—who was Lindsey Lohan? Apparently, Farrah Fawcett had slipped into the ether while Bern wasn't looking. He was surrounded by too many young people.

"Catch you later," Murphy said. "Thanks."

Bern said, "Sure."

The basement specs were uninspiring. Bern phoned the building's owner and made an appointment to survey the place three days from now when he'd survived his colonoscopy. He stuffed his light scoop sketches into a drawer and spent the rest of the afternoon arranging and rearranging the drawing implements on his desktop.

American Venus. German Fabers. The Conte charcoal leads. Resilient steel nibs for his pens.

Various moods required a graphite arsenal. Differing shades of hardness. Was this a "dark line" day (after all, he'd begun this morning thinking of Marla), or was Bern feeling more delicate than that? What kind of mark would suit him in this moment? He picked up a pencil, rejected it, tried another, and wound up drawing nothing.

Early that evening, in his apartment, he read the "Before the Procedure" brochure his doctor had given him on his last visit. Tomorrow, clear liquids all day, but nothing was forbidden him tonight except foods peppered with whole seeds (popcorn, berries, nuts, breads, cereals, tomatoes). Twenty-four hours earlier, he had stopped taking his blood-thinning pills. On the kitchen counter, he set out the disposable bottle and the pouches of powder to be mixed with water when the time came. He'd leave work early tomorrow, come home around two, and begin the purge.

He took the elevator down to the lobby. Outside, he moved past the Clinton, the old brownstone next door housing the elderly and the blind. At Sixth and West Twenty-third, a gray-haired man sold knockoff watches, wallets, and cell phones next to a row of newspaper dispensers: Gay Singles ads. Three steps away, on the corner, two army recruiters stood in front of a rickety folding table, passing out pamphlets.

The sidewalks glistened. They were dry: no water, film, or oily substance. *With existence*, Bern thought. *Glistening with existence?* Could this be joy, he asked himself. If so, why did it flood him now? He was alone. His last love, a delightful young woman, had just returned to *her* former lover (maybe Bern really *preferred* being on his own?). He was facing an invasive procedure, possibly a layoff (*damn* that young man!)...

But here he was in the world. What joy!

Gum cast from the mouths of others, ground into the concrete, pushed against the rubber bottoms of his shoes. The air was as green as sea water. Bern glimpsed rust and peeling paint, cracks in glass, chips of fleshy pink in the faces of fire-red bricks. The back of an old warehouse blazed azure in the low-shooting sunlight, shimmering, insubstantial.

Chatter. Argument and song. Everywhere, the talk on the streets was loud and vital: a huge collective breath riding a smell of burnt pretzels and car exhaust. The city would talk all night.

Across a thronged avenue, a glass wall fronted another glass wall around a bank atrium, milk white and coolly fluorescent: "ephemeral architecture," a style favored by Bern's younger colleagues. Transparency, a blurring of outside and in. Bern liked the lightness; on the other hand, it seemed to him undeniable that one of the things people sought in their surroundings was the illusion of permanence. To admit, up front, that nothing will stay, the steps, the floors, the streets... all we'll ever know...

Bern shivered. Victor Serge, it was—a Russian writer he'd read and admired in the past—who said, "What is terrible when you seek the truth is that you find it."

Huddle and cling, behind cheap walls. It's what we have, Bern mused. At least that. The thought encouraged him.

He hurried along the streets, the primeval urban forest, while all around him, in bright headdresses, beads, and skins, the city's savage children, young and old, danced with one another, whooping, howling.

By the time he reached Bleecker Street, his heart galloped: not from physical exertion, but rather from anxiety, anticipation about his upcoming procedure. His future at the firm. His senses were keen tonight! He would wander, relish the air—do whatever he pleased.

He had read in the paper about a place called Fish, an unpretentious new eatery at Bleecker and Jones with a waterfront ambience. This evening, before tomorrow's monkish diet, he would live in style—yes, by gum (as his grandfather used to say)!

Salmon on ice in the front window; dim lighting; a worn mosaic floor. The waitress's quick, graceful gestures pleased him. He ordered Blue Point oysters and Angels on Horseback. A glass of chardonnay. He took his time, savored every swallow. The waitress was in training. She neglected to take the empty oyster platter from his table until he was nearly ready to leave: the ice melted, and when she picked it up, water splashed all over the floor and into Bern's pant cuffs. "No problem, no problem," Bern told her as she blushed and scurried back to the kitchen.

On the street, afterward, Bern passed a scruffy man on the corner, in cutoffs and no coat, shouting at passersby, "You've all had *your* dinners! Now give me some money so I can have mine! Jesus wants you to, Goddamn it!"

His heart beat crazily. He ambled past the Village Vanguard and saw the name Paul Motian on a handbill posted by the door. The drummer and his band were scheduled for a nine o'clock show: thirty minutes from now. Beneath the club's red awning, Bern hesitated. He was fading. It had been a hard day and tomorrow would be harder. Did he still have the gumption to mingle with strangers?

A figure emerged from the shadows, a mummy wrapped in a khaki jacket. Bern's heart kicked. "Fuckface," the man mumbled, holding out his hands. Bern slapped a dollar into the fellow's grimy palms and, to end the encounter decisively, hustled down the steps into the jazz lair.

The dark basement room hadn't changed much—not in years. Red floor-to-ceiling curtains hung behind a piano, a set of drums, and three or four microphones. A smell of beer-soaked cotton rose from cushions along the back wall seats. Black and white photographs of musicians formed crooked rows over the tables, reflecting thin blue beams from spotlights near the stage.

Abandon hope, all ye who enter: a distinct Underworld, the Vanguard, a journey out of—into?—a dark wood. Fleetingly, Bern imagined finding venerable Dante (surely a jazz lover) at a table here, nursing a beer with Virgil or, if the moon and stars aligned just right, his old flame Beatrice. The poet would be wearing his red robe and laurel crown, maybe sporting a Brooks Brothers tie. Bern paid his cover and found a sturdy chair against the wall away from the door. From here, he had a view past the floor tom-tom to the bass drum's pedal. Good. He liked to watch a drummer's feet: the music's anchor.

At a table next to him, two girls he took to be in their early twenties sipped tall, orange drinks. Their talk, full of academic jargon, pegged them as New School types. Creative writers. *Back story*, *deconstruction*, *narrative arc*—at the moment, they seemed to be deconstructing the erotic potential of a boy with whom they shared a class. Hardly angels—but then, this was the Inferno, was it not? Bern relaxed with his beer.

An old co-worker of his, Pete Somebody, a man who'd passed away many years ago, used to brag to Bern that he'd seen the famous Bill Evans sessions here in June 1961. Paul Motian on drums, Scott LaFaro on bass—just days before LaFaro died in a car wreck. "It was the last set of the night, few folks left in the club," Pete would say (his story, well rehearsed, never varied). "The trio went into a lovely little tune called 'Jade Visions.' Evans lowered his head—he almost touched the keyboard. His hair, soppy with sweat, raked the tops of his fingers. Then he reared back, shaking. I was in the front row and, man, did I get drenched! In my eyes, on my lips. At first, I thought, 'How disgusting!' But then I realized, 'Jesus! This is *Bill Evans*'s sweat!' I didn't wipe my face all night."

Bern smiled, recalling poor old starstruck Pete. Apparently, the New School girls mistook his smile for flirtatiousness, and flashed him loopy orange grins. He bent to his beer. His heartbeat had slowed, but disturbing pulses rippled through his chest and upper arms. He knew this wasn't angina—but the mild ache he felt in the middle of his back now, right between the shoulder blades, worried him. Maybe it *was* better to sit here, surrounded by others. Just in case.

He looked up, squinting into the dim light, his fellow patrons gaudy silhouettes...how many here in '61, on the night Pete loved to recall, had died since then? Pete. Evans and LaFaro. How many objects in the room remained from that time? The curtains? Some of the chairs? The photographs on the walls? Traces of Evans's sweat on the floor, preserved under layers of wax.

What was it like for Paul Motian, now an old man, to return to the club night after night, a space he'd played regularly for more than forty years, so many of his band mates missing or dead?

Now, Motian appeared behind the drums. Wiry. Bald. Wearing shades. The curtains whispered. *Don't look back*, said his ghosts (or so Bern imagined). The corners of the drummer's mouth curled down. "Okay," he said. The word seemed to conjure his fellow musicians. Bern was aware of the instruments' sounds before he saw fingers and lips manipulating pedals, keys, and strings. But in an instant there they all were: arms, legs, and heads, pumping, swaying, kicking. Breath. More breath. A flitting rhythm filled the room.

Motian played smoothly, occasionally lunging toward his cymbals, always guarding his chest (maybe Bern was projecting). Recently, when one of his clients learned that Bern had survived double bypass surgery, seven years ago, he exclaimed, "Me, too! Last year—and guess who I met, afterward, in cardiac rehab? Weird jazz guy, drummer—Motian is his name. I never heard of him, but my buddies tell me he's famous. He never said much, just did the treadmill. I hear he's back playing now."

Motion waved his sticks, counting the band into another tune. Bern rubbed his chest. No, not angina. Right before *his* surgery, what he felt was a slow constriction inching like thick, hot oil through his arms and lungs. If that's what he experienced again tonight, he'd take himself straight to St. Vincent's. This, he figured—the ache, the elevated heartbeat—was the anxiety he'd felt all evening. Agitation about work. His colonoscopy. Seven years ago, when the boiling oil choked his arteries and he couldn't catch his breath, he had taken a subway to the hospital (a ride he didn't remember). The doctors laid him on his back. They hooked him to a heart monitor and fed him nitroglycerin pills, which gave him a grainy headache. He stayed there overnight, dreaming of Nicaragua, the last place, and the last time, he'd thought he was going to die. Nicaragua. He was thirty-one years old then. On a bus one evening, on an architectural tour of the northern half of the country, he had wound up in a town called Ocotal, near Honduras. From across the border, Contra rebels lobbed mortar shells into the mountains east of town. When the blasts began, Bern was standing in a grungy motel john, staring out the window at a Red Cross ambulance. His ears popped. His bladder blazed. He couldn't stop the stream. As the bombs fell, he pissed himself and the walls. I'm going to die holding my dick, he thought. God bless my tax dollars.

All night, in his New York hospital room, his dreams replayed that absurd and terrifying moment, from a war long forgotten.

The next day, in a large white room vibrating with primal rock music, several young male nurses prepped Bern for an angiogram. He felt a sting in his right leg, near his penis. Immediately, dizziness overcame him. Someone turned his gurney so he could see a television monitor hanging from the ceiling: there, on the screen, the interior of his heart, an intricate, tidy design. The arteries resembled cascading streams—*Fallingwater*, Bern thought. *God bless Frank Lloyd Wright*. "Left main," someone remarked. "Eighty, eighty-five percent blockage."

The next thing he recalled was cool liquid, head to toe; a dim blue light, and the hands of beautiful women tending him, shaving his chest and legs. His soul had passed over, beyond the Fixed Stars, into the Empyrean.

He awoke in a lake of pain. *He* was the lake. Plastic tubes stuffed his mouth and throat. "You made it," someone said. He didn't like the note of surprise in that voice: had there been some doubt about whether or not he would make it? *What have I done to bring this on myself?* Bern thought. "Breathe," said the voice. "Stay awake, now." Later, he learned the surgeons had collapsed his lungs during the operation, to get a better angle on his heart, and he wasn't breathing on his own. Those first few hours after the operation, a machine did the work for him. Once the machine was off, if he drifted toward sleep, his breathing got too shallow, and the nurses shook him awake. For months after leaving the hospital, he dreaded slumber.

In the ICU, he was a Frankenstein's monster of pacer wires, IVs, and yellow tubes draining fluids from his chest into a humming plastic container. A young doctor—my god, were they letting children into med schools these days?—explained to him that he had rerouted Bern's left mammary artery. Then he had "harvested" a saphenous vein from Bern's right leg and sutured it to the aorta, to bypass the blockages.

Now, Motian tapped the crown of his ride cymbal. A crisp ping. A tolling bell.

"So, technically, you were dead, right?" a colleague said to Bern the day he returned to work, his chest still tender and aching. "I hear they pack the heart in ice, then afterward, shock it back into rhythm." Bern went numb, and spent the rest of the day gazing through his office window at Lower Manhattan, the various construction zones.

The song stopped. Another—"I Have the Room Above Her"—began. Bern had been mistaken. *This* music had nothing to do with the drummer's quick feet. Motian barely touched his bass drum. No timekeeping. Piano phrases wandered around the melodies as though lost on a forest path. The tenor sax keened like a distant bird. Motian's brushes whispered across the snare: *over here; no, over here; let's take a look over there.*

Midway along the journey of our life.

In those rare interludes when a beat held for a bar or two, Bern tapped his foot, a clumsy, mocking echo of the pattern.

If Motian had slowed after *his* surgery, he had whipped himself back into shape. On stage, he was a rapacious storm. Generally, Bern was happy, too, with his adjustments since his illness. At first he'd been afraid to eat (no fried foods, no more eggs, red meat, or cream), fearful of exerting himself, but then he'd found a balance:

careful moderation. As he recovered more strength, he stopped restricting his activities. And he didn't brood on what had happened to him—though whenever he felt his heart rush or experienced the slightest twinge in his arms, chest, or back, naturally he wondered.

On his last day in the hospital, a weary doctor had told him, "Usually, the veins we use in bypass operations, like the one we took from your leg, have a good ten-year track record."

"Wait a minute. What are you saying?" Bern responded, shooting up in bed. Cool plastic tubes wrapped his body. "Are you saying I'll be back here in ten years?'

"Well," the doctor said, "you'll let us know, won't you?"

Two of Bern's colleagues who'd fallen ill in the last three years seemed to fare much less well than he did. Chris Henderson, trained at the University of Oregon, a good anodized aluminum man, had beaten leukemia, at least for now; ever since, he'd become tentative, delicate. In the office, he drove everyone crazy. Did I make the coffee in the break room too strong, he'd ask. Was I talking too loudly with my client just now? Bern wanted to tell him, Don't worry about it, Chris. Do whatever the hell you want, just like before.

Raymond Davis, a lung cancer survivor, had become creepily buoyant, a bon vivant. After work, he'd try to herd everyone to bars for tequila shots. "Live it up, man! What's the matter with you?" he'd admonish anyone who turned him down. Bern liked Chris and Raymond but mostly avoided them now. It seemed to him they had not recovered from their traumas, that their maladies had taken root in their brains and warped them, terribly. They had shrunk; friendly leeches, polite and earnest, feeding on others' concern. They targeted Bern, especially, if he let them: a fellow sufferer. He feared that to spend time with them would be to stay sick.

On the sidewalk outside the club, after the set ended, Bern flipped up his coat collar against the night's chill. Behind him, the New School girls huddled against the wall, sharing a hand-rolled cigarette. Motian appeared in the doorway wearing his shades. He glanced past the awning at the sky—skeptically, as though the air's calm was deceptive. "Mr. Motian," said one of the girls, stepping forward, smelling of sweat and sugary alcohol. "Mr. Motian, we think you're brilliant." Motian appraised her, nodded exhaustedly, said "Okay," turned, and shuffled down the stairs.

From the shadows, the mummy lurched at the girls—the man to whom, earlier, Bern had given money. The girls fell back against the wall, and the mummy lumbered down the street toward the darkened windows of the Village Cigar Shop.

Bern headed up Seventh. The mannequins of Fantasy World, standing in the window wearing teddies and leather boots, offered him synthetic, come-hither looks. Come-hither-big-boy-and-squeeze-my-plastic-butt.

He wandered past Abingdon Square—the children's swings creaking, empty, on their chains. West of the square, candlelight dithered sweetly behind the lace curtains of a small Italian restaurant. It had a new name these days. What was it? Ah, yes: Valdino West. Bern remembered its old incarnation, Trattoria de Alfredo. When he and Marla first moved to the Village, they spent a couple of romantic evenings munching melons and prosciutto at a window table here. On Bern's starting salary, the place was too expensive, so they didn't come here often. Bern stopped on the sidewalk now and gazed in the window. The décor hadn't changed significantly: large wine bottles on a shelf lining the tastefully painted yellow wooden walls. White tablecloths. Flowers in bottles. Couples holding hands.

On Marla's thirtieth birthday, Bern had brought her here. As a gift he had bought her a gorgeous rare edition of Dante's *Vita Nuova* translated by Dante Gabriel Rosetti, with hand-painted pictures of lovers in gardens, churches, or at feasts (*that* purchase had set him back a month or two!). He had found the volume at the old Gotham Book Mart. "To our new life," Bern toasted his wife. Inside the flyleaf, echoing Dante's words to Beatrice, he had written, "Happy birthday, to the lady to whom my master has named me."

Marla would be fifty-one years old now. Bern wondered if she had ever made it to Tuscany, always a dream of hers. With whom might she have gone? Her new best friends, her lover or lovers (to his knowledge, she had not remarried), were people he had never met.

The night of her birthday here, they had experienced one of their first New York celebrity-sightings, though like most New York celebrity-sightings it was disappointing, a minor event involving a man only a few folks in the crowd knew anything about. At a table next to them, someone pointed out the window at a pale, portly fellow on the sidewalk, and said, "That's Max Frisch! He's a writer!" The man seemed confused, and scurried away from the restaurant when he noticed people staring at him. Since then, Bern had meant to read Max Frisch. He never had.

He strolled up Tenth Avenue, not a route he usually took. The street seemed fresh and alive to him: friendly looking neighborhood bars, where people brought their dogs and appeared to be left alone if they didn't want to engage others. Bern passed a parking garage he knew had been stripped of its Romanesque moldings. A former horse stable, built in the nineteenth century, it had gradually been whittled down into a stucco box. Preservationists had hoped to salvage it—in the 1890s, this avenue, especially north of here, where it became Amsterdam, was known as "Stable Row"; now, most of the old horse-and-carriage barns were gone—but the garage's owner had taken advantage of the city's ponderous bureaucracy. A few months back, as the case for protecting the building worked its way to the top of the public hearings docket, the owner destroyed the last of the structure's historic ornamentation. By the time the Landmarks Preservation Commission considered the case, nothing authentic remained of the former stable. What was the point of saving a bare, empty shell?

In front of the garage now, a drunk, middle-aged woman wearing a very short skirt yelled at a pair of boys—late teens, early twenties, perhaps. Bern didn't catch her words, nor could he decipher the boys' attitudes toward her: threatening, playful? Anger flared in him...disgust at the situation's irrationality. A tense encounter—whatever its core dynamic—that could have been avoided if the woman had acted her age, had known her proper place on the streets of New York. She was as foolish as the New School girls, Bern thought, but she was seasoned enough to know how to behave.

Well. He was being unfair. He could be such a scold in his head! Really, he surprised himself sometimes. Why *shouldn't* this lady wear a mini and have a snort if she wanted? The boys laughed at her and walked away. She vanished inside the garage.

Why was Bern so furious? So quick to denigrate the woman and the girls in the club? He turned and saw his thin frame reflected in the window of an Irish pub. Inside, a woman in a parka served the remains of a pint of beer to a white bulldog. Marla. Or him. Surely, that was the source of his anger. This wasn't about the woman in the garage. He was feeling lonely, regretful, and—let's face it—gloomy about aging. Sorry for himself. The cliché of a midlife crisis. Talk about *old enough to know*...! In the bar, the bulldog, hammy, stiff, wove among the legs of happy drinkers.

New lives, Bern thought. Then newer lives, still.

That night at the trattoria, Marla's thirtieth birthday...she informed him that her sister-in-law, Becky, a woman he barely knew, had been diagnosed with Lou Gehrig's disease. In the coming months, Marla said, she would want to spend more time with the woman in Houston. But, Bern countered, reaching for her hand, he had just started work here, it would be hard for him to get away, lonely for him without Marla in the apartment. Of course he understood, of course, terrible, terrible, poor Becky, but...

And so, after several days, he'd talked Marla out of making regular trips back to Texas, just as he'd later talk her out of having a baby. Meanwhile, Becky's range of motion diminished, stopped, until she was a husk in a wheelchair breathing with the aid of machines. One day, she breathed no more.

Marla had *allowed* herself to be dissuaded from helping her sister-in-law in the last weeks of her life; to *that* degree, Marla shared culpability. But Bern's selfishness then…

And why? He gazed again at his reflection in the window. He knew damn well why.

Yes. Okay. He could admit it now. After all, what choice but to live with the past?

The spring before Marla and Bern's summer trip to Europe, before their move to New York in the fall, Bern had worked part-time for an architectural firm in Houston noted for its projects with nonprofit organizations, its designs for public schools and social service offices. He was a junior member of the team, but that spring, the firm's principals entrusted him with what was, for them, a minor project south of the city: an elementary school in Brazoria County on the edge of a large rice paddy, crowded beyond its capacity with the kids of low-wage workers. The school district had engaged the firm to design a few new classrooms, a more usable space. The budget was twenty thousand dollars. Bern cut corners wherever he could, doubling the functional role of almost every structural element. The light diffusers also diffused the heat. He designed the corridors to a larger-than-usual scale, to form play areas. He clad the exterior in a glass and marble curtain wall. Inside the building, he showcased the ventilation ducts, placing them out in the open, in the ceiling, rather than hiding them inside the walls. This had the effect of breaking up broad surfaces inside the rooms, reducing the sense of mass. Cheap. Efficient. Just what he'd been hired to provide. And he'd come in on time.

Later, he would wonder about sabotage. He knew he had pissed off the contractors—they weren't used to seeing the architect on site. Young, just getting his toes wet, professionally, Bern wanted the experience. And too, maybe he was arrogant (enjoying the firm's faith in his abilities, seeing his sketches *actualized* for the first time!). Nervous. Micromanaging. He showed up each day and insisted the builders test each weld. "We can't risk being sloppy," he'd tell them.

If a fellow failed to meet Bern's window specifications, he made the guy rip out all the frames. To Bern, this was only reasonable, good and careful work, but word got around the site. Demanding. Obsessive. Bern remembered inspecting the school's roof with the head contractor, a willowy man named Al. They checked the air-conditioning units, tightened bolts. "I gotta tell you," Al said to Bern. "Me, I sort of admire a Suit like you taking time to look over the dirty work. Most architects won't do that. Living-in-their-heads types of guys." With an oily wrench, he scratched the back of his neck. "But the thing is, with you peering over their shoulders all the time, the men here... it bugs them, do you know what I'm saying? Like you don't trust them to do their jobs. My advice to you, young man? In the future, back off."

He had, and three weeks later a section of the roof collapsed above the school's gymnasium, killing a fifth grade boy and a third grade girl. Bern still remembered their names: Matthew Wein and Sue Ann Brownly. Afterward, for over two years, the courts tried to apportion blame. Lousy design? Shoddy workmanship? That summer before New York, the incident shadowed Bern all the way across England, France, and Spain. Once he'd settled in Manhattan, he had to fly back to Houston, twice, to testify at trials. Finally, he and the firm were exonerated; engineers, coached by lawyers—or vice versa, who could tell at that point?—determined the fault lay in construction, not design. Bern took little satisfaction in this. Should I have dogged the workers even harder? he thought. *Did* those bastards set me up?

No. With every nail, nut, and bolt, children's lives were at stake. He couldn't believe anyone would pursue a personal vendetta that far. And though the courts cleared him, Bern would never escape the fact that his first built project resulted in the deaths of two kids. In his mind, and for the sake of his marriage and career, he tried to shove Brazoria County into a bottom drawer.

Throughout the ordeal, his bosses in New York championed him. They had studied his plans for the building and found nothing wrong with them. All along, they felt confident he would be vindicated. This fact secured his loyalty to the firm, even after he started getting passed over for promotions and merit raises. At first, Marla had also been supportive, though her eyes were often downcast around him (did he imagine this?). Bern couldn't believe that none of them—Marla, his colleagues and bosses—didn't harbor *some* passing doubts about him. He had much to prove. Thus, his focus, his drive, his commitment to public projects (*see, I'm not in it for the money! Forgive me, forgive me*), his strictness with Marla about taking care of Becky, or the possibility of a baby. He tried to micromanage his marriage the way he'd overseen every weld in Brazoria County. In neither case did the connections hold.

The beer-drinking bulldog approached the pub's doorway and let out a bark. Bern feared he had caused the creature's distress, but then he noticed the woman in the miniskirt. She had emerged from the darkness of the stripped-down garage and was yelling at passersby. They screeched back at her. This scene perturbed the dog. What *was* her agony? Momentarily, Bern entertained the fantasy that she was a lonely preservationist, distraught at the loss of the old stable and the new use to which the structure had been put. "A car is not a *horse*!" he imagined her shouting at officials in a meeting of the Landmarks Preservation Committee. Over the years, Bern had attended numerous planning hearings where the fate of a building was at stake, or the development of pristine land—emotional issues—and it was easy to make fun of folks whom sentiment seized in public, citizens nostalgically attached to a parcel, with no conception of complex legalities. In truth, Bern thought, watching the woman struggle with herself, people slammed by emotion are usually clear about what they want; they're heartfelt and sincere and they tend to say what they mean. The ones to watch are the Haircuts and Ties who learn the rules just to shatter them.

You're a fine one to talk, Bern thought: What did you do in Brazoria County, shaving every angle…

The woman in the parka pulled her bulldog back into the bar. He whimpered until she gave him more beer. Bern crossed the street, approaching the garage-woman slowly. She slumped halfway down a wall, searching for something in her purse, shivering from the cold. "Excuse me?" Bern said. "Ma'am, do you need some help?" The woman tried to look his way. She aimed her gaze at the windows over his left shoulder. "I need you to go fuck yourself, buddy," she croaked. Her mouth never stopped grinding, even when she'd quit speaking.

"All right," Bern said. "Just checking."

"Check *this*, asshole!"

Bern braced himself for pepper spray, a penknife, a can of mace. The woman made no move. She just stood there, working her mouth. A faint musk wafted from the maw of the garage—a trace of the old stable?

In 1880, fifteen thousand horses dropped dead, of various causes, in the streets of New York.

By the mid-1900s, five hundred thousand pounds of horse shit were piling up in the streets each day. The gutters ran with forty-five thousand gallons of horse piss.

Bern had read all this when he first came to the city and, obsessed with origins, taught himself the lay of the land.

He left the woman at the entrance to the garage and ambled up the sidewalk toward home. As he walked, he recalled the first planning meeting he'd ever witnessed. It was back in Texas. He was a teenager. A Dallas real estate outfit had purchased the land north of Houston where the cemetery sat, his grandfather's burial plot. Condos was the plan: six of them, each with thirty-six units. Four shared parking lots. The outfit's lawyer claimed that plenty of open space, including the graveyard, would be preserved within the design, but few locals believed this. Bern's mom dragged him to the hearing, at which she railed against the project. "All those moss roses," she said, her voice rising, "acres and acres of orange and yellow blossoms... irreplaceable..."

As he moved along Tenth, he paralleled the rusty High Line,

caught a glimpse of the new Frank Gehry building (a shining, multistory banana float). He was tempted to stop for a nightcap at La Luncheonette, its simple décor a powerful lure, the warm yellow light a balm to his eyes. But no, he'd imbibed quite enough tonight.

On Twenty-third, a pink plaster pastry the size of an old Volkswagen beetle revolved on a pole above a bakery. To bed, to bed, Bern thought. This city is too much! A young couple kissed in front of the Big Booty Bread Company. A high-tech boy (slick hair, Armani suit, iPod plugged into his ear) rushed from a pharmacy with about an aisle's worth of Tylenol in his arms.

Deep golden light swept through the Hotel Chelsea. Bern paused by its glass doors then stepped into the lobby for warmth. The large fireplace loomed, cold and sooty, but the ceiling chandeliers radiated electric heat, palpable if unfelt on the skin, a spiritual condition (Bern thought) rather than a physical atmosphere. The chandeliers glistened, icy. Dark, murky paintings brooded on the walls above the gritty carpet. Given the hotel's storied past and his slight inebriation, Bern expected ghosts: ectoplasmic raging against the dying of the light.

The lobby was empty except for a young Japanese man sprawled on a leather couch, Googling images of Condoleezza Rice.

He dreamed he was living with Marla again in her house, sleeping in her bed, but everything was wrong. He didn't want to hurt her feelings, but when she opened her arms to him, he pulled away, gently. "We can't do this," he said. "Of course we can," Marla replied. "I've made us a reservation at that little Italian restaurant." "I'm promised to someone else," Bern said. Marla wept. "Who?" she said. Bern didn't know. No one. Marla asked again, "Who?" He was doomed to a sad and freighted love. For the rest of his life, he would sleep chastely next to Marla, wounding her night after night with his presence—somehow, this was the arrangement now.

He woke, shaken and parched. He reached for a glass of water on his bed stand, recalling his fears of falling asleep in the hospital, in the worst days of his illness. He sat on the edge of his bed, breathing deeply. Then he paced the room to try to steady his heartbeat. At the window he watched four blind men from the Clinton flash white canes by the curb. As they laughed and talked, they moved around one another in a circle, like ponderous players in a midnight hockey game.

3.

"No," Murphy said. "Whatever we build, it has to challenge its context."

Landau, Chris Henderson, Raymond Davis, and Bern were sitting in the break room at work, sipping coffee, "getting to know each other," Landau had chirped. The room smelled of bananas and wet coffee grounds. Weak sunlight slanted through the single, east-facing window, onto the portable fridge, microwave oven, and scarred wooden table. As Murphy held forth, Bern stared at three drops of half-and-half spilled on the tabletop. One of the drops was about to seep into a scratch in the wood.

"Self-reflexive gestures," Murphy continued. "An open space, say, just off the street, reminding us of the city's disorder by offering a break from it. Public sculptures evoking industrial decay—"

"Why?" Henderson asked.

"Social criticism. You know. Through aesthetics."

Landau clapped. "I just *love* the way this guy *thinks*!" he said.

Henderson stared at his arms. Before this meeting, he had told Bern his white blood cell count had dropped drastically in the last few days, and his doctor feared he was anemic. He was slated for further tests this week, and worried about a recurrence of his cancer. The left side of Davis's face swelled, purple and black. Yesterday, he had fallen in the street. A stranger had helped him home, and now he had no memory of the incident. As for Bern, his stomach sang murky arias. Per instructions for his colonoscopy prep, he had eaten no solid food this morning. Here we are, he thought. The morgue.

The half-and-half was viscous and blue, its movement toward

the nick in the table tantalizingly slow. "What about daily life?" Bern said.

"Daily life?" Murphy repeated.

"Well, while you're scattering industrial waste on the streets, how are we supposed to go about our business? Let's say I'm an old woman, all alone here in the city, running late, trying to catch the A train—how are your sculptures going to teach me anything? I certainly don't have time to contemplate their 'lessons.' Besides that, they're blocking my way."

Landau scowled at him. You're penning your obit, Bern thought. Shut up, old fool.

Murphy smiled. Bern was sure some of his colleagues had taken Murphy aside and told him how they teased the "Old Man—Bern, the Utopian." "Here's the deal, Wally. Most of us are bored in the city now. We have to strain to find mystery on the sidewalks."

"I don't think we're bored with cities," Bern said. "I think we're afraid for them."

Landau turned away from him, clearly irritated, and went all dewy-eyed, staring at his Boy Wonder. He was a sucker for this faux-theory grad school crap. You really *must* shut up, Bern thought.

The half-and-half found its groove. Bern was strangely thrilled. His stomach *grrr*-ed.

"I'm thinking probably nothing maps our challenges more than memorial designs, am I right?" Murphy said. "Witness the WTC site. I mean, these days, in American culture, nothing goes uncontested. You know what I'm talking about. Everything is politicized. Even war memorials, tributes to our dead...they can't be designed straightforwardly, because you risk offending someone. What does 'straightforward' even mean nowadays? So we get mute black walls. Maya Lin's Vietnam. Silence. Ambiguity."

Oh please, Bern thought. Let me out of the goddamned Seminar Room. "The 1930s were an extremely politicized time in this country. Maybe you didn't study that in school," he piped up, goaded by the smile on this little *macher*'s face. "No one agreed on solutions to the Great Depression, impending war...but WPA murals seized the nation's imagination: those blocky figures of working men and women. You've seen them, I assume. And why were these murals so powerful?"

Murphy held his smile, but the corners of his mouth trembled.

"They showed the dignity of human labor," Bern said. With his fingers he brushed away the half-and-half. "But we also had the feeling we were witnessing something ancient, about to go extinct. Frankly, I don't know many young designers with the courage or the skill to pull off that sort of thing." He licked the liquid from his hands. Well, Cro-Magnon. If you're going out, go out with a bang, he thought.

"Okay, okay," Landau said, rising, tossing his Styrofoam cup into a wastebasket by the window. "It's good for us to kick around ideas, keep the old nervous systems humming, but we want it to stay constructive." He glanced at Bern. "A spirit of cooperation, got it? I expect you all to make Sam feel welcome."

"Thanks, guys," Murphy said. "I enjoyed it!"

In the narrow hallway outside the break room, Davis tugged Bern's coat. "How about it, Wally?" he said. "Tequila, after work? Kiss the old green worm?" Bern wondered if booze had caused the poor bastard's recent stumble. As he spoke, Davis held his jaw stiff. He resembled a shabby wooden marionette. Bern explained about his procedure and said he'd take a rain check. "Me, I don't believe in diagnostic tests anymore," Davis said. "Who wants to hear bad news at our age? Better to just whistle past the graveyard until the day you stumble into the hole."

"Maybe so," Bern said.

Davis slipped away.

Behind Bern, Henderson made loud clicking noises with his lips. Bern turned. "Oh. I'm sorry," Henderson said. "My gums ache. It's the GVH. Side effect from the bone marrow transplant and all the goddamn medications I'm taking. I just wish I could taste food, you know? Well. No complaints, no complaints." He smiled unconvincingly.

By the time Bern reached his office, his chest hurt. Too much time in the Sick Ward. Whatever happened to routine? he thought. The taken-for-granted? We are bored with the city? Boredom is possible only when you're healthy.

"Wally?"

Murphy stood in his doorway.

"Yes?"

The young man laughed self-consciously, put his hands on his hips, and glanced at the floor. "I mean, you *really* don't like me, do you? What's the deal, man?"

Bern stared at the pencils on his desk.

"Is there something I can do to... I don't know, make peace?" Murphy said.

Bern's mouth went dry.

"I'm really not here to get up in your grille. Really. I'm not."

"Fine," Bern said. "That's fine."

Murphy shook his head. "All right, Wally," he said. "Have a good day." He drifted away, down the hall.

Oh, go after him! Bern thought. Apologize. The boy is making an effort. What the hell *is* my problem? But he stood by his desk, gazing at the tragedies on his wall. I am what I am, he thought, tightening his rectum. If I trailed that boy down the hall right now, I'd be brick masquerading as oak. A false front, whose only recourse is to crumble. He remained standing, uncomfortably, until his feet hurt; as he sat, he congratulated himself, half-heartedly, on his dignity.

On his way home, studying storefronts, traffic islands, and billboards, he realized he had come to like the look of flat, gray, unadorned concrete: its reassuring rigidity. Did this preference indicate a coarsening of his sensibilities?

He passed a Greek deli. In the window, under red heat lamps, skewered lamb shanks and pork loins rotated on a metal contraption. The motion reminded Bern of Aristotelian models of the universe he'd seen in old philosophy books. The meat looked singularly unappetizing.

Perhaps because he was a step or two slower today, having skipped his meals, he was startled by his fellow strollers' aggressions. Few of them waited for "Walk" signals. They appeared to dare trucks, buses, and cabs to run them down. The defiance of the foot. For all the cockiness implied by this behavior, Bern took it as a sign that most people felt helpless in their surroundings and rebelled in small, meaningless ways.

Was he projecting again? Regretting his treatment of Murphy in the break room?

The lobby of his building was vacant. On his way to the elevator, he passed through a cloud of old woman—a scent of wool, dry skin, and faint, sweet lavender perfume.

In his apartment, he mixed his purgative. The instructions told him to drink eight ounces of the disgusting stuff every fifteen minutes, until no more remained. Then he had to swallow sixteen ounces of water. An hour and half later, repeat. A flat, lemony taste. Immediately, he felt bloated. He paced his kitchen, sang to himself, switched on his radio. Two NPR announcers led a pledge break. Strangely, their droning money chatter cheered him: a predictable, distracting rhythm keeping him from dwelling on his belly.

From his bookshelf, he pulled a paperback copy of the 1930s *WPA Guide to New York City*—dated but still a fine overview of Gotham. He forgot his stomach, further, by studying prints of the murals he had extolled to Murphy in the break room. One of them, entitled "Chelsea Shape-Up" showed gaunt men in baggy pants rioting outside a street-side factory gate.

By early evening, he had blasted his insides into the toilet. He was certain he could not leak any more. A cramp seized his belly and he rushed to the bathroom again. The phone rang. He let it go. No one could possibly want him like this.

4.

His gastro man had a small clinic on the east side of Washington Square Park. At first, Bern had worried that a doctor who wasn't located on the Upper East Side or around Union Square might not be worth his salt. But he had overcome this prejudice (after all, several of his colleagues—Henderson and Davis among them—swore by the guy), and he had learned to trust Nadelson.

Bern left his apartment early in the morning and took his time getting to the clinic. Normally, at this hour of the day, in this part of town, he would have stopped at the Café Reggio and admired the green and brown walls and the tin-plated ceiling while enjoying a latte and biscotti. The smell of steamed milk bubbling through the open doorway onto the sidewalk as he passed the place weakened his knees. In just a few hours, once the procedure was finished, he could return to the buzzing human world.

In the park, two boys sporting dreadlocks pounded plastic buckets with drumsticks. Behind a row of chess players sitting at concrete tables, a young man straddled a bench next to a young woman. Together, they ignored a preacher shouting at passersby, "Sinners, the End is gnawing at your bones!" The couple concentrated on a screenplay the woman had written. "Well, I meant him to be a cliché," she said. "Well, I can see that," the man replied.

"The End is a pit bull," screamed God's emissary, wagging a finger at Bern. "And it will drag your bent and miserable carcass to Hell."

Am I bent, Bern thought, sidestepping the man. I'm not bent, you old nuisance. He straightened his shoulders. Poor Henry James, he thought, turning with relief to the arch at the park's far end. In *The American Scene*, Bern remembered, James had called the arch "lamentable"—"lonely and unsupported." Generally, the Great Man's architectural criticism had more to do with his emotional states than the intrinsic values of objects. Fair enough, Bern thought, fair enough. On his return from Europe in 1904, James said he missed the "mild and melancholy glamour" of the area around the park, which had been buried by developers. James's birthplace had been "ruthlessly suppressed" (i.e., torn down), its castellated, gabled façade fiercely "amputated." The city would never feel the same to him.

The preacher continued to harangue Bern from a distance.

In Nadelson's waiting room—plastic flowers, mediocre seascapes on the walls—Bern read a magazine article about newly discovered planets orbiting an "ordinary" star in Pegasus. "This is a window onto what our solar system might have looked like sixty million years ago," an astronomer was quoted as saying. Bern recalled the mnemonic he'd learned as a kid to remember the names of the planets in the order of their distance from the Sun, *My Very Educated Mother Just Served Us Nine Pickles*, and he giggled when he came to the "naughty" sphere. No matter how you pronounced it—*Urine-us* or *Ur-anus*—you soiled the cosmos.

It's your anus today, Bern thought. He swallowed another giggle, and a woman sitting across the room cut her eyes at him, disapprovingly.

Nadelson, a thin, balding man, was chatty this morning. He and his wife planned to visit Paris next week, a short vacation. As he prepared Bern's IV—"This anesthetic probably won't knock you out completely, but you'll feel no pain," he said—he went on and on about Notre Dame, the excursion he intended to take down the Seine, the sights he hoped to see in the Marais. "I hear there's a great kosher butcher shop there, in the old district," he said, and Bern's stomach pitched.

The drip began in his IV tube, and soon the lower half of his body seemed to have turned to stone while his head floated off, in search of a light to orbit. All was fire, but not unpleasantly so. The fluorescent bulbs in the ceiling blurred, milky rainbows. Paris burned. Was someone talking about the City of Light? Construction is combustion, Bern thought, drifting. Here's a piece of wood. Do you burn it to warm your limbs or do you use it to build shelter?

Was civilization a matter of huddling around a fire or congregating under a roof? He was vaguely aware of Nadelson hovering over his haunches, some kind of business going on behind him. A nurse may have entered the room. Or maybe not. Bern didn't care. Vitruvius. Yes, it was Vitruvius who'd called fire a "civilizing trauma." Lighting hits a tree. Flash. Boom. Terror. But the flames bring heat. Together, we press around them, holding out our hands. "Now we see the splendor of the stars," Vitruvius said. "One more pass," Bern heard Nadelson say. Sunlight moved along the wall, incandescent as a jellyfish.

"Mr. Bern? Mr. Bern? Wally?" Nadelson bent above him. Bern was lying on a gurney, in a different room than before. How had he gotten here? When? A god-awful pink curtain swayed in noisy air currents behind Nadelson's shiny head. The metal rings attaching the curtains to a rod suspended from the ceiling clattered like automobile gears. His hearing and sight were fuzzy. The room smelled of mercurochrome. "You did just fine," Nadelson said. "Flying colors. No sign of polyps." He handed Bern a box of apple juice with a straw stuck in it. "As soon as we check your blood pressure and you're feeling a little less wobbly, you're free to go. You're a healthy man." He patted Bern's knee.

Twenty minutes later, sure-footed, dressed, declared fit, he stepped outside and inserted himself into the stream of swift, determined bodies on the sidewalk. "Sudden death," he had heard Murphy say to another young colleague in the break room the other day. "That's the reality of city life, right? A speeding car coming around a corner. A stray bullet. A building crane falling on top of you. A gas main explosion. I favor designs that peel away the city's skin, revealing the raw nerves underneath..."

You're a healthy man.

Across the street from him, the window of a thrift store featured rocking horses, bird mobiles, inflatable punch clowns. Momentarily, their odd shapes disoriented Bern, and he recalled a number of men he had read about over the years who had designed not only buildings but also strange contraptions, synthetic creatures, automata, fanciful animals made from found materials... Jacques de Vaucanson, who made one of the world's first lathes, revolutionizing building practices, but who also manufactured a mechanical duck that could digest and excrete. The maddening certainty of architects, dissatisfied with the world as it is, confident they could do a better job. Bern pictured Murphy's face. It's not enough to make homes for the world's creatures, he imagined the young man saying; we have to remake the creatures themselves.

The anesthetic had worn off, but Bern felt preternaturally sensitive and alert; he moved through the city as though it were a museum filled with relics whose functions weren't clear.

He strolled past the Stonewall Inn, crossed the street, and found a spot on a bench in Sheridan Park, next to the life-sized plaster casts of two women, one with her arm relaxed across the lap of the other. The first one resembled a young Mrs. Mehl—well, on second thought, maybe not. But wouldn't it be nice to see the old woman this happy? He should take her strolling sometime. Get her outside. Sunlight bathed Bern's lips, brows, cheeks: he was certain he could feel each part of his face separately as it was anointed by this spectacular day. He took a long, slow breath. A healthy man.

The Pont Neuf came into his head. Why was he thinking of Paris? Had someone been speaking about Paris? Yes, yes, of course—Nadelson, right before administering the anesthetic. That summer after Houston, when Bern was in a pall following the school kids' deaths, he and Marla had come to Paris by way of Barcelona. In Barcelona's Barrio Gotico, its gray walls still pocked from Civil War machine-gun fire, they had run across the ruins of the oldest synagogue in Europe (or so it claimed to be), dating from the thirteenth century. A few old stones, visible through holes in the floor of a new synagogue, were all that remained of the ancient structure, but after days of reading only Spanish, Bern felt comforted by the signs in Hebrew (the writing familiar to him from childhood) and charmed by the young woman behind the gift shop counter, who wished him mazel tov in a lovely Catalan accent. In Paris, Marla had stopped him in a crowd, in the middle of the Pont Neuf, and kissed him because, she said, "This is what lovers do in Paris."

For Bern, the city's romance came alive when he was surrounded once more by Hebrew, in the Marias—the signs on shuttered delis, the shouts of old, bearded men kvetching at one another in alleyways, in the midday heat, amid slightly sour smells of meats and oils. Bern had never been religious, but he recalled feeling profoundly Jewish that summer, traipsing through the old quarters of European cities, trying to outrun the tragedy that threatened his future, his career. His day of release—the day he first felt sure he could crawl out from beneath the fallen roof—was the one in late August when he and Marla visited the Empire of the Dead: the Catacombs of Paris, nearly two kilometers of dank, twisting tunnels underneath the city's Left Bank. He wasn't prepared for this unearthly realm. Millions of human skulls, symmetrical walls of bones, carted here from the city's overcrowded cemeteries during Baron Haussmann's nineteenth-century redesign of Paris. The tunnels were cold and dark. White niter covered the ground, his shoes. The sound of dripping water. Bern's lungs tightened. What seemed like hours later, he and Marla emerged into the sunlight—as warm and welcome as it was today—and felt reborn. He saw it in Marla's eyes and, drawing painful, grateful breaths, knew he experienced it too. Death had reminded them how rare it was to be awake, ambulatory, and famished. Chalky niter tracks smeared the sidewalk—thousands of traces left by the netherworld's shaken escapees. Arm in arm, Bern and his wonderful wife rushed to a nearby Vietnamese cafeteria and wolfed down spring rolls, cabbage salad, soup.

Now he sat among lovers turned to stone: these statues commemorating gay liberation. Not literally stone—plaster and copper, Bern recalled reading somewhere. But certainly, the figures resembled people caught by surprise, frozen in the midst of mundane acts, talking, touching each other casually, like the men and women in Pompeii, their intimacies seared into everlasting pathos.

He recalled the *Inferno*—Dante, outside the City of Dis, threatened by Medusa... Virgil shading the Pilgrim's eyes so he wouldn't become petrified, his chance at salvation calcified, crumbling, lost...

(*Bad Jew!* he remembered his grandfather telling him, once, only partly in jest. *What is it with you, all the time with this* saving *of things ... buildings, neighborhoods... what's next? The body? You want a resurrection? Tell me, boy, are you a secret* Christian*?*)

A healthy man. I am a healthy man, Bern thought. That's what I am. A man easily stimulated, a prisoner of my impulse to witness... but surely, for this, I can be forgiven. It's a benevolent impulse, based on a desire for the world's improvement. Is it egotistical to believe one man's sentience can shape things for the better? Well, that's the pact we make with ourselves to prevent our dissolution. It's true, Bern thought, I'm driven by beliefs (Judeo-Christian, and more) insufficient to meet present-day challenges; I shrink in the face of power; I evade my deepest feelings. A flawed man. A flawed and healthy man.

One of the most moving artifacts recovered at Pompeii, he remembered, was a stone fragment with the impress of a young woman's breast in it.

A man moved to tears by ghostly breasts.

A girl walked through the park, singing "Across the Universe."

Was it silly or noble to take personal responsibility for the world's history?

Surely, it was dangerous to feel so much inner stimulation. But the excitement made him happy. His good health left him reeling. Overjoyed. He sat as still as he could, a conserver of energy—a quiet, elegant form. Next to him, the inanimate women enjoyed one another's bodies.

For a while longer Bern sat, content and unmoving, with stone.

Art and Architecture

The building seemed to shudder with the sigh of the opening door, and a dusting of snow blew into the lobby. Bern stepped inside with the kitten in his arms.

"Oh no," said Ryszard, the super. He was standing by the elevator doing nothing Bern could see.

"You didn't witness this," Bern said. "It won't concern you."

"No?" Ryszard scratched his belly. "We'll *all* be cat watchers. Day and night. She'll have us on our hands and knees."

"She's a lonely old woman."

"I've swept this floor for eighteen years. Loneliness? It's like utility bills. Slip slip slip. In your mailbox. Every day."

The kitten, golden, gray, purred against Bern's chest.

On the third floor, listing precariously inside the doorway of her apartment, Mrs. Mehl wept. Bern knew she'd never gotten over the loss of her previous cat.

"I thought you'd like the company," he said. He'd always wanted to do more for her than help her upstairs, now and then, with her grocery sacks. She wore a wool nightgown, now, exposing her veiny ankles. Her skin smelled of Vaseline. She held out her arms and the kitten nuzzled her neck.

"What do you call her? Him?" she said.

"Him, I think. Whatever you want."

"No. You. Please."

Names imprinted on Bern during his Torah studies back in Tex-as came to mind. Childhood lessons with the rabbi. Ishmael, whose moniker means *Heard by God.* Isaac, *He Who Laughs.* And who does the Almighty anoint as the Chosen One? The joker. Go figure.

"How about Jacob?" he said.

"Thank you, Mr. Bern."

"I'll run out and get you some fresh cat food, okay?"

What he didn't tell her was that the doorman on East Fifty-fourth who'd been offering, all week, free kittens from his building's overrun basement had found Jacob this morning pawing six of his brothers and sisters. They lay asphyxiated, curled in a heap near a leaking gas pipe. Through tears, the doorman said, "Well, *this* little fellow's a survivor. Maybe I should keep him. What happens to him if your old woman keels over tomorrow? She's pretty frail, you say?"

"I'll bring him back to you," Bern said.

The man nodded and bagged up the others. "You see something like this," he said, "and you don't know whether you're meant to hold on to the tragedy part or the miracle part."

When Bern returned to Mrs. Mehl's apartment with the cat food, he found the kitten, eyes closed and purring, in her lap. "I'll just set this over here," he said, and left the bag on the kitchen floor. The austerity of her place always startled him. The first time he'd carried her groceries up from the lobby, he'd expected Miss Havisham: Old World knickknacks, newspapers and spider webs in the corners. Instead, the space was mostly bare of furniture. A simple hutch displaying blue willow china. Two Eames chairs at a square oak table. A love seat with green and blue embroidered cushions placed neatly on each arm. The décor bespoke a straightforward, elegant life. It struck Bern as admirable.

"Thank you," said Mrs. Mehl.

"Can I do anything else for you this evening?"

"You can pour me a brandy," she said. "And have some yourself." She pointed. Bern located the bottle and two small glasses. "Herbert, my husband, got me in the habit years ago," she said. "One small shot each night." He drove a bus for a living, she said, until the morning his heart signaled it had done all the work it was going to do. "I miss him every day," she confessed, taking a spot on the love seat. Bern sat in one of the chairs.

"And you?" she asked. "I always see you by yourself."

"Long divorced," Bern said. "But solitude isn't so bad."

"I suppose not. Though you're young yet, from where I'm perched. Getting old... loneliness isn't the worst of it. I have happy memories. The worst is being useless. Knowing the world has passed you by with its brand new gadgets and manners. I can't tell you the number of things I don't know how to do anymore because the packaging has changed or the mechanisms or the requirements or—ach!" She raised her glass to Bern. "I'm less patient than I used to be because I don't understand how people can be so shallow. I don't like this in myself. It's condescending of me, and I realize it's because young people are simply inexperienced, and me—I've been through so much, I'm barnacled over and can barely move. But still." She shook her head. "Simple things, like reading the book review. Do you know, last Sunday, in the *Times*, one reviewer said of a book's author, 'He seems the kind of man I'd like to have a beer with,' as if this were a serious critical judgment, a sound way of evaluating a book's worth. No. I don't understand the world anymore."

She had confused several issues, Bern thought, but she was magnificent in her indignant melancholy. And her brandy tasted fine.

"After Herbert passed, my nephew, Bob, took care of me and tried to keep me up to date. Then drink swept *him* away."

"I'm very sorry."

"A fine painter, Bob. Abstract stuff. Not my cup of tea, but even *I* could see the boy had talent, and everybody who knew anything about those fellows—Pollock, Rothko, the lot of them—drinkers, too, you know—said Bob was just as good as they were. Did he care? Oh no. No, no, no. Wouldn't promote himself. Just wanted to paint, he said. The purity of the artist. Pah!"

"Is his work available?" Bern asked to be polite.

"Scattered from here to Kingdom Come. All over Manhattan, in peoples' apartments, warehouses..."

"And no one's tried to collect it?" He was getting tired now.

"Are you kidding?" said Mrs. Mehl. "He never kept track of anything. If I had the strength I'd try to find them. I'm sure, if his work was presented to a gallery, those rich old poofters in their penthouses would give him his due. Oh well. Too late now."

"Bob, you say?"

"Bob Mehl. Could have made something of himself, believe you me. Instead, he left me all alone here with my cat. And then my cat ran away."

She stroked Jacob, who stretched his short hind legs.

"There are a lot of galleries here in Chelsea. I'll ask around," Bern promised.

A little civility at the end of the day. It did wonders.

Pipes howled inside the walls as they usually did when someone turned on a steaming shower in a nearby apartment. The building was ancient, crotchety, full of groans against the naked weight of its occupants.

Architecture, Bern thought. Did it ever *really* comfort anyone?

Mrs. Mehl leaned forward to breathe the kitten's fur. Bern washed out his glass. Gently, he pressed the old woman's hands. He said, "Have a very pleasant evening, Mrs. Mehl."

"You, too, Mr. Bern."

The following morning, in his Eighth Street office, Bern sharpened pencils, preparing to make preliminary sketches for a small brownstone renovation. A new task, however humble, was always a joy. What was it Cezanne said? *With an apple, I will astonish all of Paris.*

Raymond Davis, one of his colleagues, about Bern's age—maybe a bit closer to sixty—poked his head in the doorway. "That's it," he said. "Finito."

"Raymond?"

"They laid me off."

"Oh no." *Restructuring*: a gloomy refrain in the hallways lately, as the firm brought more youngsters into the fold and enticed or forced retirements at the other end of the scale. Bern figured his time was coming soon.

"What do you say, Wally? An early lunch? Join me in a valedictory shot of tequila?"

"Well—"

"What the hell, eh? For old times' sake?"

Since he'd had a malignant tumor removed from his right lung two years ago, Davis finished every spoken sentence with an unspoken *Tomorrow we die.*

"Haven't I been your pal?" he asked Bern now.

"Yes you have, Raymond."

Davis said he had to make a stop at the Municipal Archives to check some lot numbers. One last job. "From there, we can walk to Chinatown."

"Chinese tequila?" Bern asked.

"Let me tell you, you haven't lived till you've imbibed Mandarin firewater."

Thirty minutes later, Bern stood with Davis in the security line inside the municipal building downtown. The female guard who inspected their IDs and took their pictures, a pretty black woman with long dreadlocks and a smile promising naughtiness, flirted with the male guard who oversaw the metal detector, a tall white man with a gut the size of a housecat. Amid their horseplay, the woman asked Davis and Bern, "What's your business?" Her boredom was as palpable as the Lysol sting rising in waves from the clean marble floors.

Bern stepped through the metal detector trouble free. Not Davis. No matter how many times he emptied his pockets of change, paper clips, and pens, he set off the alarm. The technology knew: something is wrong with this man. The guard ran a wand over his arms and legs and let him past.

Inside the archives, a bald man in a bland uniform barked at people lining up for birth, death, and marriage records. While Davis leafed through books, Bern stood by a grimy window, dispirited.

"*No tenemos*," the bald man snapped at a confused Hispanic woman. She held a slip of paper covered with names and dates. Probably the only links to her past. "You understand me, lady? Go home."

Davis scribbled the information he needed into a notebook and motioned he was ready to leave.

At the intersection of Park Row, Worth, and Mott, one of the city's most guarded spots, ringed with traffic barriers and armed officers, the New York Ironworks advertised "50% Off All Rifles and Pistols."

From discussions of permit requests at the firm, Bern knew restaurant owners were trying to add extra outdoor seating in Chinatown—a push by the city for greater economic stimulus. In genteel neighborhoods, this could be an enhancement. Here, it blocked not only walkers but also deliverymen and cargo loaders. Add to this extra trash bins and the bollard posts erected after 9/11, and you had, Bern thought, an ambulatory crisis.

Davis led him to a modest shop beneath the Manhattan Bridge next to plywood stalls hawking international calling cards and bus tickets. In the shop's back room, accessed through a thin curtain Bern wouldn't have noticed on his own, cigarette packs lined the walls. Shuanxshi, Yes, Seven Wolves, Marlboro. "Knockoffs," Davis said. "Imported illegally. Cheapest smokes in the city." He bartered with an acne-faced Asian boy over a box of faux Marlboros. Bern wondered how he had discovered this place; Davis had become increasingly reckless after his encounter with the scalpel.

They found a dark bar beneath street level, down sloping concrete steps: forty-year-old American black-light posters (Bern recalled them from his adolescence—peace doves, Adam and Eve naked on a mountaintop), leafy incense. Davis ordered two shots of tequila and lit a cigarette.

"Raymond, should you be smoking?" Bern said.

"You going to be a scold, Wally? Is *that* why you're all alone?"

"Sorry."

"What the hell, you know? Who cares?"

"How *is* your health?"

"Don't know. Feel like shit most of the time. What else is new?"

"What are you going to do?" Bern said.

"Beats me." Davis raised his glass. Bern toasted him. "Eighteen years. And what? One day you're here, next day *poof*. Ah well. I should never have gotten into this racket in the first place. I blame my dad."

"Was he an architect?"

"Ham radio operator. Back in Indiana. He planted an enormous steel tower in our front yard so he could yak at Sweden. Or Australia. Damn thing threw a huge shadow on my bedroom wall. I was afraid it would topple, some night, in a thunderstorm and crush me. I think I've always longed for a safe space."

The tequila numbed Bern's lips. He felt his mouth hover an inch or two from his face above the paper placemat with its cryptic Chinese horoscopes.

"Dad thought *talk* was a nuclear deterrent," Davis said. "Make enough friends worldwide, we'll all be okay." He threw back his drink. "What a nut. One more?"

"No," Bern said. "I really should—"

"Right. *You've* still got a job."

"Low blow, Raymond. So do you, technically. Unless you want *me* to take those numbers in."

"Sorry, Wally."

"It's all right. Shall we?"

"I'm going to stay for another."

"You're sure?"

Davis grinned like a Halloween skull. Bern laid two bills on the table. "Okay. On me," he said.

"Wally. You trying to belittle me?"

A crazy impulse—the alcohol and the incense: Bern grabbed the back of Davis's neck and kissed the top of his head. "Take care of yourself, Raymond."

A walk to clear his mind, a chocolate shop for an espresso and a cherry truffle, a CD store (the only one remaining in this neighborhood). Some late-night music: Ahmad Jamal, Abdullah Ibrahim. And *this* nifty little item: Jordi Savall. Medieval ballads. Dreams of sacred order.

It was a relief to ascend to the thin crust of legal amenities after witnessing the world's *actual* business, the scrabbling, seething backdealing underneath the streets.

He passed an old water fountain, long out of service, in a locked-up city park. No more dipping into the public well, because no more public wells.

A couple of subway trips and he found himself in Chelsea again: a gallery district. He remembered his promise to Mrs. Mehl. In a swift stroke, the thought of her made him lonely, a thudding sensation like losing his breath.

The first two docents he spoke to had never heard of her nephew. The third place he entered, the Pavel Zoubok Gallery, displayed four or five Joseph Cornell boxes. An apple-cheeked girl with short black hair was quoting prices to two apparently serious buyers. Waiting, Bern observed the boxes: *Celestial Navigation*, a star map, sand, delicate clear drinking glasses filled with marbles, stamps, and driftwood. *The Storm That Never Came*, paper cutout sparrows nestled among grasses beneath a map of the constellation Scorpio and a textbook scrap demonstrating wind patterns. Bern wanted to crawl inside a box and cozy up to the universe. He overheard one of the buyers call the docent Nora. When they left, he asked Nora if the owner was around. He was not but she knew about Bob Mehl. "Oh yeah, his stuff was legendary," she said. "Me and my friends at NYU used to hear about him. He didn't have a studio of his own. He'd hang out in his friends' lofts in SoHo, paint like a madman, two or three a day sometimes, and they were brilliant, just brilliant, and he'd leave them with people or give them away."

"Have you seen his work?" Bern asked.

"Not personally, but everyone says they're knockouts."

"Where might I find his paintings?"

"Oh my." She scratched her head. "I wouldn't know where to start. A lot of his friends—that '70s–'80s art crowd, you know—they're gone now. AIDs. High rents."

'70s–'80s! Bern had assumed '50s–'60s—Mrs. Mehl had mentioned Jackson Pollock—but of course, now that he thought about it, it didn't make sense that her nephew would be that old.

"Okay, thanks," he said. As he turned for the door, he was dazzled by the wings of an angel, sitting in one of the boxes along with a thimble, a gold coin, and a clear glass cube.

That night, Mrs. Mehl confirmed that her nephew was younger than Bern imagined. She looked better late in the day than she did in the mornings before she'd had her breakfast and a session at the makeup mirror. Still, she complained. "Osteo *and* arthritis," she said, rubbing her calves. The kitten lay on a cushion and lifted its head reluctantly when Bern approached.

"Would you like me to make an appointment for you with the doctor?" he asked.

"No no, all that fuss and nonsense."

Bern considered her sagging skin and the backs of his own rough hands. Maybe she was stronger than he thought. Stronger than *he* was. Possibly, kvetching kept her alive.

Who could *he* complain to? Maybe he should get a cat.

He realized that taking care of Mrs. Mehl these days was his best and most lasting achievement—certainly more substantial than anything he conceived at work. Well. Good enough, he reasoned.

"Pleasant evening, Mrs. Mehl."

"You too, Mr. Bern."

* * *

In the next few days—*solitude isn't so bad, really it's not!*—he tried a couple of other galleries with no success. One night, walking home, he passed an IRS office, stacks of 1040 forms in its window. That time of year again: reach for the coffee spoons, measure out your life.

No dependents.

Nothing to depend on.

Really, it's not so bad.

Turning a corner, he glimpsed a newsstand headline: rockin' sockin' Earl Palmer had died. "Tutti Frutti," "You've Lost That Lovin' Feeling," "I Hear You Knocking." Bern couldn't count the tunes whose spines Palmer stiffened with his backbeat. It was years ago, during the Torah studies with the rabbi in Houston, that Bern had learned of the drummer. Each week, once the lessons were over, he walked home with other teens discussing their favorite songs. King David's sexcapades aroused the boys, but not like rock 'n' roll.

What a contrast! The barrenness of Rebekah followed by wet dreams of Dizzy Miss Lizzie. Bern believed the 45s he bought helped him find depths in the Five Books of Moses he wouldn't have noticed otherwise: Hagar, Sarah's abused servant, decked out like Lady Day. Strange Fruit in the Garden. Goin' to Kansas City, surely the Promised Land. Sarah scoffed when the Lord told her she would bear a son: "Am I, a withered old woman, to experience pleasure again with my dried-up old husband?" And God's flirtatious reply: "Do you think anything is beyond *me*—your Lord? On your knees, woman! Get ready!" Oh yeah! You give me fever!

These days, you couldn't buy a 45 single to save your life.

Whenever Bern got home after meeting the rabbi, his grandfather, who had insisted on the lessons, saw the happy flush in Bern's cheeks and knew something was wrong. The lessons must not be taking. If they were, they wouldn't be so exhilarating.

Frequently, after dinner, he waved a photograph in Bern's face—a sepia portrait of Bern's great-great-grandfather, Jacob, taken in Budapest. No one knew when. A wheatlike, long white beard, a slender Ashkenazi nose, a round black hat. "His namesake wrestled an angel!" Bern's grandfather admonished him. "*He* wrestled fascists in Europe! And you? You lie in bed at night, with that jungle noise grinding on the radio, and tug on your little *petseleh*! Aren't you ashamed?"

The picture of Jacob was one of his grandfather's few possessions at the end. Bern recalled seeing it in the rest home just before his grandfather died, his last raspy gasps buzzing like a Passover plague.

The old man had once traveled to Budapest and found the graveyard where family lore said Jacob had been laid. The headstones were inscribed in Hebrew; Bern's grandfather, who did not read the language, had failed to foresee this eventuality. He couldn't identify Jacob's resting spot or even prove he was there. Ever since, he'd said, he felt more rootless than ever.

Tell me about it, Bern thought. Earl Palmer dead. Jesus.

At Fifth and Fifty-third now, he faced St. Thomas Church and recalled his first defiant moment as a Jew. It coincided with a feeling that he would live forever and always be loved. After Torah study one night, Bern and his friends were walking home down an oak-lined avenue. They passed a bland building shadowed by a spire topped with an iron cross. Bern stared at the place. It confused him, architecturally. Apparently a Christian church. He had never really noticed Christian churches, but he thought they all had, as a matter of course, stained glass windows. The windows here were smudged and plain. While he stood, a nun appeared on the doorstep, the wings of her habit flapping like a gull's. She looked like Natalie Wood. Her beauty stunned him. "Wouldn't you like to join us for mass?" she said. With the force of a tsunami welling up from Eastern Europe, Bern blurted, "Shalom!" Laughing, his friends ran down the street. The young nun smiled at him. "Shalom," she said. "May the Virgin be with you." That night he dreamed of an Ashkenazi Miss Lizzie with Natalie Wood's big eyes.

* * *

Mrs. Mehl saw him in the lobby late that Saturday evening and told him a joke. "What do you call a pile of cats?"

"I don't know," Bern said.

"A meow-tain." She laughed and laughed, spry old thing. Jacob seemed to be doing her good.

Bern wished her *shuvua tov.*

The following Monday at lunch he checked another gallery on her behalf. Or his—after all, the quest for her nephew gave him something to do. In the guest book by the entrance, visitors wrote to the featured artist, "Always a pleasure!" "Such joy, reacquainting myself with your exquisite compositions!" The work was a series of black and white photographs of an S and M parlor, men and women binding and hitting one another.

Murphy, one of the firm's new hires, caught Bern when he returned to the office. "Hey," he said. Bern's supervisor had asked him to collaborate with Murphy on a low-income housing project over in Little Italy. "I like your latest sketches," Murphy said. His hair touched the tops of his ears—shaggier than Bern had seen it. He was working hard, keeping long hours. He won't rest until he's nailed *my* job as well as his own, Bern thought.

"Thanks," he said.

"I admire your patience, Wally. Really. Your attention to detail. I'm too restless for my own damn good. More of an ideas guy."

"We all have our strengths," Bern said.

"Maybe by the time I've been here as long as you have, gotten married and settled down... are you married, Wally?"

"No."

"Isn't it funny I didn't know that?" He fiddled with his hair. "You work with someone for months, maybe even years, and know so little about them."

"Yes."

Murphy looked at his shoes. "So. I guess it's been hard on you. I can't imagine."

"What do you mean?"

"This thing with Raymond."

Bern shrugged. "His productivity had slipped. We all knew it."

"Yeah, but..."

"What?"

"Well, the—"

"*What?*"

"Oh shit. Well... oh shit. I'm sorry to be the one to tell you."

"Tell me what?"

"Wally, they found Raymond—"

Bern groaned.

"Yeah. In a little B and B over by the Bowery. Two or three days ago. Apparently, it happened in his sleep. Heart attack or a stroke. Maybe the booze."

"They? Who's they?"

"I don't know. The owners, I guess."

"What was he doing there?"

"Beats me. He was always sort of a loner, huh?"

"I don't know," Bern said. "Honestly. I didn't see him much outside of work."

"He sure *talked* an edgy game."

"He was never the same after his..." Bern touched his chest.

"Well, anyway. I'm sorry." Murphy patted his arm. "The sketches look great. It's a neat little project. How does it feel?"

Bern glanced at the pencils in his pocket: the erasers he had chewed and chewed again. "Fine," he said. "It feels fine."

He didn't know Davis well enough to grieve. He didn't seem to know anyone anymore except Mrs. Mehl. How had he come to this? Had he stopped trying? On the subway he distracted himself eavesdropping on two men sitting nearby. They were discussing a boxer they used to watch on television. "I loved that guy," one of the fellows said. "He was synonymous with taking it in the face."

A Hispanic lady sat beside Bern, her patient expression reminding him of the woman in the Municipal Archives ("*no tenemos*") as well as of pictures he'd once seen of the sainted Catalan architect Antonio Gaudi. In Barcelona, years ago, in a perishingly hot museum, Bern had seen some of Gaudi's models. He had suspended strings, like webs, from the ceiling using weights, and then he'd studied the designs in a mirror he'd placed on the floor, to see how buildings constructed that way might look: as though the structure were suspended *from the ground up*.

Strings and mirrors, Bern thought. Simple huts, as spare as Mrs. Mehl's apartment. Surely there is still need in the world for humble objects, humble surroundings.

Thinking of Davis—would anyone say Kaddish for such a man?—he remembered the temple in Houston, a modest A-frame, as humble a structure as you could find, where he attended evening services with his grandfather during the Days of Awe. It overlooked a trickle of Buffalo Bayou; amid the singing and chanting, Bern heard water. His favorite part of the service was Ne'ilah, holding hands with others in golden candlelight, asking God's forgiveness. "The gates are closing," the rabbi intoned. For Bern, even as a child, this was an architectural detail embodying many thoughts: the past shut away, chances lost, belonging (enclosed inside a sweet, holy space).

And the hut... each year, following Yom Kippur, his grandfather took him to a placid bend of the bayou. There, men constructed Sukkot—temporary shelters filled with bread and fruits in honor of the huts in which the Israelites had dwelt in the desert. Some of these huts were made of plywood, some of aluminum, as precise as a Joseph Cornell box; Bern saw tents made of sheets (to evoke the Cloud of Glory in which the Children of Israel were said to have been shielded by God). He prayed with his grandfather and watched men haul water from the stream in ritual echoes of ancient pleas for rain. They quoted Isaiah: "And you shall draw waters with joy from the wells of salvation." Buffalo Bayou was hardly a Well of Salvation; it was clotted with mud and trash; the scum on its twiggy surface stank of organic decay.

"According to the Talmud, the minimum height of the Sechach—the covering of the Sukkot—is ten tefachim," the rabbi told him once. "In terms *we* understand, that means the height of a man seated at table."

From that moment, human scale had been, for Bern, a central design principle.

"The walls can be made of any material," the rabbi said, "but they must be sufficiently strong to stand in an average wind." *Average?* The bayou was an elm-lined Corridor of Storms. Nothing average about it. Already, as a boy, contemplating the beauty and necessity of shelter, Bern pondered escape hatches.

Buildings rise. Buildings fall.

Friends and colleagues come and go.

But in any arrangement, he thought, there were openings.

The gates are closing?

No. Solitude doesn't *have* to mean the end.

On tax day, Bern proved his existence by signing forms and slipping them into an official drop box on the corner of Twenty-third and Fifth. The box slammed shut with a *thwack*.

He was on his way to the Larissa Goldston Gallery. Prickly people swarmed the space. On display, a late series of prints by Robert Rauschenberg. The visitors were quick to take offense with one another, grumbling at the slightest nudge or obstructed view. The tax man had crushed everyone's spirit. Bern felt a draining away of his faith in humanity, but then a stone goat's head in one of the collages, side by side with a purple lotus blossom and a bright Chinese billboard featuring a smiling mother and her child, charmed him. He stared for several minutes until a woman in a fake fur coat bumped him out of the way.

The docent, an anorexic named Tamara greeted him at her desk. On the phone, the day before, she had told him she'd known Bob Mehl and owned his most significant paintings. She kept them in a back room at the gallery. Now Bern introduced himself. She tugged one of her earrings, a large gold loop, as though she'd tear her flesh. "I guess you want to see 'em, huh?" she said.

"If it's not too much trouble."

He followed her into the next room and helped her pull two big canvases (as tall as Bern) from a storage closet. On each surface, a yellow bloom of paint spread across three red lines placed vertically in the center. "Yeah, I know," said the girl, watching his face. "Not bad, but nothing special, huh?"

"This is it?"

"Far as I know. The Complete Works. The Mehlian Oeuvre."

"But I've heard—"

"I know what you've heard. We've *all* heard it. For years." She shook her head. Her slick black hair didn't move. "It's why I've kept these. If the rumors get frenzied enough, the perception—well, who knows what these could be worth, though frankly I'm not holding my breath. You're friends with his aunt, right? I'm not in the business of stirring false hopes." She popped two pieces of Spearmint gum into her mouth. "It's possible these paintings could bring in some money someday. But it's not likely. Her nephew was a drunk. And, in my opinion, a middling artist. What he's got going for him are stories. Buzz."

"Radiant genius. Tragic hero."

"Right. The art world loves that shit. We all do. But that's what they are. Stories."

"How did they get started?"

She shrugged. "Isn't it usually a lover? Trying to make *herself* feel important?"

"All right," Bern said, as weary as he'd ever felt. "I'll tell his aunt." In fact, he wasn't shocked. From the beginning, the excitement generated by Bob Mehl's name, in gallery after gallery, had a strained and surrealistic quality to it.

On his way out the door, he jostled a man's shoulder. "Watch it!" the fellow growled. Bern gave him a goat smile.

* * *

Businessmen rushed up the streets, waving sharp envelopes high above their heads. Their nefarious schemes calculated to the penny. Bern dodged them, to keep his bones intact.

What would he tell Mrs. Mehl?

My *feelings!* he cried in his head. What earthly good do they do? For me, Bob Mehl? Anyone? Day after day, this whipsaw submission to moods! Now I'll go to work (passing Raymond's empty office); I'll smile and expect smiles in return. Too much!

Isn't solitude a preferable mode of being?

Yes. Believe it.

Walking swiftly, he passed an internet café. Grimy. Newspapers piled on the floor. Chaotic images inked on wrinkled paper. Not a single female in the place. Pale, underfed boys hovering around clamorous screens. The room smelled sweet: stale aftershave. *I am your future*, Bern thought, staring straight at the kids. To buoy himself, he stepped inside the open doorway and bought a bar of chocolate.

That evening, tired of his self-burden, surely the price of his solitude, he entered the lobby of his building and ran into Ryszard. He snapped apart the chocolate bar and handed half of it to the mumbling old grump. Ryszard leaned on his broom.

Bern told him about Bob Mehl.

"Well, now the Queen will have something else to bellyache about," Ryszard said.

"Admit it," Bern said. "You kind of like the old girl."

"No. Absolutely not. Anything that is going to outlast me gives me the shivers."

"You may be right about that."

"Trust me. My grandchildren will be feeding her cats."

"How long are you going to sweep these floors?"

"It's true, my tochas aches every night," said Ryszard. "But, you know, this is my home now. I must say, it's been a good life, all in all. My father was a fruit peddler in Poland. Cold winter mornings.

Second-hand wagon. Always a busted axle. The horses had pleurisy. Me, I guess I can manage a cranky old woman. Speak of the devil…"

Mrs. Mehl bumped through the door grappling a grocery sack. Lettuce and turnips. Bern hadn't seen her up and about in a week. He rushed to help her. She relinquished her grip and the bag fell into his arms. Without a word she waddled to the elevator. Then she stopped, turned, and said, "Mr. Ryszard, you have a disgusting and childlike smear of chocolate on your upper lip."

He covered his mouth. "Sorry," he whispered.

"You may take Jacob for his evening walk in half an hour."

"Yes, ma'am."

Suppressing a smile, Bern followed her into the elevator, clutching her groceries. He still wasn't sure how to broach the topic of her nephew, but he would find a way. There was always an opening. Mrs. Mehl seemed to thrive on this certainty, and had for many years.

"A brandy, Mr. Bern?"

"Thank you. I'd love one, Mrs. Mehl."

She pushed a button. The building engaged pulleys, cables, and gears to lift them.

II

◇◇◇

Signs

I hitched to Port Arthur on the advice of an art professor, convinced I wouldn't stay long. At the time—1970, my sophomore year—I was thinking of becoming a painter. "In our day, the central principle of art is collage," the professor said. "Image-bits. Like a series of little road signs reflecting our country's fragmentation." We were sitting in his tiny office at UT. He pulled a book from his shelf. "Currently, our finest collagist is this man, a former Texan named Robert Rauschenberg. Ever heard of him?"

"No."

"Well then, son, you need to patch some holes in your know-how."

The collages consisted of ordinary objects: pieces of cardboard boxes, bus tickets, laundry lists, newspaper clippings.

"He's mostly in New York now—where you'll have to go if you want to make it in the art world—but you'd do well to breathe the air he did as a pup," my teacher said. "Go to Port Arthur. Find the heart of Texas. Its uniqueness. Its peculiarities."

Port Arthur was a gob of mud. Crooked houses sank into bayous. Silkworms—"tree devils," in the local patois—slithered up mossy trunks. Refineries ringed the town: roaring fire-tongues.

I checked into a "Monthly Rates" motel. The Wayfarer. Hookers hung around the parking lot. Petroleum tankers pulled off the highway onto a gravel shoulder underneath the motel sign ("Heated Pool / Cable TV"). Their brakes hissed. Catcalls in the dark. The girls, in gold sequined skirts or purple hot pants, ran to the trucks and hopped inside.

Rauschenberg had cleared out of here as a young man. What remained of the places he knew, soda fountains and dance halls, had been eaten by the petrochemical air. They were barely recognizable as human habitations. Texas was no place for a painter. I've got to get to Italy, I thought. How do I get to Italy?

My love of portraiture had solidified in middle school when my English teacher, Mrs. Hollins, introduced us to Botticelli during our reading of Dante's *Divine Comedy*. Botticelli had illustrated scenes from the poem. I cherished the artist's name. Sandro Botticelli. Saying it was like singing opera.

Mrs. Hollins showed us black and white slides of Dante's lady spirits. They looked like spider webs freshened with dew. With one line, Botticelli could evoke a person's history. His illustrations gave me a glimmer of what preachers meant, in their sermons, by "Grace." My favorite was Piccarda Donati, a former nun forced by an evil brother to leave the convent and marry against her will. Dante meets her in Paradise, on the moon. Though her soul has been saved, an air of defeat clings to her. Botticelli posed her with a slightly upturned face, a leaflike gown, a modest, prayerful attitude. Her sepia eyes were tightly contemplative, her hair a brush-back of two or three pencil lines, and her mouth a dark dab welling up from the page like a wayward drop of ink. This is how I tried to draw the girls I liked.

Now it was eight years later and I was casing Port Arthur for signs I was meant to be an artist. Each evening, I'd grab a burger or some soup in a twenty-four-hour café and retreat to my room, sketching things I'd seen: tractor tires, antique lanterns, mailboxes made out of irrigation pipe.

One night my mother phoned me from the Panhandle. "You okay?" I asked. In the parking lot just outside my room, the sequined ladies huddled.

"Same old six and seven," Mom said. I pictured her standing on the scuffed red linoleum in our boxy old kitchen.

"Dad?"

"Sits in his study, staring." Two years earlier, he'd suffered three hemorrhagic strokes. He didn't say much now. Once or twice a month he'd claim he'd got a visit from an angel. In that part of Texas—the northwest, blustery winds, blistering sun—it took massive infusions of faith just to get through the days. We had almost as many churches as bars. But angels? Dad said they looked like Dallas Cowboy cheerleaders. "Frankie, I'm sending Mildred to you," Mom said. "I don't know what else to do. She's adrift here."

I closed my sketchbook. "Is she sober?"

My sister had dropped out of high school, senior year.

"About half the time," Mom said. "It's too depressing here. She has to get out, away from your dad, get a fresh start. Look after her, son."

Through my dirty window I watched a girl in the parking lot toss a busted shoe at a tumbleweed tangle. "Mom, right now, you know, I'm not really in a position to—"

"Frankie, don't do this to me again. Okay?"

Nothing to say to that. She blamed me for Dad's angelic silence.

2.

On a late Monday evening, a week later, I met Mildred at the Greyhound station. People rushed off the bus, glancing back, as if to escape something. And then she appeared. The last to get off. I remember she tripped on the bus steps, catching herself on the door. What did she wear? My memory isn't clear, and I can only see her now as she looks in this sketch on my desk. I made it a few weeks after she arrived in Port Arthur: purple bell bottoms, a paisley see-through blouse, a feather boa around her neck, and a black felt hat whose floppy brim hid her eyes.

She smelled of rum and Coke. That I recall.

"Frankie!" she croaked. She flipped off her fellow passengers. "Goddamn prigs! Let's get a drink."

I took her to a place called Derrick's next to a Texaco natural gas plant and a meat-packing outfit employing Vietnamese refugees, probably illegally. In the old days, I'd heard, Derrick's was notorious for bar fights: on Saturday nights, the Baptists and Catholics went after each other. In time, Derrick's customers learned to self-segregate and drink in relative peace. In this boisterous crowd even Mildred in her getup might slip by unseen. On the sidewalk she stopped to light a cigarette. "This fucking air," she said. She stared at the flaming orange sky. "It's like eating burnt matches. Kind of interesting, really."

We found a table under naked red bulbs swaying from the tin-plated ceiling. Behind us, a shrimper's net hung on a pinewood wall. On the table, modified drill bits served as ashtrays. Mildred filled one with half-smoked Luckies. The light flattened her face. She looked like wax. The room smelled of insecticide, and the thump of a muddy electric bass, from the jukebox, shook the floor.

"So, Frankie," Mildred said. "Rembrandt, eh?"

"Something like that. What about you? I mean, I'm glad to have you here—"

"Mom. She's freaking. I guess I don't blame her, with Dad and all, but... basically, she kicked me out. Probably just as well. We'da wound up killing each other." She laughed, phlegmatic and raw. "She said I needed a new start. Lucky you. You get to be the chaperone."

"Not much work here, except maybe waiting tables." Me, I'd been living off my dwindling summer wages.

"I can do that."

"How *is* Dad?"

"Fuck." She lit another Lucky. "Waiting for an angel to come give him a cosmic blow job. Who the hell knows?"

"Does he *ever* make sense?"

"Shit, Frankie." She rubbed her eyes. "Listen, Mom can say whatever she wants about me being a fuckup and all, which is true, but damn it, I stuck with her to take care of Dad. I mean, that's what I did."

"I know. I'm glad. I'm sure Mom's grateful."

"She's got a hell of a way of showing it."

"She's worried. She doesn't know what else to do."

"Oh, like *you've* got a genius plan."

"You're on your own, Mil. I'm not going to tell you what to do. You know that. I'm just here, that's all."

"Yeah, well." She grinned. "Mom thinks you're squatting in a hole. The starving artist."

"It's cheap. They've got rooms. I've reserved one for you."

"Good. Sit tight," she said. She shambled to the bar for a second round of Lone Stars.

Before his first stroke, our dad installed septic tanks (he was "Shit Man" to our classmates). One day, Mom told me he needed my help after school. Instead, I stayed late, smoking with friends on the track around the football stadium. Mom sent Mil to get me. We went to find Dad.

His Honey Wagon, tiny as a Tastee Freez ice-cream truck, was parked in front of the Landis's. Irreducible solids had settled inside their system and gradually filled it, destroying the clarified liquid effluent. Filthy people, I thought. They didn't deserve my father. His gentleness. His care. He'd never been like other men in town. He liked to read books. He was devoted to Sunday school.

Mil found him in a hole in the backyard among screwdrivers, wrenches, and a dying yellow flashlight. He lay twitching in mud.

I jumped in beside him. Rain spattered his face. "Dad? Dad?" I said.

His mouth hung slack. He was freezing, his overalls soaked. Mildred crouched above us on the lip of the pit. "Dad, look at me!" she barked. "*Look* at me!" His eyes drifted up then sank back down. "What's he doing?" she said.

"I don't know."

"Fuck, Frankie, what do we do?"

"Guh…guh…" Dad said. He was skinny, but his weight caused my shoulder to spasm.

"All right," Mildred said, swatting wormy wet hair from her eyes. "Stay with him."

"Where *you* going?"

"Up to the house. Here." She pulled a lighter and a hand-rolled cigarette out of her pocket. "See if this soothes him a little. Hell, who knows?" She lit the cigarette, took one long puff, and handed it down to me.

"What *is* this stuff?" I said. Back then, pot was still a rare little item in Nowhere, Texas.

"Just try it."

Dad couldn't hold the joint in his mouth so I passed the smoke beneath his nose. His eyelids fluttered and his face *did* seem to soften. Mildred tossed a Baggie into a tree. "I'll be back with someone," she said. "When you hear us coming, get rid of that thing, okay?"

"They'll smell it."

"Well shit, Frankie…"

"Okay, okay, just go."

She slogged off into the dark.

I rocked my father, fanning him with the smoke, looking for signs that he knew me.

Do you know what it's like when the man who made you no longer registers your face?

It was hard to move my feet: stuck in my neighbors' waste. Is anyone finer than a Shit Man, I wondered, staring at my father's open mouth. Cleaning up after others. Purifying. Isn't that what the body does, moving its bowels: casting itself from itself?

"Uh," Dad said. "Guh."

What would I tell my mother? If I'd done what she'd asked, could I have prevented this? Crazily, I remembered Mrs. Hollins in class, saying the lake of shit in Hell was set aside for the flatterers. The ones who lied.

* * *

Last call at Derrick's. Mildred sipped her beer.

"I should have realized how hard the last few years have been on you," I said.

"Well, you had your own thing to do. Your drawings and stuff. No biggie." She sniffed. Her hands shook. "It's just that I miss the sweet old bastard. The way he used to be."

"I know."

"Frankie. What I'm afraid of?" Mildred said. "I'm afraid I'll be a lunatic, too."

"No."

"Maybe it runs in the family?" She cackled sadly and squinted through the smoke-haze. "What *is* that twaddle—wonder if they've got any Janis on the box? Not fucking likely."

"Sure they do. It's her hometown."

"Right. She's the biggest star this goddamn place ever produced—"

"Well—"

"—and they treated her like crap. You hear she's coming back? High school reunion. Next month. Janis may come. She said so, in *Rolling Stone*. Can you believe it?"

"Really?"

"TJ High. Thomas Fucking Jefferson!"

"So *that's* why you got on the bus."

She laughed. "No, no. I didn't know nothing about it. I read the interview on the way down. But if she really *does* come... man, I've got to find a way in there."

We drained our mugs, toasting Dad, and then walked six blocks to the Wayfarer. A full moon rose above hissing blue refinery flames. On the way, Mildred pulled a flask from her macramé bag. At the motel, I made arrangements for her with a man at the front desk. He was bald, wore a wife-beater, and flashed forearm tattoos proclaiming eternal love for someone named Slit.

Mildred's room was next to mine. We said good night and I stood in the parking lot inhaling what little breeze there was, staring off into the dark, where, not far away, Louisiana sank into syrupy swamps. The hookers had fled to the trucks. A profusion of grays tainted the sky, streaked with yellow and green.

I was here because I wanted to be an artist. Damn you, Sandro Botticelli!

The television in my room didn't work. Neither did the radio. The carpet smelled of foot powder. I peeled off my shirt. I reached beneath the lamp shade—bruised with tobacco stains—and switched off the light. Through my window screen I heard Mildred slurring "Piece of My Heart," exactly the way she used to sing to Dad to get him to sleep.

3.

She slept in. I spent the morning strolling, sketching, taking notes. When I returned to the motel, around noon, Mildred was sitting in her open doorway in a fraying nylon lawn chair dressed in the same outfit she'd worn the night before. She was smoking. She had a black eye and a jagged cut on her forehead.

"What happened?" I asked. "Did one of these truckers take you for—"

"Some asshole over at the breakfast place down the road. Showing off for his friends."

"Why?"

"He said I looked like Janis."

"You do."

"And then he said they didn't want no white trash 'round here and he gave me a pop. Probably didn't help that I called him Shithead."

I didn't phone Mom with this news. Instead, I told her Mildred was settling in just fine. Yes, yes, of course, I'd keep an eye on her.

"My guardian angel," Mildred joked.

Days before the first stroke—a thunderhead in the brain, one doctor said—Dad had been reading St. Augustine for a Sunday school class he attended each week. We found a marked-up copy of *Confessions* in his study while he was in the hospital. The angels were "pure form," said the book, and they arrived in a blink. Their "perfect task" was to gaze at the face of God.

If I interpreted Dad's markings correctly, what bothered him, as it troubled the saint, was the Fallen Angels. Were they *born* with a sinful nature or did they spurn God within a few seconds of existing? In the margins, my father had scribbled, "Their tumble from Heaven, covering the span of the cosmos, must have taken thirty seconds or less."

I imagined Dad shoveling shit, squatting prayerfully in a pit hollowed out by an angel's impact with Earth: feathers floating in air like arteries tangled in the back of a brain.

After his third stroke, he regained the use of language, more or less, and spoke of visitations.

"Ain't he just like a Texan?" Mom said. She was born in Oklahoma. "Them ol' Texas boys always *did* take sternly to church."

He described a sort of heavenly pep squad. When I pressed him for details, he handed me another book from his Sunday school class: Henry James Sr.'s *The Redeemed Form of Man*. On the title page, beneath the author's name, Dad had written, "American Original." Then he pointed me to a passage he had underlined in red:

> I remained seated at table after the family had dispersed, idly gazing at the embers in the grate, thinking of nothing, and feeling only the exhilaration incident to a good digestion, when suddenly—in a lightning-flash as it were—"fear came upon me, and trembling, which made all my bones to shake"...some damned shape squatted invisible to me within the precincts of the room, and raying out from his fetid personality influences fatal to life.

What did these words mean to my father? Why *in red*? I looked up at him. "American Original?" I asked. "They're all around us," he said and then he simply nodded, as if now—an ignorant Okie, like my mom—I knew all I would ever need to know.

4.

In six weeks I'd filled two sketchbooks. My throat was always sore (the air smelled of sulfur). I planned to leave Port Arthur soon.

In the meantime, I got a job waiting tables in Derrick's. Mildred washed dishes at a place called Dusty's. Right away, with a combination of chutzpah and cracked charm (people either wanted to kill her or kiss her), she made friends with folks who had pull on the high school reunion committee.

In an interview on *The Dick Cavett Show*, Janis confirmed she planned to return to Texas. Mildred and I watched the interview one night on a jumpy RCA set in the motel lobby.

In the afternoons, walking to our jobs, we'd cut past "Thomas Fucking Jefferson." The high school was a physical afterthought to its football stadium. On the television show, Janis said the school was staffed by people whose only goal was to buy a new car each year. "What's happening never happens there," she said.

After work, I'd hear Mildred singing in her room as she stirred her Scotch and sodas, and think of Dad—his early convalescence, before I'd left home. He enjoyed the sounds of our voices. It didn't matter what we said or read to him as long as we kept a steady cadence.

He especially liked newspaper stories on the space race. He signaled his excitement with birdlike hand signs, his palms gyring up, his fingers fluttering wings. Eventually he'd fall asleep and I'd assume his rounds in the Honey Wagon, circling town in the truck with a stack of overdue job orders.

I redesigned leach beds, pumped out waterlogged tanks, poured root killer into clogged-up drains, advised homeowners about bacteria to put into their tanks to eliminate sludge. I didn't like the work, but by sundown I felt good to have done it.

I thought my father and I might talk about Dante—after all, we had angels in common—but he didn't take an interest in my schoolwork. One day, Mrs. Hollins said the holy pilgrim had climbed out of Hell on the Devil's body toward Mount Purgatory. The turning point, where he left the Evil Realm and moved toward Heaven, was Satan's anus. Like excrement expelled from the body, Dante flowed through one tunnel after another, increasingly purified until he saw the face of God.

As I repaired my neighbors' plumbing, I pondered the labyrinths of the upper and lower intestines, the mazes of brain and heart.

One night, Mom went shopping for supper and I was reading to Dad. A sharp smell forced me to throw back the bed covers. His bowels had let go. Soft masses of shit smeared the sheets and his skinny white thighs. Down the hall in her room, Mildred heard the groaning. She appeared in the doorway. The smell staggered her. With one hand she covered her mouth and nose, stepped into the room, and helped lift him into a sit. We peeled off his shorts. She went to the bathroom and readied five or six wet cloths. Together, we swabbed his legs and his withered penis. We tore the linens off the bed. While I sanitized Dad with rubbing alcohol, Mildred wadded up the leaking mess and took it to the basement, to the washing machine. Throughout the ordeal we hadn't said a word. We didn't look at each other or Dad's tear-streaked face. For days, he had registered little, but now he was clearly upset. Shame—the last emotion to vanish? Maybe, swabbing our father, Mildred and I bonded on some unspoken, unspeakable level. We felt Dad's wordless horror as well as the necessity of what we were doing. But afterward, we drifted to our separate rooms. We never spoke of the incident. Our mother didn't mention it, either, though she was the one who eventually retrieved the sheets from the washer and must have guessed what happened.

One afternoon, a week or so later, I came home from a particularly nasty job at the Methodist church—waste had backed up from the downstairs toilets—to find Dad in front of the television watching John Glenn. "He saw something," Dad said. He made his little hand sign.

"What do you mean?"

"Out the window of his space capsule. Something he couldn't explain. Thousands of flashing lights."

"What do the experts say?"

"Frank," Dad said. He placed a gentle hand on my shoulder. "This is way beyond the experts."

5.

A week before Thomas Jefferson's reunion, TV trucks began to appear in Port Arthur. The reunion's chief organizer, a rather snippy young woman, went on a local television program to say, "This is *not* a reception for Janis Joplin. I'm getting just really tired of hearing about Janis Joplin and all the really nasty things she's said about Texas and the kids I went to high school with. There are 566 other members of TJ '60, and the reunion is for everybody to have fun, not just for Janis Joplin."

"Bitch," Mildred said. We were sitting in the motel lobby. She was sipping vodka from a Dixie cup. She wore Day-Glo eyeliner, a string of plastic pearls, and jeans with a peace sign sewn across the butt. She turned off the television, stepped into the parking lot, raised her fist, and shouted at the truckers parked along the gravel strip, "Janis Power!"

The day Janis got to town she gave a press conference in the Petroleum Room of the Goodhue Hotel. Mildred and I watched it live on a black and white set in the Pelican Bar, down the street from the high school. Junkers cruised past the school, full of boys. I sketched them as I drank, watched Janis, and glanced out the bar's tinted windows.

Later, a journalist named Chet Flippo said Janis wore enough jewelry that day for a "Babylonian whore," and the room stank of the peroxide in her hair. She made a crack about the press table. It was covered with a big white cloth. "Looks like someone's about to serve the Last Supper," she said.

No one laughed.

A local reporter asked her, "What have you been up to since 1960?"

"Trying to get laid. Stay stoned."

"Right on!" Mildred shouted, sitting beside me. People stared at her.

"What do you think of Port Arthur now?" asked another reporter.

"There seems to be a lot of long hair and rock," Janis said. I'd seen none of this. "Which also means drug use, you know."

Mildred toasted the screen, but it seemed to me the cocky star was a very hurt soul, still stuck in the tenth grade. It wouldn't do to mention this: Mildred and I would probably fight about it.

"What do you remember most about the town?" someone asked Janis.

She stuttered and frowned. "I don't really remem... no comment."

"You were different from your schoolmates, or were you?"

"I felt apart from them."

"Did you go to many football games?"

"I think not. I didn't go to the high school prom and—"

"You *were* asked, weren't you?"

"No, I wasn't. They didn't think... they... I don't think they wanted to take me. And I've been suffering ever since." She gave a ghastly smile, but it was clear she wasn't joking. "It's enough to make you want to sing the blues."

Mildred picked up her bag. "Frankie, can you cover my drink? I'm going to the high school now."

"Sure."

"Head on over later. Behind the gym."

"I don't think so. It doesn't seem right."

"Don't worry about it. I told you. I can get you in. These guys I met—"

"No, thanks. Have a good time. I hope you get to meet her."

After she left, I stayed for one more beer. In town, men ran up the streets hauling microphones and cameras. Goateed disc jockeys gave away radio station T-shirts and 45s, bands no one knew. Steam drifted from the Texaco plant. This stuff will kill me, I thought. Don't breathe. It'll show up in your belly years from now. A drunk stopped me in a vacant lot. He pointed to the smudgy air. "Smell that, boy?" he said. "It's the smell of money, and don't you fucking forget it."

I wound through darkened streets past the Pompano Club and a Walgreen's, cut behind City Hall and over to the Inter Coastal Canal. In a narrow alley, Vietnamese dishwashers smoked in the doorway of a tiny seafood joint. Wet boxes, shattered crabs lay at their feet.

Around 4 a.m., Mildred woke me, pounding my door. I unbolted it and slid back the chain. She staggered in with a bottle of Southern Comfort. Her clothes smelled as smoky as the town.

"Well, did you meet her?" I asked. I slipped into a shirt and buttoned it halfway.

"Damn straight."

"What was she like?"

"Beautiful. Want some?" She held up the bottle.

"No, thanks."

"Don't be a goddamn prig, Frankie."

"Okay, just a little, in that glass over there—there, next to my sketchbook. What did she say?"

"Said people here had laughed her out of class, out of town, and out of Texas."

"I believe it."

"Her classmates, Frankie—they're fucking pigs. Still! Nothing ever changes. The world will always be high school. They gave her a tire because she had traveled the farthest to attend. 'What am I going to do with a fucking tire?' she said. And then. Oh, Frankie. Then some asshole said she was still the ugliest girl in class."

"No."

"Yeah. But she was cool. She said, 'Everybody lay whoever you're sitting next to.' I wouldn't have touched *any* of those suckers. But guess what? I got to hug her and get her a drink. And Frankie, you know what she told me?"

It was the finest night of Mildred's life. I raised my glass to her. "What?"

"She told me stardom was nothing but riding a bus."

History records that, three months later, in Room 109 of the Landmark Motor Hotel in West Hollywood, California, Janis Joplin lay dead of "acute heroin-morphine intoxication." Apparently, she had spent the evening in the Sunset Sound recording studios working on a track entitled "Buried Alive in the Blues." At the end of the session, Janis and her band made a cassette recording of "Happy Birthday" to be sent to John Lennon for his thirtieth on October 9. Then she went to her room at the Landmark. Earlier, she had bought an unusually potent supply of smack; in the course of the weekend, it killed eight people. Janis shot up. Her eyes rolled backward in her head. She pitched forward onto the floor, busting her lip on a nightstand.

In New York, the night before she had flown to Port Arthur for her high school reunion, her fellow Texas exile, Robert Rauschenberg, had split a bottle of tequila with her. "I knew the reunion was going to be a disaster," he told a reporter after she died. "But I couldn't convince her not to go." He blamed her death on Thomas Fucking Jefferson. "She was devastated," he said. "She needed confirmation from home and that's what got her into trouble. She wanted to be loved."

Signs (1970), one of Rauschenberg's finest collages, features Janis Joplin ("the voice of her generation," he said) and an Apollo astronaut. Also in the picture: RFK and JFK, Martin Luther King Jr. in his casket, peace marchers, soldiers in the swamps of Vietnam. I've hung a copy of *Signs* in the art room of Ely High School, in my old hometown, where I teach now. The collage is meant to "remind us of love, terror, violence," Rauschenberg wrote. "The danger lies in forgetting."

6.

Appropriately, given my father's obsessions in his final, mostly silent years, the last time I saw Dad was the day Neil Armstrong stepped on the moon. This is so neat, it sounds like a trick of memory, but I swear it's true.

That day, I'd left the house early. Bob Mitchell, out on Farm Road 60, had a problem with runaway waste in his yard. His tank lines were old, and the D box seemed to pump most of the effluent into only one line at a time. Tree roots and a jerry-rigged system made it hard to find the actual problem. The leach beds were poorly designed.

I removed the D box lid to re-level the outlet pipe. I didn't have the tools I needed or a cap with an offset hole in it, so I tried to align the holes by sight. I kept missing the mark. This went on for hours. Finally, frustrated and angry, I kicked the pipes and sliced my knuckles on a tree root. I climbed out of the hole and told Mitchell I'd come back tomorrow for another go.

When I dragged into the house, my father met me at the door. He looked me over—spattered overalls, muddy boots in my hands, bloody knuckles. He placed his palm on my shoulder. "Frank," he said. "You can't open a flower with a hammer." He patted my back and went to sit on the couch.

Mother and Mildred sat raptly in front of the set: a blurry moon. "The Eagle has landed!" Mildred shouted.

I stood behind them. Whatever I touched, I'd soil. Mildred held her nose and laughed. "Mr. Beaver says this is America's finest hour," she said. "Mr. Beaver" was her name for the heavily jowled Dick Nixon.

I squinted at the screen. A shifting white mass. Piccarda, are you there, I thought. Has your eternal soul been saved?

Armstrong bounced down the spacecraft's ladder.

Gingerly, my father stood, approached the set, and touched the screen's curved glass. "The gate is closing," he said. Then he walked to his study.

Mildred rolled her eyes.

I moved down the hall toward my father's oak door. Lamp-glow spilled into the hallway. "Dad?" I said.

"Frank. Come in."

He sat at his desk in a wedge of light. The rest of the room remained dark. I sat in a chair opposite him, careful not to dirty the cushion. "Dad?"

"Yes?"

"Are you happy?"

He smiled at me. "Of course I am."

"What do you recall of the night we found you?" I asked. "Anything now?"

He stared at the ceiling. "Moonlight. Rain," he said. "You and Mildred."

I nodded. I didn't know why I'd followed him in here. Perhaps I knew I wouldn't see him anymore. I'd applied to college. In honor of my father, I'd been tempted to write in my application essays, "Martin Luther's enlightenment came to him on the toilet. 'It is God's justice which justifies and saves us,' he declared. 'This knowledge the Holy Spirit gave me on the privy in the tower.' "

Now Dad leaned toward me over his desk. "Frankie. Man is spreading contagion to the moon and beyond."

I stared at him.

"Evil. You know what I think? I think it's a fellow clutching something tightly in his fist," Dad said. He paused for a minute as if searching the shadows for something. "Everyone around him wants to know what it is. They're convinced, whatever he has, they can't live without it. 'Please!' they call. He laughs and opens his hand. And do you know what he's holding?"

I shook my head. He must have read this somewhere and memorized it, I thought. I listened to the wind.

"Nothing," Dad said. He slumped, exhausted.

I rose, came around the desk, and kissed the top of his head. "Okay. Okay, Dad. Good night." I thought: *I will not let you go until I have blessed you.*

7.

"She was a goddamn saint. And they fucking crucified her," Mildred said.

We had rented a little blue canoe. A Friday afternoon. We were paddling down the Sabine River—in part because it was a crazy thing to do, and Mildred was always up for something like that, and in part because she wanted quiet time to grieve for Janis. She'd brought a bottle of bourbon and two paper cups.

We drifted past Gulf Island and the Rainbow Bridge. Along the banks, sooty brick walls of World War II–era factories rose above knotted kudzu. The factories' windows were smashed. Fire broke above the trees, from the smokestacks of nearby refineries. Ahead of us, a blue heron skimmed the surface of the water.

"Who the hell invented high school?" Mildred moaned, filling our cups.

"Some sadist."

"Dickie Nixon is king and Janis is toast. Tell me about a world like that, Frankie, 'cause, I gotta say, I don't think I can find my way around in it."

"I don't know," I said. I took one of her hands.

We didn't see each other for nearly three years. I moved away from Port Arthur, returned to the university. My art professor was disappointed that I'd picked up few new skills, and I began to avoid his courses.

One semester, I met a girl named Lori in a class on the American Puritans. After our first night making love, she asked about my family. I told her Mildred's story.

"She's still in Port Arthur?" Lori asked. She propped herself on a pillow and rolled a joint.

"Yeah. Washing dishes, waiting tables. Caring for Dad—it seemed to knock her off her rails and she's never gotten back." Mom blamed me for *that*, too. "She calls me for money now and then. Booze and cigarettes."

"Still, you'll regret it if you cut her out of your life, Frank. You should go see her."

"Go see her," Mother insisted on the phone.

And so, over Spring Break, I arranged to visit Mildred.

She didn't show up at the Greyhound station. I shouldered my duffel, checked the address—Mildred had moved out of the Wayfarer, into an apartment—and walked along the canal. Her place was up the street from TJ High, in the shadow of the auditorium and the gym, ugly round buildings dubbed "Twin Titties" by the high school students. Her apartment, a one-bedroom on the second balcony of a crumbly complex, was dark. The door, painted red over a layer of blue over another layer of yellow, stood open. "Hello?" I called. I dropped my duffel and fanned the door to keep from gagging: a combination of rat poison and spoiled meat. I switched on the overhead. A poster of Big Brother and the Holding Company was taped crookedly over a hound's-tooth couch, next to a poster of George Harrison with a long beard and flat felt hat. He looked like a monk. A portable TV sat, unplugged, on a green shag carpet in the center of the room. In a corner, by the kitchen, a purple beanbag chair bled Styrofoam pellets from a gash in its side. "Hello?" I called again.

I stepped outside and leaned against the balcony's iron railing, breathing deeply. The balcony overlooked a weedy courtyard. As I stood there, a sailor pulled a weary woman in high heels and a miniskirt toward a ground-floor apartment. He kicked open the door. I had no experience with such things, but it occurred to me: this was the kind of place that might be called a Shooting Gallery.

For over an hour I waited for Mildred. Finally: "Oh shit." Her voice at the bottom of the stairs. I heard her scrabble in her bag.

"You don't need your keys," I called. "It's open."

"Who's there?" she shouted. "What the fuck do you want? I don't have anything."

"Mil, it's me."

She straggled up the stairs, an unlit cigarette locked between two fingers. She wore only one shoe. Her hair, dirty brown, branched in all directions like an unpruned ivy plant. "Frankie!"

"The door was open."

"Come in, come in! Welcome to *mi casa*!"

The apartment smelled a little better since I'd aired it out. In the light, I saw Mildred wore a rope for a belt over a tentlike dress. Bangles and beads. A rattan wrap with a pattern like rattlesnake skin. She smelled of garlic, sweat, incense. "What happened to your shoe?" I said.

She glanced at her left foot. The nail of her big toe, but only the big toe, was painted black. "I don't know," she said. "I hope I donated it to a good cause!" She rushed me, affectionately, and shoved me into the beanbag. Styrofoam sprayed the room: confetti at a sad little party. "Frankie! It's so good to see you!"

"You, too."

She stood. "So here's the thing. I didn't meet you because... because..."

"It's okay."

"Well, anyway, before you judge me—"

"I'm not judging you."

"All I'm doing?"

Her breath was a blast of gin-soaked cherries. I'd count our meeting a success if I could get her to bed without any fuss.

"All I'm doing—"

"Let's talk in the morning, okay?"

"—is my Daddy-thing."

"Mil, what the hell are you talking about?"

"Frankie, did you ever see Dad in a suit and tie? I've been thinking about this. Listen. The proper, paunchy, hotshot bit? No! That wasn't him. Dad went his own way! Frankie?"

"Yes?"

"Frankie, listen, listen to me." She frowned, suddenly serious. "It's about ignoring the so-called outer reality and seeking the inner light. *Feeling* it, man, as much as you can. The bullshit pain as well as the highs. I mean, Frankie, it's all about opening yourself to the whole fucking range of being a human goddamn person. You know?"

I struggled to rise from the beanbag. "Right," I said.

"You *are* judging me. You're pissed that I didn't come meet you. But that's what I'm trying to say—"

"Really, Mil. Let's get to bed."

"You're judging Dad, too, you know. Don't deny it." She swayed on the shag carpet. "You laughed at him just as much as I did."

"Dad? I never laughed at him. What's this about Dad?"

"And *I* am on—" She nearly fell into my arms. "—I am on a goddamn spiritual path, Frankie, okay? So don't screw with me."

"This is pointless, Mil. In the morning. We'll talk then, okay?"

"You don't know what it's like, Frankie. Never even tried. Too goody-goody."

"Who's judging who now?"

"You'll never know what it's like to dig so deep into yourself, you're like the wick inside the candle wax—the *candle wax*, man—knowing part of you's burning somewhere, burning you up from the inside out, and one day all the wax will melt and you'll be as free as the ash in the air!"

I stepped away from her, tried to make a joke. "Well, Sister Mil, eh? Can we get some sleep now?"

She picked up her bag. "I'm leaving," she said.

"Mil, how did we get into this? I didn't mean—"

"I'm going to sleep with a friend. This place is too small for both of us. I'll see you in the morning. We'll get some breakfast or something."

"Mildred—"

"There's food in the fridge." She stumbled toward the door, stopped and turned. "It really is good to see you, Frankie." And then she was gone.

I couldn't sleep. When I'd left her here and gone back to school, Mom scolded me. "You're letting me down again, Frankie. You need to look after her."

"Mom, she's a grown woman," I'd said. "I've got myself to think about."

Now, I surveyed the room, the squalor to which I'd condemned my sister. No one was going to mistake *me* for a saint.

I'd gotten used to the smell. I picked up the loose Styrofoam pellets, but the trash can in the kitchen was full so I left the pellets in a pile on the floor. I dragged my duffel into the bedroom. The sheets were stiff and yellow. On the red-striped pillow sat Mildred's old teddy bear, the one she used to sleep with as a girl. He smelled of old milk. I clutched him to my chest and stretched out on the floor.

Mil didn't show for breakfast. Or lunch. I couldn't find a key so I left the door unlocked and wandered into town. Students tossed Frisbees on the high school grounds. Downtown, I sat on the steps of a boarded-up Savings and Loan and watched men across the street, on the curb, share a flask. I had brought a drawing pad and a charcoal pencil but nothing inspired me. How had Rauschenberg made anything of himself, coming from here? He had once said, in an interview, "Painting relates both to art and life. Neither can be made. I try to act in that gap between the two." I'd never understood what he meant.

Late in the day, when I returned to Mildred's apartment, I found the door wide open, the television gone. I rushed to the bedroom closet. My duffel was missing, too. A few pairs of pants, shirts, a transistor radio. "Son of a bitch!" I yelled. It occurred to me Mildred might have taken the things and pawned them. In any case, I had my wallet, and I'd kept my bus ticket in my pocket.

The stuffed bear stared at me. George Harrison stared at God. "Hell," I said to the room. "I guess that's it." I stuck two twenties on the freezer door with a fridge magnet. Maybe Mildred would get them, or maybe I had just made some crackhead's day. I picked up my drawing pad and walked to the bus station.

Lori and I spent the next day in bed, getting high, making love. She was the perfect ministering angel, her blonde hair a festival of light.

Six months later, Mil disappeared. Mom was frantic on the phone. I went back to Port Arthur. It seemed I could never escape it.

The apartment manager told me Mildred owed him nothing. He thought she'd gone someplace with an out-of-work oil man. She didn't want to stay in touch, fine, I thought. I was tired of the burden of her. Mom was furious at me, but it was a quiet fury. "Texans," she said. "How is it I raised a couple of damn Texans?"

Of all the ways I feared Mil would die, asthma was not a candidate. Cigarettes, I guessed. Alcohol. An overdose.

When we finally got the autopsy report, we learned that just before her death Mildred's lung capacity had dropped to nearly zero. For at least a week she had been a walking corpse.

A jogger discovered her body in the south end-zone of the TJ High School football stadium. Apparently, she had scaled the fence around 2 a.m. For what purpose, no one knows. She had, on her person, a pack of Marlboros and an unopened bottle of Old Charter. She weighed ninety-seven pounds.

It's not clear where she'd been living. She had given her teddy bear and the George Harrison poster to a friend at work. None of her other things were found.

Mom left me to make the funeral arrangements. She'd exhausted herself when Dad died just a few months earlier (she'd buried him quickly, giving me no time to make it back for the ceremony). "I asked you to do this one thing for me, to look after your sister," Mom told me. Her voice was brittle, faint. "Just this one little thing."

I had Mil cremated and scattered her ashes on the Sabine River.

8.

The moon is shrinking. I read that yesterday in the paper. My father would have appreciated this. Scientists at the Center for Earth and Planetary Studies at the Smithsonian's National Air and Space Museum announced they have "deduced the moon's dwindling size from cracks on the surface seen in images taken by NASA's Lunar Reconnaissance Orbiter." As the moon's core has cooled and contracted, the outer crust has fragmented into faults, with one side of each fracture slipping over the other, reducing the moon's size by about two hundred yards, or the length of two football fields.

On the surface of the moon, just before he meets Piccarda Donati, Dante does not know what substance he inhabits or how his body can mix with Heaven's insubstantiality. How can "one dimension contain another?" he asks. The moon "took me into itself / as water does a ray of light / and yet remains unsundered and serene."

These days, the elements I once moved through so effortlessly have evaporated. My world has shrunk. Lori and I divorced a decade ago. My mother died last year in Amarillo in an assisted-living facility. In truth, she had diminished for me, little by little, as my father's memory erased her. I buried her next to him: my final link to the past.

I'm comfortable now teaching high school art classes, eating takeout in the evenings, still dreaming of getting to Italy. I'm fond of my American Originals: Rauschenberg, the intriguing shadows cast by homeless men huddled in the parking lot of the empty Astrodome, an occasional high school freshman who scrawls an arresting sentence on an exam. You never know what you'll come across in the great state of Texas.

I do a little painting, culling images from my sketchbooks, and sometimes exhibit in a local gallery. Solitude contents me, and most of the time I don't wrestle with loneliness. I would not claim to be living a saintly life, but at least I am living lightly on—in?—the world, and doing no harm that I can see. And so I go about my days. As with Janis: *Nothing left to lose.*

Except for this. One last cherished memory. *The danger lies in forgetting.*

That day on the river. After we'd drifted a while.

Mildred said, "I keep thinking, where did everything turn? When did I realize I couldn't get back to *before*? That night...you know the one I mean...I've always wished I hadn't been so high. I've wondered if I could have helped Dad more."

"I wish...well, I wish a lot of things about that night," I said. "And you did okay. Really."

Mildred nodded. "Our lives didn't end then, did they?"

"No. Of course not."

She nodded again. Mosquitoes troubled her face. She brushed them away. Old wooden pilings, abandoned since the Civil War, poked up out of the river. The water had a variegated sheen, thick and pale. People had tossed hubcaps, busted microwave ovens, and U joints into the stream. Mildred and I held hands and floated past the remains of a Weed Eater. A heron rose fluttering from the water.

"Bless Janis," Mildred said.

◇◇◇

The Magnitudes

A dream of birds.
And then I wake recalling my father.

Later, just before my morning show at the planetarium, I catch a crosstown bus to Oak Cliff. After a few short blocks, the bus pulls up to a dusty intersection separating a residential neighborhood from a small business district. A tennis-shoe army gets on: half a dozen Mexican women, on their way to housecleaning jobs in south Dallas neighborhoods. They've come from a 7-Eleven parking lot, where they kissed their husbands or boyfriends goodbye. As the women board the bus, pickups come for the men, taking them (I imagine) to construction sites or distant fields for a day of strawberry- or apple-picking. The men remind me of my father, an oil man when he was younger: stringy arms, the permanent squint characteristic of field workers and drillers exposed to the sun. Some of the women are accompanied by children. They nestle crusty noses between the ladies' breasts, loose inside faded print dresses, and fall asleep. A dark-eyed boy in a stained T-shirt, sitting across the aisle from me, gives me a beautiful smile then closes his eyes. Two stops later, the women gather kids, rags, spritzers, and toilet-bowl brushes. They get off the bus and march toward unpainted, ramshackle houses, places whose owners, from all indications, can't afford housekeepers. The homes are old, ornate in their decay. Possibly the occupants are clinging to some lost glory, a proud history, refusing to accept changes of fortune.

My stop is surrounded by hobby shops, pawnbrokers, hardware

stores, and bail bondsmen. The Yucca Theater sits in the middle of the block. An old-fashioned place, like the Oklahoma City theaters my mother took me to when I was a child. On the dirty, cracked marquee above the entrance, a set of plastic letters: O A T. *Patton? On the Waterfront?* I can't remember recent titles. I haven't seen a memorable movie in years, though my ex used to drag me to matinees every Sunday. Nothing stuck with me. I have no idea what Karen and I saw. Am *I* the problem or is the film industry not what it used to be?

A torn John Wayne poster sags in a glass case—"Now Showing"—next to the ticket booth. I step through the open doorway. Dust, Lysol, stale popcorn. An air conditioner rattles in a corner, but the lobby is hot and close. A man in a red vest slumps beside a flickering Coke machine, which casts the only light in the place. The glow turns his jowly face green. "Come right in," he says to me. He sounds like Vincent Price. An elegant croak. "Everything goes. If you see something you like—concession equipment, carpets, seats—make an offer."

I nod my thanks, step past him into the auditorium. Empty. Dingy rectangular screen. A leopard, a lion, and a wolf are painted among stone arches on the walls—the animals are badly faded. Broke-backed seats. Sticky aisles. Someone has swept trash into a pile near a door with a cobwebbed EXIT sign: ripped ticket stubs, business cards, partial phone numbers scribbled on slips of paper. The air conditioner shudders to a stop.

Eggplant-colored curtains line the sides of the screen. I came here hoping I could use the material to replace the fraying drapes in the Star Room's entryway: my last grand gesture before leaving the planetarium. The curtains are dusty but nice and thick. I finger their folds, listen to a critter—a mouse? a rat?—skitter beneath the seats.

Not Vincent Price. Lyndon Johnson. *That's* who the fellow in the lobby reminded me of…and it occurs to me: an old theater in Oak Cliff. What was it called? The Texan? Yes. The Texan Theater. Grassy knoll. Officer Tippett. It all comes back. When Lee Harvey

Oswald ducked into the Texan Theater after allegedly shooting Officer Tippett, two old combat movies were playing: *War Is Hell* and *Cry of Battle*. Why do I know this? It's my Lone Star legacy. But also, in graduate school, during study breaks, a group of us traded conspiracy trivia—a mindless relief from the chaos theory we were to be tested on at the end of the term. "Chaos or conspiracy?" someone would say. "Chance or plan? You decide." JFK ruled these sessions. His assassination offered a depthless pool of conflicting possibilities. Chaos or conspiracy? Burch Burroughs, the manager of the Texan Theater, claims Oswald paid to attend the double feature at 1 p.m. and bought a bag of popcorn at 1:15. What do the Dallas police records say? Oswald snuck in *without* paying at around 1:30. Chaos or conspiracy? Bernard Haire, a shop owner next to the Texan, claims he saw officers detain Oswald—or someone who *looked* like him—in the alley behind the theater. He didn't resist. The Dallas police? Oswald was pulled, kicking and screaming, out of the front entrance before a gathering crowd.

Oswald. Ruby. An American revolution. Right here in Big D, my father used to joke.

Well. Dad's murderer would have a thing or two to say to those boys.

I step away from the curtains and take a seat in the front row. In bas-relief, in the theater's cheap stone walls, next to the leopard, lion, and wolf, sketchy figures stand and sit. They appear to have been painted once, a lavish mural, but the colors have worn away. The figures remind me of classical nudes—Titian, maybe—abstract forms melting into one another.

Titian is dead.

John Wayne is dead.

So is Vincent Price.

Behind me, a shuffle, a creak. I turn. A man lingers in the back row. He says hello. In the dim light it takes me a moment to notice he's wearing a priest's collar. I rise. "I'm buying the curtains," I say.

My voice echoes in the high-ceilinged room. "I mean, just so you know."

He raises a hand. "It's all right. I'm not here to scavenge. I used to watch pictures here as a boy. I'm just looking around. Remembering. Sorry to disturb you."

I start to head for the lobby. The priest looks me over. "You're about my age," he says. "When we were kids...the Beatles' first movie. *Day for Night? Night and Day?*"

"*A Hard Day's Night.*"

"Of course. How could I forget? I saw it four times, right here!" He grins and for a moment I see the child in his middle-aged face: pudgy cheeks, pale brows. He probably wore a bowl haircut, Beatle-style, as I did. He's wearing a too-sweet aftershave. Tall, stooped. "I remember thinking, No one has ever had as much fun as this fellow, Ringo," he says. "Pounding out anger, frustration... just whaling away on the drums. Utter joy. I couldn't sit still." He pats one of the seats. "Watching those guys sing...such a *kick* after months and months of Kennedy Kennedy Kennedy."

"Funny," I say. "I was just thinking about that."

He looks around. "Well. Old theaters. End of an era. I guess a joint like this brings it all back."

"I guess."

" 'All you need is love,' " he says. "If only."

I smile and nod goodbye. He sinks into a seat, for all the world like a lonely kid.

In the lobby, I tell the man in the vest to hold the curtains for me (I'm not sure, yet, how to transport them to the planetarium). We negotiate and I hand him a check.

On the bus to work I hum "A Hard Day's Night." The bus is nearly empty and I sit in the back, away from the other passengers, so as not to disturb them with my tune.

John Lennon is dead.

The day my mother took me into Oklahoma City to see the movie (we lived in Holdenville, nearby; I had just turned seven), the city never seemed finer, clear and lovely, vibrating to light-hearted melodies.

For weeks afterward, I drew the Beatles on everything: newspapers (crossing out JFK, LBJ—the Scrabble-like headlines following the president's murder), scratch pads, my Golden Books of Science.

I didn't see headlines so bold again until the Murrah bombing. An American revolution.

My father's dead, my mother—

No. Not here. I bite my lip and sit on my hands till they hurt.

At the planetarium, I find in the day's mail a letter from a former patron, a crackpot who writes every week. Two or three others write, too, about their conversations with God or their visits from aliens. Shedding these folks is the one perk of forced retirement. ("We can't afford to maintain a human host, especially with our attendance dropping," the museum board informed me last month. "Across the country, planetariums are becoming digital sky-theaters, with prepackaged shows narrated by Robert Redford or Tom Hanks. This will be our new direction. We thank you for your service.")

> Sirs [the letter says]:
>
> The Good Book tells us Abraham's father came to Palestine from across the flood—i.e., from west of Egypt, which is obviously a reference to America. The USA, then, is the origin of all life on Earth, which should surprise no one. Uncle Sam was there in the Garden, giving that serpent hell, believe you me, and the Tree of Knowledge was draped in the red, white, and blue. But more important than that, where *scientists* are concerned, is what first scrambled the continents (except for America, which has always been right where it sits today). I know you theory-boys have been chewing on that, but here's my two cents: check out the comets. They're the work-horses of the solar system, roaring past the planet, shifting the land masses, due to gravity

(what you might call the Jigsaw Effect), throwing the world's lesser peoples into confusion, from which they have never recovered.

In a file box in the storage room I save the letter with others like it (a cultural record, for good or ill) and start to prep my show.

This morning, the ten o'clock audience consists of three old men, two of whom are hard of hearing. I press a button on the Star Room console (round and metallic, like the clunky robot in *Lost in Space*) and Glenn Gould's version of the *Goldberg Variations* trills through tiny speakers. First, then second, canon. The repetitions put me at ease. As the sun sets in the room and the brightest stars appear, about the size of nail heads, I see in my mind's eye, written against the planetarium's dome, the music's mathematical equivalent, a string of elegant functions: *if performer* a *produces note* b *at time* c, *then the second canon commences at* c+(a–c)d, *where* d *equals the interval between successive entrances of—*

From the console I dim the cove lights. Dusk is a red button, sunset a silver lever next to the music's volume knobs. The sun sinks fast or slow depending on the show, the crowd's mood, or my whims. These old dodderers will be disoriented after sitting so long in the dark, I think. Keep an eye out.

"In Canto Twenty-eight of *Paradiso*, Dante describes the Primum Mobile," I begin. "The abode of God and all the angels. Remarkably, his fourteenth-century conception of the universe is eerily modern. It accords with contemporary physicists' notions of the three-sphere, a finite object lacking edges—"

A light snore from the front row.

"—in other words, a sphere with fixed volume and immense magnitude, but one in which every point is interior—"

Now, a *chorus* of snores.

"Mathematically, this can be depicted as…" With the slide projector I throw the equation onto the dome, bright yellow numbers fluttering across the ecliptic:

$$x^2 + y^2 + z^2 + w^2 = R^2$$

"Dante put it like this: 'From this point hang the heavens and all Nature.' "

The old men slump in their seats. There's no point going on. I stop talking and let the music play.

The two o'clock show has been advertised as an "Introduction to Space." I have options. The Catastrophe of Creation. The Copernican System. Journey to the Arctic and the Mysteries of the Northern Lights. Time Travel (in only half an hour).

I drop a slide marked "Kodiak bear" into the projector: a bright, bad painting of the sort nailed to walls in roadside motels. The bear stands by a stream, slapping at fish. My supervisor swears images like this are audience pleasers—"Every state-of-the-art installation does this sort of thing. It helps viewers picture Ursa Major when you superimpose the bear on the stars"—but it's discombobulating to hurl an animal into the void.

The projector's bulb is weak. I replace it. Boxes, bulbs, armatures. Tracks, rods, gears. Our astral engine needs a tune-up.

"Excuse me?" someone says behind me.

I turn to see a tall, auburn-haired woman standing in the entrance portal, surrounded by the ratty old curtains. Beside her is a little girl.

"Are we early?" the woman asks. She combs the girl's hair with her fingers. Her hands are flecked with dried yellow paint.

"Not to worry," I say.

"You're the man who makes the moon rise," says the girl.

"That's right."

"Hey! There aren't any *bears* in the sky," she says, glancing at the dome. I think I've seen her here before. She's ten, maybe. Eleven.

"No."

"Then I don't understand why he's there."

"Me, neither," I admit.

"You know, you're supposed to show the truth."

"What's your name?" I ask.

"Anna. It's an *obligation*."

"You're right, Anna."

She bounces on her toes. "*I* know something true," she says.

"What's that?"

"The earth is younger than the rest of the universe."

"That's right!" I tell her. "Earth was born not long ago, as long agos go."

Anna laughs. Her mother smiles. "She loves it here, ever since her class came to visit. Told me I just *had* to come see it," she says. "I'm sorry we got the time wrong. We'll take our seats and wait."

"Are you a painter?" I ask her.

"Why, yes."

"I noticed your hands."

An embarrassed grin.

"Is your work on display?"

"I'll be showing soon in a little gallery down the road."

"The new one? Out by the airport?"

"Yes, that's the one."

"I pass it each day. On the bus home."

She lingers by the curtains. She's self-conscious about her height, frail, slouching a little, folding her arms.

"Well," I say, "it's wonderful. Good luck with the show. Are you on our mailing list?" I hand her a pen.

By 2:05, the auditorium is only a third full, but no one else appears to be coming. William, one of my regulars, has arrived carrying a hard-boiled egg and a tub of cottage cheese. "The stars always make me hungry. I don't know why," he says. He's a sweet man, but the sight of him deflates me. Not a crackpot, but he takes a lot of work. I had hoped to get through this day with no awkwardness or strain.

Anna and her mother—Susan Hayes, she's written next to her e-mail address—sit in the back row. I peek at them as I draw the curtains and cue the music: an instrumental version of "Norwegian Wood"— "Good afternoon, I'm Adam Post," I say—followed by Brian Eno: sparse, extended tones, highlighting silence.

In addition to William, Susan, and Anna, middle-aged couples round out the audience: vacationers, early retirees. None of them looks happy together. A few gruff, solitary men. No other kids.

I tug the sun from the sky and simulate the stars' brightness over Dallas fifty years ago, twenty, ten, five. As we approach the present, the heavens become progressively harder to see. "An endangered night sky," I say. "As cities grow, and artificial lighting spreads across the globe, we're increasingly cut off from the magnificent sights our ancestors used to yearn toward and dream on. Does this make us fundamentally different from ancient peoples?"

Coughing. Creaking seats. Tough crowd.

They want more drama? Okay, here we go, then. "Recently, the Hubble telescope, orbiting Earth, has glimpsed the last spasms of matter before it's sucked into a black hole." Button-press: a vortex spreads from the dome's center, like motor oil leaking from a car. Raspy gasps. "Black holes are dying suns, collapsing in on themselves. Their gravitational fields are so powerful, they cannibalize all surrounding space, gulping nearby objects—other stars, say—into their maelstrom."

I click on my pointer. A bright red dart speeds across the dome, a little pilgrim among the galaxies. It touches a star in the neck of the Swan.

"Astronomers have long speculated about what they call an 'event horizon'—that is, the boundary of no return around a black hole, where *what is* cannot escape oblivion. The Hubble has now provided hard evidence of this, photographing ultraviolet light from gas clumps as they were breathed into a compact sun known as Cygnus X-1, right here."

I conclude by indicating 47 Ursa Majoris, a star fifty-one light years from Earth reportedly orbited by at least two planets larger than Jupiter. Pleasurable coos as I cast the Kodiak bear into the bowl of the Dipper.

Sunrise. A partly cloudy new day.

"Any questions?" I say.

A buzz-cut guy raises a tattooed arm. His T-shirt reads "I Lost It in Memphis." "Yeah, what about them crop circles I keep readin' about, over in England? Aliens messin' with our wheat?"

I sigh. "So far, all other planets we've seen outside our solar system appear to be gaseous, and in orbits either perilously close to their stellar hosts or outside what we believe to be habitable zones," I say.

"So no, in other words?" His smirky arrogance reminds me of my brother when we were kids.

"So no."

He looks skeptical.

As the crowd shuffles out, a man says to his lady companion, "I would've liked to have seen more bears."

"Yes," the woman agrees. "Bears are really cute."

I catch Susan in the portal, next to the dusty curtains. "I hope you and Anna will come back."

"Can you make it rain?" Anna says.

"Sure. And I do a pretty good job with the sun and the moon, right?"

She looks me over: a frank assessment of my uses and limits. "I guess," she says.

Susan smiles, waving long, painted fingers, and thanks me for the show.

William stays to eat his egg and cottage cheese and to watch me clean the Star Room. His face is a desert of wrinkles. In his late sixties, he's still a handsome man. Leafy eyebrows. Thick white hair. He sits on the edge of his seat.

"What's up, William?"

"Well, Adam, it's very exciting. I've refined my afterlife theories."

"Wonderful. You don't mind if I straighten the place while we talk, do you?"

"Not at all." He spoons some cottage cheese into his mouth.

"I'm listening," I say. In fact, I'm picturing Susan naked. I haven't slept with a woman since Karen left me six months ago.

William's hand shakes. He's told me he comes here because the planetarium provides a hushed, contemplative atmosphere. He's no longer allowed to keep an office on the college campus where he used to teach. He hasn't said so, but I suspect his unconventional work drove him from academe.

"The key to the whole thing is simply this," he begins. "Almost all of space-time lies in the future." He runs a napkin across his mouth. "The universe will last for at least 100 billion more years—probably longer than that. Plenty of time for all the elements to fall into place."

"What do you mean?"

"I mean, to prepare for the resurrection of the dead."

I've heard him speak this way many times but the words never fail to startle me.

"Here's the short of it. Earth is doomed. Humanity is doomed. The sun will eventually fatten and engulf us. You know all this, Adam. I'm just totting up."

I nod. I pull a small ladder out of the storage room and dust the base of the dome.

"But here's what we can do. Mechanized space vehicles equipped with antimatter engines can travel to nearby star systems at approximately nine-tenths the speed of light," William says. "There, we can colonize the planets, or failing habitable worlds, build orbiting space stations."

I sweep around the console.

"I calculate it will take about six hundred thousand years to populate the Milky Way, a drop in the bucket, then it's off to Andromeda—three million years. By the time ten billion billion years have passed, we will have seized control of the universe. With a series of strategically placed explosions, we can force the cosmos to contract in certain places and build up vast energy reservoirs in others."

Explosions and revolutions. "What does this have to do with an afterlife?"

He smiles. "At the Big Crunch, enough energy will have been amassed in the universe—under *our* control—to perfectly emulate every creature that ever existed. Because, you see, all information generated in time will exist in that energy. The universe will shrink to a final singularity of infinite density and infinite temperature, the End-Point, in which all creatures, great and small, with their memories intact, all their *potential* selves, will be brought back to life."

I tap my chin with the tip of the broom. I have no idea what he's saying. "What about Hitler? Timothy McVeigh? We'll have to mess with *those* assholes again?"

"Yes, well. An annoying side-effect. Can't be helped. " He wads up his food sack.

"Excuse me, William. I think I see a problem," I say. "For your theory to work, wouldn't *all* information, from the beginning of time, have to be available at the end? What about black holes? Information is lost forever inside an event horizon. Isn't it?"

"Hm." He folds his hands in his lap. "Hm. Well. Good point, Adam. I think—yes. Yes. I'll have to get back to you on that."

"I'm sorry, William. I don't mean to—"

"No no. I'm certain I'm correct. I just have to work out the bugs."

He's confessed to me that the death of his wife, Lily, from a heart attack three years ago had sent him into a downward spiral ("We were in love until her very last breath, Adam, our very last *kiss*!"). His immortality work, an amusing sidelight to his more serious projects in plasma physics, became all-consuming.

"In any case," he says. "You'll be reunited with your parents. Didn't you tell me you'd lost your folks? In the bombing?"

"Yes. Of course, I hope you're right, William."

"Trust me. Well. I suppose I should mosey on and leave you to your work," William says, tossing his lunch sack into the trash.

I straighten his collar. "Take care of yourself, okay? Don't work too hard on your theories."

"Adam, could we...some night..." He stops in the portal. His thin lips tremble. "Would you like to have dinner somewhere? I don't get out much, now, and since Lily died I can't speak to many people about things that interest me."

I realize I've never seen him outside the planetarium.

"Certainly, William. I'd like that," I say.

"Fine. I'll call you?"

"Sure."

"And I'll work out the, uh...the, uh...what was it?...oh yes, the black hole problem. I'll have an answer for you, I promise."

"Good."

He gives me a shaky wave and walks to the bus stop. In the wind, tufts of white hair swell on his head like toy parachutes, right above each ear.

Alone again beneath the dome, I run my fingers across Susan's name on the mailing list. Then I set the star ball spinning. "You had an *obligation*," I whisper. Virgo, Pisces, Sagittarius. Careening, colliding. Chicken Little, that little shit...he had it right, didn't he?

"You had an obligation," I say louder, watching planets fly among dark matter, "not to be *blown to fucking bits*."

The sky falls.

Bird dreams.

In one, beneath a swift black flock I pace beside the chain-link fence blocking the hole where the Murrah building stood. The fence is adorned with teddy bears left to memorialize the children. With me is Timothy McVeigh. "Why did you do it?" I ask him. He won't answer. I reach to touch a bear. "Leave my stuff alone!" McVeigh screams. He slaps my arm. "Little creep!"

The dream shifts. Now I'm standing in a field very much like the one behind the planetarium. Hawks circle overhead. My father, wearing overalls and a green Mobil Oil cap, is lying in the charred ruins of a granite building. He gets up, dusts himself off, and walks to me over broken tinted glass. He's grinning. I take his hands. They're chalky and cold.

"Father—" I say.

"All I wanted—"

"Father—"

"It was a beautiful morning in the city, remember?"

I whisper, "You didn't make it, Father. I'm sorry."

"Oh." He looks at his body then back up at me. "I see. Are you in touch with your brother?

"Yes."

"How is he?"

I shrug.

"The two of you...what was it, son? Was it your breathing? All those inhalers and pills...I always worried about you."

"I know."

He kisses my forehead. Then he turns, walks back to the ruins, and lies down among the blackened stones.

2.

A nuthatch, I think now. It was lying like an old potato skin on the asphalt.

One night, when I was about Anna's age, maybe a little older, my father took me out to eat, just the two of us. Some special occasion I can't remember. Maybe I'd done something worthy in school. Baked potatoes, macaroni and cheese. Dad offered me a sip of his wine. Afterward, beneath moth-hazed lights in the restaurant parking lot, I noticed a tiny bird the color of a sewing spool. It blinked rapidly, stretching its legs. One of its wings was bent. My father tried to talk me into leaving it alone. There was nothing we could do for it, he said, best let Nature take its course. I was inconsolable. "Moral obligation," I muttered. From the time we were small, Dad had lectured my brother and me: moral this, moral that, boys, understand?

Finally, he gave in, rummaged in the car trunk until he found a box with his golf shoes in it. He removed the shoes. We placed the bird in the box and drove it home. For the next week, we hydrated the bird with water from an eye dropper, fed it seeds from Pets Aplenty. It didn't eat much. One morning, when I woke struggling with asthma I got up and found the box empty. My father told me the bird had been so eager to join its friends, he took it into the back yard and let it go. It swooped over our peach tree, waving its gratitude with two firm wings. He laughed and I did too—or tried to, between wheezes.

Now, with Dad no longer here to tell me stories, I'm certain the poor thing died overnight and he threw it into the trash.

3.

Fanning out from the planetarium: feeder roads, cargo routes, latticed grids. Birds wheeling overhead. The first glimpse of distant runways. None of it—the comforting, open flatness, the strobe lights bordering landing strips—is meant for us ground-dwellers. It's supposed to be seen from the sky.

It's Friday evening, my third-to-last as the planetarium director. I've just concluded the day's final show.

On the bus, my breathing shallows out. I pull my inhaler from my shirt pocket, take a hit. A cool Albuterol rush. Over there the gallery, nearly finished, where Susan Hayes will show her paintings. I take a deep breath.

The bus exits the International Parkway and bumps over an unpaved road reserved for service vehicles. The airport is expanding. No new runways have been built, but each year fresh shopping outlets appear near the ticket counters and airline gates (a testament to greater volumes of delayed flights, more time to kill?). In the waiting areas, on boxy white televisions attached to the ceilings, a regular ad between CNN newscasts promotes DFW's "goal to provide exemplary customer service and innovative new concessions to increase passenger satisfaction with their airport experience."

I'm never a passenger, but I've come to depend on the "airport experience." It gets me through evenings when I know I can't sleep and so I often stop here to pass the time before heading home from the Star Room.

The bus pulls up to Terminal B. My fellow riders fold their *USA Todays* and grab their bags, all of which look more or less alike. I squeeze past them, slip unencumbered through the automatic sliding doors (an almost erotic *hiss!*) and into the concourse, past the gleaming silver counters—the ill-fitting coats and strained, may-I-help-you smiles—of Continental, British Airways, Frontier, Korea Vanguard, Lufthansa, and Mesa. I head for the TRAAIN stop, past out-of-order ATM machines, telephones, Internet kiosks, travel insurance booths, a copy shop ("Second Looks"), and the warmth of rust-colored heat lamps nurturing rows of melted cheese sandwiches wrapped in gold tinfoil, French fries, pizza.

On a thin, pesto-colored carpet, restless travelers reset their watches. A dozen or so of us crowd against a wall of sliding glass doors. "Stand back, please," says a robotic female voice. Boredom perfected. "The train will arrive in two minutes."

I like the double A in the TRAAIN sign above the doors—as if this were no ordinary train, but a supertrain, a train to end all trains.

And it *is* remarkable: completely mechanized, running in a constant loop from Terminal A to Terminal B to Terminal C. Sometimes I ride it for hours, circling, circling, lulled into a temperate daze. The pale green light inside the compartments (what is its source?) softens our flesh tones, turning us all the color of vanilla yogurt. The computerized voice, warning us every few minutes to keep clear of the doors, soothes like the ticking of an antique clock once you key into its rhythms.

Everything about the airport is designed to be as automatic as breathing. Glitches, failures, weather, unpredictable situations agitate the plan, but for a nontraveler like me, with no destination, no time pressures, no agenda, it's easy to shut down and be carried along, easy just to *function*, which is what I seek on evenings like this.

At the same time, I desire a heightened awareness of sights, smells, sounds, emotional dynamics (none of which involve me directly, so I can observe them disinterestedly and take abstract pleasure in their unfolding). Like a chemical reagent, the airport's tedium works with my own exhaustion to produce sharper than usual perceptions. No analysis. No expectations. For a few hours—on my best nights here—life occurs solely on the surface, and when the surface is all there is, its contours emerge in a stunning display.

The doors open—a torpid exhalation—and we step onto the train. The plastic seats are cold and hard, made for short journeys only, but I've accustomed myself to sitting without moving, and without comfort, for extended periods.

I shake my inhaler and swallow another gust. Across the aisle from me a pig-tailed girl—three or four years old—plays with a brown and white Beanie Baby. A puppy or a gopher, I can't tell. I think of Anna. Perhaps *any* female child, right now, will make me think of Anna: a little Force of Nature. On the other hand, the girl's mother, in black slacks and pumps, reading a *Business Week*—her rich blonde hair and bemused mouth remind me of my ex.

The bus slides through blue-lit underground tunnels, climbs until it parallels a highway. Jets idle in the dithery glare of sodium vapor lights.

"Aeromexico, Air Canada, Air France," the train says. The voice is too flat to be seductive, but it's as persistent as memory. This quality gives it a haunting, sexy power.

Business Week and her daughter get off. I decide to follow them. Not *follow*: take their cue. I hang around an American gate, a 9 p.m. to Houston, wondering if I'll glimpse Karen. She's a flight attendant. We met here three years ago. Sometimes she scurries through this concourse dragging her bag-on-wheels, preparing for her next leg:

Seattle, Portland, San Francisco. Occasionally, she has time for a cup of coffee and we'll sit on wobbly metal stools at waist-high tables in a fast-food court, catching up with each other. Naturally, when I spot her, or recognize anyone I've seen before (I'm familiar now with a few steady travelers), the safety of my "airport experience" is broken; I'm forced to marshal my energy and be social again, which is precisely what I'm hoping to avoid after a busy week. Still, her pretty face remains a pleasure and a comfort. The hem of her jacket rides the tops of her hips, just so...

In the waiting area, ticketed passengers skim paperbacks as thick as house bricks. Legal thrillers. True Crime. Every third man barks into a cell phone. One particularly noisy fellow in a high-sheen suit says twice, into his mouthpiece, "Dude, did you check today's digits? The high techs crashed!"

Headlines in the newspaper bins: "Attorney General Okays McVeigh's Execution." "Credibility of the Nation's Law Enforcement at Stake."

A sweating young mother in a blue halter top yells at her little boy to stop popping her bra straps, which keep sliding down her shoulders. She's got a wad of sticky napkins in one hand and a crumbling ice-cream cone in the other. A baby watches an escaped yellow helium balloon bob against pale ceiling lights. Another man with a cell phone says, "I don't *do* lunch in Tacoma anymore. Worst lunch town in the West. I mean, Christ, *goat*-kabob?"

By a plastic trash barrel a woman pauses, glances at her watch. "I have to get to Cleveland," she says loudly to no one in particular. "I have to get to Cleveland *right now*."

"—welcome all our first class passengers as well as our special Mileage Plus travelers," says a cool announcer.

I walk the concourse, past gift shops selling Cactus Jelly, Lone Star belt buckles, Dallas Cowboy refrigerator magnets, licorice drops in cardboard containers shaped like oil derricks. A Muzak version of "Norwegian Wood," with cellos performing the sitar part, drones between flight announcements and CNN weather updates. The airport's subculture—janitors, store clerks, security men, wheelchair assistants—sails through its tasks. Most people don't notice it, it seems, except for the annoying gate guards. But I'm aware that these workers keep the environment clean, predictable, efficient. I understand we're all in their hands. It feels good, sometimes, to relinquish control. The sun can set without me.

Frizzy blonde hair beneath a dark blue cap. "Karen!" I call. I wave wildly, surprised at my eagerness. The woman turns—a stranger—and dismisses me with a scowl. I stand beside a security gate, at a loss for what to do with myself. A man empties coins from his pockets into a liver-colored bowl. He steps through the portal and sets off the alarm. Uniformed men converge on him, flapping metal wands. *Hocus pocus! Danger, vanish!* Somewhere down the line, another alarm brays.

I'm about to make my way to the Ground Transportation exit when an elderly gentleman collapses in front of me. He falls against a candy rack in a gift shop doorway—chocolate mints shower his chest and head. Immediately, three security officers surround his body, alerting paramedics through their sleek walkie-talkies. Within minutes, two young men arrive with an oxygen tank. They strap a plastic see-through mask on the fellow's face and he begins to revive, his eyes drifting, his hands flitting nervously in the air. He looks like my father. The same thin chin. My chest tightens and I'm tempted to ask for a mask-suck. A boy in a Star Wars T-shirt tries to pluck a mint off the floor, but his mother, swift, determined, tugs his hand and whispers, "No! Make me proud!"

Take me with you. Wherever you're going. Boise? Bristol? Birmingham? Don't leave me here with nothing! I'll make you proud. I promise.

The old man sits up, shaking and pale. "Tell my children I love them," he says. "Tell my children I'm sorry." The paramedics assure him everything will be okay.

4.

"You're crazy," Marty says. He laughs, a bark, and I jerk the phone away from my ear. "We're talking literature. Not real life." I had told him Dad's spirit seemed to be haunting me lately—in dreams, in the airport just now. Immediately, Marty assumed I was thinking of his work: his assertion that the ghost in *Hamlet* was Shakespeare's nod to Purgatory. When the Protestants banned Purgatory in the mid-1540s, the deceased were stranded searching for purification between Heaven and Earth, Marty says. "I am dead," moans Hamlet's father's ghost, and he means *dead.*

As usual, Marty had missed my point. The point was, Dad was suddenly a presence in my life again.

"You're stressing, Adam," he says now. "McVeigh's back in the news. That's all it is. The bastard's finally about to get what he deserves."

"How will that help anyone?" I ask. I'm sitting in the dark in my sparse apartment.

"It'll help *me*, the minute they stick that needle in his arm."

"Will it?"

"Sure."

Marty and I have never been close, but he worries if I don't check in once a week. He's a good big brother, that way.

"Well, anyhow," I say. I don't want to argue with him. Not tonight. "What about your theater?" Marty teaches at Sul Ross State, several miles south of here near the Mexican border. For the past year he's been spearheading the university's construction of a replica of the Globe Theater in the West Texas desert.

"Sucker's really going to happen. Can you imagine?" Marty says. "Thank God for donors with holes in their pockets."

"How'd you sway them?"

"Sold our fucking souls. It's TV money. Couple of our drama grads went to Hollywood, made it big in the sitcom world. Writing, producing. I'm in the wrong damn profession."

"You and me both," I say, thinking of Tom Hanks's prerecorded lessons on stars.

We've agreed that as soon as I've finished my tenure at the planetarium, I'll drive down to stay with Marty. We haven't spent much time together since our parents died. I'll use the occasion to clear out of my apartment and ponder new starts. I ask him again if he's sure it's no trouble. "You're not, uh...sharing your house with anyone now?" I know of at least four exes over a five-year span.

"Nope. What about you? Any moon maidens?"

"No, sorry to say." What's wrong with us, I think. Two grown men.

"Well, damn it, bro, get out and grab some ass!"

Underperformers, Dad used to say, patting our chests. *Don't let those lungs of yours hold you back. Embrace the world*, he said. *Just like me in the oil fields.* We'd roll our eyes at him. *I'm telling you: Breathe it all in, boys, better or worse!*

"And you," I say. "Good luck with the Globe."

"All right, Star Man. Keep it spinning."

The moment Marty clicks off, the telephone chirps again, startling me. "They're back," says Lila—like William, a Star Room fixture. I'm fond of her but wary in her presence. She often calls me late at night. I'm never prepared for her.

"Who's back?"

"Adam, don't you ever surf the net?"

"Of course."

"Then you must have read about the new crop circles?"

"Lila..."

"Two formations appeared overnight in wheat fields near the radio telescope at Chilbolton, England." Her voice is high and thin. Her *manic* voice. "A man's face looking up, and an abstract pattern similar to the binary message sent into space by the Arecibo radio telescope in 1974."

I groan.

"The difference is, in this returned message, Arecibo's double helix DNA pattern is partly a double helix and partly a triple helix," Lila says. "Like nothing we've ever seen. Quite significant, don't you think?"

"No."

"Adam, Chilbolton has a bank of security cameras. They failed to detect any nighttime activity in those fields. If *human beings* had been out there making those patterns, the cameras would have caught them. Plus, this work couldn't have been completed in just one night. It's too elaborate. And the patterns are only discernible from the air. How do you explain all that?"

"I don't know, Lila. I can't." She breaks my heart. She swears she was snatched one night, raped and impregnated by Andromedans. Or Arcturans. I don't remember. She claims they continue to follow her, dressed as nuns: "They don these harmless masks. Benign, you see. Smarmy little smiles." Before she walked into the Star Room, I'd never encountered a true believer—of *anything*. In time, I persuaded her to see a therapist, who convinced her that she'd watched too many *X-Files* episodes. Her problem wasn't space travel. It was Hollywood. Gullibility. Unresolved issues with the Church. She improved for a while. Now her painful delusions, including her conviction that she miscarried late one evening, come and go. She used to piss off Karen. Lila is attractive when she isn't paranoid. I've never flirted with her. I don't want to shock or encourage her, nor do I want to romance a will-o'-the-wisp. But Karen was jealous of her, anyway.

"I think these things are hoaxes, Lila. I've told you that. I don't know what else to say."

"Adam, can we get a beer next week? I really need to debrief with you."

"Okay."

"I don't mind telling you I'm scared. I mean, you know. All I've got's a dead bolt. Inferior technology. I'm afraid they're going to come for me again."

"No one's going to come for you, Lila. Stay off the Internet, okay? It's crazy stuff. I'll see you next week."

"Okay." Timid, unsure. But basically solid, I think. No danger to herself. "Goodbye, Adam." Her voice says, *Don't let me go. Please don't let me go.*

I set the phone down. A jet rumbles out of DFW, a mile or so away, shivering my windows. Lights flicker, high in the sky.

Birds.

I wake remembering the Murrah site, an early morning shortly after the bombing. I met a medical examiner there, by chance. Hawks circled above us. After high heat, he explained, what's left of the human body is the canine maxilla, facial and palatal bones, occipitals, the calcaneum, the talus, fragments of the parietals, vertebral drums and spine, perhaps the tibial and humeral shafts.

5.

"Have you been crying?" Karen asks.

Her blue cap, perfectly square, perches on her upswept yellow hair. She sits across a round table from me, on a slender chair in the middle of the fast-food court. Coffee steams in front of us.

It's late Sunday night.

"No. Why?" I say. I'd seen her the minute I arrived at the airport. When I asked if she could chat, she told me she had only thirty minutes to spare: "I'm working the Seattle flight." Breeziness. Distance.

I admit, "I *have* been pretty down lately."

"What's going on?" she asks.

The coffee tastes of its Styrofoam cup. My lips burn. I surprise myself: "I miss you," I say.

She glances away from me at a flickering Delta monitor. "Well."

I imagine a crisp new bra beneath her blouse. "I don't know ...weird dreams. I'm having trouble concentrating," I say. "My shows have not been good. I seem to have lost the feel for the audiences, lost patience." I brush my eyes. "To be honest, I don't *know* what's going on beyond, of course, the fact that they're forcing me out..."

Behind her, a chubby boy drops a slice of pizza. Smoking cheese grips the floor.

"Passengers for Denver should now be aboard Flight 111, departing from Gate Seven," says a crackling speaker in the ceiling.

Karen picks at a smudge of lipstick on her cup. "Actually, Adam, you know what? A lack of concentration might be good for you," she tells me.

"What do you mean?"

"You use your concentration like a shield."

"I don't know what you're talking about."

She sighs. "Tim McVeigh."

"What?" I say.

"Now it's *his* turn, right? *Of course* you can't concentrate."

"I don't think that's a— "

"No? It doesn't affect you? Jesus, Adam. Just once, can't you drop your guard?"

"Honey. Please. All right, it's true, every night I go online, scrolling through updates on his trial. I figure if I could just understand—"

"*Understanding* is not *feeling*, Adam. That's your problem, okay? I've told you that."

"Karen—"

"And, anyway, the Internet...it gives me the creeps. You and that Lila woman. You're made for each other."

"Please."

"I'm sorry. I'm sorry." She shrugs. "Okay. So. How *are* your friends?"

"You know."

She nods, reaches for my hand. "You're a lovely man, Adam. I just—"

"Karen, listen—"

"And it's sweet of you to say you miss me, but you don't. I mean, all right, maybe you do a little. I miss you, too. We've had some nice times together. But you're lonely, that's all. You and me, we were never..."

"I know."

She squeezes my fingers. "And you're grieving. Adam, you've never really dealt with it. You realize that?"

"I'd like it if you'd come home with me again some night," I tell her. "Your next layover?"

She fusses with the napkin in her lap.

"What is it?" I say. "I don't mean to upset you, honey, I'm just hoping—"

"I'm thinking of relocating to Portland," she says. "Oregon. Next week, the week after? There's this guy."

"Ah. A pilot?"

"Yes."

"Of course."

She laughs. "Maybe that's our trouble, Adam. I've got *you* figured out, and you've pegged *me*."

I laugh, too. "Well. That's great, I guess. I'm happy for you."

"No you're not. But thank you."

We finish our coffee without saying much more, but the minutes pass agreeably and I start to relax.

She checks her watch, reaches for her carryall. "Seattle calls," she says.

I walk her to her gate. "Portland, eh? I hear it rains a lot there."

"Rain can be nice."

"I can make it rain for you. I can make the sun shine. Give you the stars."

She smiles and nudges my shoulder.

How will you spend your life? I think. *With whom? Will you be happy? Will I know it if you're happy? How will we remember each other?*

"Goodbye, Adam. Thanks for the coffee."

Will *we remember each other?*

"Take care." I peck her cheek.

"Catch you next time around," she says.

May you eat well aboard your lengthy flight. May the in-flight movie be a romance...

Not here. No tears. Not now.

Don't leave me with nothing, damn you.

A man with a plastic ID badge and a set of keys opens a heavy door for her: "Authorized Personnel Only." Her jacket hem brushes the tops of her hips. A pair of pilots slips past me. Is one of these fellows her lover? Should I smack him? Smack them both? I turn again for a final wave to Karen but she's gone.

I stroll past empty gates, closed gift shops, and rows of newspaper dispensers. Analysts predict the Dow's joyride is over. Experts declare genetically altered foods "safe as milk."

The coffee I drank earlier sits badly in my belly. I realize I haven't eaten. In front of a vending machine, I pull out my wallet and buy a package of peanut-butter crackers.

On the TRAAIN, going in circles, I watch frantic parents prepare their children for wearying trips. Some families are headed for freezing weather. Mothers tug jackets, coats, and sweaters past resistant little arms. "Believe me, when we step off that plane back east, you'll want to be wrapped up tight," one woman tells her son. Other families are westward bound. They strip their infants down to diapers. One man smells of beer. Another sips coffee. A woman eats a bean burrito. Another tells her husband she's craving scrambled eggs. The train makes its endless loop, neither here nor there, early nor late, in the blackness of its tunnels, a fixed sixty-five degrees (I estimate), suffused with a steady bright green. From time to time, when we emerge from under ground, we see highway cloverleafs curling into the distance, rows of parking lot lights marching toward vast invisibility at the horizon.

6.

I go through the motions of the morning show but it lacks pizzazz. The small crowd is as restless as I am until, on a whim, recalling Karen's hair as it curled beneath her cap last night, I point out the star cluster Coma Berenices—according to legend, the hair of an ancient queen. The astronomer Garrett Serviss, describing the constellation in one of his atlases says it has a

> curious twinkling, as if gossamers spangled with dewdrops were entangled there. One might think the old woman of the nursery rhyme who went to sweep the cobwebs out of the sky had skipped this corner, or else that its delicate beauty had preserved it even from her housewifely instinct.

The audience seems pleased, and afterward, as I'm cleaning the building, I tell myself I've recovered my equilibrium.

Outside, the sun glides behind clouds (sloppy clouds, irregular, thick; in *my* sky, they would never do).

7.

"All right, bro. I've cleaned out the back bedroom for you," Marty says on the phone. He calls more frequently now. Maybe he really *is* eager for me to come. "Meantime, hang in there. Grab some ass!"

"Will do."

"Little creep!"

"I didn't touch your stupid old toys!" I'd shout. This wasn't always true. As kids, Marty and I would end up fighting, wheezing, both of us. Our room was like an infirmary. Shade drawn. Leaden air. No sun. Mom always came running. She'd whisper and sing, hold Marty then me.

Tonight I sit in my dark apartment, missing Karen, thinking of Susan Hayes, contemplating last things at work, and wondering if Marty and I can really share space once more.

Our stuff. It was all over the house.

One afternoon, Mom forced me to hide my Beatle drawings in a closet. She said we had to straighten up because Dad was bringing guests home for supper. She collected my sketches in a neat little stack and told me to put them away. Dad's guests—sullen but gracious, dark skinned—spoke little English. Two of them were missing fingers on one or both of their hands. They inhaled my mother's mashed potatoes, roast beef and gravy, green beans. My father didn't say much. He smiled and gestured with his fork for his friends to eat, eat, by all means try seconds. Grab thirds.

Marty and I stared across the table at each other.

After the meal, Dad showed the men the small collection of core samples, drill bits, and fossils he kept on a shelf in his study. Jealousy seized me. His geologic oddities and oil field souvenirs were *our* treats, his and mine. Each evening, I'd ask him to tell me about them again, take them down so I could touch the rocks' porous edges. This was our private, intimate time together. I'm sure it sparked my love of science. Now, he was letting these silent strangers handle *our* trilobites, *our* schist, *our* shale (one man nearly dropped a piece—he had only three fingers on his right hand!). I retreated to my room and furiously scribbled John, Paul, George, and Ringo in every library book Mom had checked out for me that week. *Charlotte's Web, Little House on the Prairie, Have Spacesuit Will Travel.*

At one point, I put down my pencil and raised the stiff yellow shade over Marty's bed. Through the window screen I heard my father's laughter from the porch. I plucked an empty jam jar off my desk, ran outside, and chased fireflies through the yard, all the while keeping an eye on my father and the men. They smoked cigars. Marty sat at their feet, listening closely to the visitors' fractured talk. I could see my mother, through the bright kitchen window, washing dishes. Steam rose around her face, her dark brown hair.

Later, when she put Marty and me to bed, she said the men worked for the same oil company our father did. Roughnecks, she called them. "They've come all the way from Mexico, leaving behind their families. They're not familiar with our language or our customs. They don't earn much money and they don't have good places to live. Your father wanted to offer them some hospitality tonight. They don't get many home-cooked meals."

"What happened to their fingers?" Marty said.

"I don't know, honey. Oil field work is dangerous."

"Did you *like* having them for supper?" I wanted to know.

"To be honest, I was a little uncomfortable. But your father feels a moral obligation to lend them a hand, and I respect that."

"What's a moral obligation?" I asked. "He's always talking about it."

She rubbed my belly. "It's the feeling you get in here when you see something that isn't right and you want to change it."

"Their *fingers* weren't right!"

"Well," she said. "Life makes lots of demands on people."

Dad walked into the room. He thanked Marty and me for our politeness at dinner.

"You showed those guys our rocks," I said accusingly.

"It's okay, kiddo. It's good to share, right?"

"I guess so," I said.

Patiently, and without a word, Mom erased my rock 'n' roll scribbles from the library books.

Dad tousled Marty's hair. "Goodnight, mop-tops," he said.

Mom. She didn't like rock 'n' roll but the Beatles, she said, seemed "wholesome." I remember sitting with her in the plush movie house in Oklahoma City—bright lobby chandeliers, silver spigots on the soft-drink machines, crushed velvet curtains by the screen. It was nicer than anything I'd ever seen. It smelled like a new car, leathery and polished. I held my mother's hand. When the songs played, every hair on my body (not many back then) leaped to attention.

I'd never witnessed four young men happier than the Beatles.

Lord. I'd forgotten all this until the empty old theater. The priest. My mother . . . my mom . . . such a lively young woman . . .

In the middle of the film, when the band broke free of its cramped rehearsal hall and scampered like puppies through an open field—when the boys ran, as Marty and I never could—I thought I'd faint from pleasure. My breath caught in my chest. Mother looked at me, worried. I reached into my pocket and gripped my inhaler, but I managed to settle down and didn't have to use it.

After the show, in the car, I hugged my mother hard: her belly's soft heat through her pink cotton dress, the fluff of her breasts against my cheek. She took me to an ice-cream parlor for a chocolate sundae with candy sprinkles and nuts. Sunlight shattered off my spoon onto her pretty, lipsticked smile.

Late at night, online (like, right about now), Murrah survivors share their raw edges. But for the most part, the bombing belongs to the conspiracy nuts now. They play it over and over in their chat rooms—a wild and familiar cartoon.

> Timothy McVeigh kicked ass!
>
> You scum-sucking maggots, you got exactly what you deserved!
>
> I have proof that Princess Diana masterminded the bombing so British agents could swoop in and be heroes, solving the crime. (She's still alive, by the way, living with Dodi Fayed in Costa Rica.)
>
> The One World Government needed a new patsy—so they created Tim McVeigh.
>
> Sodom. Gomorrah. Oklahoma City. When will we ever learn?

Words flicker, not quite *on* the computer screen but floating in electronic space at an indeterminate distance from my eyes. Messages dance. I remember the first time I ever logged on to find out what happened.

Here's what happened.

At around 8:45 a.m., on April 19, 1995, my mother and father walked into the Social Security Office of the Alfred P. Murrah Building in Oklahoma City. My father had retired from Mobil Oil the previous summer and wasn't receiving his government checks. He'd written Social Security many times, trying to solve the problem. Finally, he decided to confront an official. He made an appointment. He and Mother drove to the city from their home in Holdenville.

I had just started working at the planetarium. That morning, I roughed out a script for my first show, to be performed the following night. At lunchtime, I turned on the console radio and sat beneath the dome with a ham and cheese sandwich I'd made in my kitchen at home. Initially, I thought the news was a hoax. OKC? Nothing ever happened there.

The rest of the afternoon (Oklahoma phone lines were jammed), I played with the meteor projector, crashing fireballs on the empty horizon.

Ma Bell got me nowhere. Oklahoma seemed to be quarantined. Marty called. He didn't know anything either. He hadn't heard from our folks. Television and radio offered sketchy, conflicting reports. So I turned to the Internet. Its updates were puzzling, too, hard to verify, but they appeared more detailed than the usual news sources. Accurate or not, the web's chaos made its information feel strangely more honest—closer to actual experience—than Tom Brokow's practiced schtick.

> 10:20 p.m. CST: Rescuers confirm fifteen dead; hundreds injured. Red Cross has responded. The search is on for survivors in the rubble. Witnesses report several infants trapped in debris.
>
> Word is, cops at Will Rogers Airport have stopped two Arab men who may have been responsible for the bombing.
>
> Those killed were mostly civilians. No FBI agents. No members of the BATF. This suggests that government employees may have been

tipped about the bombing, and stayed away from the building. Dare we ask: did the U.S. destroy its own facility so it could blame local militias and confiscate our guns?

Twenty-four hours later, Marty and I still didn't know if Mom and Dad had survived the inferno. I decided to push ahead and go to work. My mother had been proud of me for getting the planetarium job after more than a decade of adjunct teaching in community colleges. (In 1979, I'd earned a master's degree in astrophysics from UT Dallas but, post-Reagan, most of the nation's space funding went to SDI-related projects. Soft money was hard to come by, and I saw no point in pursuing another advanced degree.)

The morning after the bombing, weak with worry, clumsy and dazed, I went about my business. Mom would have expected me to carry on. I prepared the slides and the star ball, and at 8 p.m., while the crowd whispered in buzzy anticipation, I leaned into the mike. "The universe," I said, fighting to steady my voice, "is full of unsolvable mysteries."

8.

"Such a puzzle," Karen used to say, touching my face. Poor girl. I suppose I was always a mystery to her.

One night, I remember, shortly before she left, she told me, "Did you know the Chinese believe we store grief in our lungs? A businessman told me that once, in a karaoke bar on a layover in Sacramento. He said we ingest the world and hold it in our chests: a box of sloshing tears."

The night she mentioned this was one of many evenings I'd risen from bed and sat and stared at my computer screen, puffing on my inhaler. She couldn't get me to talk. I see now how hard she tried. "It must be awful, the way people go about their routines while everything's changed for you," she said.

"It is."

"What's it like?"

"I don't know how to describe it."

"Can you try?"

"I don't think so."

"Adam, please don't shut me out," Karen said.

"I'm not."

She looked at me and sighed. "You won't even admit to yourself what you feel."

It's like snow falling all the time. Snow on snow.

Would that have satisfied her? Was it true?

Now I sit in the dark, on the bed we used to share, staring out my window at refinery lights just beyond the airport: eight thousand, five hundred thirty-two light bulbs on sixteen smokestacks, twelve storage tanks, two cokers, two distillation towers, one hydrocracker, and eight security gates. Over and over I count the lights, imagine my father among the hard-hatted men.

On the eastern horizon, the healthy gleam of finance: more than two hundred thousand mercury vapor lamps burning in downtown Dallas.

It's a clear night above. Stars as round as buttons. I pour myself a glass of wine and imagine unhooking the buttons. One by one by one…

Nebulae, as delicate as a woman's aureoles.

A star falls.

Gracefully. Across the sky. Nestling in a pocket of the land.

We said this as kids.

Our mother taught us. We chanted it back to her.

Make a wish, boys. Boys? Once upon a time.

9.

One night, between midnight and after midnight, I looked up and there was a white path in the sky, soft as lamplight, wide enough for three people to walk on, side by side by side. A troubled congregation. Oh death and trouble have spilled their icy laughter on our town. The path pointed north, and I asked my children, Children, is this a path we should take, and they said, Mother, what does it mean, should we ask the aldermen, ask the selectmen? And I said, Who knows, children, maybe at path's-end, pain is just a plaything.

"I don't get it," Anna says. "Adam, I don't *get* it!"

"Me, neither," I admit. Carelessly, I'd left one of our crackpot letters out in the open, sitting on the console, and Anna discovered it following today's show. Her mother stands smiling, embarrassed, in the portal.

"To be honest, I think this person is pretty disturbed," I explain.

"So then... it's probably not true?"

"Well, what's she *talking* about? But, you know, it's interesting, the responses the sky prompts from people."

Anna shakes her head, disgusted. "You're supposed to tell the truth, Adam."

"I'm sorry."

"It's an *obligation*. I've told you that."

"Yes, you have."

Susan apologizes for her daughter, nudges Anna's shoulder, and says they have to go now. "Thank you for the show." Asteroid formation: always a winner. "It was lovely. We'll be back." She's wearing a cream-colored blouse, black jeans. Her hair hangs loose around her shoulders.

"No need to rush off," I say. "The next show's not for another hour. If you like, I can demonstrate for Anna how the star ball works..."

Susan shakes her head. "My opening's scheduled next week and I need to check the place. It's worrisome. They're not quite done refurbishing the gallery, and it's hard to imagine the carpenters and electricians will be ready in time."

"I'd love to see your paintings."

"That's sweet."

"No, really."

"Well..." She bows her head; her hair hides her face. "I'm supposed to hang the first few tomorrow in the finished rooms," she says. "Eight a.m. If you're truly interested, I could give you a sneak preview. In exchange for your space tours."

"Great."

"Really?"

"Yes. I'd like that."

"Don't be sure." She laughs. "It's selfish of me. I could use some help. Some of them are quite big, with large—I mean really humungous—frames."

"*Humungous*," Anna repeats, nodding, as if her mother is either a genius or a loon.

So I find myself, before Wednesday morning's show, on the steps of the small art gallery. One step is purple, one white, one red. On a mat inside the doorway I wipe the dust from my shoes. As Susan talks, she keeps her head down—still trying to hide behind her hair. She *leans* into her sentences, chasing definitions. "As a child," she tells me, "I stared at my father's architectural drawings and wondered what kind of magical maps I was seeing. Were these skeleton-sketches, animal anatomies? Were they shellfish?" She laughs. "When I realized I was looking at representations of buildings, I remained intrigued by the designs. But—I'm not sure how to put this—what they *were* was not as mesmerizing as *what they could have been.* When I was free to imagine the diagrams as many things at once, it was like I was holding in my hands... I don't know... the blueprints of the universe." She laughs and shakes her head. "Anyway, when I knew these sketches were only of rooms, spaces filled with simple objects—flowers in a pot, a china cabinet, a couch—they lost much of their spell for me."

Talking takes a toll on her. She's willing herself—driven by need to share her work?—to overcome deep reticence as we speak.

"One of the things I want people to feel, when they look at my paintings, is the magic I experienced when I saw those architectural drawings for the first time," she tells me now. "But of course, for the magic to happen, you have to *not know* what you're looking at. There has to be confusion."

"What I see is an affliction to me. What I cannot see a reproach," I say.

Susan cocks her head.

"Lévi-Strauss. My first week on the job, I thought of engraving that line on a plaque and hanging it above the planetarium doorway," I say. "I don't think my bosses would have liked it."

For forty minutes or so, I help Susan unpack paintings from crates and lean them against the walls. They're huge and heavy, and Susan struggles with them. Many of the paintings are on hollow-core doors linked to form panels, and they're as tall as she is. She's incredibly thin; perhaps not entirely healthy, I think. An aspect of grief (or am I projecting?).

"I believe I was probably dyslexic as a child," she says, standing back to study a particular image. "I couldn't understand two-dimensional plans of elevations. Also, our household was pretty hectic."

I listen closely, enchanted by glimpses of her face.

"My parents didn't care if I made a mess, if I built, say, a volcano on the dining room table out of whatever materials I found around the house. I could leave it there for weeks."

"A kid's paradise," I say.

"It was. My grandfather was an architect, too. My babysitters were drafting supplies. I could take things apart—like clocks—and no one would even notice. I didn't put them back together successfully. I tried. But I found it was interesting to dismantle something, try to reassemble it, and come up with a completely different object."

"What about Anna?" I ask. "*Her* environment?"

"Oh, my husband's a neat-freak. Anna's parameters are *very* strict." She laughs.

We work a while longer. She doesn't do small talk. To break the silence I tell her I'll be leaving the planetarium soon. "Really? Oh. Anna will be so disappointed," she says.

Sheetrock clutters the floors. Susan breathes heavily. I ask if she's okay.

"I need to rest for a moment," she says.

"Can I get you some water? You look a little—"

"I should tell you, Adam. I'm sick."

"I wondered. Here, sit down. Let me get you—"

"No, I mean *really* sick."

I look at her.

"Leukemia."

"Susan…"

"I'm doing chemo, you know, but frankly…" She trails off.

I realize she's wearing a wig.

"So this show is very important to me. Do you understand?"

"Yes."

"I appreciate your help, Adam. And your interest. Really."

I nod. Silently, we work another thirty minutes. Then I gather from her body language she wants to stop and survey the paintings.

Layerings and erasures. Thick surfaces. Grids (echoes of her father's architectural designs?), nonsense (childlike scribbles in crayon). "I think I lost faith, at some point, that anything can ever really be finished," she says quietly, pacing the room. "No, that's not it. It's what I said before. I want to try to tell everything about an object. What it was, what it might be. I guess I lost interest in things that *could* be finished."

Pale yellows, blues, and greens. Ziggurats and spirals, like Dante's Purgatory, Heaven, and Hell. She's not after the beauty of shapes, I think; she's probing their deep structures, taking them apart with little hope of putting them together again.

We make a right turn, into a larger room.

"How do you get this texture?" I ask her.

"It's an encaustic process, pigment mixed with hot wax." She moves in beside me. She smells lemony. "I didn't know how to do it at first, and I learned different ways to make really dangerous fumes.

I almost blew myself up a couple of times." She shrugs. "It's not a good idea to heat turpentine on a hot plate."

"I love what you do," I tell her. "You've found a way to paint ideas, and to paint everything at once. But the uncertainty... it's as if your hands were trembling as you worked." I amaze us both by lifting her fingers to my lips. "Congratulations on really fine work."

I've embarrassed us.

"Thank you," she mumbles.

"Susan—"

"Y'all are gonna have to leave pretty soon," a workman interrupts us. He's hauling a dusty Skilsaw. "We got some ceiling work to do. We'll cover your paintings, ma'am, and take good care of them, but it might get rough in here if you don't have a breathing mask."

"Yes, all right," Susan says. "We're on our way." To me she adds, "Anna had a sleepover at a friend's last night." She checks her watch. "I need to pick her up."

"Susan, can I ask: what are your doctors telling you?"

She bites her lower lip. "I don't..." Her eyes moisten. "I just need to do this show."

"All right," I say, a near whisper.

"Thank you, Adam."

"I feel privileged."

The Skilsaw starts to whine. As we move toward the door, I glance at the titles of the paintings. They're written on paper wall-tags we've placed beside each image. *The Angel of Forgetfulness, Vacillating Measures, Expectations of Distance, Notes for a Talking Cage, A Chronology of Skin, Language Mechanics.* They read like entries in a fevered encyclopedia, lost among dusky labyrinths in a library. Tales of astronomers madly dreaming, spirit becoming flesh, a lover's body breaking into bloom.

10.

The radio wakes me as sunlight hits my bed. Behind my eyelids, an after-streak of birds.

"After several delays, appeals, and a flurry of legal motions, Timothy McVeigh died today with his eyes open," a female reporter announces solemnly. "He was declared dead at 7:14 a.m., Central Time, Monday, June 11, 2001. Witnesses on site said he looked stoic, calm, resolute. Many of the bombing survivors and victims watching the closed-circuit feed in Oklahoma City swore he looked defiant. Hate-filled. Arrogant."

I dress and catch a bus to the airport. For forty-five minutes I ride the TRAAIN, trying not to think—or to think vividly, I'm not sure which. This is the announcement I've been waiting for. The balm of justice. Permission to move ahead.

The train's doors slide open. People come and go. The motion soothes me. I remember riding in the backseat of my father's car one day as we cruised toward Oklahoma City. The car's purposeful movement. Its smoothness. My mother poured chicken soup from a thermos, and handed a steaming plastic cup to me over the top of the seat. "Don't spill it, honey," she said. "Don't hurt yourself. Steady, now. Okay?"

"It's impossible," a man says now to a little girl sitting next to him across the aisle from me.

"But *why?*" the girl screams.

The train stops and I step off near the copy shop. In the concourses, I find I can't watch flight attendants without a catch in my throat. Head down (I've let Karen go; really, I have), I hurry toward the Ground Transportation Exit. Outside, on the sidewalks, people jostle one another, glancing at their watches.

I stop at a pay phone next to the sliding-glass doors.

"The bastard got what was coming," Marty tells me. His voice is faint on the line.

I reposition the receiver so it doesn't hurt my ear. "It's just another death, piled on other deaths. How does that resolve anything?"

"Don't think about him anymore. Move on."

Move on. Yes, that's what they say. But *moving on* is precisely what Marty would never do—"Don't touch my stuff!"

A limousine driver signals to a business traveler. Two pilots hustle past me, laughing.

In seventh grade, when I came home from chemistry class with straight As on my projects, Marty took it personally (he'd gotten all Bs). He turned his attention to English. In high school, he'd never introduce me to his dates—what few he had—fearing I'd steal his girls (an irrational fear, to be sure; I was as painfully shy as he was).

And now I'm going to stay with him? Are we crazy? If we've managed to be civil as adults, I think it's because we've kept hundreds of miles between us.

"Anyway, bro, forget the planetarium, forget that asshole," Marty tells me now. "Get your butt down here. Unwind."

"Right," I say. "I appreciate it." I watch a young couple with twin infants flag a taxi outside.

"We'll have a ball together," Marty says.

What *were* our flare-ups about? I mean, really? Proximity? Private space? Competition for Mom and Dad? Well. Not a problem *now*.

"You're not worried? Even a little? You really think we'll be okay?" I ask Marty.

"What do you mean?"

"All the fights we used to have."

"What fights?"

"You're kidding, right?"

"No. What are you talking about?"

It can't be that he remembers a different past than I do. "Ah, you know, the usual stuff," I say.

"We'll be fine," Marty says somberly: a signal, perhaps, that he *does* know what I'm talking about. "Let me know your schedule. And get here soon."

After I hang up the phone, I work with a Hertz representative to rent a car at the end of the month and drop it off at a dealership in south Texas (I haven't driven a car in years, though I've dutifully renewed my license). I pay an advance, sign a contract.

Upstairs, I get a bagel and stroll past "Second Looks." Inside the copy shop, a teenaged employee tugs pink and purple sheets from a Xerox machine. He's wearing a blue apron, a baker pulling pies from an oven: a word-maker, a confectioner of reproductive delicacies. Photostats and duplicates. Posters, bills. Notes and invitations. I pause to watch the process. The shop's copiers clack with a steady, soothing rhythm; pages emerge with a reassuring sameness from the printers. The boy feeds job résumés, birthday greetings, swap-meet fliers, alumni newsletters through the copiers' plastic slots: a frenzied information-quilt recording the city's buzz. No—more like splitting cells, I think: the culture's basic units proliferating and replicating, spreading throughout the community like strains of a virus. What was it in Timothy McVeigh that wished to deny, that *thought* he could deny, all this energy? Behind me in the Terminal A concourse, travelers rush toward the ends of the earth in a colorful blur, some toward destinations listed on the fliers. This boy, it seems, is casting destinies.

For an hour I ride the TRAAIN. Loop after loop, the riders look exhausted. An old woman coughs uncontrollably into a Kleenex. The train's automated voice says something inaudible and therefore faintly threatening.

At the planetarium, I place the mailing list on its wooden stand just outside the Star Room. With the tips of my fingers I caress Susan's name.

The latest missive:

> Gentlemen:
>
> There are holes in the sky, if you know where to look. Sometimes you can stare through them and glimpse the nations of Heaven. Heaven is industrious and efficient, and its citizens are busy plugging the holes so we can't see in. This is not a malicious effort—they know we would be utterly bereft if we saw too clearly what is beyond our grasp. Still, it is your duty as scientists to expand our knowledge, even into the

areas God deems forbidden. You must hurry. I suggest you train your cameras and 'scopes on Lyra, now, tonight, before the angels spackle all the gaps.

I toss the letter in the trash.

Turn up the cove-lights. Time for the afternoon show. No one has arrived. For my own pleasure, I whisper into the microphone:

In this world
we walk on the roof of Hell
gazing at flowers

The poet Issa. I quoted him often in the old days.

The energy, the excitement!—before blockbuster movies, laser light-shows, video games, and computer simulations primed people to expect extravaganzas we can't afford. (On the south side of the dome, I notice now, a small aluminum panel has peeled away from the surface: a jagged edge pricking Scorpio's heart. Our universe looks a little ragged.)

Once, early in my tenure here, I invited a guest lecturer, a NASA man who'd done some artificial intelligence work, to address an afternoon group. Human beings are "finite state machines," he said. Genetically, we are capable of generating only a fixed number of responses to any stimulus: at most, a person can experience no more than 4×10^{53} changes of state per second.

That day, a woman in the audience wore a T-shirt proclaiming SO MANY MEN, SO LITTLE TIME. When our speaker saw it, he did a brisk little skip in the aisle. "Yes, yes!" he said. "That illustrates *precisely* what I'm saying!"

No one's coming. I shut out the lights and lock the doors.

11.

A sweet note from Karen, postmarked Oregon: "I read the news. May that awful man's passing bring you peace, Adam. With warmest wishes—"

* * *

The plan this evening was to meet William at Terza Rima, his favorite Italian restaurant, as soon as I finished up at the planetarium, but just as I'm putting away my broom, Lila phones: "Adam, I know we were going to meet later this week but I've got to see you *tonight*!"

"Lila! I'm sorry," I say. "I have a commitment."

"Cancel it! I'm desperate. I'm scared. Please, Adam."

She'll be angry, but I don't have the pep to see her alone. I call William and ask if he'd mind delaying our dinner for an hour. "Meet me first for a drink at Call Me Later?" I ask. I tell him about Lila. Graciously, William accepts the change of plan. "Sounds like an adventure," he says.

Call Me Later is a sports bar at the edge of an industrial park west of the airport, catering to computer geeks, electrical engineers, and telemarketers like Lila. It's close to where she works, so this is where we always choose to meet.

A big man bumps me, sloshing a pitcher of beer. His T-shirt reads, "My Alcohol Team Has a Soccer Problem."

I grab three chairs by a large-screen TV: dirt bikes, flying black mud. On the wall, behind glass frames, there's an Emmit Smith jersey, a Troy Aikman jersey, and an autographed photo of Jerry Jones. Seventies disco blares through hidden speakers. A smell of stale peanuts in the air.

"...outsourcing our solid-state production...Indonesia..." a businessman says to his partner behind me.

"Layoffs?"

"A few. You know. Minor collateral effect."

William appears in the doorway. He stumbles. I grasp his elbow and help him sit. "Thank you, Adam," he says. In the video light, his skin is the color of morning snow.

I apologize to him. "This woman, Lila, is extremely needy," I say. "But maybe, whatever's troubling her, we can dispense with it quickly. Then you and I can get to the restaurant."

"It's all right, Adam," William says. "I understand. You're surrounded by needy people."

"Well."

"Like me, for example."

"William—"

"No no, it's true. I've seen it," he says. "You're a very kind man, Adam. Patient. A good listener. People sense this and they cling to you for dear life. It's one of the reasons you're in trouble with the museum board, isn't it? They like to keep things 'professional'—their word for 'impersonal.'" He reaches across the sticky tabletop and pats the back of my hand. "Well, relax, Adam. Screw the board."

I'm startled to hear such language from him.

"It was the same with me and the university. To be sure, my colleagues looked askance at my research—'Immortality Studies' was not proper copy for their recruiting brochures—but mainly it was the time I spent with students, especially after Lily died. My peers said it was unseemly of me to eat and drink and talk with kids outside the classroom. I protested that kids were our jobs; nurturing the young. No, said my colleagues. The institution wanted to be recognized as a major research center—more grant money, that way—so *aloofness* was the ticket. Head down over a lab table in some darkened corner somewhere. Pooh."

I order us a couple of beers and a hard-boiled egg for William.

He says, "So I 'followed my bliss,' as the writer Joseph Campbell used to say."

"And the university shunned you."

"It doesn't matter." He sips his Rolling Rock. "My studies have sustained me, as will yours." He lifts his glass to toast me. "I'm sorry you have to leave, Adam. I'll miss you. Shame on the board for exiling you. But I have faith in your resiliency."

"Thank you, William."

"Now, before I forget, and before our guest arrives," he says. "Those pesky black holes? The flaw you pointed out in my theory?"

I laugh. "Tell me." I reach over to straighten his shirt collar.

"Order up!" a bartender yells at a waitress.

"Centaurus," William says. "An exception to typical black hole behavior. The Hubble has discovered an intense glow *outside* its event horizon. Apparently, energy is pouring out of it like pasta flung from a bowl!" William cracks his egg.

"Congratulations," I say.

"Adam!"

"Lila. Hi." I reach for her arm. "Here, give me your purse. Please, have a seat."

William stands precariously. He offers Lila his hand. "Hello, hello," he says. "Very nice to meet you, young lady. Sit down. Relax."

"Thank you," Lila says, flustered, straightening her hair. "I'm sorry to call so last-minute, Adam."

"Take your time," I tell her. "Catch your breath." I order her a beer.

She leans over and whispers to me, "I wanted to see you *alone*."

"I'm sorry," I say. "I had no choice. I told you, I already had plans when you phoned."

"Shit. Anyway, anyway, they're back," she says, a little louder. She sinks into her chair.

"Lila—"

"And please, Adam, don't ask about my medications, all right? This isn't *me*! It's *them*!"

She's pale and disheveled. She scratches her right ear—her headset at work forms a rash there. Forty hours a week, phoning strangers with offers of revolutionary new kitchen appliances. "I don't even know what the hell they do," she's said. "I mean, how many ways can you dice a carrot, anyway? *This* is what I went to college for? To expedite soup?"

Her shapeless blue dress spreads like a tent in her chair. She looks like a child. I urge the beer on her and leap to cheer her up. I say, "By the way, you'll be happy to know I finally did some investigating on the crop circle thing."

"You did?"

"Absolutely. It's an old practice," I say, "dating all the way back to seventeenth-century China. Yes, really. Listen. Historians have found remnants of manmade circles on the Sino-Mongolian border. And these more recent examples in England...at least three different London-based groups, trickster-artists, have hinted they're responsible for the pranks."

"But Adam—"

"Wait," I say. "The security cameras at Chilbolton? Turns out, the latest circles weren't terribly close to the telescope facility. With a little planning and a tractor, these things are surprisingly easy to make. Takes about five or six hours, that's all. So you see? No mystery. No aliens." I pat her chilly hand. "Feel better?"

She frowns, glances at William, starts to talk, sips her beer. Then, meekly: "Okay. Well, then. What about the cow mutilations in Montana?"

"*What?*"

"Yeah." She's energized now. "Herds of cattle drained of blood, no visible wounds, with their *faces lifted off*."

"Lila. Lila. What do you get from this?" I say.

"What do you mean?"

"You seem to *need* something to fear. Isn't that what your therapist suggested? I confess, I don't quite—"

"Adam, damn you, don't you condescend to me." She throws William a mighty chilly look.

"I'm not," I say. "I'm sorry."

"If you won't believe me, you should at least try to grasp what I'm going through. Always, you throw up this...this...*screen* of fucking reason."

"Understanding is not feeling?"

"Exactly."

"Okay. But I *have* to ask you. Are you taking your Zoloft?"

"Yes."

"Good."

"I'm telling you, Adam—I've told my doctor—my depression isn't chemical. It's the memories of the anal probe."

I nod. My eyes hurt. What do *I* get from this? The flattery of being trusted? Pleasant, I admit. The easing of the constant fluttering in my belly... a distraction from my own vague fears? I don't know, don't know.

All I know is, I'm sitting here tonight in a bland, noisy bar listening to a reasonably intelligent woman talk faceless cows and anal probes.

Well. It's easy, and little enough, to listen.

"The memories get clearer every day," Lila says.

"Tell me."

"The lights. Remember the lights I told you about?"

"Of course." When she first showed up at the planetarium, a year or so ago, she lingered after my performance, asking about the possibility of life beyond Earth. By her third or fourth visit, she was telling me her UFO traumas. Standard tales, popularized in the media: late night, lonely road, strange lights behind the pines... "I saw the lights more than once," she says now. "I'm certain of that. The first time, it was after work... a triangular pattern, no color I'd ever seen. I can't describe it, even now. I opened my car door and stepped out. Next thing I know, I'm back behind my steering wheel, but three hours have passed. My ears hurt. I reach for them." She touches her right lobe. "And there's dried blood, like someone has ripped out my earrings, then replaced them."

I've heard this before, more or less the same details. William seems entranced.

"The second time. After work again. But now, when I come to myself in my car, I'm on a completely different road, about sixty miles away, and I'm wearing someone else's clothes. I mean, they don't even fit me."

I order us another round of drinks. She's looking better. Talking helps.

"I try to recall what I can, but all I remember is a birthday celebration in the office, right before I left the building. One of my colleagues had turned forty and we'd bought a cake for her. I remembered her holding a gift in her hands, a box about the size of a book, gold wrapping paper, pretty blue bow... it's only recently, when I look back... when I think of her lifting that present, what I see... suddenly, what I *remember*... is a pair of charcoal-brown hands, paws really, or fins, webbed and with three fingers, gripping a mechanical box, blinking lights, shiny buttons, and I feel a pain..." She pats her rear. "... right here."

I lean across the table and take her hands. "Lila. Whatever you've experienced or—forgive me—imagined, I know it's real to you, and that it torments you, and for that, I'm so very, very sorry."

"Thank you, Adam." She smiles, scratches her ear, and looks at me warmly. Then, bashful, she glances away at an autographed football on the bar. "I only wish sometimes... I wish I had someone to stay with, you know, someone to keep me company."

I nod. The truth is—how can I ignore it?—Karen was right about Lila. Karen was always right. If I gave this girl an opening, she'd fly into my bed. I don't flatter myself that Lila is in love with me or that she even finds me particularly attractive.

Her smile widens. I squeeze her hands and let them go.

"So anyway. Now they're back," she says. Across the room, a bow-tied fellow thrusts his pelvis against an old-fashioned pinball machine. "Get *in* there, baby! Yeah!" he shouts. Squeaks and blips blast from hidden speakers.

"Excuse me. May I ask? Who are 'they,' exactly?" William says.

"Andromedans!" Lila blurts. "And it's none of your fucking business, old man, all right?"

"Ah." William nods. "No one believes you, right?"

Lila glances at me, blushing. "Right."

"William, maybe I made a mistake here," I say. "Perhaps, if you don't mind, Lila and I should—"

"*I* believe you," William says. He takes Lila's hand.

"You do?"

"Most certainly. It's one of the travesties of our time that our government and our scientific institutions aren't prepared to handle the inevitable intermingling of extraterrestrial life and homo sapiens."

"Fuck!" Lila says. "Yes!"

"I belong to an academic task force, the Strategic Initiative to Identify the New Paradigm," William says. "Its goal is to insure that humanity doesn't react with bellicosity to representatives of extraterrestrial civilizations whenever they make themselves known to us. We could very well find ourselves in the position of Native Americans in their first encounter with Europeans, and we don't want that to happen, now do we?"

"So," Lila says, "you don't think I'm crazy?"

"Not in the least." I see, now, why students liked William. "My friends in the university thought *I* was rather wobbly to pursue all this, but their vision is far too narrow, poor souls. I think it's irresponsible for scientists not to prepare for this eventuality. *Clearly*, we're not alone in the universe, the numbers don't lie. It's only a matter of time—"

"Hey, let me tell you, the time is *now*," Lila says, gripping his arm. "Trust me."

"Oh yes, Inflation Theory, coupled with recent M-brane models suggest, without doubt, that we're part of an enormous galactic civilization," William tells her. "I'm even persuaded that meteorites are life's transportation system, a series of buses, if you will, carting panspermia through space."

"Panspermia!" Lila says. "Lovely word!"

"You know, my wife's name was Lily. Lily. Lila. Charming." William beams at her. "Now, young lady. Tell me more of your story."

I might as well be at another table. I excuse myself to go to the bathroom. Afterward, for a few minutes, I stand in the parking lot, breathing deeply. A scent of freshly mown grass in the air. Through the tavern window I see William and Lila sitting knee to knee. Something tells me William won't mind, now, if we cancel our dinner.

A volley of laughter sweeps the room. I step back inside. By the bar, a man drops a pair of quarters into a flashing big machine. Worlds explode.

"Adam, where have you been hiding this charming woman?" William asks me.

"We've got so much in common!" Lila says, blushing prettily.

I touch her wrist. "You're all right?"

"Much better now, thanks." She smiles at William.

"I'm glad." I sit and order another beer.

"So, anyway, what this means is, the End-Point will see us as we sit here tonight. We'll be together forever," William tells Lila.

"Lovely," she says.

"Tell me. Have you *always* wanted a child?"

12.

The John Wayne poster has vanished. So has the Coke machine in the lobby. Most of the theater's seats have been removed. The manager stands behind the empty snack bar beneath a handwritten sign: "Everything must go! Last three days!"

He waves a small silver shovel in my face. "Popcorn scooper?" he asks.

"No, thanks," I say

"Plastic catsup bottles? We've got a whole slew of them."

"Sorry. Can't use them."

"They'll shoot any and all liquids sixty, seventy feet."

"Nope." I arrange for him to FedEx the theater's curtains to the planetarium. I write him another check. As I turn to go, a man in a striped shirt and khaki pants appears in a doorway at the bottom of a wooden staircase, just to the right of the snack bar. He cradles a tattered old poster. "Are you sure about this?" he asks the manager.

"Absolutely," the manager says.

"You could auction this on eBay."

"No. Take it."

I realize the man with the poster is the priest I met here before. After a moment's hesitation, he recognizes me, too. Together, we walk out of the theater into a cloudy afternoon. "I didn't know you, at first, without your collar," I tell him.

"I quit."

Down the block, a street crew is repaving part of an intersection: shovels, boiling tar. Nearby, a restaurant manager shouts at four Mexican boys to stop loitering in front of his place. One of the boys flips him off. The kids scatter into an alley.

The ex-priest turns and points at the theater's dusty marquee. "This is a special place for me. I've been coming back every day, mourning it. It kills me they're tearing it down. I used to love seeing movies here as a kid. Always felt happy and safe." He offers me his hand. "Robert Hipkiss."

"Adam Post. Quitting the priesthood? Pretty momentous." Oh, don't get started, I think. He'll wind up as one of your crackpots. What signals do I send to draw such people to me?

"Well, naturally, my decision was a long time coming," he says. "The day I met you, I was wrestling with myself." He taps the poster against his thigh. "I was thinking, that day, of the catechism, the part that says, *How to deal with the educated. Temptation and scandals to be faced by the candidate during his catechumenate*. I suppose most people who leave the calling do so because they lose their faith," he says. "*The chief reason for Christ's coming was to manifest and teach God's love for us. Here the catechist should find the focal point of his instruction.*" He scratches his head. "I have no problem with that. I did, and do, believe it. It's that other phrase. *The educated. How to deal with them.* It always stuck in my craw. There are many ways to interpret the catechism, of course, but I always heard in it a deep suspicion of thought... as though faith and education were somehow incompatible. I've never wanted to be the type of man who feels that way. I want to be contemplative *and* be a servant of God."

"But surely it's not necessary to leave the priesthood?"

"No. Of course it's more complicated than that." He unrolls his poster, careful not to tear its edges: Ringo's big, baleful eyes. "I don't think the theater manager knew what he had," Hipkiss says. "These old *Hard Day's Night* ads must be worth a fortune. He let it go for fifty bucks."

"So, are you telling me that, as a priest, you couldn't indulge in rock 'n' roll?" I ask.

"No. Though there was a certain... *humorlessness* in the parish, a shrinking from pleasures of any sort. I *am* too attached to the world, I admit it." He grins. "I felt closer to Godly serenity in this old theater, watching Ringo tap his hi-hat, than I ever did behind the altar. Whenever I wore the collar and the rabbat, I felt *that* part of my identity, the happy part, had to be bound and gagged. Tucked away behind the pipe organ."

The street crew hammers pavement with pick axes.

"The truth is, I fell in love," Hipkiss tells me. He rerolls the poster. "I was assigned to a small church in this area, ministering to poor Mexican families, immigrants from Nicaragua, El Salvador. Lots of mothers working as housekeepers."

"Yes. I've seen them on the buses," I say.

"My heart went out to them all."

"Naturally. A moral obligation."

"And to one woman in particular. She's married."

"Well."

"I'm not sure what we'll do." He chuckles sadly.

Here's a man who's ceased to be an alien, an awkward stranger to himself, I think. He's tumbled back to Earth and fallen hard.

"I haven't put much money away," he says. He waves the poster. "And here I am, spending what little I have on silliness."

"It's hardly silly. Not to you. 'All you need is love'? I think God would approve."

He's a gentle, amenable man, but no, I think. Not another one. Not when my *own* orbit is rapidly deteriorating. I move away from him, slightly.

He gets my drift, reaches to shake my hand. "God bless you," he says.

"Be well."

He walks away, humming.

13.

For Susan's opening at the art gallery I've bought a dozen red roses.

Her husband will be there. Is it inappropriate for me to offer his wife flowers? Will my gesture be misconstrued? What *is* the meaning of my gesture?

A dying woman. Another man's wife. The astronomer's curse: straining for the unattainable? I kidded Karen about this whenever she flew away from me.

But tonight it doesn't feel like a joke. What's wrong with me?

What the hell is wrong with me?

I straighten the Star Room. Only three people attended this afternoon's show, but they left an unholy mess: mud, Styrofoam cups, paper clips, loose change.

I sit beneath the setting sun, staring at my flowers.

The late bus is nearly empty. The art gallery is locked and dark, the show long over. Above me, a waning moon in an untroubled sky. I pause on the gallery steps. Through a window I glimpse a row of folding tables stacked with empty food trays. Candelabra top the tables. In that perking, low light, Susan must have dazzled everyone! Past all this, beyond the corner of a doorway, I see one of her paintings, a tall panel coated with oil and impasto, bright reds, somber yellows: a purifying fire.

I lay the roses by the door.

14.

On one of my last nights alone at the planetarium, I revise my farewell script, hang a portion of the theater curtains in the portal to the Star Room. A note from the board, received this morning, tells me to plan my final performance a week from now and then remove my belongings from the premises.

The curtains shimmer in dim blue light reflected off the dome. A faint trace of eau de cologne wafts from the velvet. I imagine, muffled deep within the soft worn furrows, sewn inside the seams, the voices of cowboys and femme fatales, lovers' whispers, the Beatles' "Yeah yeah yeahs!"

In addition to the curtains, I'd hoped someday to add to the dome's base a scale model of the Dallas skyline, giving viewers a sense of the sky's immensity stretching over our city—a city bright and safe, measured, with clear and manageable paths.

Well. My tiny Dallas is not to be.

I look around: the dome's bleak and toneless color, a cool ceiling over all of creation. Alone in here at night, I relish the lifeless vacancy of my space, its beautiful, mechanical boredom, which puts me at ease. It demands nothing of me. It doesn't need my help.

The star ball—like the jar I used to carry as a kid, with holes punched in the lid to keep captured fireflies alive, only *this* jar, the A3P, contains all of the flashing galaxies. Everything patterned and neatly tucked away until I release the universe, its edges blurring above me, the Star Room becoming the same size as the cosmos. *Becoming* the cosmos. The delicacy of Order. Totality, held like a caught breath inside a small, sealed case.

I extinguish the stars, pull the curtains to, step outside the building, and lock the glass doors. Headlights sweep the wall. A car pulls up behind me. I pocket my keys and turn.

An old Honda hatchback. Susan rolls down the passenger window. "Adam, can you sit with me?" she asks. She nods toward the back seat. Anna's asleep there. "We can talk if we keep it low. She'll snooze through anything."

I slide into the car. The engine idles. A Talking Heads CD plays quietly through the speakers. In the dashboard's green and yellow light, Susan's face floats as a series of cool, soft planes. Her hands are caked with dried purple paint. A cardboard air freshener, shaped as a tree, sways from the rearview mirror, scenting the car like oak.

Susan rubs her bare arms. She's wearing a white sleeveless blouse. She has goose bumps, a summer chill.

She says, "You didn't come to my opening."

"No."

"I looked for you. All night."

"I'm sorry."

"Did you leave the roses?"

"Yes."

"I *thought* it was you," she says.

I stare at my feet. "I know what an important night that was. How did it go? Splendidly, I hope."

"I wish you'd been there."

"Probably just as well," I say.

"Why?"

Is this it? Our event horizon? The point of no return? "I would have felt funny about, you know... your husband."

Susan slumps, her face an open question. "Adam, have I given you the impression—?"

"I don't know," I say. "Well, no. I mean—it doesn't matter. How *are* you? How do you feel?"

"Shit." She thrums her fingers on the steering wheel. "We've met, what? Three times? *Three times* we've talked?"

"Susan—"

"Okay," she says forcefully. "Here's the thing, Adam." She glances over her shoulder at Anna. "Daniel—my husband—is a very kind man, but he views my painting as a hobby. Not serious, you know. It doesn't pay the bills. In the last few years, as I've made my way, well... the short version is, I was liking my new independence, the friends I was making, and Daniel was more and more unhappy that I wasn't home taking care of, well, everything. To be honest, we were on the verge of splitting. And then I got sick. For Anna's sake..."

Her eyes glisten.

"It's okay," I say. "I understand."

"Anyway, anyway... the day we talked in the gallery, the care you took, just *looking*... I hadn't had that in a while, not since the treatments began. I felt an immediate connection."

"Me, too."

"I was so hungry for it. Maybe that wasn't fair to you."

"My admiration was genuine, Susan."

"You've been so kind to Anna and me."

She reaches across the seat and takes my hand. The coarseness of the dried paint on her fingers reminds me of my father's old core samples.

"And now you're leaving?" she says.

"I'm afraid so. My brother—he's all the family I've got left, and we've gone a lot of years without really talking. And you?"

She smiles sadly. "I stay as strong as I can for as long as I can. And make sure Anna and Daniel are fine, going forward. That's it."

I squeeze her hand. "It's cruel," I say. "It's cruel for us to meet like this. Now."

"Oh, Adam, I don't—"

"I know, I know. Would anything have been possible under other circumstances? Who can say? But *this*—"

"Yes. I feel it, too."

"I'm sorry," I say. "I'm being selfish." I turn to watch Anna sleep. "Poor little girl. Does she know?"

"She knows I've been seeing a doctor. Not the prognosis."

"She's too smart, Susan. She'll figure it out before you're ready. She deserves to know."

"Yes. We'll tell her soon."

"Is your husband a good father?"

"He is."

"Good. Good."

She turns my hand over and over against the car seat, touches my fingertips as in a child's repetitive game.

Anna stirs, a low whine like the star ball makes whenever it moves into position. She slips a thumb into her mouth, falls still. "Should you get her to bed?" I say.

"We haven't resolved this."

"It doesn't matter. The only thing that matters is that you take care of yourself now."

"Three times!" She laughs. "I can't believe that's all it was! I'm going to miss you, Adam."

"Stay in touch? I'll give you my brother's address."

"Of course."

I nod.

We sit silently for several more minutes. Then she asks, "Can I drop you off?"

"You need to get her back. I'll walk. My final show is next week. Will you bring her?"

"I will."

I kiss her lightly: the left temple, where her hair fans away from her skin. Then I reach behind the seat and squeeze Anna's arm. "Good night," I say.

I stand and watch Susan's taillights pull away, as red as the scribbles my pointer leaves among the moon's rubbled craters.

15.

Tonight,

Final Show:

A Possible History of Forever

. . . or, *Is That All There Is?*

William and Lila are the first to arrive. He's looking dapper, in a red pullover sweater, neatly pressed khakis, and shiny cordovan loafers. A healthy ruddiness colors his cheeks. His eyes are keen. He links fingers with Lila.

"You two look happy," I say.

"He's a wonderful man," Lila tells me.

"And she's a delight," says William. "Thank you, Adam, for introducing us."

"Glad to be of service."

Lila hands me an invitation for a potluck to promote local awareness of the Strategic Initiative to Identify the New Paradigm. "I've invited some of the group's national leaders here to meet with a select bunch of forward-thinkers," William says. "As we know, Dallas is woefully unprepared to encounter new worlds."

I tell them I hope they'll enjoy the show.

Susan and Anna step through the curtains. I hug them both. Susan looks regal against the velvet folds. Anna's eyes are red. She slouches, and I figure Susan has told her the truth about her illness. She confirms my hunch with a nod. "I've got something for you," Anna mumbles.

"Oh?" I say.

"A letter to keep with your others."

She hands me a sheet of notepaper:

It's not fair to take the sky away from people.

Signed,
Anna

"Thank you very much," I say. "You know, honey, only *I'm* leaving. Not the sky. But I'll be proud to save this."

"When you make the moon rise tonight, do it real slow," Anna says.

"I will." I look around the room. "All my friends," I whisper. My sweet old crackpots.

A few strangers wander in—maybe twelve in all. No one from the museum board.

I push a button. *Music for Airports.* The lights dim. "The artist Odilon Redon once made a lithograph—a hot air balloon in the shape of a wide-open eye," I say. With the cove lights I indicate a brittle balloon, cast by the slide projector. "Redon entitled his piece, 'The Eye like a Strange Balloon wafts itself towards the Infinite.' So. Tonight, as we travel together through space, may your eyes be strange balloons. I'm your host, Adam Post."

The sun sets.

"As you know, our little cosmos is calling it quits," I say. "But before it's done, let's rejoice one last time at its marvels, along with the poet Gerard Manley Hopkins, who once wrote, 'Look at the stars! Look up at the skies! / O look at all the fire-folk sitting in the air!'

"Some say the souls of the dead are cast into the skies. There, they live on as stars, lighting the dark woods for those of us struggling on Earth. So perhaps endings aren't so sad, after all." Minor chords drift through hidden speakers. "Other myths say falling stars are souls returning to Earth, bathed in a purifying fire, where they walk among us as angels.

"In any case, for six years now, here at the planetarium, we've endeavored to suspend ourselves in a state of possibility. Whatever we can envision, perhaps someday we'll create it. We are builders. We are dreamers. We are once-and-future fire-folk."

This is the last time I'll stand at the center of my universe. No more control. *Move on*: Marty's voice in my head.

I make the moon rise.

Let them go, I think. Let them all go.

A rumble of thunder. Lightning. Anna laughs and claps.

I press a yellow button and an aurora borealis explodes across the northern arc of the dome. Cascading blue light overflows the dipper's tipped bowl. "May your lives blaze," I whisper into the microphone.

Now, one final time, sunlight pours through my space.

Music for Airports fades into distance. I bring the house lights up. For a moment, no one moves. Then, one by one, the patrons wish me luck and pass silently through the curtains.

Standing in the portal, Susan catches my eye. "Call us?" she says. With her fingers, she brushes Anna's hair.

"Of course," I say.

Anna won't look at me.

"Will you be all right, honey?" I ask her.

"My mama's sick," she says.

Susan closes her eyes.

"I know," I say.

Anna shuffles her feet. "My mama is sick and they're taking away the sky."

"So you've got to be really strong now."

"I don't know how."

"Sure you do."

"I don't!"

"For your mother. You'll learn. Won't you?"

She puffs her lower lip. Susan and I lock gazes, helplessly.

Finally: "Adam?" Anna says.

"Yes, honey?"

"Can you make it rain?" She grabs my hand. "One more time, for me?"

And I do.

16.

I snag a bus to the airport, pick up my rental car—a new, white midsize (I don't know one automobile from another)—and return to the planetarium. I place Glenn Gould, Brian Eno, and other music CDs into a small cardboard box; fill a paper sack with constellation slides and star charts; remove the pen-sized pointer from the console and wire it to a battery from the storage room. Now I can aim a red, lighted arrow anywhere I wish (a pointless activity—pun intended—but one I'll relish). I unlatch the curtains from the Star Room's portal and fold them into the car's backseat.

A new letter has arrived. Should I leave it for the kid the board has hired—at a paltry wage—to activate Robert Redford for their fancy new shows, the voice of Tom Hanks? I unseal the envelope:

> If you ever get up there, please know that the moon is pure pumice, straight from the earth's core. I have proof, and I don't need the Bible for this, that Earth was once much bigger than it is at present, but it busted apart upon collision with some unholy solar debris. The Bible doesn't say so but I can prove this is accurate, if you would like a demonstration at my home (I'll be gone next month, but any time after that is fine. Tuesdays, around three, are best).

I slip the letter into my box, a keepsake.

At home, I swaddle my computer in a series of blankets and set it in the trunk. I throw my clothes into a suitcase, along with a family scrapbook. The apartment is paid for until the end of the month, but I've informed my landlord I'm leaving. One last look around. My radio. I click it on as I dust the countertops. A debate about the death penalty. None of the show's guests, whose loved ones have been murdered, are in a benevolent mood. "There's no way that thug can atone for what he did to my family," says one man, sobbing. "Killing's *too good* for him."

"I want that mother to *fry*," a woman shouts.

I swallow a gust of Albuterol. *Forgive me*, I think, staring at a cobweb in a corner of my ceiling. I can't reach it even with the broom. I picture my parents' faces. Marty's face. *For everything I did, please forgive me. For things I didn't know I'd done, please forgive me. Forgive me.*

I step outside. "Forgive me," I say to the wind.

I drive to the airport, intending to hang around the concourses one last time before hitting the road. By the side of the highway I spot a slender stick and almost stop to pick it up. It might be useful. After all, from a vertical stick in the ground, you can learn the exact time once a day (when the sun is highest in the sky and the stick's shadow is shortest), you can mark the summer and winter solstices, and you can determine the sun's altitude. There are quicker, more accurate means of making such calculations, but none simpler or quite as graceful.

Ingenuity over drudgery—much to be desired.

In 250 BC, Eratosthenes used a stick, the sun, and the stick's shadows to measure the size of the earth; hundreds of years later, scientists determined Eratosthenes' figure—a circumference of 46,250 kilometers—was accurate to within 15 percent. Much harm, much good can come from a man with a stick.

I decide to keep moving.

At the airport, I park the car and make my way to Terminal A. The copy shop clatters with motion, the dull fertility of repetition. All day, a stay against Nothing (though the world is ending every minute!): relentlessly, the machines duplicate anything anything anything anything anything anything anything anything anything anything anything any—

I head for the TRAAIN. "Please clear the doorway," says the train's robotic voice. A crowd of people rushes in. A crowd of people rushes out. "Standing in the doorway can endanger yourself and others."

I ride for half an hour. Then I give Marty I call. "I'm setting out," I say. "I think I'll take my time. Look around."

"Beautiful West Texas? Rattlesnakes? Tumbleweeds?"

"What is it Dad used to say? *Embrace the world?* I don't know. I'll be there in a couple of days."

"Okay, bro. Hey, we finally poured the foundation for the new theater," he says. "You'll get here just in time. You're going to be impressed."

"Look forward to it."

I go to find my car.

17.

Night-driving. Its great pleasure is the odd radio fare. For a while, I listen to a BBC production of *King Lear*. The king wanders the heath in exile. "Howl, howl, howl! O, you are men of stones!" he shouts. "Had I your tongues and eyes, I'd use them so that heaven's vault should crack."

Lear at midnight, in the middle of the Lone Star state. Who'd have imagined it? Seek and ye shall find!

When the performance ends, a broadcaster delivers the latest news: thousands of Iraqi children are reported dead as a result of U.S. food sanctions; the Atomic Energy Commission *does not know* where the nation's nuclear waste should be stored; former Beatle George Harrison—the "spiritual" Beatle—has been diagnosed with throat cancer.

I hum "A Hard Day's Night"—if not the Music of the Spheres, at least a pleasant little tune.

Near McDonald Observatory, there used to be a globe factory. Several years ago, I toured it and watched the sure-fingered women on the factory floor paste hemispheres together, as if arranging apple slices on a blue china plate. The women were serious, intense—laboring, it seemed, with a strict moral purpose (and for much less than minimum wage). Not long ago, I read in a newspaper that the factory had moved south, across the Rio Grande. The production of the planet, outsourced to Mexico.

I pull my battery-powered pointer from a paper sack and aim it out the window. With my lighted arrow, I touch hummocks of hay, horses, cows, and sheep. Cloud-bottoms. Rotted barns, coffee shops ("We never close!") crumbling into dirt. Within seconds, I've circumscribed the earth.

Just as I'm thinking I need a nap, or at least a break to stretch my legs, I see a neon sign by the highway up ahead. Flickering pink letters: Paradise Motel.

How can I pass it by?

I turn left, off the highway, and park. The motel consists of three single-story brick buildings in a row. A drive-in movie screen, isolated from the motel by a wire-mesh fence, angles toward the rear parking lot. The swimming pool is filled with air. A green lamp blazes in the office window. Above it, an electric sign says, "Cable TV!"

The moon—marred all night by clouds—shines briefly in the east, its craters dark, like pieces chipped from a pane of thick smoked glass.

Behind the office desk stands a man who—damn if it isn't so—looks like my father, with this difference: he smiles easily and broadly.

No. Looking closer, I think I'm making this up. I'm tired. This guy looks nothing like my father. Too swarthy. Too short.

"Howdy. Pulling an all-nighter?" he says to me.

"I got a late start." I sign the register.

"Breakfast comes with the room: coffee and doughnuts here in the lobby, seven to ten," he says. He hands me a silver key.

He's assigned me a corner room facing the movie screen. An auto salvage yard sprawls across a barren field to the west of the motel lot. Hundreds of hubcaps hang on a cinder-block fence in front of the main office. I unlock the door to my room, flip a wall switch. Light explodes onto a thick orange carpet, a single bed, a tiny TV, and a lamp with a yellow paper shade.

I remember a statistic from one of my shows: 98 percent of the universe remains invisible to us.

Dear God, that's not nearly enough. I switch off the light.

It doesn't take long for my eyes to adjust to the dark. With my red, flaring arrow I write my name on the walls. *Adam Post.* The light's afterglow remains in my eyes for several seconds.

On the bed, I wrap myself in part of the Yucca curtain. The velvet is soft and warm, a ghostly heat I imagine radiating from the auras of Hollywood stars, amazing black and white light from the screen penetrating the curtain. Ingrid Bergman, Audrey Hepburn. Happily, I hug my pillow.

On the nightstand, I find the TV remote and a Magic Fingers box. I slip two quarters into the box and the bed begins to vibrate. It hums and whines like a flying saucer in an old sci-fi flick. I turn on the television. The reception is awful. I click through the channels and settle on a Hedy Lamarr movie. Snow obscures the figures on the screen: reflections in a small, tarnished mirror.

Birds all night. All night, birds.

It's three in the afternoon when I wake. I'm soaked beneath the curtain. The TV wheezes: an evangelist with white, poofy hair yelling, "Hell!" I turn him off and stand at the window. Somewhere nearby, children are singing, a song within a song. One voice holds a high note while others chant melodies. I remember Fridays at the planetarium, the noise and excitement of the kids as they gathered outside the Star Room.

The window is dusty. So, it appears, is the sky.

I shower and shave. Outside, on the sidewalk in front of my room, sunlight blinds me. I'm afraid to move. I shield my eyes with my arm. The sky is immense. I realize I'm used to a much smaller version of it.

In the office, the manager—Fred Davis, says a sign on the counter—slaps price tags on cellophane-wrapped packets of postcards. "You missed breakfast," he tells me. "Lunch, too."

"And you?" I say. "You don't sleep?"

He laughs. "My shift started last night just before you pulled in. I'm clocking out in an hour. My wife'll take over then."

"I guess you don't see much of each other."

"Secret to a long, happy marriage," he says. "Might be half a sweet roll left on that table over there. Otherwise, if you're hungry, you'll have to walk down the highway a bit, just past the auto salvage. There's a Sure-Mart there."

"Thanks."

"You missed your checkout time. I'm afraid we'll have to charge you for tonight."

"It's okay," I say. "I could use the extra night, anyway."

I set off down the road. A short walk to stir the blood. Kids chase each other across the motel lot. Aside from my car, I see four station wagons parked in the gravel slots. In the auto salvage yard, a man welds something onto a car bumper. He's propped the bumper across two rusty barrels. Sparks jitter from his torch, rise a little, float to the ground. Sunlight blares off the hubcaps attached to the fence.

The Sure-Mart is dim inside, and my eyes are so dazzled by the outside light, I'm helpless for a moment. Slowly, forms appear: outlines of boxes, bags, glass freezer cases. Colors complete the lines now, and textures, as though matter was a paint-by-numbers game, filling the world's given shapes. I stick a frozen hot dog in a microwave oven in a corner of the store, next to a rack of girlie mags: *Angels of the Desert Southwest*!

Back outside, walking by the highway, I tear open a small bag of Fritos with my teeth. I'm light-headed, sweating. Two jet trails cross each other overhead, perfect, half-circular lines, as though the ecliptic and the celestial equator had twisted together like pretzels. A praying mantis leaps from the dirt and brushes my forearm. A flash of green against startling blue sky. A delicate touch on my skin. The air smells of sage.

I breathe, slow and easy.

In the motel office, Davis stands with a pair of binoculars, staring out the window.

"What are you looking at?" I ask.

He scans the flat horizon. "Nothing," he says. "But you never know when something's going to turn up out there."

Back in my room, I hear children shout, "Ha ha, you're it!" from the parking lot. A beautiful little girl, as tall and dark as Susan, flies past my window, followed by three or four other girls, laughing and singing. They form a ring on the sidewalk and do a fast, frenetic dance.

For supper I finish the Fritos and munch a Power Bar. On television, a man eats a bowl of worms in order to win a prize.

Shadows in the evening light reveal the textures of my room's rough walls: moonlike in the unevenness of their surfaces. It's hot. I stare at the telephone. Finally, I pick it up and call Susan. "I'm glad I caught you at home," I say. "How are you feeling?"

"A little tired today. Anna's been a problem." Her voice awakens me like sudden heat or ice. "Daniel thinks we need to take her to a therapist. He doesn't think she's handling my news very well."

"Listen," I say. "Listen." Wrong. Wrong. What's wrong with me? "I hadn't planned to say this, but it's so nice to hear your voice, and I... I think I made a mistake, Susan."

"Adam, what are you talking about?"

"I think I want to come back for you," I tell her. "I want you with me."

"That's impossible."

"Why?"

"For all the reasons you already know. Adam, please."

"Is your husband there? Can you talk freely?"

"Yes, I can talk, but don't do this."

"I knew I'd miss you. I didn't know how much," I say. The words make it all true, whether or not it *was* true before. Who knows *what* comes *when* and *why*? The dome spins this way and that. "I haven't felt anything, not a thing, since—"

"Me, neither," she admits. A shallow, raspy breath.

"So?"

"Nothing. So nothing. You know that."

"Susan, can I call you again? Tomorrow?"

"Of course. Yes. I want you to stay in touch. But please don't say these crazy things... or pity yourself... or whatever's going on, Adam. All right? Where are you, by the way? Some terrible old motel room?"

"Exactly. Susan, do you at least think about it? About *us*?"

"I won't answer that. How can you ask? I'm tired. I need to lie down."

"I'll call you tomorrow."

"Please respect me on this. You know the situation. For God's sake, Adam."

"I know."

"And I don't want to hear the word *obligation*. I'm not one of your crackpots. I'm a dying woman."

"Don't say that."

"It's the truth. Anna has to accept it. *You* have to accept it. And none of this is fair to my husband."

"But as long as—" Wrong wrong wrong.

"Let me hear you say it. I want to hear you acknowledge the truth."

The truth? For some reason, I flash on the bird my father and I found years ago in the restaurant parking lot. Fleeing on two firm wings? "Yes," I whisper.

"Yes what?"

"You're dying."

"Okay. Thank you. Thank you. So no more nonsense, all right?"

"Susan?"

"What is it?"

"I'm—"

"You're lonely, Adam. That's all it is. Stay out of crappy motels. You hear me?"

I rub my eyes. "Sleep well, then. My love to Anna."

"You too. Good night. Adam?"

"Yes?"

"Thanks for calling," she says.

The receiver burns my palm.

Numb, I sit on the curb outside my room, fanning my face with a sheaf of stationery. Fireflies twinkle in the night. The hubcaps on the fence at the salvage yard shimmer in blue moonlight. The color reminds me of Susan's palette, of our day together in the gallery when she told me she was sick. *I've lost interest in things that could be finished…*

Apparently, the drive-in behind the motel specializes in classics and second-run movies. Lauren Bacall flickers across the screen. She was one of my mother's favorites. I remember, in that clean new theater in Oklahoma City... no. Imagine instead Robert Hipkiss as a boy, sitting dreamily in the Yucca. Don't feel. Don't try to understand.

In the parking lot, a boy runs in circles, blowing bubbles with a bottle of soap and a pink plastic wand. The bubbles rise, brightening as they catch the film-light. Clouds smudge the sky, but I can make out the constellation Crux, its upper star a clear orange.

"Mommy, look!" shouts the boy with the bottle of soap, as a cluster of bubbles floats toward Lauren Bacall's wet lips.

18.

Ahead of me as I drive, the sun rises and then appears to rise again—the brightness spreads so fast, cutting through a nearly cloudless sky. Rocks in fields on either side of the road absorb the light and shine like mirrors: flecks of sky, chipped and dropped to Earth.

I've tuned my radio to jazz, a program entitled "Drummers' Extravaganza": Cozy Cole, Chick Webb, Big Sid Catlett, Zutty Singleton, Dave Tough, Baby Dodds, Gene Krupa, Buddy Rich, Louis Bellson, Shelly Manne, Panama Francis, Jo Jones, and the great Kenny Clarke.

I check the map. I can stay on the highway or I can turn here and take a country road. No doubt, the highway is more efficient but not as elegant as the road. I turn. Up ahead, a splintered wooden structure, the base of an old windmill, perhaps. As I approach, I see it's part of a much larger ruin: an old aviary, according to a faded painted sign. Oak poles cluster together, some leaning badly in an octagonal pattern; wire-mesh screens—sagging now to the ground. Large wooden dowel pins (perches for the birds?) lie scattered like bones in the dirt. A few red and yellow feathers—green and blue ones, too—rustle from nails or splinters on which they snagged long ago.

I stand and sip water from a bottle. The feathers twist in the wind.

I check the map once more. The sun is blinding now, the land a lake of light. On the horizon, hills: soft crevices filled with shade or illumination, strong here, weak there—as varied as the thick encaustic surfaces of Susan's paintings. This morning, I'm feeling a refreshing distance from her, a mild embarrassment about the call I made last night. Or maybe I'm just trying to talk myself into experiencing nothing. A cloud uncurls like a sash around the sun.

I set out again, brightness cascading over bushes, billboards, rocks. They all appear to move. On the outskirts of a small ghost town, a naked mannequin, missing an arm, lies beside the road. Empty hamburger bags blow against her torso. Up ahead, a tattered sign says, "Re-elect Edwin Low, Sheriff." Seven or eight sparrows perch on a sagging telephone wire; a new bird arrives, settles among them, and they all begin to preen in pleasure and excitement.

On my radio, Jo Jones pounds out a drumbeat as steady as a pulse.

Squinting against the glare, I nearly miss a curve in the road. I've entered the desert unprepared for the vigor of the sky. At a gas station–café, I buy a cheap pair of sunglasses and give Marty a call at a pay phone whose cracked glass door won't close. Just inside the restaurant, a waitress stands behind a cash register slurping lemonade, reading a *Screen Secrets* magazine. Behind her, a calendar on the wall rustles, open to the wrong month.

"Hey," I tell Marty. "Looks like I'll get there tomorrow afternoon sometime. That okay with you?"

"Fine, fine," he says. He sounds harried. "The architects are squabbling about our theater," he tells me. "Stage measurements. Windows and doors."

A tumbleweed blows against the phone booth.

My brother's voice rises and I hear a bit of the old hair-trigger Marty, the one who always accused me of stealing his toys. "Anyway, I'll be glad when you get here, bro. Take my mind off this stuff."

An invitation to disaster, I think: he'll count on me to make things better, and when I can't, he'll turn on me. We'll fall into our old patterns and this time Mom won't be around to save us from ourselves.

No. I'm not being fair. He isn't all *that* angry. And his annoyance is justified. Maybe *I'm* the problem, I think. Little creep.

I pass a farmer in a field pounding dirt with a shovel to no apparent purpose. Clouds crowd the sky, reeling like silver clock gears. Another nameless town, full of trucks hauling cattle feed. Wind scatters hay from the trucks' open beds. The streets seem made of straw. At a high school, a marching band rehearses on a practice football field. Farther on, in the middle of a flat, shadowless field, an abandoned fairground sprawls: an off-kilter merry-go-round, rusting in the sun, an old loop-the-loop ride.

Evening. Thunderheads. A faint water-smell in the air. Flash-lightning shoots through the sky; the electrical charges appear to overflow the clouds' limits and burst toward Earth. Then, just as quickly as the storms gathered, they're gone. The sky begins to clear. At dusk, a single cloud changes color with the sunset; one by one, cirrus wisps, like mirrors, take up the hue—a faint orange-pink—and sink with the sun.

The night is warm. I find a rest stop and kill my engine. Crickets *skreek* in the weeds—here, there, then a whole chorus. *If you prove that there cannot be motion without cause, you've proved the existence of God*, said Thomas Aquinas. I open my door. One cricket hushes. Soon, others follow suit.

Bootes, Aquila, the Little Dipper (like the tiller of a ship). Saturn and Mars. A star cluster, low in the west, too faint to have been etched on the planetarium's star ball.

Though the air is warm, I figure a fire would be nice. An aesthetic pleasure. One should never forego an aesthetic pleasure. I gather twigs and sticks and, using the car's cigarette lighter, start a little flame. Sparks flit here and there, mingling with lightning bugs. A meteor spikes through Cassiopeia. Antares, in the heart of the scorpion, shines like a candle flame through a little patch of alabaster.

I must have slept, stretched across the hood of my car. The ground is moist with dew and the air is chilly. I've got a crick in my neck. I wander into a field and take a piss. Meteors *zizzle*. In the south, a few stars rarely visible in this hemisphere poke above the horizon, their light as faint as a far-off lament.

On my radio, a newsman says New York's World Trade Center will host an important economic summit tomorrow: "There'll be much excitement around the Twin Towers. Following the '93 bombing incident, security, naturally, will be tight."

More jazz. The Bill Evans Trio, from the Village Vanguard sessions—recorded, says an announcer, just days before Scott Lafaro, the bass player, was killed in an automobile accident.

Castor and Pollux gleam above the road: a pair of quarreling brothers. The moon begins to rise. The sky is many colors: black, silver, yellow, deep blue. A faint eggplant tint, over in the east.

I turn off the radio and crawl into the back seat, wrapped in the Yucca curtain. At dawn I wake. Sunlight streaks across the remaining stars until even the most gorgeous are gone.

19.

"The prodigal brother," Marty says. "In the bosom of his family at last!"

"Don't start with the literary allusions," I say.

"Deal—as long as you promise to keep the cosmos out of our conversations."

I laugh. "Neither of us will be able to play by these rules."

"Come in, come in. Let me look at you. You're thin. Don't you eat?"

"It's been stressful."

"You always *were* a-quiver, as the poets say."

"There you go again."

"How 'bout I whip us up some spaghetti? We'll unload your car later. Scotch, vodka, beer?"

"Red wine?"

"You got it."

Since I saw him last, Marty's brown hair has thinned at the temples and he's gained six or seven pounds. Otherwise, he's the same: slightly bowlegged, long-faced and prematurely jowly, like Dad. He's wearing khaki pants, a white shirt, and black cowboy boots. His house is austere. A hound's-tooth couch, a couple of wooden rocking chairs. A plain deal table in the center of the dining room. On it, *The Riverside Shakespeare*, open to a page of *Hamlet*, and the rough drafts of a pair of Marty's articles.

As a sign of his hospitality he's displayed on an otherwise empty shelf a book I sent him one Christmas on the work of Joseph Cornell. I thought it might be a point of connection between us, science and art, though as I recall he never said a word about it. The book offers photographs of Cornell's shadowboxes: *Toward the "Blue Peninsula,"* a simple white container filled with wire mesh. Behind the wire, a tiny window opens onto startling blue sky—a glimpse of infinity in a claustrophobic space. *Cassiopeia #1*, only fourteen inches wide, its inner walls plastered with star charts: heaven folded into the equivalent of a cigar box. *Solar Set*, a box featuring sketches of the sun and of Earth's orbit around it, behind five fluted glasses, each holding clear yellow or shadowy blue marbles—phases of the moon. Staring at the book, I'm struck with a fierce and piercing homesickness for the planetarium.

Charmingly, a small brick fireplace occupies the northeast corner of Marty's living room. On the mantel sits a china doll in a glass bubble. I'd forgotten Marty took it when we sold our folks' house. It used to belong to our grandmother. "Grandma would be pleased," I call to Marty. He's uncorking a smoky bottle in the kitchen.

"What's that?"

"Her doll. It would tickle her that you kept it."

"Oh, nothing satisfied that old woman."

"True."

"It comforts me to have it there. You know. The familiarity."

"You never struck me as sentimental," I say. I join him in the kitchen.

He's poured himself a whiskey. "Sentimental? No," he says. "I like order. Continuity. That's all."

On the pantry door, by the stove, he's taped a newspaper headline: MCVEIGH DEAD. "Like I say," he says, catching my stare. "Order."

" 'Move on.' Wasn't that your advice to me?" I ask.

"Absolutely. But we can't pretend it didn't happen."

We take our drinks to the table. He shoves aside Shakespeare. "Once the theater's finished—*if* we can get the damn architects to agree—we're thinking *Hamlet* will be our first production," he says.

"Been busy," I say, nodding at his drafts.

"Doing okay. If nothing else, I've got good work habits. I've become a set-in-his-ways old man."

"Hardly old."

"Dad was like that. Remember?" Marty asks. "He loved us, but he was happiest, I think, on his own, puttering around his tools and that junk in the garage."

"No. That's not how I picture him at all." I sip my wine. "It seemed to me he was always making an effort to help other people—his 'moral obligations.' Remember? Like those roughnecks, those Mexican guys."

"Who?"

"Seriously?"

"Seriously. When was this?"

"Oh, we were seven or eight. He had them to supper. You really don't remember?"

He shakes his head and laughs. " 'Moral obligations'? All I know is, he acted so aggrieved whenever I asked him for something. Extra allowance, the car keys."

"Hm. You didn't keep his core samples, did you? His rock collection?"

"I think it got tossed when the house sold."

"I always loved those pieces."

"Yeah, well, that stuff...that was *your* thing with him. 'Nother drink?" Marty asks.

"I'm fine. And you?"

He pours himself a second whiskey. "Me?"

"*Your* thing with Dad?"

He laughs. "In college, when I told him I was going to major in English, he didn't say a word. Later, I found out he'd phoned my professors, asking them, 'What the hell can an English grad do?' "

"That's sweet."

"Sweet? Meddling, is what it was."

"He was concerned about you."

"More about him than me. I was his obligation, but I don't think morality had anything to do with it."

Down the block, a lawnmower whines. A clock ticks in the kitchen.

"I appreciate you letting me stay, Marty."

He toasts me.

"Even if the board hadn't forced me out, I'm not sure I... I mean, I was struggling."

"With what?"

"Women. Work. You know." Susan's face floats like a pane of light in the air in front of me. "But mostly..." I glance toward the pantry door, at the killer's bold, familiar name.

"Still?"

"Don't tell me you don't feel it, too."

He shakes his head.

"It's funny to hear myself say this." It would take an 82-inch telescope, shoved down my throat, to locate everything I'm feeling now. "I've been trying to ignore it, but... maybe it took seeing you to pull it out of me."

Inconsolable?

"Adam, we've talked about this."

"You said it yourself. You can't pretend the past didn't happen."

"Yes. But you put it behind you."

"How?"

"File it away."

"Fine. But *how?*"

"I don't know. You work. You fuck. You drink." He stands. "You cook. I'm going to put the spaghetti on. And you should take a shower. What did you do, sleep in the car last night?"

"As a matter of fact."

He looks at me and sighs.

"All right," I say. "I won't be long."

In the back bedroom, I slip out of my clothes. A bed, a night table, a chair, a set of dresser drawers. No curtains on the window, overlooking a small backyard. No pictures on the walls. I shower quickly, comb my hair in the dresser mirror, pull on a pair of jeans and a blue cotton shirt. Gingerly, I open a dresser drawer. Empty. Another one, the same. In a bottom drawer I find a handful of faded snapshots: Marty and me as kids. We're dressed in dark shorts and black and white Oxfords. Quintessential 1950s geeks. All that's missing are the Davy Crockett coonskin caps. The grin on Marty's face—wide, slightly crooked—I saw only minutes ago, in the kitchen.

The spaghetti is clumpy and thick. Marty apologizes. "Actually, I don't often cook," he says. "On my own, you know, it doesn't seem worth the trouble." My poor, fucked-up brother. Something *is* wrong with us. Dad knew it. Something has always been wrong. Maybe Marty's inconsolable too. Perhaps he just hides it better. "I usually grab a burger on my way home from school."

He tops off my glass.

"I used to eat at the airport," I tell him. "I liked the bland atmosphere."

"You're a weird duck, bro, you know that?"

"I could relax there. No demands."

We laugh awkwardly.

"So," I say. "We're going to be okay?"

"You and me? Sure. Why not?"

"Do you remember how angry you'd get at me for messing with your toys? How Mom had to run to our room and make peace?" I ask. "Tell me you remember that."

"I remember."

"I'm relieved."

"I don't have toys any more. We'll be fine." He chuckles. "Though I'll tell you…as a kid, I remember thinking life was great till you showed up, bawling, pissing, and shitting." The truth at last! "For a while there, I thought you were going to take away everything I had."

"Great. And here I am again," I say.

"At *my* invitation." The whiskey has loosened him up. "The thing with you was, you had such a *rage* to know everything. To put your hands on it, like a blind person." He reaches for the bottle. "Honestly, Adam, it wasn't the *stuff*, the toys and such…I worried you saw things—the truth of them—in ways I never could. I was in awe of you, bro."

"Bullshit."

"It's true. And of course I hated the hell out of you for it."

"I couldn't see *anything*, Marty. I was too busy anticipating your next meltdown."

He gives me an oh-so-innocent look.

"Honestly. Every move I made, I knew it upset you. Cards on the table? I remember our childhood as a series of little explosions."

"Well. Two little geniuses together, what do you expect?" Marty grins.

"But you *did* make the sun rise," I say.

"Come again?"

"When you pulled back the bedroom shade, real dramatic. Told me to sit up, get ready. Remember?"

He drains his whiskey. "You were a pain in the ass, little bro."

"So were you," I say.

We stand and clap each other's backs.

As we unload the car, he doesn't say a word about the theater curtains or my pointer. Once we've arranged my stuff in the guest room, he yawns loudly, a bit theatrically. "I'm bushed," he says.

"Me too."

"Got everything you need?"

"I'm fine," I say. "Thanks."

In the dark, I see the first edge of moonlight slide across the floor from the bedroom window. I set my things around the room; fill the dresser drawers with my underclothes and socks. Yesterday, the sky expanded above me. Tonight I'm safe and snug.

I won't sleep.

I sit on the edge of the bed, thinking of Susan.

Through the walls I think I hear—yes, exactly, as in the old days—Marty's light snores.

In the morning, Marty goes to teach his classes. He lives on the east side of Marfa and commutes a few miles to his college in a little town called Alpine. I tell him I'll poke around Marfa for a while, and we agree to meet at lunchtime. He'll take me to the desert to see the theater.

Before I leave the house I phone Susan. She's not doing well today. "Nausea and headaches," she says. "It happens."

"Can Anna help you?"

"She tries. She's doing more of the grocery shopping for me. Daniel's very kind, but he wasn't prepared for this, of course. We were pretty distant already and under these circumstances... well, everything's a little forced. Hard to find our balance together. Especially knowing what's coming."

"I'm so sorry, Susan."

"And you? You made it to your brother's?"

"We're fine. It's very comfortable here. He couldn't be more accommodating. Susan, I apologize for my call the other night. The last thing I want to do is add to your pressures."

"It's okay. Let's not talk about it."

Move on, I think. *Everyone's always moving on.* Except they aren't. Not really. "Yes. All right. But if I decide to come back to Dallas after spending a little time here, can we, I mean, do you think—"

"I don't know. For me, right now, it's one minute to the next."

"Yes, but promise me—"

"I can't promise *anything*, Adam! I have to be here for Anna."

"The feeling you get in your belly."

"What?"

"It's how my mom described a 'moral obligation.'"

"That's beautiful. Adam?"

"Yes?"

"I think I need to lie down now."

"Is someone there with you?"

"Daniel's just a phone call away."

"Okay."

"Really. I'll be fine."

"Are you sure?

"Call me later," she says. "I love to hear your voice."

Howl, howl, howl!

In downtown Marfa, I turn in my rental car and buy a batch of postcards: garish red sunsets. I stand at the counter next to the cash register and write to Lila, William, and Anna. Near the postcard rack, a stack of pamphlets: *The Birds of the Davis Mountains.* Cassin's Kingbird, Clark's Nutcracker, White-throated Swift.

I scrawl Marty's return address on the cards, buy stamps, and drop the cards into a mail slot. Outside, the sun is straight overhead. I cool myself off by imagining night on the other side of the planet. A plane passes and I think of Karen, floating around somewhere... or maybe not. Maybe now she's firmly grounded. Does she think of me? The plane crosses the sun. The wings become shadows; on land, their outlines sparkle with light reflected off the body of the jet.

Marfa, sixty miles north of Mexico, was named for the family servant in *The Brothers Karamazov*, the novel the railway overseer's wife was reading when her train paused here in 1881. Marty tells me Marfa is famous for three things: its World War II prisoner of war barracks; its use as a backdrop in the Elizabeth Taylor movie *Giant*; and its transformation into an arts mecca.

Oh yes: and the Marfa Lights, unexplained flashes in the evening sky whose source has never been discovered. Theories suggest everything from luminous methane gas to UFOs.

I dodge tumbleweeds in the streets as I stroll past the Paisano Hotel where, apparently, Liz Taylor romped during the filming of *Giant* (she is said to have swum naked in the pool), coffee shops (only two—Mike's and Carmen's), a bookstore, and a gallery featuring smashed automobile sculptures. They look like wadded-up paper, as tall as a man. The colorful textures are lovely, but there's no denying the violence of a twisted automobile.

A U.S. Border Patrol truck, massive, olive-green, parks by a curb. Two men in camo clothes, wearing steel helmets and gripping rifles, leap from the cab of the truck and run down an alley. Somewhere, a dog barks.

Two men pass me on the sidewalk wearing combat boots and sweaty felt cowboy hats. The thing to do, one tells the other, is to form an armed militia in the hills. Then we attack government installations—"McVeigh style"—until the governor resigns and Texas secedes from the country. Then this place would be a fucking paradise.

Before I stop and think: "McVeigh was a punk," I mutter.

The old warriors pause, turn, stare at me. "What the hell?" says one, but nothing's going to happen. These guys are made of straw. I walk away. A young mother hurries her child past me and into the safety of a dime store. That's right, ma'am. Just another stranger in town. Who *knows* who I might be?

At lunchtime Marty picks me up in his Camry and drives me to the construction site. Clouds like ocean waves. The desert is gold-going-pink in gauzy light, with patches of green where grasslands rise from the sand. In the distance, the Dead Horse Mountains and the cone of an ancient volcano. "Pavement Ends, 32 Miles," says a big yellow sign.

Marty's car smells of fast food. Fries. Overdone beef. "It's true. Most of those fellows are harmless. Sunday soldiers," he says when I mention my run-in. "Crackpots. The hills are full of them. But one in ten turns out to be a psychopath. Be careful." He swings us down a side road. "Maybe it's because there's so much space out here, and the air is clear, but this place draws a lot of dreamers," Marty says.

"I saw the border patrol. Dressed like paratroopers."

"Oh yeah. Mexico is tanking. They've got a drug war on their hands. We've had a huge influx of illegals. Everyone's nervous. About a month ago, a couple of feds stumbled on a boy who'd crossed the river. In the dark, they thought he'd raised a rifle—it was just an old stick—and they blew him away. Big stink, as you can imagine. Investigations, court cases. It's just added to the tensions." He spreads his arms. "Welcome to my world, little brother."

"The Republic of Texas."

He laughs. We pass an old Hispanic woman leading a burro with a rope. Strapped to the burro's back, a portable television set and a microwave oven. "We're here," Marty says.

We park next to a group of men gathered around a concrete slab in a clearing surrounded by mesquite bushes. The men are wearing white shirts and dark ties, sleeves rolled to their elbows. Young professionals. Bright futures. I wilt in the heat. A makeshift drafting table straddles two sawhorses.

Marty introduces me to the team: architects and contractors, all from Houston. Together, they ponder a set of blueprints on the drafting table. A mild breeze curls the edges of the paper. A scent of lilacs in the air. "Here's what we're dealing with," Marty tells me. From underneath the blueprints, he pulls a copy of a drawing made in 1647 by a man named Wenceslaus Hollar. A view of London. I'm reminded of Susan's circles, grids, and swirls. "This is one of the historical documents we have, showing the theater's location, relative shape, and size. Not much to go on. What's depicted in this other drawing, here, is the *second* Globe, built after the first one burned. They moved it across the river—see the building with the flag?—and constructed the new theater out of the surviving timbers of the old. We have written accounts, performance contracts and the like, to supplement our knowledge. But overall, the theaters' layouts remain a mystery."

Over his shoulder I glance at the drawings.

"Shakespeare viewed his stage as the earth," Marty says. "The balconies, sky."

"A magic space."

"Right."

"I'm not sure..." I say.

"What?"

"Well, I was just thinking... a year or so ago, for one of my planetarium shows, I did a little impromptu research. The Elizabethans invested a lot of power in the zodiac. In triangulations *based* on the zodiac. If the theater was open to the sky..."

Marty removes his shades.

"Triangulations," says one of the men. "The zodiac. Interesting." He tugs a calculator out of his pocket. Below us, a rustling rises from a narrow ravine, the crackling of dry, brittle brush. A crunch of gravel. I peer down a rocky slope to see a Mexican family, a man and a woman probably in their midtwenties with two small children, all dressed in long pants and heavy shirts, trundling through dust. They startle when they spot us. We stand silently. The wind is a razor of heat. The blueprints ripple. Eventually, the family walks away.

"Broad daylight," Marty says, shaking his head. "They're getting bolder. More desperate, I guess."

"Where do they go?" I ask.

"Who knows? Lots of shoe factories on the border, auto manufacturing. And there's always the East Texas fruit fields, if they can get that far."

In the car later, on our way back to town, Big Brother says, "The *zodiac*?"

"You're not mad at me, are you?"

"No," he says. "But that'll be all, right? No more pearls of wisdom?"

"I was just trying to help, Marty."

He smiles at me. "You are who you are," he says.

"I'm meddling, you mean. Like Dad."

He drops me at the bookstore. A little tense, we agree to meet for supper at the house.

"So I talked to the chair of our math department," Marty tells me. He's reheating spaghetti on the stove. "There may be some adjunct positions opening up in the spring."

"I don't think I can go back to teaching. But thanks," I say.

"What'll you do?"

"Don't worry. You won't get stuck with me."

"I'm not worried."

"Maybe I'll go back to Dallas. You know. After I've licked my wounds."

"If you need any money…"

"I'm okay for a while. I live pretty frugally."

We laugh. He turns off the burner.

"Listen," Marty says. "I gave some thought to what you said this afternoon. Here's the problem with your suggestion." He drains the pasta water in a colander. "If we look at the breadth of the zodiac and make equivalent measurements, scaling it down, we get an elegant and workable set of numbers for the theater's *large* spaces."

"But not for interior doorways or the stage," I say.

"Precisely. You fucking love to mess with my world, don't you?"

"What else have I got to do?"

"The Globe was primarily a summer theater. Most of the performances were given in June, July, and August," he says. "My guess is, the stage was oriented toward the midsummer sunrise, facing the cosmic center, as it were, along the azimuth of the solstice, as many churches were."

"I'm impressed," I say.

"So. If Shakespeare wanted his stage aimed at the center of the universe, as he perceived it, it probably reflected the core of his true concern."

"Man," I say.

"Exactly. The proportions of the human body."

I pour a glass of wine and toast my brilliant brother.

"In Shakespeare's day, anatomy theaters—you know, those pits where doctors performed surgeries?—were built according to ancient drawings of a man on his back, with his feet and hands extended, describing the circumference of a circle," Marty tells me.

"Will your architects know what to do with this?"

He shrugs. "In *their* theaters, surgeons explored the body's ills," Marty says, drizzling into a yellow dish a little pool of olive oil. Extra Virgin.

"Virgin, just like me!" I remember we said as kids.

Once upon a time, making our mother laugh.

I picture Susan lying in an old anatomy theater; in the office of her doctor; floating in the space of one of her paintings.

"I imagine Shakespeare, in *his* theater, saw himself doing something similar. Exposing melancholy. Joy," Marty says.

"Beautiful, brother. The birth of the Globe."

"Okay," he says, raising his glass. "Let's eat."

20.

I tell Marty it's *my* turn to make supper (I can't take another night of his noodles). I'll get steaks and potatoes at the market and fire up the grill when he comes home. "Deal," he says. After he leaves for morning classes, I shower. As I'm about to walk into town, the phone chirps.

"Adam?"

It's Anna.

"Hi sweetie. What's up? Shouldn't you be in school?"

"You knew my mama was dying."

"Is everything okay?"

"You knew. Didn't you? I only thought she was *sick*."

"Anna, honey, tell me. Has there been a change? What's—"

"She throws up a lot. My daddy took her to the doctor this morning."

"Does she know you're at home? *Are* you home? Does she know you're calling me?"

"I skipped class. And no, she doesn't know I have your number. I found it in her purse. She told you, didn't she?"

"Yes."

"You should have told me you knew."

"I didn't think—"

"We were friends, Adam. You had a responsibility to tell me you knew. Something that big—"

Damn this kid!

"Okay. I'm sorry. Are you taking good care of her?"

"She won't let me. She thinks *she* should take care of *me*."

"You're right. She *does* think that. How about your dad? Is he good with her?"

"They don't get along very well. They just pretend they do so I won't be upset. You knew that, too, didn't you?"

"I don't know much. We never really talked about your dad. You get upset anyway, huh?"

"I think you should come back here." She says this wearily, as if acknowledging I'm a last resort, not the kind of man who can make it rain when the desert really *needs* it.

"What does your mama think?"

"She's sick. She doesn't *know* what she thinks."

How did she get so smart?

"Your mom and dad have a plan, Anna, for going forward."

"It's not a very good one."

"You don't know that."

"I know she's not happy. I know she misses you. She talks about you. She liked it that you liked her paintings."

"I miss you guys, too."

"So?"

"It's complicated."

"Adults always say that. It doesn't mean anything."

"I guess you're right."

"Of course I am."

"I'll tell you what, Anna, if you go to school, I'll promise to think about it and to talk to your mom again."

"If you talk to her, she'll tell you not to."

"But I *have* to talk to her, honey. You know that."

"I suppose."

"Get to school?"

"Okay."

"I'm really glad you called me. Phone me again sometime."

"Come home, Adam."

"We'll talk," I say. Home? *You're not the center any more.*

I lock the house and walk into town. Small clouds move swiftly together, like animals in a herd. On a telephone pole, a flier announces a performance of Samuel Beckett's *Endgame* to be performed at the Chinati Foundation. Posters for a coffeehouse appearance of a local folk duo: Scapegoat & Martyr. One Way signs. Here, there. In these narrow alleys, I imagine, picturing men in boots, people could die in an instant.

21.

I stick to the center of the streets. A faint buzzing overhead. Electrical wires. A smell of dust, of overheated car engines, barbecued beef.

We met, I imagine whispering to Susan on the phone. *We had some time together. For a while, we made each other feel more alive. That's something—maybe more than most people get.* Would she believe me? Give me her trust? Would it be enough to overcome sickness and a life of grief afterward? Could I handle a life of grief? Like Dante and his beloved Beatrice? I haven't done well so far.

Does grief explain Susan's pull for me? Hell, since OK City, perhaps grief is all I'm capable of feeling.

There's a smell of old tires in the air. Far off, toward the mountains, the *whish* of cars on a road. Mesquite twigs scrape the cuffs of my pants.

Late afternoon. I cut through a field of brittle weeds. Crickets leap. The architects have lengthened the theater's foundation. They've pieced together a partial prototype of the stage: a wooden box with a trap door at the top and an entrance and exit to the Underworld.

I sit on the edge of the Globe and peer down a limestone slope filled with fissures. Mud, pinyon powder, some kind of white and red mineral deposits in the faces of rocks. A faint humming in the earth. Do unseen caverns stretch beneath my feet? Underground streams? Hidden fires, hidden lives? Many old stories, legends, must have sprung from this land. Mexicans, Native Americans, European missionaries. The ghosts of the dead, passing from one world to the next.

Come home.

Our home is death.

Is death our home? Mother, Father, Susan.

For a moment, I'm dizzy at the edge of the stage. A hawk circles overhead, its gyre a steadying pattern. My eyes focus.

A grainy scraping below me, in a little ravine. A rain of pebbles. I turn. Huffing up a weedy incline, a young woman hikes, carrying a baby. She's wearing black cotton pants, cut midcalf, a dark blouse. Purple yarn ties her long black hair. Skin the color of wet clay. She's wrapped the baby in a brown cotton blanket. The baby squirms. The woman stops when she spots me.

I start to say something—I'm not sure what—but she shakes her head. Her eyes dart. "Town," I tell her. "If you're looking for town—something to eat?" I point. My movement makes her flinch.

Men's voices. Nearby. The barking of dogs. Metallic clinking—belts, keys? The voices rise and fall, coming closer. The woman whimpers.

I don't think. I open the trap door in the floor of the stage. "Hurry," I say. It's too obvious, the first place they'll look if they see it. I crawl in after the woman, pull the door shut, and sit beside her in the dark. I should have stayed outside, talked to, distracted the men. What am I doing?

Too late now.

An odor of loam and sweat. The baby gurgles, a low moan. I urge the woman to silence her child. From underneath the blanket she pulls a mesh bag. Inside it, a plastic bottle, a little book filled with pictures of angels. The woman turns the pages of the book and the baby settles, watching.

Boots. Crunching gravel. Men laugh casually, some moving past us. Maybe they're not pursuing this lady. Maybe they haven't spotted her. Routine patrol? The baby makes a guttural sound. Above us, on the stage, a radio crackles. "North perimeter," someone says. "A whole damn family." The men march away—or so it sounds. Is it the woman's family they're after? Has she been separated from her lover, father, mother? What terrible thing has erupted in the center of her life? Where will her pilgrimage lead?

In light through small cracks in the wooden floor above us, I see her face now that my vision has adjusted to the dark. She's very young. A teenager. She starts to stand. "No," I whisper. "Wait a while longer. To be safe." I can tell she doesn't understand me, but she grasps my gestures. She sits back down and rocks her baby in her arms. "My name is Adam," I say, placing my hand on my chest. "You?" I point at her.

"Maria," she says.

"And *la niña?*"

"Anna."

I laugh. She looks at me, puzzled. "Maria," I say. "I think you got lucky this time. But I don't know if I've done you a favor. Did I?"

She stares at me.

More movement outside. Maybe just the wind, but for a long time—I begin to lose track—we wait. Marty will wonder what's happened to me.

Finally, Maria stirs and I know I can't stop her. I nod, put my fingers to my lips. Slowly, I open the trap door. The sun has set. Night air touches our skin. I breathe deeply. The world. Here we are in the world. Maria scrambles up, pauses, looks down at me, smiles. Then I hear her run through the weeds. The baby cries. Or laughs. I can't tell. They're bound to be caught soon. Forgive me. But then I think: I took care of this woman. Briefly. Unwisely, perhaps. Badly. But: I am capable of taking care of someone. Maybe even my brother, no matter what Marty feels about me. No matter what Susan thinks is best for the two of us. No matter what Anna believes about the fraying limits of my powers.

Does it matter that my parents are ghosts? *Forgive me. An American Revolution. I didn't stop it. If I could have, I would have...*

God knows my brother needs care. Susan could use me. With the crackpots, I always held something back—my tithing to grief? *Taking care of someone.* Giving willingly, not surrendering to need. A pair of eagles passes overhead. I don't feel burdened or sad.

I emerge from the hole. A disorienting mesh of odors and sounds. A bright flash. The Marfa Lights? The deep unknown? Dirt. Sage. Leaves. Come home? Above me, pulsing steadily, the stars.

III

◊◊◊

Basement and Roof

McGee's, next to Bern's building, sold many strange and wonderful things: high-end kitchen implements, ladies' perfumes, pets. Bern wasn't sure what this combination said about his West Side neighborhood. One day, he popped into the shop for an extension cord. He meandered up the aisles past Spanish combs and plastic flowers, old water pumps, shower nozzles, hat stands, paintings of bullfights on velvet, and bins of used yarmulkes. The narrow pathways smelled of foot powder and sweetened toilet water until he reached the animals. In a back corner, an oppressive odor of fur and pine-scented air freshener hung like invisible webbing. In a cage, four black terriers wrestled one another among shreds of the *New York Times*. Kittens slept nearby in a tall-sided box, unperturbed by the canary calls showering down on them. Bern noticed a saleswoman, a dark-haired beauty wearing a plastic nametag: "Marietta." He smelled the mint flavoring of the gum in her mouth. Behind her, frantic scrabbling. In a large cage, a big brown bird with gold talons and chest feathers the color of wheat rattled the enclosing wire with stringy wings and his beak. A sign on the cage said "Macaw."

"Your sign is wrong," Bern told Marietta. "I grew up in Texas and I used to see these birds. This is a roadrunner."

"Nuh-uh," said the woman. "Imported from Brazil. A rarity."

"I'm telling you," Bern said. After its flurry, the bird drooped, perfectly still. "And it looks sick."

"He's fine." She shuffled a stack of receipt books on a counter littered with newspaper ad supplements.

Bern peered between the wires, into the bird's dark eye. The pupil glistened. Your time is short, Bern thought.

He bent closer to the cage, hands on knees. Fifty years old. Something is trying to talk to you.

No. Not the bird. The angina he'd felt again last week; the stress test he'd taken, which turned up nothing; the impatient young doctor who implied that Bern had wasted his time despite bypass surgery eight years ago. "Just monitor yourself," the young man said, dismissing him. "Pay attention, and let me know if you feel any changes."

Not the bird. But the creature stirred Bern. Its feathers resembled grass clippings, yellow and thin. All flesh is grass, Bern thought. Hang in there, old fellow.

For some reason, on Friday morning, the 4, 5, and 6 trains weren't running below Eighty-sixth Street. Bern hiked. Finally, with a speeding heart, he caught the M2. He stuck his MetroCard backward into the pay slot—he wasn't used to riding the bus—and pissed off the driver. It takes an enormous capacity for shame just to get across town, he reflected. I am blessed with such a capacity.

On East Fifty-fourth Street, near the river, a small fruit stand was temporarily abandoned. Perhaps the seller had taken a bathroom break. Bern watched an old woman pass the stand, place her hand on a bunch of grapes as though to snatch it, and apparently change her mind. In the end, her gesture appeared to be a sacrament instead of a near-theft.

In the middle of the block, he found the brownstone whose basement Landau, his boss at the architectural firm, wanted him to renovate. The building was faintly Tudor, with cream-colored window trim. One of Bern's new young co-workers had told him a pair of television stars lived in the place. He named them, but Bern didn't know who they were. Before leaving the office this morning, he'd encountered Landau in the coffee room. Landau warned Bern to "get the lay of the land quickly. The only way we can turn a profit on this one is if you don't spend too much time on it. Don't screw it up, okay?"

"Jerry, when have I screwed things up lately?" Bern asked.

Landau stood nose to nose with him. "I used to be able to count on you, Wally, to work quietly, unobtrusively."

"And you still can."

"You've been a pain in the ass with these new hires, especially with this kid, Murphy. You could try to be more welcoming."

Bern said nothing.

"I know, I know," said Landau. "*He's* a pain in the ass, too. They all are. But what do we do? These kids are going to take this firm into the future. You'd better get used to it, Wally."

So he'd been banished to a basement.

Inside the assigned building, the cherry wood moldings nicely complemented the dark yellow walls and floor tiles, pink with pigeon-gray borders. In the lobby, a plum-colored carpet led to the doorman's desk, lighted from above by a tiny chandelier shaped like an old gas lamp. The doorman, wearing black pants and a white shirt, no tie, was a friendly young fellow named Brian. His head was shaved like an NBA player's and he wore thick red glasses. He called across the room to another young man in black pants, standing by a marble-topped table near a row of mail slots, and asked him to take the front for a while. He was going to show Bern the basement.

The bowels of the building smelled of laundry detergent, bleach, Lemon Pledge, and oil paint, with a trace of old taffy and roach powder. The space's dimensions were hard to determine. The dim yellow ceiling lights, tucked among heating pipes, were not much help, and the clutter was befuddling: decades' worth of discarded furniture, appliances, radiator shells, and sports trophies. Propped against the wall beside the elevator were two framed movie posters, presumably removed from apartments when the tenants decamped or died years ago: *The Woman on the Beach*, starring Joan Bennett—"Go ahead, say it, I'm bad!"—and *Call Me Madam*, with Ethel Merman.

Brian kept up a constant patter, following Bern as he moved

among rows of musty boxes, toeing piles of paper, stacks of letters, mismatched shoes. "Must be interesting to be an architect in this city," he said. "Though I bet you wish you were in on the World Trade Center sweepstakes, eh? Some folks are going to make scads off whatever goes on downtown. Best thing that ever happened to them."

"No," Bern said. "I'm content to stay small. Sketch my little huts and things."

Brian laughed. The sound echoed in dark corners crammed with fishing poles and cobwebbed skis. Several pairs of children's socks lay in a sea of green and white powder on the floor in front of a busted dryer. On top of the machine, a tower of phone books radiated mildew. "Look at that," Brian said. "No one uses those anymore." He pulled a cell phone from his pants pocket and held it high. "I haven't given a thought to telephone books in five years."

"So the owner... he wants to expand the laundry room, is that right? Over here?"

"That's the plan."

"Shouldn't be a problem." Bern stepped behind a rusty oil container. Several poorly conceived abstract paintings, heavy on browns and midnight blues, leaned against the wall behind the old metal drum. As he maneuvered around a three-legged coffee table, he heard a kitten whine.

Brian smiled. "We feed them," he said, watching Bern's face. "Keep the rats under control. Though now *their* numbers are getting out of hand. Need a cat?"

"Don't think so," Bern said, remembering the melancholy creatures in McGee's.

Brian slid his glasses to the tip of his nose and gazed over the bright red frame at Bern. "Funny. You *look* to me like a cat-daddy."

"What does that mean?"

"I don't know," Brian said. "Like you could use... *something*."

2.

He ran his hand across his chest, breathed deeply, shedding the basement. The river's waves were as thick as hair gel. Squinting at the southern tip of Roosevelt Island, he glimpsed through the trees a corner of the Gothic madhouse, designed by the same architect who'd conceived St. Patrick's. Angels and the damned. Well, any city worthy of the name was built on the shoulders, horns, and wings of a vast population.

Cigarette butts bobbed on the surface of the green and black water.

Bern remembered the rest home in east Houston where his grandfather had lived out his days, in a shadowy room at the end of a long hall swollen with the maddened moans of men and women. In his room, his grandfather kept only a tattered copy of the Five Books of Moses, a family photograph, and a blue glass swan smaller than a fist. Where had it come from? It was an unlikely keepsake for this rough and tumble giant, a yellow-pine salesman on the back roads between Longview, Lufkin, Nacogdoches. A remembrance of Bern's grandmother, long dead? Or of some other woman? A family heirloom? The swan's eyes and the point of its beak had worn away from too much touching. It appeared to be hollow inside, a container for yesteryear's chills. Slowly, over time, Bern's grandfather, too, had lost the sharpness of his features. Now, in the rich loam of a field north of Houston, more and more encroached upon by condominiums and gated communities, the old man's definition was further abraded by earth-acid, the lime and spoors of the land he had loved and worked. That a glass creature, for all its fragility, could prove more enduring than this man's enormous and immovable body (or so it had seemed to Bern as a boy when, in games, he rushed against his grandfather's legs) was as imponderable to Bern as the composition of an interstellar cloud.

The East River burbled, thick and mucoid. He turned a corner. In the street there appeared to be a huge chocolate milk spill. Three coatless businessmen conferred by an ash can. "Two percent of two billion is a big number," said one. In the window of a little market, a rack of the day's papers: the *Irish Voice, France-Amerique,* the *Guardian, Amsterdam News* ("New Black Faces"), *India Abroad, Jewish Week* ("The Difference between Non-Jewish and Un-Jewish").

Appropriately, he saw at a bend in the river the Secretariat's mirrored green façade. Ordinary and bland. Bern hated to admit it, but across the street, Trump's World Tower filled him with more global optimism than the United Nations. Taste or no taste, at least Trump tried to proclaim *something*—even if it was only the arrogance of wealth.

Bern ate in a steamy sushi place whose antiquated sound system played Warren Zevon: forceful anthems of self-destruction, bitterness, divorce. As he listened, he thought about his ex-wife, to whom he hadn't spoken in over a decade, as well as recent flings with women (one of whom he'd met through a dreary personals ad). In the end, either Bern or the women worked too much, felt exhausted on weekends, and called things off. There just wasn't much interest, all around. Is this what happened to people when they reached a certain age? Or was it him?

He wondered if he had given up on sex and love. Briefly, he imagined the thin, dark face of the saleswoman he'd encountered days ago—Marietta. He chewed his edamame. Was he disappointed in himself? Not the prize-winning professional he'd thought he'd become? The saint in his personal life? What would late life hold in the absence of women, their laughter and often embarrassing questions? He shoved his plate away. His wasabe had no *zing*. When Zevon sang "Reconsider Me," Bern thought him malevolent and untrustworthy.

After lunch, he spent another three and a half hours studying specs in the basement, trying not to brood on his solitude. The stuff here reminded him of a taxidermist's shop he'd seen on vacation with Marla, his ex, in Paris's Seventh Arrondissement (their last trip together). One afternoon, in a Beaux Arts building smelling like rich red wine, Bern had discovered row after row of dark wooden cabinets housing butterflies (aqua and gold), horned beetles (so black they were purple), peacock feathers, yellow birds no bigger than sewing spools. Fossils. Fish skeletons. In the back, in a vast space arrayed like a furniture showroom, stuffed zebras, ostriches, tigers, and giraffes. A swan stood in a corner, its tail feathers singed the light brown of caramelized sugar. The shop's owner explained to Bern and Marla that the bird had been rescued from another taxidermist who had lost most of his inventory in an accidental blaze. At the time, Bern hadn't flashed on his grandfather's swan, but since he had been thinking about it this afternoon, he wondered at the connection his mind must have made that day among the stilled animals—for, leaving the shop, he had been crazed with the need to rush back to the hotel with Marla and make love for the rest of the day: a stay against wearing-away, he figured now, though at the time it felt like a response to the thrill of unapproachable creatures brought near.

On his way home that evening, he peered through McGee's front window. The store was closed and dark. He couldn't see the pets. He pictured the roadrunner crimped in its cage, dying, perhaps, from the mixture of perfume and artificial fresheners in the air, still experiencing in its olfactory memory (did birds possess such an attribute?) dust from the back roads of Texas, bluebonnet blossoms, fresh peaches on sun-baked trees.

In his apartment, he poured a glass of wine, disappointed to find no messages on his phone. Not that he'd expected to hear from anyone. He thought of the boxes in his closet. The basement had reminded him of family cast-offs he hadn't combed through in years. He rose from his couch, picked a box, and untaped the lid. Dusty wool. Mildewed paper. Right away, he found what he'd hoped to discover—the item nagging at him, just below consciousness, most of the day.

He would need to get a turntable. He hadn't owned one since '95, '96.

On his lap he held the record album. His grandfather had given him this recording one birthday, when Bern was just a boy: *The Sounds of Texas*, an oddball assortment of noises and effects. A strange and ridiculous gift, Bern always thought. Now, tonight, far from home, from childhood, it made more sense to him: "Track # 1: 'The Yellow Rose of Texas,' Performed by the Kilgore High School Marching Band," "Track # 2: Railroad Cars Uncoupling," "Track # 6: Sawmill Blade," "Track # 8: Prairie Dogs Digging," and "Track # 12: Road Runner."

In Houston, his family had lived near the lip of a bayou. Roadrunners roamed wild down there, among muddy, twisted oaks. Every night, Bern went to sleep to their sounds, which he couldn't quite remember. A whistle, a call? His parents were gone now, along with his grandfather. He sat back, remembering them, closing his eyes and rubbing his chest.

3.

"Wally, how come you haven't built anything?" Monday morning at work. Young Murphy blocking Bern's doorway. At his desk, Bern hunched over sketches of the building on East Fifty-fourth, pencils strewn like pickup sticks. "What do you mean?" he asked, irritated. He had been trying to grasp the *essence* of *basement*.

"Well, at Landau's suggestion, I've gone through the company files," Murphy said. "Getting up to speed on the institutional history. I didn't mean to snoop or anything, but I notice you tend to take the renovations you're assigned—and the designs are usually wonderful, by the way—but then you hand the initial plans off to others, who finish the projects and take most of the credit. Why is that?"

"It's the way things are done," Bern said.

"No. I mean, that doesn't appear to be the pattern with others. Landau isn't pressuring you, is he?" Murphy said. "I mean, he doesn't force you to surrender your—"

"No, no."

"Then why don't you build?"

I like things that already exist better than things that do not. Who said that? "Naturally, the permits—"

"You know what I'm talking about, Wally. And—forgive me—I saw some of your speculative work. The plans were tucked into the files," Murphy said. "Really innovative. Your ideas for that old factory uptown? The curtain wall? Very nice."

Bern remembered those sketches. Many years ago now. An abandoned aluminum-sided cube beneath a railroad bridge on 125th Street. A meat wholesalers' district. Men smoking on uneven sidewalks, wrapped in smocks as bright as marbled fat. A smell of blood in the air, pressurized steam from coiled hoses, river rawness—bracken and bones in the tidewater. Everywhere, a sting of meat-dust, stirred by passing traffic. In the late afternoons, the bridge cast structural shadows on the west side of the building and on the reflective sides of delivery trucks, a crisscross pattern suggestive of propeller blades, which Bern had used, along with the corrugations in the preexisting aluminum, as the basis for an airy design.

"Why didn't that project go forward?" Murphy asked. "If I were Landau, I would have championed it."

Bern shrugged.

"When's the last time you brought something to fruition?"

Another shrug.

"You're far too modest, Wally."

" 'The builder is trapped between error and obsolescence.' Someone said that once."

Murphy laughed. "Listen, can I take you to lunch? I'd like to pick your brain, hear more about your experiences here over the years."

"I have this basement." Bern tapped his desk.

"Don't worry, Wally. I don't expect you to be my buddy."

The kid was trying. Give him that. "Maybe another time."

"Okay, Wally. Suit yourself. I admire your work. Really. You should *build*."

Maybe Landau was right. Perhaps Bern shouldn't push back so hard at his new co-workers. Still, he didn't entirely trust this preening Mr. Murphy. Too much ambition. Did Bern even *remember* ambition? It could make a man ruthless.

On his way to the washroom, he ran into a colleague, Chris Henderson, in the hallway. They'd been hired at the same time: the Dark Ages, before Murphy's first diaper. The poor bastard looked quartered and beaten. "How are things, Chris?" Bern asked. Henderson had just finished chemo.

The man picked at his lip. "Wally, I've been meaning to ask. Do you suppose on Thursday, you could swing a couple of hours to go with me to the hospital? They're going to run some bone marrow checks and I'll probably be a little woozy afterward. My wife's out of town, my other arrangements have fallen through, and I might need assistance on the subway, getting home."

Bern owed Henderson for help, recently, pricing a brownstone renovation. "No problem, Chris. I'll clear my desk," he said.

"Thanks, Wally. Thanks a lot." He turned away, pinched by internal shadows.

Bern dearly hoped the bathroom would be empty: a moment's solace. These days, the briefest encounters rattled him. Murphy. Henderson. But a tall, bald man in blue overalls stood at one of the urinals, legs apart, pissing like a thoroughbred. From the back, Bern recognized him as one of the regular maintenance men. He didn't remember the fellow's name. He had once given Bern a tour of the attic when Bern bumped into him after-hours one Friday and expressed interest in the man's extensive knowledge of the building. At his feet now sat a sweat-darkened leather tool bag. The man nodded hello. "Keeping busy?" Bern asked, unzipping at the end of the row.

"Oh, you betcha. When are you geniuses going to come up with a place takes care of itself, so I can prop my feet up on a big desk and kick back the way you do?"

Bern laughed.

"Like today. Fucking birds."

"What's that?" Bern said.

"Oh, migration season for some species or another. I don't know. This morning, I get a call—the lights on the roof are disrupting their damn flight patterns at night. Disorienting them. Something about the angle of our particular building. I gotta go up and disconnect."

"How do you get up there?" Bern asked.

"Ah, yeah. That's right." He grinned. "You're the fellow likes to know the ins and outs." And *he* liked to be the Big Shot. He picked up his bag. "Come on. I'll show you."

Bern finished his business, washed his hands, and followed the man—Simpson, he remembered now—to a freight elevator, out of sight of the normal business corridors. The elevator smelled of fiercely polished iron platings, not to mention the earthy sweat in the creases of Simpson's leather bag. The door opened onto a narrow concrete room where another door, with a wire-reinforced double-glass window in it, led to the building's roof. Twelve stories up, in a mild breeze with a scent of snow, though the day was sunny and dusky blue, Bern (his heart cantering!) surveyed the foliage, patterned grids, and movements below. From this perspective, everything looked orderly and random all at once—a healthy sign, Bern thought, for surely a city dies when it strays too far from its pathways or deals strictly in necessities. He stepped forward, stood steady. He was glad he had bought, last week, a firm new pair of shoes.

A pale full moon, the color of chardonnay, bobbed in an orange dust cloud in the vicinity of Battery Park. Already, pier lights sparkled on the water. Greenhouses, jails, administrative centers. Church spires rose among circles of stone.

Simpson pulled from his bag a paint-crusted screwdriver and fiddled with spotlights the size of snare drums. The lights were disported every few feet around the inner edges of the rooftop. Opaque plastic plates, red, green, and white, filled the fixture's barrels. Simpson mumbled and cursed. Bern searched the sky but saw no birds. He thought of the roadrunner wilting in the back of McGee's.

To the north, the Cloisters, the delicate medieval buildings, the very top of Manhattan, a place Bern hadn't visited in years.

He leaned over the south-side parapet. All around him, windows like picture slides—each slide a life superimposed on many other lives. The old medieval argument: is the world as perfect as it can be? Could the Lord improve it if He wanted to? God could grant trees the power to think and talk. But would they still be trees? This would not be perfecting the world, but rather, producing another world entirely. A splendid idea—but, Bern thought, gazing at dashing scraps of color below, surely we would miss this sad old place.

"All right. Now the damn birds can see where they're going," Simpson said, rising. His joints creaked. Loose tools jingled in his bag.

"Thanks for bringing me," Bern said.

Simpson glanced at the streets. "Don't seem so awful up here, eh?"

"Sweet, really."

"Well, now, I wouldn't go that far," Simpson answered, shouldering his bag. "Hell, I just improved your odds of getting smothered in bird shit on your way home."

4.

The mild weather broke. Snow blurred the gold domes and display windows of the neat, well-mannered shops along Madison Square Park. It clung to the black trees and grayed the air where cheerful men swept sidewalks and shook the park's shrubbery free of ice; burlap wrapping made snug the delicate plants beside the benches. Soft office lights in the upper-story windows of pale-blue buildings turned violet in the twilight. Everywhere, bells seemed to ring: the chiming and crackling of frost. Smoke and chestnut-flavored breezes greeted walkers rounding chilly corners. A woman with a big white dog appeared to be strolling in the company of a polar bear. At the edge of the park, a man wearing a fig-colored coat, with his fine shoes mired in slush, stood waving at a woman in a curved window halfway up the Flatiron. The light behind her head was the purple of plums.

The quick cold, and the giddy shock of the snowfall, reminded Bern of his very first trip to the city, alone, for his job interview, over twenty years ago now. Early February. Marla still had her job in Houston. The firm had put him up in a small room at the Gramercy Park Hotel, then a dim, if venerable, corridor of steady drafts and clanking pipes. Wall-to-wall carpeting in the lobby. Swedish meat-balls were served in the bar, and you could smell them outside as you struggled with your umbrella (bought on the street, on the fly, unprepared as you were, a naïve Texan believing the newspapers' promises of mild days ahead). Inside the bar (dark wooden beams curved like canoes, musty red drapes), the ghost of S. J. Perelman seemed to drift in a corner, next to a shelf of amber whiskeys, but this was just the breath of the patrons, visible in the chilly, convivial space. Bern's room was freezing: a broken radiator and a cracked window bandaged by duct tape. At midnight, he huddled beneath his bedspread, figured food might warm him. He sprang for room service: a simple order of toast. Forty minutes later, a shivering boy tapped his door. As it turned out, the hotel's room service came from a restaurant two blocks away. Through the snow, this kid had tramped in the middle of the night to hand Bern two slices of bread wrapped in a sopping napkin.

A sweet, pathetic welcome to New York. Bern had chewed his rubbery toast and stared out the window at the ice crystals pelleting the small park below, yellow in circular lamp-glow. For Bern, the hotel would always be drifted in snow. These days, its gaudy reincarnation—the bronze and salmon décor, the Aubusson rug stretched across the lobby floor—had vanquished the place's gentle spirit. He felt himself swoon as he envisioned, again, flakes falling against the smeary glass panes of his dreadful, yet charming, old room.

In this nostalgic mood, he stopped as he was strolling after work one day at a shop in the Village called Left Bank Books. He had glimpsed in its window a blue and gold volume the size of an old-fashioned men's smoking case: *The Latin Works of Dante*, translated into English and published in 1904 by a modest London firm. Rare, but not too rare. The bookshop owner offered it to Bern for fifty dollars. Bern had no pressing interest in reading these minor pieces, but he recalled buying Marla the *Vita Nuova* shortly after she'd joined him in New York, a gift for her thirtieth birthday, and, seduced by the snow into sentimental recollections of his own new life in Manhattan—heady youth!—he gripped the book as though it were a swatch of his personal history. Besides, the volume was lovely, with an inset tissue covering the title page and stamped reproductions of details from the Lateran Mosaic: Peter and Constantine receiving their authority from Christ. The shop was a precarious maze of book towers about to topple. Bern spent an enjoyable twenty minutes chatting about reading with the owner, a spry, bearded former college professor who had given up tenure at a southern university to buy the store and indulge his lifelong passion for book collecting. The move had been a terrifying financial gamble, and he admitted he was struggling: he sold most of his books to fashion models who dropped in with photo crews to use the space as a quaint backdrop and who felt guilty enough to purchase something in return. But clearly, the man loved what he was doing, and Bern left the store abuzz with contentment.

Warmed, he settled on the couch in his apartment next to *The Sounds of Texas*, propped against a lamp on his table. He opened *The Latin Works of Dante*. Most of the pages remained uncut. For more than a hundred years, this book had gone unread! Bern retrieved a small knife from his kitchen and ran it gingerly along the seams, freeing the poet's words from their seals. In the back of the volume was Dante's treatise on land and water. What is the planet's noblest element? Dante asked. Where can it be found? The bottom or top of the globe? What *deserves* to be closest to Heaven?

Basement or roof, Bern thought. Where is our proper place?

A faint onion smell clung to the knife's edge, and now to the sides of the pages.

That evening, Bern popped into McGee's, just before the manager locked the doors. Marietta was not around. He approached the roadrunner's cage. The bird slumped beside its red water bowl, barely breathing. Its feathers were dusky and hunched. The air smelled of fake pine. Bern whistled softly. How did roadrunners speak? He should know this. All he could conjure was the *beep beep* of the cartoon creature. He whistled again. In cages swinging from the ceiling, canaries exploded into sound, but the roadrunner stayed as it was, eyes shut.

5.

The waiting room in the lab at St. Vincent's overflowed with teenagers and children sitting with their mothers. Two or three old men with splotchy red faces.

Henderson had trouble fishing his Blue Cross card out of his wallet. Bern gave him a hand. "It's very kind of you to come with me, Wally," Henderson said.

"Happy to help."

"My wife scheduled a trip to visit her mother in Connecticut, knowing I had more tests coming up. Poor thing. It's worn her down, caring for me. You appear to be doing well. How's the heart?"

"Who knows?" Bern smiled. "Seems to be working." Soon after Henderson started chemotherapy, Bern admitted to him he'd had a bypass. The fraternity of the middle-aged. Now, he was wary of walking the Trail of Suffering—glorying in one's infirmities in order to feel special. But this was unfair to his friend, who was genuinely nervous, and had reason to be. Besides, illnesses *were* isolating. Look around.

"I hear they're tearing this place down," Henderson said. "St. Vincent's, I mean."

"Preservationists are fighting the plans," Bern told him.

"Maybe that'll stall them for a while. I've lived in this city thirty-eight years. I know. When people want to build something, they build. Well. I suppose it benefits you and me, eh? Got to keep things moving, or the whole shebang clogs up."

"We are not who we were," Bern said.

"No."

A nurse called Henderson's name. Bern identified himself to her, said he'd be walking Henderson home. She informed Bern his friend would be responsive after the procedure, but he wouldn't be steady on his feet, and later, because of the sedation, he probably wouldn't remember this afternoon.

Bern sat back down in the waiting room. A copy of *Theatre News* lay on the table next to him. He leafed through it, looking for the byline of one of the women he'd met, and stopped seeing, several months ago. He didn't find her name. He thought again of Marietta. The smell of her gum.

An hour and a half later, the nurse emerged from the lab arm in arm with Henderson. His skin was the color of bread dough. She told Bern to remind him, later, his test results would be ready next week. She handed him off.

"Pizza," Henderson slurred. "I'd like a slice. I'm starving."

Gripping his arm, careful to avoid the spot where the IV needle had pierced his skin, Bern guided him a couple of snowy blocks to a nearly deserted pizzeria. A teenaged boy, whose clothes reeked of pot, tended the wood-fired oven. He stared at the flames and cackled to himself. An elderly couple sat at a corner table glaring suspiciously at the twists of green pepper strewn across their deep-dish pizza. The woman appeared to be drinking a pitcher of beer all by herself. Her head lolled. A second empty pitcher sat beside her. Her companion, a bald, toothless man with a moldlike mustache, did not seem to know where he was. Henderson stared off into space. Bern realized, with more dismay than he would have imagined, he was the only *functioning awareness* in the place. Perhaps that was overstating things, but he was struck with loneliness, akin to the feeling he'd had as a kid (nine? ten?)—a memory still vivid to him—when one day he'd stared at his family's house and wondered how others saw it? Did they see the same details he did? The off-white paint on the eaves? The slant of the roof? The exact same number of windows? Did they hear the birds in the bayou?

Later, at Henderson's apartment, he helped Henderson strip down to skivvies and a T-shirt. Then he tucked him into bed. He brought him a glass of water. "Thanks, Wally. I owe you," Henderson mumbled, and drifted off to sleep. Bern left the key on the kitchen counter, next to a slip of paper with his home phone number on it. As he let himself out, he glanced at framed family photographs on bookshelves next to the door. Elderly men and women, children, teens. Foreign cafés. Graduation gowns, wedding dresses. Beyond work, Bern knew little of Henderson's life. The photos opened angles onto worlds that Bern, through his association with Henderson, nearly touched, but didn't, and never would. He buttoned his coat and shut the door behind him.

God plans and man laughs. Bern recalled this Talmudic teaching from the Hebrew lessons his grandfather made him take as a child. Or was it *Man plans and God laughs?* He couldn't remember now.

He was standing in Henderson's office doorway. It was midmorning. Henderson sat behind a large oak desk, gripping a pencil, staring at the ivory-colored carpet on his floor. "Chris? How you feeling?" Bern asked.

"Oh," Henderson said, hands trembling. His hair was parted sloppily in the middle. Bern had never seen it combed that way. "Oh."

"You doing okay?"

"Thanks, yes. I'm always woozy for a while after they've had their mitts on me. Wally?"

"Yes?"

"Look at this." He wagged a finger. A gold wedding band slid around the base of the digit. "A week ago, it fit me," Henderson said. "Maybe it's just as well. I think my wife's had enough of sickness." His face looked green. His shoulders drooped.

Bern wasn't sure what to do. "Chris, you need a little break or something?"

Henderson didn't move.

"Yes, let's get some air," Bern said. He set his coffee cup on the desk then led Henderson to the freight elevator—"I didn't know this was here!" Henderson said—and onto the roof. The man's cheeks reddened. He laughed, delighted, at the dizzying heights. "Ah well," he said softly, gazing out over the city. "There it is. Where I misspent my youth." He scanned the rooftops. "Were you ever in the service, Wally?"

Bern shook his head in the wind.

"Neither was I. I used to think I was lucky. The draft ended right before my number was called. But you know what I've thought lately?" He approached the building's north edge, next to one of the spotlights Simpson had disabled. For an instant, Bern worried about the roof's resilience. "My father—dead all these years. A World War Two vet. Normandy. He used to tell me he couldn't talk about what he saw over there. But when he got into his seventies and eighties and suffered all sorts of ailments—heart, lungs, joints—he began to admit he'd never felt more alive than he did during the war, the exhilaration of the danger. Though he loved his family, and all of us children and grandchildren, his life since then had been one long anticlimax." Henderson twisted his ring. "A common experience, I suppose. Now, that generation is gone, and no one gives a shit about the Second World War. Soon, Wally, our generation will be gone, too."

"Not all that soon, I hope."

"Soon enough. You know? I'm tired, man. I don't ever want to feel nausea again. But I will."

"I hear you," Bern said.

Henderson surveyed the streets. "The only reason I go out anymore is to prove to myself I can. I don't remember the last time I really enjoyed a restaurant or a movie or a play. I worry about the day I'll go into a hospital and won't be able to make it out again on my own. I worry about my kids. Not a single one of them has a head for money. How are they going to get along without me?"

"You can't think about that, Chris."

"I can't *not* think about it. I worry about just marking time. About the fact that I've probably lived longer than I should have. I worry about the cure being worse than the illness. Wally?"

"Yes, Chris?"

"It's fucking cold up here, you know that?"

"It is."

They stood together, shaking, not talking. The rooftops reminded Bern of a half-waking dream he'd had in the hospital, after his heart surgery: a dream of flight over vast western canyons, gorges, rivers. Someone had left a Carlos Nakai CD in his room (the previous occupant? Had he or she recovered or died?). The nurses played it for Bern on his bedside player: soft Native American flute music, soaring notes, the breath of high but gentle winds. His imagination followed the music up, up and as he lay in bed he willed himself over grassy plains and rapid water, gaps in the ground washed orange with sunset, shadows on the rocks cascading like colors freed of their substances, floating off into space. Purple. Black. Forest green. He glanced at Henderson. If he could clutch the man, leap with him into the air, carry him into the timeless safety of that pleasing old dream . . .

"I'm freezing my ass off, Wally."

But no. This was a heavy time for them both.

He had to buy a turntable. He ought to get that poor sick creature out of McGee's.

"I'm sorry. I'll take you back inside now," Bern said to his friend.

For a long time that night, after setting up the turntable (he'd found it for sale buried in old clothing on a back shelf in McGee's) and listening to the "co-co-cooing" of the roadrunner on the record—a more grating sound than he had recalled—Bern couldn't sleep.

When he did, he dreamed of Marla. She told him she had found a new house for them. "You and me," she said, touching his arm. He wanted to tell her they couldn't do this, but to say so would destroy her. She'd burst into flames in front of him. The dream shifted, then, to the house—a shack at the top of a long flight of loose wooden stairs overlooking a Houston bayou. Bern climbed the steps. When he opened the door and moved inside, he began to tumble through space, his arms whipped by kudzu. "Goodbye," he said: a farewell, he knew, to all the women in his life. Then he was no longer part of the dream. He saw Marla, naked, curled on a gray mattress, weeping.

6.

Saturday. *Good Shabbos.* When had Bern last uttered those words? Last night, *The Sounds of Texas* had reminded him powerfully of his grandfather, the old man's insistence that Bern take seriously his Hebrew lessons and his mitzvoth to others.

Midafternoon. A glorious return to mild weather. With Texas tolling in his head, Bern stepped into McGee's. In the pet section, Marietta was yelling at a bald man in a sagging white suit. Some poor schmuck who had asked an innocent question, Bern thought. But no. Apparently, this man was her boss. "Even the ferrets are croaking!" Marietta shouted.

"That's not your concern," the man said. "We have people looking after that. Your concern is moving product."

"No. I quit. You hear me? Enough. The animals can't flip you off—see, look at their little paws, they're just dying to give you the finger—but I won't take this shitty treatment."

The man was ready to slap her. Bern stepped forward. "I'd like to buy this bird, please." In fact, he had no idea what he was doing.

"Which one?" the man grunted. "The macaw?"

"The roadrunner."

"Imported from Brazil. It's a—"

"Coo," Bern said. He approached the dusty cage. "Co-co-cooo."

The bird lifted its head and flicked its long black tail. Its front toes wiggled, along with the four large toes (two on each foot) in back. Marietta laughed. "Our sign is wrong," she told her boss. "I'll ring this fellow up. Then I'm out of here." The boss walked away, windmilling his arms.

"So," Marietta said to Bern. "Finally. A man of action."

"Cage come with?"

"You're not going to keep him in it, are you?"

"I'm not sure what I'm going to do. Do you want to come with me?" It wasn't the bird. Maybe his heart—his heart was doing the talking.

"What do you mean? A *Free Willy* sort of thing?" She laughed at him. "Jesus. You're serious?" For an instant, she seemed to consider his offer. "You're a nut, you know that?" Then she held out her hand and took the bills he proffered.

"Thank you," he said.

"No, thank *you*. Truthfully, I was beginning to worry about him."

"Good luck."

"Oh—young girl, unemployed in New York? What can go wrong?" She gave him the nicest smile.

Out on Twenty-third Street, Bern hailed a cab, hiding the cage behind his legs. The bird was maybe two feet tall.

"Whaddya got there? Is that an animal?" said the cabbie.

"A bird in a cage. Perfectly safe," Bern said. "Just a few blocks, and then I'll be out of your hair."

"Goddamn right!"

The roadrunner bit the cage's bars. Behind each eye was a patch of blue skin. Bern admired the white crescents tucked among the round brown feathers of its wings.

"So where we going?" the cabbie asked.

Where indeed? Bern cooed to the bird.

The approach to Brooklyn Bridge always confused him: a maze of chain-link fences blocking pedestrian paths from winding streets and the sprawling, trash-strewn parking lots of nearby government compounds. He made his way past weedy patches of grass (garbage bags, abandoned tires) and stone façades. A dumping ground at the base of a national monument. Well, welcome to New York, Bern thought. A smell of wood and earth.

He found a staircase with iron banisters and climbed past half-moon windows in the bridge's brick face. A toilet bowl lay overturned in the grass beneath him. Long ago, the bridge's underside used to house printing shops, grocers' supply stores, and ship chandleries. A buzzing hive. When he crested the stairs, the sky snatched his breath, vaulting behind tense, harplike cables. He set the cage on the ground. In the distance, in blue-gray haze, the raised arm of Miss Liberty. A warning, a wave. The outline of Ellis Island: a piled-up old overcoat. On the other side of the bridge, behind the former New York Post building, patterned enclaves of public housing, old TB infernos that Robert Moses had hoped to eradicate ("When you operate in an overbuilt environment, you have to hack your way with a meat ax," he said). Knickerbocker Village, where Julius and Ethel Rosenberg kept family secrets and lived in mortal terror. Bern lifted the cage again. The bird was silent and still. He wove among mothers with children, among laughing and crying young lovers. Prisons. Bern had forgotten how much of Lower Manhattan was marked for detention. Public plazas, federal buildings, the dead zone around City Hall. It was always a relief to walk up Centre Street, past the official buildings and into the clamor of Chinatown and Little Italy (on such a walk, the Twin Towers' absence, he realized, would be a constant, quiet pressure over your left shoulder) and then over to the Bowery, teeming with kitchen supplies. It was like stepping out of the Empire of the Dead, back into colorful life.

The water was green, cleaner than it used to be (the city did *some* things right). Bern had a sudden craving for oysters. The erotic smell of bracken. Tankers; to the north, beyond the Williamsburg Bridge, the tiny pyramid of a stark white sail. Buildings should never be taller than ships, he thought. The brick and wood of the bridge's Manhattan side gave way to the stone of the Brooklyn end.

Above the shoreline, he paused for a brief look around before turning and walking back. Next to a grocery store and a butcher's shop, he saw a small sign on a house: "Madame Olympia, Reader and Advisor." The future! A bored-looking woman sat on the stoop, sizing up passersby.

Your time is short, Bern thought.

He spun around, fell in love again and forever with Manhattan. Damn the place. It trembled with searing, reflected light. Strips of emblazoned filth echoed with the music of concrete-mixing trucks, rhythmical pile drivers. The city raising, destroying itself. Intimate avenues, great open trenches. Sunlight painted the bridge's girders, purging them of their materiality, making them shimmer. The raw smell of the tidewater—fusty, bloody—made Bern dizzy. A sexual swoon. He didn't understand himself and he wouldn't pause, now, to try.

There were ghosts on this bridge. He had stood here on September 11, on his way to Brooklyn for a site visit. A breathtaking sky—and then billowing white smoke, variegated and rolling. The sweet, fleshy odor... like fried something-or-other in a Chinatown food cart. People on the bridge whipped out handkerchiefs and tissues, covered their noses and mouths. In the distance, fluttering paper: migrating geese, suddenly blind. In an astonishingly short time, hucksters began prowling the bridge, offering organic pills to assist healthy lungs in dissolving tainted air particles. An instant conviction—though no one knew, yet, what had happened—that many were missing. Bern didn't know whether to be grateful or sad he had no one to make love to at home, for he understood sex would be different tonight: sweeter for some, dogged for others. But not the same for anyone.

On the edge of the bridge, now, he was nearly overcome by the smell of onions and roses wafting from a wire-mesh trash can, whose sagging plastic lining called to mind the word *uterine*. Theatrical gestures on the streets: playful shoving and pushing, heads thrown back, arms raised. A reflection of pickle-green light on the side of a passing bus. At a makeshift fish market, old women plunged their arms into crushed ice. Fish scales flashed in the sun, like hundreds of tiny mirrors appliquéd to handbags. From the ice's vapors the women pulled gritty shells, bloody tentacles.

He made his way up Allen Street. Newsstand headlines: "U.S. Senate Tries to Force Vote on Pulling Troops Out of Iraq—Fails to Win Republican Support," "Mayor's Traffic Plan Crashes." Next to Bluestockings Bookstore (a poetry reading was in progress, hosted by "the hardest-working guinea butch dyke poet on the Lower East Side," the emcee said), Bern set the cage on the sidewalk and rested. His arm was sore from the weight. He needed to sit. He had to figure out what to do. What in Christ's name had possessed him to purchase this bird?

He headed for Katz's Deli and took his ticket by the door. The place was so busy, no one noticed—or if they did, no one cared about—the cage. It tugged him toward the floor. He was sweating and his heart beat rapidly. On his table someone had left a Xeroxed flier, an incoherent rant against the "Sons of Ishmael and their Hatred for America." A sign above the meat counter said, "Send a Salami to Your Boy in the Army."

Around the room, he recognized familiar features, the Jewish faces he had known, growing up—Ashkenazi, Sephardic—light and dark, long and wide. Smiling, frowning. When he had first come to New York, he would wander from the Gramercy Park Hotel in the evenings and visit this deli. He felt its hominess, the kvetching, the noisy chewing, the aggressive nose-blowing, sneezing, and coughing. Behold our humanity, in all its goofiness, grime, and glory. Now, looking around, sipping his tea, Bern knew intimately the bully, the good son, the placating middle child, the rabbi. The damaged girl who would damage others in return. The boy who would succeed in spite of himself. He saw intransigence, forbearance, anger, and love—everything but the wisdom that could only be had through the long patience of being dead. And, of course, he figured, glancing at the roadrunner, admitting, at last, how lonely he had been in his quiet rooms (architecture no solace!), how much loneliness he had to look forward to: wisdom was what he was after.

Another cab to Central Park. By now, it was early evening. He got out at Strawberry Fields. A half-moon appeared to burn a hole among the bare limbs of a tree. Twittering and scrabbling in the bushes. A lone teenager sat on a bench, singing "Instant Karma." He was dressed in white, a baggy shirt—the eternal harlequin, straight out of a history book. Bern headed into the park with the bird in its cage.

In a clearing surrounded by holly bushes, he set the cage on the ground. A pain in his chest: close to the surface of his skin. Perhaps it was only muscular. Monitor yourself. Let me know.

What does a roadrunner eat? This bird was domesticated, weak. Its chances of surviving out here...

An owl hooted in a linden tree. At the clearing's far edge, above a sculpted outcrop of rock, moths bounced off a softly glowing lamp. They looked like snow. The air smelled of rotting wood. Bern knelt and opened the cage door. The ache grew stronger in his chest. Then it subsided. The roadrunner poked its head out, took two looks around. It darted into the bushes. Bern's heart leaped. He didn't know whether to feel happy or sad. What had he done? He stood and set the empty cage on a rock. The bird's slurring echoed in the darkness—the music of Bern's boyhood rising in the center of the city, hanging there in the trees.

7.

"Chris is on the roof," Landau said.

Bern was seated at his desk, staring at his sketches of the basement and wondering what to buy for supper (now that his favorite haunt had closed—to make way for a block-long condo—and he worried again about scrabblings in his chest): milk, veggies, fruit, and water? He focused his eyes on the deep shade and blinding sunshine in the doorway. "What did you say?"

"Somehow, he discovered the freight elevator. Go talk to him, Wally."

"What's the matter with him?"

"I had to let him go. You knew that, right? These youngsters ...they're...we need room to...please, Wally."

Bern stared at his pencils. "Why me?" he asked.

"Because...I don't know, you started work here around the same time. You're the same generation. You share similar sensibilities. I don't know, Wally. Just get your ass up there! Please!"

The elevator was maddeningly slow. It smelled of old, cold coffee.

Henderson stood with his hands in his pockets, rocking on the balls of his feet. He was near the north edge, facing, in the distance, the Flatiron and the Empire State. He watched a plane glide low over the Hudson. Hair whipped around his eyes. Bern approached him from behind. "Chris?" he said.

"Oh. Wally. Hello."

"How's it going, Chris?"

"Pretty day."

"You're not, uh..."

Henderson laughed. The sound caught like a slip of paper in the wind. It died instantly. "Thinking of doing something foolish? No."

Bern didn't know if he should trust him. He stepped close. His shoes felt thin.

"Did you know, Wally, that most of the manhole covers in Manhattan are made in Haora, India?"

"No."

"West Bengal. They're forged in unsafe foundries, I'm afraid. Molten steel. Workers barefoot, nearly naked..."

"I didn't know that," Bern said. If something happened, would he be responsible? After all, he'd shown Henderson this migratory path.

"I have a friend over at Con Ed who does some of the buying—roughly three thousand covers a year—and he's told me this. He's been over there. Every six months. When he asks the operators about the terrible conditions, they tell him, 'Accidents do not happen here.'"

Bern craned his head, but the streets were too far below for him to see anything.

"Just as, I suppose, layoffs don't happen here. We live in the City of Oz, right? Happily ever after. For everyone."

"I heard. I'm sorry, Chris. Really. I suspect I won't be far behind."

A chilly gust.

"Well. We look on the bright side, right?" said Henderson.

"Right," Bern said.

"My cancer's in remission. So far."

"That's right," Bern said, patting Henderson's shoulder.

"And I took my wife out last night. Our first real date in years."

"Good for you, Chris."

"Took some convincing. But we had a nice time, in the end. McCoy Tyner at the Blue Note. He's about a billion years old, but man oh man, can he play! Did a splendid version of *A Love Supreme*. I think I was nine years old when I first heard that album." He smiled and closed his eyes. "Before the show, there was this fellow in front of the club. A junkie, I suppose. I don't know what a junkie looks like, but this was my idea of one, gaunt and sinewy, hollow-eyed. He was hawking CDs. His own. 'You probably heard of me,' he said. 'My stage name is—' and he muttered some African word. My wife was appalled by him, but me... I sort of admired his fortitude. Night after night, out on the streets. It all depends on how you look at it, eh?"

"That's right," Bern said, shivering. From here he could see the green-gold fringe of Central Park. The Cloisters, up north.

He wondered where his roadrunner was.

"It's freezing, Chris. Let's go in," he suggested.

"I like it. Go ahead, Wally. I'll be there shortly. It's kind of peaceful up here."

"No. No, I'll wait for you."

"Don't you find it peaceful?"

"I'm cold."

"I'm not going to jump. I promise."

"I know, I know. I'm just..."

"What?"

"Come inside, Chris. Please."

"You think?"

"I think so. Yes."

When the elevator door slid open, Landau greeted them with raw relief. "Hey hey, Chris!" he cried. He slipped his arm around the man. "Everything good?"

"Fabulous."

"Fine! Well, that's just fine! Let's... well... listen! How about we step around the corner for a drink? On me, eh? Wally, join us?"

"No, thanks."

"You sure?"

Bern heard the pleading in his voice. "I'm sure," he said.

Landau scowled. "Chris, ever had a dirty chili martini?" he asked rapidly. People had gathered in the hallway. New young faces. Bern didn't know any of them. When had they been hired? They stared at Henderson, each other, the floor. "Hot peppers. First sip makes you wish you were never born. By about the third, you're never so glad you're alive."

Henderson gave Bern a wry little grin.

"I'll give you a call sometime," Bern said. He wondered if he would. There was no malice in this thought, just an intimation of awkwardness. A fear that, from here on out, the two men would have nothing to say to each other. He watched Landau lead Henderson away. People turned to look at Bern. Murphy appeared at his side. "Is he okay?' Murphy asked.

"I don't know."

"Well." Murphy glared at the others. They disappeared into their offices. "I'm sorry for him. It's hard on us all."

"Yes," Bern said.

"How about you?"

"Me?"

"Are *you* okay, Wally?"

"I think so."

Murphy watched him closely. "Okay. Well. I hope so. Listen, Wally. I've got some ideas about a project I'd like to kick around with you. You know. Maybe work together some more. I've even spoken to Landau about the possibility."

"You have?"

"Get our focus back. That's our challenge, right?"

Bern turned to look at him. "Tell me. How is it you're so interested in my work?" he asked. What he really wanted to know was, How can you be who you are? So jaunty when some of us see every reason to jump?

"I *know* good design. My mother was an interior decorator." Murphy grinned. "I was the sort of privileged, cultured snob everybody hated in high school."

"People still hate you," Bern said. He tried to make it sound like a joke.

Murphy squeezed his arm. "I give them good reason," he said. "And I confess, Wally, I'm damn proud of it."

He left Bern alone by the break room: a smell of Cheez-Its and cold pizza. Bern walked back to his office. Until early in the evening, he worked on the basement, with the lights of Lower Manhattan burning yellow and blue in his window.

Murphy's project, a series of apartments, came in at ten mill—more than Bern was used to spending, but low even for a small-scale undertaking. The apartments would be managed by a non-profit housing trust. Murphy suggested galvanized metal and lots of plate glass. Bern saw the wisdom in these choices. The kid wasn't half bad. An emphasis on communal spaces (at Bern's insistence): open-air walkways overlooking courtyards that connected to common rooms and shared kitchens, brightly lit stairwells. The key for a population of elderly, disabled, and mentally challenged—the target demographic, here—was to foil isolation however possible. Bern agreed with Murphy that the first floor should be devoted to social and medical services, the hub of the enterprise. The one aesthetic fillip Murphy clung to was to "answer" the "surrounding fabric of the city—the rough-and-tumble of the neighborhood"—with oddly pitched stair railings. As long as safety was not an issue, Bern felt fine with this.

To be working again, working at all, was good.

One Saturday morning (*Good Shabbos!*), after refining some sketches, he decided to visit the Cloisters. Perhaps, he thought, he could find inspiration in the buildings there. The old medieval arguments. Perfecting the world.

The sunshine was glorious. He caught the M4 at Broadway and West Thirty-second. As the bus moved up Madison, finely dressed people toting massive shopping bags boarded and enforced an awkward decorum, sitting stiffly, staring straight ahead, saying nothing. A group of silver-haired matrons rocked down the aisle, rattling book bags from the Met.

As the driver wound north, the fashionable passengers departed and were replaced by seedier types. Then, as the bus curled through

Spanish Harlem, he saw more and more elderly folks waiting impatiently at the wind-blown stops. The infirm. The wheelchair-bound. I am a healthy man, Bern thought, feeling his chest, watching an old woman shake red pills into her palm. As the bus approached Fort Tryon Park—an unlikely Paradise at Manhattan's northernmost tip—it overflowed with people in need of rest and redemption.

In the Cloisters' gift shop, where Bern first entered, light streamed through tall, leaded windows. Indoor fountains whispered. He perused the books. *The Florentine Church. Medieval Architecture.* A biography of Dante.

He strolled from gallery to gallery, past illuminated manuscripts, jewelry, and tapestries, past a Carolingian plaque with the face of John the Baptist stamped on it, past a blackened effigy of a lady from the Loire Valley, as well as Books of Hours and Romanesque altars. Silver reliquaries gleamed in blue and yellow light beaming from stained-glass windows. Arched stone doorways led them from one passageway to another. In the cool open spaces, even the crying of children took on the solemnity and grandeur of Gregorian chants.

Finally, he emerged into the Cuxa Cloister, a covered walkway surrounding a courtyard planted according to medieval herbals and books of poetry listing flowers and varieties of bushes. Pine cones, leaves, and animals—and a mermaid holding her tail—were carved into the capitals. Bern looked up: a daylight moon, the color of rich whiskey in a startlingly close and depthless blue sky. From somewhere, a faint honeysuckle smell.

How much does the moon weigh?

Or the touch of a finger?

Things a builder should know.

In memory, Bern heard the cooing of a bayou bird. He put a hand, once more, to his chest. What perturbations skittered inside him? He did and didn't want to know.

He walked around the Benedictine columns, and then among the thirteenth-century ornaments imported here to make the museum. Gothic balustrades. Vestibules. Archways from monastery windows in the hills of ancient Paris. Peaceful—perhaps he should rethink his relationship to religion.

He came to an outdoor path overlooking New York. The roof above him appeared to be streamlined and sturdy. The birds nesting in its eaves seemed to come and go with freedom and ease. Venus, sapphire-colored, hung in the west, a precise wax seal. He remembered reading, once, probably in college, a description of a "personal experience of Eternity" (Boethius? St. Augustine?): it was, the author said, the sensation of having *complete and perfect possession of unlimited life at a single moment.* Or, as Dante put it, finding that spot where "every *where* and every *when* is brought to a point." And from here, that spot would be—? Somewhere west of Manhattan, in the middle of the Hudson River. He gazed out at the water, the buildings and trees, the people he did and didn't know—invisible to him now. He thought of his daily walks, the scenes he witnessed, and the events unfolding without him. He checked his wallet for bus fare: his ticket to join his fellow travelers yearning for rest. Soon, this meditative mood would be broken and he would dissolve again into the present. There were more sounds of Texas to recall. A building project to finish. There were vintage books to buy in quaint, failing shops. He turned to admire, once more, the colors and textures of the interlocking pieces of the cloister, designed and fashioned by warm human hands long before the city existed.

ACKNOWLEDGMENTS

"I Have the Room Above Her," titled "Bern," appeared originally in the *Georgia Review;* "Signs" and "The Empire of the Dead" appeared originally in the *Hopkins Review*; portions of "The Magnitudes" appeared originally in the *Georgia Review* and in *Gulf Coast*, titled "Magnitude" and "What It Was, What It Could Have Been," respectively (I am grateful to Tracy Hayes Harris for her observations on the painting process, which I have borrowed from here); and "Basement and Roof" appeared originally in *Southwest Review*. I am indebted to the editors of these journals and to John Irwin, for his support of these stories. Thank you to Barbara Lamb for her kind attention to the manuscript and to Mary Lou Kenney and Hilary Jacqmin for their editorial assistance. Finally, my heartfelt thanks to Glenn Blake for his encouragement and steadfast friendship through the years.

About the Author

Tracy Daugherty was born and raised in Midland, Texas. He is the author of four novels, five short story collections, and a book of personal essays, as well as biographies of Donald Barthelme, Joseph Heller, and Joan Didion (forthcoming from St. Martin's Press). His stories and essays have appeared in the *New Yorker*, *Vanity Fair*, the *Paris Review* online, *McSweeney's*, *Boulevard*, *Chelsea*, the *Georgia Review*, *Triquarterly*, the *Southern Review*, and many other journals. He has received fellowships from the Guggenheim Foundation, the National Endowment for the Arts, Bread Loaf, and the Vermont Studio Center. A member of the Texas Institute of Letters and PEN, he is a four-time winner of the Oregon Book Award. At Oregon State University, where he is now Distinguished Professor Emeritus of English and creative writing, he helped found the Masters of Fine Arts Program in Creative Writing.

Fiction Titles in the Series

Guy Davenport, *Da Vinci's Bicycle*
Stephen Dixon, *14 Stories*
Jack Matthews, *Dubious Persuasions*
Guy Davenport, *Tatlin!*
Joe Ashby Porter, *The Kentucky Stories*
Stephen Dixon, *Time to Go*
Jack Matthews, *Crazy Women*
Jean McGarry, *Airs of Providence*
Jack Matthews, *Ghostly Populations*
Jack Matthews, *Booking in the Heartland*
Jean McGarry, *The Very Rich Hours*
Steve Barthelme, *And He Tells the Little Horse the Whole Story*
Michael Martone, *Safety Patrol*
Jerry Klinkowitz, *Short Season and Other Stories*
James Boylan, *Remind Me to Murder You Later*
Frances Sherwood, *Everything You've Heard Is True*
Stephen Dixon, *All Gone: 18 Short Stories*
Jack Matthews, *Dirty Tricks*
Joe Ashby Porter, *Lithuania*
Robert Nichols, *In the Air*
Ellen Akins, *World Like a Knife*
Greg Johnson, *A Friendly Deceit*
Guy Davenport, *The Jules Verne Steam Balloon*
Guy Davenport, *Eclogues*
Jack Matthews, *Storyhood as We Know It and Other Tales*
Stephen Dixon, *Long Made Short*
Jean McGarry, *Home at Last*
Jerry Klinkowitz, *Basepaths*
Greg Johnson, *I Am Dangerous*
Josephine Jacobsen, *What Goes without Saying: Collected Stories*
Jean McGarry, *Gallagher's Travels*
Richard Burgin, *Fear of Blue Skies*
Avery Chenoweth, *Wingtips*
Judith Grossman, *How Aliens Think*
Glenn Blake, *Drowned Moon*
Robley Wilson, *The Book of Lost Fathers*
Richard Burgin, *The Spirit Returns*
Jean McGarry, *Dream Date*
Tristan Davies, *Cake*
Greg Johnson, *Last Encounter with the Enemy*
John T. Irwin and Jean McGarry, eds., *So the Story Goes: Twenty-five Years of the Johns Hopkins Short Fiction Series*
Richard Burgin, *The Conference on Beautiful Moments*
Max Apple, *The Jew of Home Depot and Other Stories*
Glenn Blake, *Return Fire*
Jean McGarry, *Ocean State*
Richard Burgin, *Shadow Traffic*
Robley Wilson, *Who Will Hear Your Secrets?*
William J. Cobb, *The Lousy Adult*
Tracy Daugherty, *The Empire of the Dead*